SOME DEAD GENIUS

SOME DEAD GENIUS

LENNY KLEINFELD

Published by Niaux-Noir Books

For Leighton Gage, whose noblesse obliged him to champion the underdog—or in this case, the underbook.

ONE / 2005

Phone calls are easy. You dial. It rings. Tesca answers. You inform the semi-simian loan shark you've got another painting you can turn into cash.

Call. Now. Before Tesca turns you into a cripple. Or fish food.

Come the fuck on, what's one more painting, this point you've already lost everything. Every penny, your gallery, your car. And as of this week, your hair; past few days your comb's been doing more harvesting than grooming. Compared to that, what's one lousy magnificent Laurie Desh canvas.

That painting. Best day of Dale's life. A Thursday. Seven years ago. Laurie's face when he took one long look and bought it. That Thursday when he discovered Laurie, and became her dealer, and her friend.

Not that she'd been so fucking sentimental about him, had no problem blowing Dale off soon as she caught fire. But, shit. It's like trying to blame a tiger for having teeth. Like most of the great ones, Laurie had the simple clear-eyed selfishness an artist needs to survive.

Survive. Good word.

Dale reached for the phone but it rang. The double *ring-ring, ring-ring*: front-door intercom.

Tommy Tesca was downstairs. Great. Don't even have to make that easy phone call. Just buzz him in and give him the good news.

Dale buzzed, waited, opened the door, said, "Hi—"

Tesca grabbed Dale by the throat and bulled him across the loft to the open-plan kitchen, where he slammed Dale against the fridge and asked, none too optimistically, "So you got any money for me—like this week's vig—an' last week, plus the week before? Heh, Dalie-boy?"

Dalie-boy made a frantic gagging noise, as verbal as he could get with the loan shark's massive hand clamped on his throat.

"What I thought." Tesca shook his head. "Look, I like you Dale, heh? So you pick what's it gonna be. We go old school, bat to the knee-cap. Or how 'bout a welding torch to the nuts. Or—messy, but really does the trick—I put a drill through your eyeball. Your choice."

Dale tried to shout through his nose, which sprayed snot on Tesca's sleeve.

"Heh, gross."

Tesca yanked Dale to the sink, grabbed Dale's arm and shoved Dale's hand down the drain, mashing Dale's fingers against the dull blades of the disposal. "Say we just get it over, heh. Save me goin' out the car for my toolbox." Tesca released Dale's throat to reach for the disposal switch—

"*Painting!*" Dale gasped, "Ga' 'nother painting—my closet in my closet!"

Tesca scowled. "Thought you were outta paintings."

"Lent it a girlfriend last year but when I asked it back refused claimed it was a gift this morning I made her give it back," Dale rattled off woodpecker fast.

Tesca smirked at the pale, toothpick-limbed *Amedagone*. American white-bread. Soft, bleached, crust-less. "*You* made her give it back?"

"Tommy I can sell that for fifteen—no twenty, twenty thousand Laurie Desh is white-hot, she—"

"Which closet?"

"Up, upstairs—*Arrrgggghhhhh!*"

Tesca grabbed Dale's ear and dragged the squealing art dealer past forlorn walls pimpled with empty picture hooks, up a short set of stairs to a sleeping loft. Only thing in it was an air mattress, lost inside the imprint left by a king-size bed; Dale's furniture had marched out the door months ago. Tesca kicked the air mattress out of the way as he strode to the closet, with Dale's ear and what was attached to it lurching after him.

Tesca yanked open the closet door. Snorted. The spacious walk-in was a ghost town, populated only by one suit, one pair of black jeans, four shirts, a flock of empty hangers, and, on the floor, leaning against the wall, a 30x20 rectangle wrapped in brown paper.

"Looks small."

"Twenty grand," Dale vowed.

The simian shark released Dale's ear. Dale stepped into the closet and carefully lifted the package.

Tesca fished out a switchblade and popped the blade.

"Let me unwrap it," Dale insisted. Quickly adding, "Please."

Tesca offered him the knife. Amused. What with both of them knowing Dale Phipps plus switchblade added up to zero threat.

Dale shook his head. "One slip and twenty grand turns to shit." He carefully peeled away the paper.

The canvas was entirely shades of dark red. Many of Laurie's early works were. Dale once teased her, *Someday this will be known as Desh's Blood-Red Period.* Now, not funny... The painting was still a trip. Laurie'd slathered on layers of pigment with a palette knife, making it look like a classic mid-century abstraction. But if you looked long enough the textured edges of slather resolved into a ghostly suggestion of a face. At first critics dismissed it as a trompe l'oeil parlor trick. But Dale knew it wasn't *what* an artist did, it was *how,* and Laurie's—

"Heh! Some asswipe pay twenty large for that crap?"

Dale realized he was glaring. He neutered his expression.

"Tommy, there are asswipes lining up to buy Laurie Deshes. I'll need a couple of days, maybe a week, to sell—"

"Ah no no no no no, that leaves here with me." Tesca shot him a shrewd look. "How much you pay for this?"

"Twelve hundred."

"Shit," Tesca complimented him. "How come so cheap?"

"Laurie was just starting out. Could've paid even less, but I wanted to put a couple of bucks in her pocket."

Tesca peered at the painting, examining it with professorial gravity.

Looked at Dale. "Didja fuck her?"

"No. Well—once—we, uh... Just a bump in the night. Maybe we were a little too drunk."

"Didn't get your twelve hundred worth?"

Dale suppressed an urge to commit suicide by throwing a punch.

Settled for throwing Tesca a sour grin and retorting: "Twenty grand."

"That'd make up for a lousy lay," Tesca conceded. Then grumbled, "But you owe me twenty-five."

Dale's heart thudded and he tried not to imagine a drill bit juicing his eyeball. "Please, Tommy, twenty is the bulk, you get that right away, just give me another week—"

"The fuck ya gonna get another five? Plus vig."

"Beg, sell my blood… Ah, shit, this is gonna—just a notion—Laurie's the rock star of young Chicago artists, if you hold that painting a year or two—"

"You owe me now, not in two years." Tesca paused. Frowned. "When'd you buy this crap looks like a wall been plastered by a spazz, heh?"

"Seven years ago."

"Twelve hundred to twenty large. So another seven years, this spazz job brings… four hundred thousand?"

"Jeez, Tommy, no one can—it's not geometry—I mean anything's possible, but even when an artist dies you can't guarantee a price bump that nuclear, I, I, I was just saying, if you did hang on—sorry, sorry, forget I—sell the painting, a-a-and I will do *whatever* it takes to get the money. What-fucking-ever."

Tesca stared at him. Gauging, Dale was certain, what level of maiming would motivate him to actually do what-fucking-ever.

Tesca still had the switchblade clutched in his paw. Dale tried to take solace in the thought the knife was preferable to the disposal. Truly.

"Wrap it up," Tesca muttered. "And careful."

The brown paper was too torn to re-use. Dale took the painting to the kitchen and wrapped it in his one remaining apron. Secured it by knotting the apron strings. Handed it to Tesca. Promised, soberly, "I will come up with the rest. On time."

"I know," Tesca said. He slapped Dale so hard it spun him around and buckled his knees. Tesca put the painting down. Yanked Dale upright and slammed him against the sink. Shoved Dale's hand into the drain. Turned on the disposal.

The gun never got old. So good in the hand. And the power. No shit we're gun crazy. It's still a recent infatuation for us thinking monkeys. A million years of flinging rocks and pointy sticks, now suddenly there's this explosion coming out the end of your arm... Mark thought he thought too much, for a cop monkey. Though he did shoot okay just now. All tens, except that one fucking eight.

Gale. Gale had popped into his mind. His ex-girlfriend. She'd moved back to Santa Monica two years ago. Two days ago Mark heard Gale was engaged. She'd met a guy named Boyd Whitsell, and decided to marry him anyway.

Detectives Mark Bergman and John Dunegan were down in Area Three's basement range, shooting qualifiers. The annual session at which a Chicago cop is obliged to fire thirty rounds at silhouettes. And to hit enough of them to assure the Department that if you discharged your weapon in the real world, there was at least a 70-30 chance you wouldn't hit an innocent bystander who knew a lawyer.

Doonie, the big shambling vet who'd taught Mark the homicide business, stuck his head around the divider as Mark reeled in his final target. Doonie took an unsurprised glance at the tight group shredding the silhouette's heart. Issued his ritual dismissal: "You were trying."

After twenty-six years on the job Doonie's own marksmanship had tailed off; a natural side-effect of age, weight, children and bourbon. Doonie claimed he was conserving energy, saving his best shooting for the street fucks who deserved it.

Lunch. They parked half a block from their usual Thai joint on Belmont. Walked, shoulders hunched forward, into an umbrella-killing squall, clutching shut their raincoats, which neither cop had buttoned despite the slashing rain and chill; it was thirty-three degrees, the temperature at which rain can't quite bring itself to turn into snow, and settles for being suspiciously thick ice water. Springtime in Chicago. At least the worst part of spring was over. That first serious thaw in early March where the icy-hard snow banks lining the sidewalks melt and release six months worth of defrosting dog fudge. It was now the third week in March, when the weather might begin to show some genuine friendliness. Except maybe for an April sucker-punch snowstorm.

Mark and Doonie peeled off their raincoats as they went through the door, knowing the room would be overheated.

Their regular waitress asked if they wanted menus. They said nah, and ordered.

She came right back with drinks. Tea for Mark, a Singha for Doon.

Doonie took a grateful, first-drink-of-the-day pull on his beer. Asked, "So what happened?"

"With what?"

"You missed a shot."

"I took that one left-handed, with my back to the target."

"Usually make that shot in your sleep. Lose a lotta sleep last night?" Doonie wondered, hopefully. Doon was forty-seven, thoroughly married, and a big fan of his thirty-five-year-old partner's busy sex life.

"Nope, none at all. Sorry. How are Phyl and the kids?" Mark was a big fan of Doonie's busy family.

Doonie answered with a dismissive grunt.

Something was up. Mark asked, "Kieran heard back from anyplace?"

"Yesterday," Doonie sighed. "Looks like my firstborn will be getting his Masters at Notre Dame."

"Congratulations."

"Gets worse. Only a partial scholarship."

"Fuck."

"Fuck," Doonie agreed.

Doonie's second son, Tom, had two years of undergrad left. Next September, Patty, the youngest, would be a freshman, which meant Doonie would continue his tuition hell streak of having two kids in college—three, if Kieran went for a doctorate.

Mark knew better than to offer help to Doonie. Have to have that conversation later, with Phyllis.

Steaming aromatic plates landed in front of them. The cops ate in silence; Doonie stewing about having let slip he was worried about doing right by his kids, Mark stewing about letting the thought of his ex-girlfriend's engagement distract him while firing live ammo. Gale would've married Mark if he'd asked. That's why she'd moved in with him.

Gale came from semi-serious wealth. Within a year the romance of embracing an alternative lifestyle—a cop's—had worn off. Gale pressed Mark to take the job her father offered as head of security for his company. Mark asked, "So instead of being his guest at Chamonix and Kauai and Tierra del Fuego, I'd be his employee?"

It ended. Case closed.

Except for him shooting that one fucking eight.

Mark's radio burbled. There was a dead guy demanding Mark and Doonie's attention.

Cheered them right up.

THREE / 2012

On the outside it was a typical 1950s two-story wood-frame, with sensible Chicago priorities. Roof and double-paned windows looked new. Paint job didn't.

Inside, the brush work was hallucinatory. The place was crammed with modern art. A number of canvases were glowing airbrush portraits of eroticized, half-nightmarish women and men, many dressed in sci-fi fetish wear. The skin tones were electric colors never seen on an Earthling. But the faces were fully human, unapologetically challenging the viewer.

"Lotta Robert Gilsons," Mark noted.

"Lotta whats?" Doonie asked.

"Chicago painter."

"Also the vic," said the young uniformed cop who'd let them in. "Robert Gilson, forty-eight. His wife, Helen," the young uni added, indicating the woman sunk into a couch in the living room.

Helen Gilson was fiftyish. Wearing a patchwork neo-hippie work shirt over jeggings. Terrific legs, but what caught the eye was her neon-orange hair. That and the fact she was doing the blank stare and the slow, gooey head wobble of the seriously tranqed.

Huddled with Helen was a tall silver-haired woman in a black turtleneck and long black skirt. She was clasping Helen's hand, gazing into her wide numb eyes and murmuring, too softly for the cops to eavesdrop.

"Her shrink," the young uni explained. "Now for the good part," he murmured, with a barely suppressed smirk.

"You mean the deceased?" Mark asked.

The young uni gave them a confident nod. He led them through the house and out across the yard to a garage.

A former garage. Long ago converted to a studio, and, according to Connie The Coroner and her magic thermometer, converted to a murder scene less than four hours ago.

When they walked in, Mark and Doonie's view of the vic was blocked by one of the TV Stars (Doonie's term for Crime Scene techs) processing the scene. The TV Star, also in his twenties, was bent over the corpse, shooting a close-up.

The TV Star saw them, gave a delighted shake of the head and stepped aside. The TV Star and the uni watched with snarky glee as Mark and Doonie got their first glimpse of the corpse.

"Yeah, that used to be Robert Gilson," Mark confirmed, as they approached the guest of honor.

"You recognize painters," Doonie complained, unsurprised.

The young uni shot the TV Star a puzzled frown, stymied by the detectives' refusal to acknowledge the hilarious sick shit right in front of them.

"I recognize Gilson," Mark told Doonie. "West Rogers Park boy, with an international rep."

"Well," Doonie countered, "I recognize the guy in Gilson's mouth. That's Ken—though a lot better hung than the one Patty had."

A naked Ken doll was stuffed, feet-first, in the dead artist's mouth. Ken had a glued-on erection that was resting on Gilson's upper lip.

Doonie leaned down and examined Gilson's wounds. "Ken didn't do these," Doonie said. The perp had clocked Gilson on the head, presumably with the bloody, jagged two-foot-long shaft of Cor-Ten steel that was on the floor nearby.

"Came from that," Mark said, pointing to a tripod-shaped steel sculpture in the corner of the studio that had two similar shafts dangling from hooks, and one empty hook.

Ugly as it was, the head wound might not have been the COD. Gilson's throat was sliced open.

"Takes him down with the bash to the head, then *zip*," Doonie summarized. "Nice and quiet."

"Uh-huh." Middle of a residential block, a sculpture and a knife make way less conspicuous murder weapons than a gun.

Indicating the Ken-in-mouth tableau, Mark asked, "Does it speak to you?"

"Not in English."

"But I sense a theme," Mark said, gesturing at what Gilson had been working on when he was killed.

The vic was sprawled next to a worktable on which there was a Barbie doll. Barbie's clothes had been removed, except for her boots, and Gilson had been painting anatomically correct details on her.

"There's more," the TV Star said. He went to a cabinet and pulled open its doors, revealing a gallery of Barbies and Kens. Sixteen pairs. Nude and semi-nude. Carefully posed.

All the Kens were painted to look like Gilson; had his curly salt-and-pepper hair and rowdy moustache. The Barbies were all distinctly different. And Ken was usually doing something foul to her.

Doonie instructed the TV Star to bag the dolls, and snuck a pleased little grin at Mark. This case did feature some promising sick shit.

They made a quick inspection of the garage; no signs of forced entry.

Time to go talk to the heavily glazed widow.

FOUR / 2012

Helen Gilson was still melting into the couch. The silver-haired shrink was still glued to her.

"Mrs. Gilson, I'm Detective Bergman, and this is Detective Dunegan," Mark said, gently. "We're sorry for your loss."

The widow, concentrating on the task, raised her head. The shiny orange hair framed a pleasant oval face, chemically drained of affect. She gazed at the cops. And gazed at the cops.

When it became obvious Helen wasn't going to hold up her end of the conversation, the tall woman in black introduced herself. "Dr. Margot Bader. Helen's therapist."

"Nice to meet you," Mark said. "Mrs. Gilson, could we speak to you in private?"

Helen slowly wobbled her gaze down to her hand, which was clutching Dr. Bader's. Slowly looked up at the cops. Nope. Not letting go of that hand.

"This will save Helen having to tell me about this," Dr. Bader offered, with a well-practiced reasonableness. "However, Helen is somewhat sedated. Can you speak to her later?"

"We plan to," Mark said. "But time is important. Whatever you can tell us now, Mrs. Gilson, will be useful."

"All… right," Helen said, to Mark and Doonie's surprise, and possibly her own.

"Were you here when it happened?" Mark asked.

Helen gave her head a slow, wobbly shake.

"Where," Mark prompted, "were you?"

"Yo… ga."

"At yoga?"

A wobbly nod. "Came… home… went to…" She aimed a gaze in the direction of the studio. "I…"

11

"You?"

"Saw him, and... passed... out."

"Then?" Mark coaxed.

"Woke... Took V-val-yumm... Then, 9-1-1... Then, took... a Lu... minal."

"Mrs. Gilson, did your husband have enemies? Or stalkers, someone obsessed with him?"

A slo-mo wobbly head shake: No.

"Do you have any debts?"

Wobbly-no.

"Do you know anyone who would want to kill your husband?"

Helen thought it over. Said, with plaintive narcotized sincerity, "It... wasn't... me."

Mark raised an eyebrow and waited.

"Eight years... ago... I stabbed... Bob. But not... very hard."

"How did it happen?"

"Was just... bad time, a... thing. W-we..."

"You?"

"Bob... a-pologized... I stabbed, and Bob... polo... gized." Tears spilled.

Which brought them to the twisted little elephant in the room. "Mrs. Gilson, were you aware of your husband's collection of... Barbies and Kens?"

A wobbly-nod. "Found them... few years a-go."

"They represent women he had affairs with?"

Wobbly-nod.

"Were you angry about all those—Barbies?"

Wobbly-no.

"That's true," Dr. Bader interjected. "May I?" she asked her patient.

Wobbly-nod.

Dr. Bader explained, "Helen and Bob are—were—a mature, realistic couple."

"Do you know," Mark asked Helen, "if any of the Barbies, or their significant others, were—less mature?"

Helen thought. Gave a mournful shrug, and sagged against Dr.

Bader.

Dr. Bader laid a hand over Helen's face, shielding it. Stared at the cops, informing them the interview was over.

As they left, Doonie shot Mark a skeptical, disappointed glance. If Helen was so mature, so un-jealous, why had she dyed her hair Barbie orange?

Despite the kinky dolls this was looking like a plain-vanilla, wife-got-fed-up-with-her-hound murder. A quickie.

FIVE / 2012

The frustration reduced Mark to playing with Barbies.

After two days all Mark and Doonie had on Helen Gilson was what they began with: She'd spent twenty-eight years married to an artist with a slippery zipper.

They'd done a follow-up with Helen, who this time was only partially encased in chemical buffering. Helen said she understood who Bob was and how life was always throwing women at him. The time she stabbed him had nothing to do with sex; it was because of something mean he said during an argument. They had a solid, loving, happy marriage.

That rosy picture was confirmed by family and friends. And by nine of the Barbies—whose names Helen provided.

Helen's alibi held up. She'd been miles away, flexing chakras.

Helen could've hired the hit. But her phones, emails and financials showed no sign she'd been in touch with Throat-Slitters R Us.

The cops confirmed Bob Gilson didn't have enemies or debts.

Both of Gilson's adult children were happily married, gainfully employed and not mad at dad.

The TV Stars turned up no unexplained fingerprints or DNA.

No neighbor had seen a throat-slitter entering or exiting Gilson's house or studio.

That narrowed the theoretical suspect list to: A disgruntled Killer Barbie, or her disgruntled spouse/boyfriend/girlfriend.

Mark and Doonie spent Day Three interviewing the known Barbies.

All had nice things to say about Bob. All but one claimed Bob had never done the nasty things his Ken was doing to her Barbie; the exception said she *liked* golden shampoos. All said their bonks with

Bob had been short flings or one-night-stands. Nothing like a romantic, slay-your-lover affair.

None copped to having a jealous spouse or partner.

Which left the seven unidentified Barbies.

Doonie packed it in for the day, went home to have dinner with his expensive family.

Mark ate at his desk, filling his stomach with kebab while he tried to empty his mind by watching a Cubs pre-season game. The Cubs kept swinging at pitches outside the strike zone, mocking Mark's at-bats on the Gilson case.

How to track down the mystery Barbies?

Go through years of Gilson's communications, contact every female.

Show Gilson's friends photos of the dolls. The known Barbies said Gilson had gotten their hair, eyes, pubes and ink exactly right. Also their clothes, on the dolls who were partially dressed… Mark could run their tats through a database. He began extracting the Barbies from their evidence bags—

Kazurinsky and Kimbrough, night-shift detectives who'd caught a case and were on their way out, paused to admire Mark's Barbie line-up. Kimmie gave him an *Aww, how adorable* grin. Mark didn't grin back. Kaz and Kimmie left, politely not breaking into giggles until they were headed down the stairs.

Mark began photographing Barbie tattoos.

Got to a Barbie wearing a red leather jacket and nothing else. But, shit, that jacket was the exact same… And she had long black hair—which was cut just like…

Mark checked her eyes. Green.

Turned the doll over.

The hair went up on the back of Mark's neck.

Left butt cheek. Six tiny green letters. Gilson had painted the tat to scale, so Mark had to use a magnifier. But his gut knew what the tat would say:

VISION

So.

Mark and the dead guy had both seen the tiny, well-placed word Janvier Dunstan referred to as her first and last piece of performance art.

Hmm. If Mark had slept with a subject the vic had also slept with, and that subject turned into suspect, Mark had to step away.

But first, the subject would have to confirm this black-haired green-eyed Barbie was in fact a Janvier Dunstan Barbie.

Mark was uniquely qualified to conduct that interview; he could confirm the subject's identity, even though she was someone he hadn't been naked with, or seen, or spoken to, in four years.

Janvier had been twenty-one at the time. Waitressing—and dealing pot and Christ knows what else—to pay her way through an MFA at the Art Institute. Now she'd be twenty-five, and doing…?

Mark pulled out his cell, found Janvier's number. Still in the address book, two phones after he'd last called her. A cynic on the street but a sentimentalist on the speed-dial.

He thumbed. Got the voicemail for a dry cleaner. Baritone, with a mellifluous East African accent. Definitely not Janvier, whose voice was husky but nowhere near that deep. And her accent, despite her French name, was pure Midwest. She was Mark's favorite thing about Indiana, and not just because there was no competition.

Janvier was six foot, easy. Nearly Mark's height. A fine full-length full-contact fit. And the sweep of that long sleek back. Insanely silky skin. Endless legs, most exciting legs he'd…

And smart, talented, funny, tons of fierce young energy, and a whole lot of rural resilience. But always playfully, defiantly stoned. Or tripping, or coked.

There'd been no way Mark could ignore the felonious recreationals. And no way she'd back off. He'd ended it.

And yet, soon after that, on her own initiative, Janvier helped Mark and Doonie leverage one of her pot customers, a woman who'd witnessed a hit-and-run and then refused to testify. Janvier set her customer up for a drug bust, and the detectives traded the reluctant witness a walk in exchange for her testimony.

Mark had phoned Janvier and thanked her. But that was all. By then Gale had moved in with Mark, and… Now Gale was gone, and Mark was sitting here remembering the feel of Janvier's legs intertwined with his, and, right, working a murder.

He searched the white pages. Found a J. Dunstan. In Pilsen. Hot neighborhood for young artists. Hot enough so it was no longer cheap. Janvier was making money. Mark hoped it was from selling more art than weed.

He called.

Someone answered.

"Maaark," Janvier said, teasing it into a lyric.

SIX / 2005

ood news, bad news. Bad news, you've lost a finger. Good news,
only lost one. Bad news, it was your middle finger," the surgeon-
comedian informed Dale. "Good news, it was your left hand—" sly
grin, "—unless you're a lefty. You a lefty?"

"Uuuhhhh."

"Okay then. There'll be some deformation and loss of function
in the adjacent fingers. The nurse will be by with prescriptions and
instructions. ER's crazy today, gotta hustle."

Dale lifted his left hand. It had no fingers. The whole hand was
encased in a softball-size glob of gauze and tape, bright white with
a red stain above the place where his middle knuckle might still be.

Good news, his head was encased in an anesthetic haze. Bad
news, a nurse showed up with a laptop.

The nurse flipped open the laptop and said, "So you don't have
any medical coverage?"

When the forms were signed and the (*Thank you, Jesus*) prescriptions handed over, the nurse asked, "Is there anyone who can drive
you home?"

Was there? Dale had burned so many bridges.

Walt Egan. Dale and Eegs went back to fourth grade at Francis
Parker. Eegs would never lend Dale another dime, but was still good
for a ride home, after something like an emergency middle finger
amputation.

The nurse went to make the call.

Dale closed his eyes.

Five thousand, plus twenty per cent vig: six thousand.

Seven days. Six thousand. How?

Ah shit. Ah fuck. Why couldn't he have gone legally bankrupt like a normal person, protected his assets? Why'd he have to go literally bankrupt, piss away what should have been a lifetime-cushion trust fund, then keep right on going and piss away his friends' money?

There was no way he could hit up his friends again.

Or family. His parents were gone. Dale was sole heir, which turned out to be only pocket-money solace; his parents' estate had been decimated by bad investments and good hospitals.

He was the only child of two only children. Had no siblings, uncles, aunts or cousins who might be guilted into sacrificing hard cash to save him from Tommy Tesca's next surgical procedure.

What quick crime might pay six thou?

Bank robbery. At this point what the fuck... Yeah sure, a guy robbing a bank with a gun in his right hand and a gigantic white lump where his left hand should be. Make an LOL security-cam clip. Especially the part where the one-handed robber tries to pick up the money without putting down the gun.

Seven days. Six thousand.

How?

SEVEN / 2005

"Oh God God God, Dale, that was like so totally the best, *bestest* sex, that wasn't sex, that was a *fuck*, you animal, an-nee-mull," Soosie chirped. Soosie, panting, slick with sweat, was trying to purr, but though Soosie was a chunky five-foot-seven, the gene factory had equipped her with wispy high-pitched munchkin pipes; chirping was Soosie's deepest, sultriest sound.

Music to Dale Phipps' ears, even the one that was swollen and purple.

Walt and Elise Egan had spent two days taking care of and feeding Dale. On the third night Dale felt un-crappy enough to be fed at a restaurant.

The Egans took Dale to *the* new Mexican place ("The Taco Goes Molecular"—*Chicago* magazine), where a reservation entitled them to a forty-five-minute wait. They headed to the bar, where—holy shit, is that—yes—Soosie Smith and two girlfriends, mainlining margaritas. Soosie Smith, daughter of millionaire Phillippa Smith (boutique ad agency), to whom Dale had sold four pieces over the years.

As a teenager Soosie often accompanied her mom to the Dale Phipps Gallery, where Soosie made it plain she considered Dale to be adorably sophisticated. He'd pretended not to notice. Soosie was too young, too shallow and the daughter of too wealthy a client.

Now, years later, over extraordinary appetizers and inexcusable entrees—blueberry-molé foam on gluten carnitas, for fuck's sake—twenty-three-year-old Soosie made it plain she was still suffering from unrequited lust.

After dinner Dale went home with Soosie and requited with phenomenal enthusiasm.

In between requitements, Dale related the broad outline of his plight. How he'd lost his business and was about to be evicted from his loft. Why his left ear was purple and where his middle left finger had gone.

Soosie wept, and offered anal sex.

This morning Dale had packed his six or seven belongings and moved in with her.

Tonight they'd celebrated with a romantic (edible) dinner, followed by dance clubs. Now they were back in bed, where Dale the an-nee-mull was fucking as if his life, or at least his kneecaps, testicles and eyeballs depended on it.

Soon Dale would let Soosie pry out some dark details he'd alluded to but refused to discuss—specifically, how the half-orangutan thug would be removing a lot worse than a finger if Dale didn't come up with another six thousand. Within three days.

Dale wouldn't ask for it. Soosie would offer. Soosie would insist. Soosie dropped that kind of money during an hour at a good shoe store.

Dale couldn't entirely relax until they'd played that touching scene and he had the cash in hand. But he'd only have one shot; had to pick the perfect moment. And then, then he'd be free and clear, starting over, with Soosie—and her millionaire mama—behind him.

Dale Phipps was back. Life had handed him a lemon and he'd made a bottle of Petrus.

Soosie threw her leg over his. Began rubbing her damp swollen labia up and down his thigh. Sucked his nipple.

Dale began to stiffen. Make that a magnum of Petrus.

Soosie fondled his erection. A jeroboam.

He pulled Soosie on top of him, grasped her ample hips and lowered her onto his jeroboam. Began to swivel, slowly, slowly, stirring the ooze—

The radio alarm went off.

Soosie giggled. "Seven-fifteen already!"

"You set the alarm?"

"Dermatologist at eight-fifteen, only appointment available. So-o-o," Soosie urged in her most carnal chirp, "bet-turh hur-ree."

"We'll be there before the snooze alarm goes off," Dale promised.

He reached for the snooze bar.

Froze.

Surreal.

Sounded like the newscaster just said: "Rising young Chicago artist Laurie Desh, twenty-nine, was found murdered in her apartment late last night. Police haven't released any details."

Jeroboam turned to magnum turned to bottle turned to half-bottle turned to stricken baby worm.

H i, Janvier."

"Hi—actually that's not my name any more. Like, legally."

"To whom am I speaking, legally?"

"JaneDoe. Capital 'D' but all one word: JaneDoe."

If ever a name change proved someone hadn't changed. "How long you been all one word JaneDoe?"

"Three and a half years. This is a business call, isn't it?"

"Yeah."

"Shit, you and Doonie caught the Bob Gilson case? You questioning everyone Bobby slept with?" Sounding amused, possibly even pleased. No, definitely pleased.

"Is now an okay time for me to come over?"

"Just you?"

"Doonie knocked off for the night."

"But you're still working."

"Always."

"Not quite true," she averred, mock-sultry. "I'm here," she added, and hung up.

Yeah, she was there, same as Mark remembered. Except now she was JaneDoe. The term for an unknown victim—or suspect. A name she'd bothered to legally acquire. Shortly after Mark stopped seeing her. Or did it have nothing to do with him? Three years ago, fresh out of art school, she'd given herself the tag for a total unknown—a name that'd go from sarcastic to ironic if she got famous.

But then again, "JaneDoe" would also make a perfect fuck-you *nom de guerre* for a killer.

Nah. The fuck was he even thinking.

JaneDoe opened the door and they looked at each other. *Looked.*

That first-time-in-four-years moment of paralysis, each soaking up and speed-reading the other, and competing to do the better job of faking being cool.

First one who's able to speak wins.

Mark said, "Hi."

JaneDoe countered with a kiss on the cheek and silence.

Score tied.

She was wearing a black long-sleeve T-shirt over frayed, paint-stained gray tights. No bra.

"You look good," Mark told her.

"I know," JaneDoe replied, just like Janvier would've. Asked if he wanted coffee or something.

Mark followed her to the kitchen. This place was a big step up from her student pad. It was a loft in a renovated factory a block off Halsted. And maybe she'd matured or maybe it was the larger space and the high ceiling, but the fusty after-scent of pot wasn't as massive as in her old place.

"Cool apartment," he said.

"Don't worry, wasn't from dealing," she replied, tamping coffee into an espresso machine. "In fact I'm so busy I've had to start *paying* for dope."

"Progress."

As the machine hissed and burbled, JaneDoe caught Mark up on her amazing four years.

While attending the Art Institute she'd been painting, making collages, waitressing and dealing dope. Six months after graduating she was still doing those same four things. So she got a job with a woman in Evanston who had a business designing and building foam-rubber mascots for sports teams and fast-food chains.

"And then, I know the bass player from The Intermittent Wipers, and they—heard of them?"

Mark nodded. "I ain't dead yet."

"But way over thirty. So, the Wipers ask me to make costumes for a Halloween gig. Next thing, Flaming Lips is on the phone and they want a herd of dancing creatures. Soon as that tour starts, my commissions go ballistic—Lips fans wanting costumes for Burning Man and Coachella, nerds who don't wanna dress up exactly like the other nerds at Comicon, and then, money money money, sex freaks bored with standard fetish gear."

Mark gave her a thumbs-up. JaneDoe poured double espressos, handed him one and headed to her work table, explaining, "I gotta get Robo-Zeeb built and boxed for a 7 AM Fedex pickup."

"Robo-Zeeb?" Mark inquired as he followed her to the table, on which was the body of a shiny zebra-stripe robot, plus a mane, a tail and two hooves.

JaneDoe held up a helmet that looked like a sci-fi mechanical zebra head. "It's for a wealthy dude in Milan who just had a La Scala-sized break-up with his boyfriend," she explained. "Can't face the world yet, so he needs a costume so he can go clubbing anonymously. But fabulously."

"You designed a Robo-Zeeb who can drink without removing his head?"

"There's an intake port in the muzzle that allows him to drink or smoke through a straw. But he can't snort—I could drill nostril holes in the visor, but that'd look like shit, and the customer didn't specify snortability... Don't know if my costumes are high art or low art, but they're sold art, more than you can say for my paintings." JaneDoe grinned. "Okay, one more brag. Last year I had two of my more bizarro costumes in the New Chicagart show at MCA—and when the show closed, a collector bought 'em. Five grand. Apiece."

"Way to go." Mark took off his jacket; JaneDoe kept the place warm.

"Gets better—this year the collector passes away, and her kids put her collection on consignment at Marla Kretz—you know the place? Hottest gallery maybe in the city."

"Take your word for it."

"Some detective. Anyway, last month, anonymous buyer scoops 'em up—nine grand apiece. Marla now has my three newest ones but wants more—she's telling collectors I'm 'redefining sculpture' and they'd better get in quick."

"The Praxiteles of our age. Compliment, not sarcasm."

JaneDoe blew a kiss Mark's way and picked up the zebra tail, which, like the mane, was made of fiber-optic filaments. She held the tail against the robot's butt, studied it a moment, then began making trims to shape the tail to a point. As she worked, she asked, casually as she could manage, "How your last four years been?"

"Okay," Mark shrugged.

With that subject covered in sufficient detail, Detective Bergman moved on to the topic that brought him here. "So, you and Robert Gilson?"

They both went to work, Mark interrogating his ex-lover about her affair with a murder victim, while she efficiently grafted a tail, mane, and hooves to a zebra robot. It was more than efficient. It was graceful. Almost hypnotic. JaneDoe's hands were independent creatures with personalities of their own, doing what they'd clearly been born for, not at all distracted by the sex and death questions their owner was answering.

After JaneDoe took Mark through the details of her two-night stand with Gilson, Mark showed her a photo of the JaneDoe/Barbie and Gilson/Ken as they'd been posed in Gilson's cabinet: Gilson/Ken was pressing a lit cigarette into JaneDoe/Barbie's bicep.

JaneDoe gave a dismissive snort. Pushed up her sleeves. "See any burn scars?" she scoffed. "Bobby got that shit out of his system in his painting, and obviously also through those Barbie totems. Never told me he was making erotic action figures," she complained.

"So Gilson wasn't all that kinky? Didn't do things that might piss off his partners?"

"Ah shit, Mark, Bobby didn't do enough to make you want to come back for seconds, forget inspire you to knife him. If anyone wanted to kill him it'd be other major male artists—Bobby Gilson was destroying the myth that being a great artist means you're a great cockster."

"Cockster."

"Sounds better than cock-star, which is just totally high-school porno."

"What would you think of a guy referring to you as a great cuntster?"

"Depends which guy." JaneDoe inserted a battery into the Robo-Zeeb's power module, flipped a switch, and colors began to course through the two glossy translucent hooves. "*Okayyy.*"

"Y'know, if I were some suspicious homicide detective, this is where'd I'd point out: You don't seem all that broken up about Gilson's murder."

"Cried for hours. And I am gut-sick, enraged, and very much looking forward to you and Doonie nailing this son of a bitch. But I have work to do." She toggled a switch, turned a dial and now colors also pulsed through the fiber-optic mane and tail. She pulled Robo-Zeeb upright. Grinned. "Wanna try it on?"

Mark held up photos of the unidentified Barbies. "These anybody you know?"

"No—wait, the natural redhead in the denim jacket might be Chayenne Tiger. Chay's a videographer, shot a doc about Bobby."

Mark wrote down the name.

"So," JaneDoe wondered, "you gotta run off now and question Chay?"

"Little late for contacting a witness—at least one I don't already know."

"Witness? *Suspect.* All us Barbies are."

"C'mon, Janv—Jane—Doe—I know you didn't murder anybody."

"You do? How?" she demanded.

"Ms. Dunstan, do you have an alibi for the morning of the murder?"

"Nope," she crowed, "I was here working, all alone." She moved close to Mark. "I'm done. You done? Can I pour us a drink?"

Mark shook his head.

"So you still think there's some tiny percent of a percent of a mini-chance I could be the murderer," JaneDoe declared, delighted.

"Nah."

"But I haven't got an alibi." She moved closer. Much. Her breasts touching his chest. "Wanna grill me?"

He felt her nipples rise. Wasn't just her legs, she also had incredibly long... Step back. Now. Leave. Now.

Instead, Mark asked, "If it's not his wife, or any of the Barbies, why would anyone kill Robert Gilson?"

JaneDoe shrugged and so did her nipples.

"Know any artists who've been attacked, maybe didn't report it?"

"No... Buu-u-t..."

"But?"

"Six, seven years back, someone killed Laurie Desh—amazing painter—kind of a bitch, but amazing painter. You should also go catch whoever did that. Pleeeease," JaneDoe implored, dragging eloquent fingertips across the bulge in Mark's pants.

Mark gripped her wrist, removed her hand.

"I'll check it out."

Mark stepped back so their chests were no longer touching. He let go of her wrist.

"No more grilling?" JaneDoe protested.

"No."

They looked at each other.

Mark sank to his knees.

"Steaming," he explained, then pressed his mouth to her crotch, and exhaled a long, warm, damp breath through the thin stretch fabric.

JaneDoe quivered.

Mark inhaled a scent he still recognized.

NINE / 2005

Could be a coincidence, Dale told himself.

Laurie Desh got killed. Got killed two days after Dale gave Laurie's canvas to Tesca and said something about prices jumping when artists die. Doesn't mean it was Tesca. Odds are it wasn't. Sick fucks break into houses and kill women all the time.

Ah, shit. Who's he kidding. No way it's a coincidence.

Except if it is.

Midmorning, the cops issued a statement. Break-in, signs of a struggle. Cause of death strangulation, probably by garrote. Also theft of some valuables. No sexual assault.

Sounded to Dale like a junkie burglar. Except for the garrote. Do junkies carry garrotes?

Fuck it. Not his problem.

Three days. Six thousand.

He needed to find the right moment to work Soosie. Soon.

A few hours later the concierge rang Soosie's apartment and said two police detectives were at his desk; they'd like to speak to Mr. Phipps.

While waiting for the cops to make the journey to the 34th floor, Dale nearly fainted; sagged into a chair, head between his legs. Soosie took it as a sign of how deeply he was grieving.

Detectives Adams and Winokurov had only a few questions.

Did Dale know anyone with a reason to kill Laurie Desh?

None.

Is it true he and Ms. Desh had parted on bad terms?

Yes, but they'd made up; it was just business, kind of thing happens all the time.

    Still, just to dot the i's and cross the t's—where was Dale last night?

"With me," Soosie said, decorating it with a salacious grin.

A reporter called. He'd heard Dale was Laurie Desh's first dealer and longtime friend. Asked Dale about Laurie, her work, her place in the art world.

Dale was eloquent, despite having to fight to control his emotions.

Soosie, touched and impressed, sat beside Dale, leaning against him. Whenever he said something awesome she squeezed his thigh and cooed.

When Dale hung up he looked at Soosie and let the tears come. She flurried his face with kisses. They rolled onto the floor. Ripped clothing. Went total an-nee-mull.

Afterward, in the post-coital float, Dale gazed mournfully at Soosie and whispered, "I have to leave tomorrow."

Soosie let out a startled whimper.

Dale raised his bandaged hand. "Man who did this is coming after me again, in three days." He caressed Soosie's cheek. "I refuse to be anywhere near you when that happens."

TEN / 2005

Side street off of Taylor. Authentic neighborhood Italian restaurant. Dale liked the vibe, first glance, before he got out of the cab.

Inside, no tourists. Only trace amounts of hipsters.

Little cramped, little noisy, smelled like momma.

Autographed black-and-white glossy of Our Tony Bennett Of The Immaculate Tuxedo, hovering above the register.

Minor imperfection: Tommy Tesca, seated with his back against a wall. Smiling. Waving Dale over.

"Amarone," Tesca boasted, filling Dale's glass, then lifting his own in salutation.

Oh God. We toasting Laurie's death?

Dale murmured, "Your health," and gave his glass a wave that stopped short of a physical, karmically binding clink. Took a sip. "Really good."

"No shit." Tesca took a big swallow. Pushed a basket of breadsticks at Dale. "I ordered. All stuff you can eat one-handed," he grinned, glancing at Dale's heavily bandaged left hand.

"Thanks." Dale took a longer pull of the hefty red.

Tesca asked, "You bring it?"

"Every penny."

"No it ain't."

Don't panic. No panic. No. "Exact amount."

A glower. "You and me, we are nowhere near even."

Fuck. Fuck. Fuck. A black hole swirled open beneath Dale's chair—

"Fact is, heh," Tesca rumbled, "I am so fucking far ahead, dinner's on me—fuck, I ain't even gonna take that envelope you got in your pocket." Tesca snorted and smacked Dale's shoulder. "You,

Dalie-boy, are one sad motherfucker. Shoulda seen your face." Tesca refilled Dale's glass. "Drink up, red wine keeps off the heart attacks, heh?"

"So far," Dale murmured, and downed a serious dose of cardiac vaccine.

A waiter delivered an antipasto platter that was dinner for four, and promised the rest of the appetizers would be arriving in a minute.

Tesca tucked in.

Dale put food on his plate. Took a breath. Asked, "So, the painting brought more than twenty-six?"

Tesca took his time chewing. Poked his nose in his wine glass, took a lavish sniff, then drained it. Finally said, "Thirty—eight—thousand. You were right, fuckin' great painting." He refilled his glass, topped off Dale's and waved the empty bottle at a waiter. Observed Dale sitting there like a lump. "Look—you tell whatever shmuck lent you that six grand, *you gave it to me*, heh? You *keep* that cash. Your lucky night, the fuck you mopin' about?"

"Tommy…"

Go on, ask. Simple question. If only his mouth could move.

Not necessary. Tesca knew. Gave Dale a world-weary conspiratorial smirk. Explained, *sotto voce*: "She died. Bad luck for her. Good luck for us… Look. If I'm not the one who clipped her, I'd tell you, *Hey, wasn't me*. And if I did clip her, I'd tell you, *Hey, wasn't me*. So what the fuck." Tesca sat back. Gestured at Dale's untouched plate. Warned, "Don't insult the cook."

Dale speared an olive. Forced himself to place it in his mouth. Couldn't force himself to chew. The olive sat there, stuck to his sandpaper tongue.

"So," Tesca asked, "with your smart taste and this art crap selling so good, how the fuck you go broke, heh?"

Necessity was the mother of mastication; Dale had to eat the olive so he could answer.

It was a delicious, calming, possibly life-saving olive. Dale began to pick at his antipasto and explain the gallery biz. How hard it was to stock your place with art you were passionate about, that was also art someone might buy. How easy it was to slide into debt. So then you borrow some super-expensive, kitschy, sure-fire commercial pieces on consignment from a friend's gallery in New York, so you have a shot at earning some cash. Except these super-expensive pieces get torched in a fire started by idiots free-basing in a gallery next to yours, and of course by this point you'd let your insurance lapse. Suddenly you're a big six figures down and process servers are laying blue envelopes on you.

Tesca said weird-ass accidents happen in his line of work, too. Gave a few examples he thought were amusing.

After dinner, Tesca insisted on giving Dale a ride home.

Tesca didn't start the engine. Looked at Dale.

"I was lyin' before, when I said we were even."

Dale blanched.

Tesca snorted. "Christ you're easy! Heh!" Tesca pulled out a thin wad of bills and offered it to Dale. "Twelve hundred. I know, you useta get twenty percent. But heh, you didn't do the heavy lifting here. You did earn ten percent—on the profit."

"No, Tommy, that's, but—I don't—I'm fine." Dale tried to push the money away. Couldn't budge Tommy's massive hand.

"Commission on your art smarts, this is how you live." Tesca tucked the cash into Dale's breast pocket. "A 'Thank you' would be good."

"Thanks, yeah, of course, but Tommy—" Dale pulled the money out of his pocket, "—I didn't handle this, you did it on your own."

"Fuck the modesty crap. We're partners." Then, sidewalk hard: "You set her up. She went down. We cashed in."

The sucking black hole re-opened beneath Dale Phipps, while above him the light bulb went on: *The money makes me accessory to the murder. If I don't take the money, Tesca has to kill me.*

Dale slid the twelve hundred into his pocket. "Thank you, Tommy. Thank you."

Tesca gave him an approving "Heh," accompanied by a love tap on the back of the head. "You're very fuckin' welcome, partner. So we okay?"

"We're okay."

"Heh. So Dalie-boy, who we do next? Gimme a name."

"*What?!*"

"I figure this time, first we buy three, four pictures, so we make some real—"

"Fuck no, no, Tommy, I ca—"

"Fuck *yes*, this is a good thing. Just settle the fuck down, think—"

"No! No fucking way. God! I'm sorry. No." Dale pulled out the twelve hundred, and his envelope containing the six thou, and thrust them at Tesca.

Tesca sighed and slammed a brick-sized fist into his new business partner's stomach.

Dale folded up. Began making gurgling noises.

Tesca reached across him and opened the passenger-side door.

"Lean out—you puke in my car, I'm gonna hurt ya."

Dale did as instructed, half-fell out of the car and deposited his authentic neighborhood dinner and surprisingly good Amarone on the pavement.

"Jesus fuck, Dale, whole life I been fuckin' guys up to make 'em gimme money. You're the first I hadda hit to get you to take money. Here, rinse." Tesca handed Dale a bottle of water. "After every score you gonna make me smack you around before you take your cut?"

Dale shook his head. Carefully. Didn't want to spew on the dashboard and find out what Tesca meant by *hurt ya.*

Not an issue. Tesca was back in ebullient entrepreneur mode as he drove Dale home.

"So okay, you make a list of which three-four these spazz Michelangelos would see the biggest price bump after the funeral. And no thinkin' small, heh—I'm gonna kick in seventy-five, a hundred grand. Remember, ten percent of what we clear is yours."

They pulled up across from Soosie's posh Gold Coast tower. Tesca gave Dale a shrewd glance. "You live better'n most homeless guys."

"Just crashing with a friend."

"Friend friend, or a broad?"

Dale shrugged. "Yeah."

"Heh! So that's how you dug up six grand. Old-fashioned way, with the meat shovel." An approving wink. "You got hidden chops, my friend." Tesca's grin turned cold. "Me too. Tommy Tesca reads minds. Right now you're thinking you run, get far away as that cash in your pocket will go. Mistake. I'd find you. You know that, right?"

Dale nodded.

"Good. And you're also thinkin', maybe you go to the cops, tell 'em the whole thing, heh, you didn't do any crime here, it was all Tesca. Very bad idea. Cops can't prove who clipped that girl. But say somehow they do get lucky and they nail Tesca? Tesca's gonna tell 'em this kill-the-artist idea was all Dale Phipps—like some goombah would think to game the art market? Tell 'em how Phipps dimed this Desh bitch then pocketed his cut... But either way, me in jail or not, you in jail or not, this would happen: Someone would stomp your head flat." A glance at Soosie's building. "Hers too, just for fun. So, okay?"

Dale managed a soft affirmative grunt.

"Awright. Hey—c'mahhhn. We, my friend, have invented a great business."

Doonie scrutinized the JaneDoe Barbie. "You recognized her from this?"

"Same hair and eyes, same jacket, she and Gilson are both artists. Seemed worth a shot."

"Why'd you go over there without me, steada waiting till this morning?"

"Night owl, best time to catch her."

"How'd it go?" Doonie asked, hoping for the best.

Mark pretended Doonie was asking about the case. "Same as everybody else—said Gilson had no enemies."

"Janvier have an alibi?"

"JaneDoe—she's now JaneDoe, all one word."

"Why?"

"She's an artist."

"How's she lookin'?"

"Old and ugly. Didn't have an alibi—but also no motive."

"She still dealing?"

"Says that's histo—"

"Hey," Doonie scowled, pointing to the tiny inscription he'd found on the doll's backside.

Well, shit, that didn't take long. Mark handed the magnifier to Doon.

Doonie read the replicated tat. Held up the JaneDoe Barbie, pointed her butt at Mark, and with a hint of anticipatory relish, inquired, "You make a positive ID?"

After a moment Mark replied, "I won't conduct any more solo interviews with that witness."

"Not until we close this thing, so we gotta move fast." Doonie grinned hungrily, a man on a mission to protect his vicarious sex life.

"We bust our humps we make an arrest in forty-eight hours."

Two days later they were in Lieutenant Husak's office delivering the daily no-progress report.

"Re-interviewed Helen Gilson, twice. Tossed the house, her permission. Nothin'," Doonie groused.

"You really think Mrs. I Only Stabbed Him Once Gently had no problem with hubbie screwing sixteen live Barbies, and playing with dirty dolls?" Husak wondered. "Having him whacked and the Ken shoved in his mouth seems a wife kind of message."

"If she hired the hit she did it telepathically," Mark said. "We just don't like her."

"We don't like anybody," Doonie admitted.

"This morning's the funeral," Mark said. "We're gonna go stare at people."

Maybe they'd get lucky. Some hinky dude would snicker during the eulogy, then piss on the grave.

Bob Gilson had taken a piss on religion, but his infirm eighty-eighty-year old father wanted a funeral mass for his son, and Helen Gilson was as obliging a daughter-in-law as she was a wife. She booked her husband's final personal appearance at Holy Name, Chicago's toniest cathedral. Bobby was a devout atheist but Helen knew he'd've been willing to do this for his dad.

Doonie eyeballed arriving mourners on the sidewalk outside, while Mark slipped inside and studied them from the gallery during the service.

Nothing. No secret gloating grins. No vengeful glares.

Only guy interrupting the eulogy was a sobbing eighty-eight-year-old in a wheelchair.

The cops tailed the cortege to the cemetery, got out and observed from a respectful distance.

Doonie perused the six Barbies who'd attended the mass and

were now arrayed by the grave. "You weren't shitting me, all six of Gilson's Barbie boinks went up to the widow in church and kissed her?"

"Takes a village to raise a child, takes a harem to bury an artist."

"Tall, long black hair," Doonie, said, indicating the most striking Barbie; four years back Doonie had spoken to then-Janvier on the phone a few times, but they'd never met. "That must be her."

"Yes it must."

JaneDoe felt eyes on her, looked up. Spotted Mark. She was wearing shades, he couldn't see her eyes. But her lips eased into a serene hint of amusement. He knew why.

The other night Mark had gotten out of JaneDoe's bed at 4 AM and started pulling his clothes on, saying, "Listen, ah… Sorry."

JaneDoe shrugged. "You have to get home to change clothes."

"Not apologizing for not staying the night. Apologizing for staying at all."

JaneDoe raised an eyebrow.

Mark explained, "Now I have to recuse myself from the case. Or hide this from my boss."

"Fine by me either way," JaneDoe said.

"And, either way… Can't see you again, in private, until the case is cleared."

"That part, what's the word, sucks."

"Lots. And it'd be best, for both of us, if you don't tell anyone about this—friends or police. With the cops, never lie, just don't volunteer. But if they do ask, always be completely straight with them."

JaneDoe broke into a teasing sing-song chant: "Marky fucked a sus-pect, Marky fucked a sus-pect."

"You're not a suspect. Still, Marky is having no luck finding a way to apologize for being stupid enough to sleep with you, without having that sound like an insult."

JaneDoe sighed, got out of bed and gave Mark a good kiss. Prophesied, "Someday you're gonna stop thinking your job is more fun than I am."

Now Mark was standing in yet another cemetery for yet another stranger's funeral and thinking, maybe JaneDoe had a point—*shit*—Laurie Desh. He'd been too busy to pull the Desh file, then it slipped his mind. Might as well take a look. Desh's alibi for the Gilson murder was that she'd been dead seven years, but maybe she'd have something interesting to say.

TWELVE / 2012

Mark got on it soon as they got back to the office after the funeral. The Desh and Gilson cases did share similarities. Both vics were painters. Murdered at home, died from neck wounds. In both cases the cops had fuck-all to show for their efforts.

The big difference: Mark and Doonie made an effort. The detectives who caught the Desh case had waved at it as if it were a passing train, then filed a report on the noise it made as it went by.

Desh's apartment had been robbed, half-heartedly; a piece of lazy theater the investigating officers chose to believe. The half-assed Homicide detectives emailed a memo to Robbery asking them to drop a line if they ever busted a burglar with a garrote in his pocket. Declared their work done.

There was one Desh acquaintance who had a glimmer of a motive; an art dealer who'd gone bust after Desh hit it big and took her business elsewhere. But he had an alibi. And he was bankrupt, so the cops assumed he couldn't afford to buy a hit.

"Not that they bothered to run his financials," Mark informed Doonie. "If they did they didn't mention it—these two weren't into cluttering reports with facts. Or words."

"Who were these guys?"

"Vassily Winokurov and Philip Ada—"

"Adams!" Doonie chuckled. "Phil and VW got away with more murder than they solved. Phil's got a Chinaman at the Hall, and his Lieutenant at the time—um, Terry Schmidtlander—Schmidtlander was smarter than to fuck with Phil Adams over small stuff like working a case the right way."

"How the hell big is Adams' Chinaman?"

"Cousin Eddie."

"Fuck," Mark commented, impressed.

Cousin Eddie Strick was a Fifth-Floor guy; desk on the same floor as the Mayor. Officially Eddie was something like third assistant sub-mayor. What mattered was Eddie was the Mayor's third cousin and go-to guy for making things happen, and not happen, and un-happen, in untraceable ways.

"Adams still on the job?" Mark asked. "I wanna talk to him, find out what isn't in the file."

"Waste of time. Sensitive type, ain't much for criticism."

"So we go at Winokurov."

"Nope. Big-time steroid-sucker. Cartoon muscles, cartoon brain, perfect partner for Phil. Until a stroke turned him into asparagus."

"So we go see the art dealer. Dale Phipps. I got his current address."

"Course you do," Doonie groused. The big man hauled himself to his feet. "After this wild goose shit, we're stopping for a Jack and you're picking up the first three rounds."

"Doonie, Bergman!" Husak barked, erupting from his office. "We got another dead artist. Area Four, but you get over there."

THIRTEEN / 2005-2006

Richard Struger."

"Why?"

"He lives in Milwaukee."

"That's his big appeal? I gotta drive ninety miles to pop him?"

"Yes. Tommy, Laurie Desh gets killed, it's a random act. But if another Chicago artist gets killed, the cops will see a pattern."

"Heh."

"And Tommy—can you, can this one look like an accident?"

"Trickier. And more expensive."

"Worth it."

"Why not stick with another fucked-up break-in robbery, like Desh? Sad shit, happens alla time."

"If two artists get murdered the same way, only ninety miles apart, it still looks like a pattern. But if it's not a murder... Much safer."

"Heh. Dalie-boy, you got a brain when you put your mind to it."

"Thank you."

"And we buy the paintings under your name. That's safer, too."

Richard Struger liked to ride his mountain bike, alone, through a rural county northwest of Milwaukee. Had a regular route.

Late one afternoon Struger apparently took a spill while peddling over a railroad crossing on a remote country lane. May have hit his head on the rail. Wasn't enough skull left to be certain.

It was dusk when the freight train barreled through. By the time the engineer saw the cyclist splayed across the tracks it was too late for anything but a quick curse and sensible braking. Derailing wouldn't have improved the poor bastard's chances.

The condition of the body parts suggested—the M.E. couldn't say for sure—Struger might have died a few hours before the train went through. Taking a hard fall and smacking his skull on a steel rail, or breaking his neck, could easily have done it.

The coroner's call was accidental death, probably caused by Struger falling off his bike. That ruling comforted his family; it was a mercy, having official sanction for the probability Struger had checked out before the train disassembled him.

Also comforted the railroad. No grounds for a suit.

For Dale Phipps the coroner's verdict on Struger was comforting, and profitable and tormenting.

Tommy Tesca had come up with the hundred grand.

Dale acquired three Struger paintings, in three cities. On behalf of an anonymous client. A common practice.

Four months after the final purchase Tesca visited Struger. With hands-on help from Dale Phipps.

Part of Dale was sickened by collaborating in a murder. A larger part of Dale was sickened by the possibility of getting caught. He hadn't liked Tommy's plan, which was to stage a hit-and-run accident while Struger was riding his bike.

The loan shark had a business to run, so the unemployed art dealer went to Wisconsin and followed the target around. Came up with a better plan. Checked train schedules. Picked the spot.

And was there when Tesca killed Richard Struger, because moving and placing the body was a two-man job.

The next day the newbie murderer considered suicide. Settled for morose lethargy, punctuated by random vomiting. Tufts of hair began deserting Dale's scalp, unprodded by any comb.

Soosie noticed Dale seemed a little down and whisked him off to Salt Cay.

Caribbean luxury did lighten Dale's mood. But not his skin. It got sun-burned. It blistered. The blisters left red blotches, which, despite determined efforts by multiple dermatologists, never went away.

Over the next six months Dale sold the Strugers. San Francisco,

43

Miami, Berlin. Net profit, ninety-four grand.

Tommy Tesca announced he'd double down, spend two, three hundred thousand on the next project. Make some real money.

Dale Phipps said that given the amount of work he was doing, including murder-planning and corpse-wrangling, they should split the profits 50-50.

Tesca glowered but Dale didn't melt.

They settled on 60-40.

Dale dove into research on artists who lived outside Chicago, and were old enough so that death might seem natural.

Dale dove even further into research on offshore corporations and accounts. No way he'd ever again put his name on a transaction. Or use a bank whose records the cops could get a peek at.

He developed gum disease.

FOURTEEN / 2012

When Mark and Doonie arrived there was a small crowd of camera jackals and gawkers outside the crime scene, a modern town-house in Wicker Park. Word had gotten out Gerd Voorsts had been murdered; this being the second killing of a major artist in a little over a week, the social and news media had leapt into serial killer heat.

One look at the corpse and Mark and Doonie took that same leap.

The murder weapon was different; this vic had been treated to a bullet through the temple. But the toy in his mouth was a persuasive bit of stylistic consistency. It was a Yellow Submarine dildo. Beatles peering out the portholes.

Wendy Hsu and Jim Montero, the Area Four detectives who'd caught the case, ran the details. TOD was about 11 PM last night. Ligatures indicated Voorsts had been handcuffed. Shooter marched him down to the basement guest suite and put him where he was found, fully clothed, in a bathtub. The small entry wound and lack of an exit wound, plus the basement bathroom location, said the weapon was a .22; turn on the exhaust fan, flush the toilet, pull the trigger and the pop wouldn't play louder than a percussive fart.

Voorsts was fifty-seven, Dutch national, here on a work visa. The body was found this afternoon by the vic's boyfriend, Hal Taylor, twenty-nine, who was returning from kayaking the Grand Canyon.

According to Taylor, Voorsts had no enemies, stalkers, threats, debts or batshit ex-boyfriends.

And no Yellow Submarine. Had to be something the killer brought with him. Which gave the cops a lead to run down. Couldn't be that many places you could buy that dildo.

Hal Taylor was in the kitchen, drinking chamomile tea and eyeing his constantly vibrating cell. He turned the phone off. If he returned even one of the calls or texts that were flooding in, he'd lose it. He was determined to keep his shit together in front of the cops. Partly because that's what the street taught him growing up black on the south side. Partly because he wasn't about to play the weepy gay. Mainly because that's how Gerd would handle it.

"Mr. Taylor?"

Two plainclothes cops. Big, disheveled, paunchy but powerful middle-aged Irish polar bear. And a thirtysomething dude with a lanky gunslinger thing going on, and a scary-smart face, starting with striking gray eyes.

Taylor stood to shake their hands—*Ants! Or was he just imagining*—

"I'm Detective Dunegan, Detective Bergman, we're sorry for your loss. We're working the Robert Gilson murder—"

No, those really are ants crossing that windowsill—Ignore the ants, just fucking ignore those goddamn—.

"—and we got a coupla questions you could help us with."

"Of course. I—uh, I uh—" Taylor couldn't control it, "—excuse me—" The rage launched him past the cops, to the windowsill where he pounded and pounded, obliterating every one of those…

Oh, fuck. Oh God. I'm a mess… Sorry, Gerd.

Taylor brushed ant fragments off his hands. "Sorry, I… When I, I found Gerd, there was… this trail of ants across his body. They were swarming… in and out of the bullet hole."

"No apology necessary," Bergman said, "little bastards had it coming."

Jesus. Cops you were glad to have around. Gerd would've been amused.

The older cop asked the questions. The younger cop observed, gray eyes reading Taylor the way they'd assess an X-ray.

Dunegan asked, "Was there anything Mr. Voorsts and Mr. Gilson had in common? Were they friends, maybe working on anything together?"

Taylor shook his head. "They barely knew each other. We met Bobby and Helen at a reception last spring. A month later we had them over for a dinner party, about twelve people. Gerd and Bobby didn't hit it off. I think Bobby found Gerd a touch pompous." A rueful half-grin. "Which he could be."

"Any friends or associates in common?"

"None—Gerd was in town five years ago, for four months—he taught a master class at the Art Institute—that's where we met."

"The Art Institute," Dunegan noted. "You were a student?"

"Yeah. When the semester ended I went to Amsterdam with him. We just moved back to Chicago last year, it's not like Gerd knew many people here…" Taylor's voice plunged into the barely audible, a whisper from the pit of his stomach. "Gerd moved here because I was homesick. And last night he was alone because I had to go fucking kayaking…" Taylor clenched his eyes shut.

"Hey," the big cop confided, "twenty years in Homicide, I learned a coupla things. First is they got murder everywhere, even Amsterdam. Second is the only one who gets to take credit for killing Gerd Voorsts is the one who killed Gerd Voorsts."

After a moment Taylor whispered, "Thanks."

"Sorry to have to ask," Dunegan said, "does the Yellow Submarine refer to some, anything, in Mr. Voorsts' life?"

"Fuck, *no*," Taylor hissed. Then, apologetic: "Not, not far as I knew."

Dunegan flicked a tiny, almost telepathic glance at Bergman, giving him some sort of cue. Taylor recognized the lived-in intimacy.

Bergman asked, "Five years ago, at the Art Institute, did you or Mr. Voorsts know a student named JaneDoe?"

"Yeah—but then her name was Janvier. How did you know she was at school then?"

"We've interviewed all of Mr. Gilson's acquaintances. So you knew her?"

"Casually. But JaneDoe was one of the first people I re-connected with when we moved back, because she and I had pieces in last year's New Chicagart show—in fact, she was at that dinner here with Bobby and Helen Gilson."

Bergman asked, "How did JaneDoe and Mr. Voorsts get along?"

"Great, this time."

"This time?"

"When Gerd gave that master class, JaneDoe wasn't allowed in because she was an undergraduate. She asked if she could audit but Gerd turned her down. She was pissed—but like I said, this time she and Gerd... Oh c'mon. JaneDoe? Kill people?"

Bergman's gray eyes went opaque.

Taylor didn't do representational art, but he knew someday he'd paint those eyes, that look.

Christ. Planning a painting while Gerd's down there with ants waltzing in and out of his skull.

But Taylor wasn't mortified. Because he knew Gerd would approve.

FIFTEEN / 2012

There weren't many ways being a cop reminded Mark of being a teenager, but one was that the car was the most reliable place guys could talk with no danger of being overheard by a grownup.

They were driving to JaneDoe's, on official business.

Mark said, "So."

Doonie gave a dismissive wave. "Filed your paperwork after you interviewed her. Then just now we brought Hsu and Montero up to speed about the JaneDoe connection soon as we heard about it. And we're goin' to re-interview JaneDoe, together. You're in policy."

"Not the part where I forgot to inform Husak my first interview with her ended in bed. *And by the way, Loo, four years ago JaneDoe and I had an affair...* Doon, she's about a quarter-inch from being a person of interest. Longer I wait to tell Husak, the deeper the shit." Mark glanced at his partner. "Not just for me. Who's gonna believe you knew nothing about it?"

"Everyone," Doonie ruled. "I never even met her, years ago she and me just had a coupla phone conversations. Far as what happened last week, you never told me you banged her, I can testify hand on a bible."

Which was no guarantee the brass would believe it, seeing how Doon had his share of reprimands engraved on his permanent record. Another similarity to adolescence.

Mark said, "Nah. Before we talk to JaneDoe I gotta tell Husak—"

"And take a guaranteed rip? Just for not mentioning you fucked a witness?"

"Doon—"

"Look, if she turns into a suspect, you'll go confess your sins to Husak and lie your ass off about how I knew nothin'. Till then fuck it, we got work to do."

SIXTEEN / 2012

When JaneDoe's door opened the cops were enveloped by the muscular stank of high-grade weed. Standing there was charred sweetness herself, green eyes gone heavy-lidded. Floppy black sweater, baggy black pants. Half-empty wine glass in her hand, sadness in her eyes, weary grin on her lips.

She gazed at Doonie, pleased. "Detective Dunegan, at last."

JaneDoe handed her glass to Mark and gave Doonie a kiss. On the lips. "You give good phone," she explained.

JaneDoe retrieved her wine from Mark and stated, with somber formality, "How nice to see you again, Detective Bartman."

Doonie laughed. Said, "So tell us you didn't kill Gerd Voorsts."

"I didn't kill Gerd Voorsts," JaneDoe agreed. She ushered Mark and Doonie inside, confiding, "Though I'm flattered you think I could be Chicago's most cultured serial killer."

"Anything you set your mind to," Doonie assured the youngster. "Gotta ask, hon—where were you between ten PM and two AM last night?"

"Right there," she said, indicating her work table, on which were the unassembled parts of a multi-hued... something. An asymmetric female something, if those seven mounds on the torso were breasts. "I'm too busy to have a life, forget go around stealing lives."

She finished her wine and poured herself another.

"Anybody confirm you were here?"

"Sure." A casual wave at her work table. "Zug," she said, revealing the creature's name, without giving away its gender.

"Any homo sapiens?" Mark inquired.

JaneDoe gave an apologetic shrug. Then asked, for real, "How's Hal doing?"

After a moment Mark replied, "His friends should call him."

"His friends keep getting voicemail, and no replies to texts," JaneDoe murmured. Then slipped back into her armor, a breastplate of cynicism topped with a helmet of intoxication. "Lemme guess what brought you here: I was at a dinner at Hal and Gerd's house with Bobby Gilson. I've been wracking my little brain and can't come up with a single fun fact about that night. Or anything Bobby and Gerd had in common besides painting the shit out of every canvas they touched. Now sit down, Detectives, ask away, I'll tell you everything else I don't know about why the hell this is happening."

They sat. Went through her every encounter with Voorsts, especially him not letting her take his master class. She assured them if she killed teachers who annoyed her, the faculty lounge at the Art Institute would've looked like Omaha Beach.

"Fucked if I can think of anything else," Doonie announced. Not true; he was signaling Mark to ask it, after the interviewee thought the quiz was over, and might be caught with her composure down.

Doonie said, "Good finally meetin' ya."

"You too," JaneDoe said.

She walked them to the door.

As they got there, Mark asked, "By the way—you own a gun?"

"No, that's you guys."

So much for the composure-loss theory. "Wanna come take a paraffin test for gunshot residue?"

JaneDoe shook her head. "Send your paraffin guy here. Gotta finish Zug."

Doonie asked, "You can work when you're this high?"

"Sure. My art's like my sex life. No mistakes I can't correct in the morning," she said, shifting her gaze to Mark.

Doonie informed Mark, "I'll be out in the car." Made his exit.

JaneDoe and Mark looked at each other.

"How you doing?" he asked.

"How you think? Someone's running around killing artists."

"Male artists."

"So I got nothing to worry."

"There someone you can stay with, or who can stay here?"

"You."

Knife in. Knife twisted. Say your line, asshole. "Not till we nail this guy."

He touched her cheek and left. There was no sound of a door shutting behind him. JaneDoe was standing in the doorway, watching him. He returned, eased her inside and closed the door. Waited till he heard the lock click.

Mark got in the car.

Doonie said, "Maybe she *should* get a gun."

"Her and every artist in Chicago... Maybe that's the only connection between our vics. They were artists. Maybe our perp's an especially serious art critic."

"Ooh," Doonie grunted, pleased.

As Mark put the car into gear Doonie took out his phone. Scrolled through the voicemails he'd ignored in the hours since this case expanded from a media snack about one dead artist into a media feast about one live serial killer. Picked the winner, Karl Winnie at the Sun-Times.

"Karl, Doonie—Look, wish I could help ya, but—... Look, it's too soon, can't say anything yet, you know the fuckin' drill... Well, shit, Karl, one detail, 'cause it's you. We're calling our perp The Art Critic."

SEVENTEEN / 2010

Usually it was the nudes. A man—almost always a man—would park himself in front of a nudie—and stare at it too long.

Maleekwa Pritchard-Varney, one of the uniformed guards stationed in the galleries at the Art Institute, wasn't surprised how many dudes got freaky off peeping at nudes, any nudes. Even that Picasso where the only good part was one triangular boobie stickin' out the side this poor woman's head. What Maleekwa didn't get—wasn't sure she wanted to—was why so many people—men, women, young, old—would get hypnotized by that crazy-nasty Ivan Albright painting, *Picture of Dorian Gray.*

Dorian Gray had clothes on, but Jesus, it was like his body was the whole Wikipedia of ugly diseases. And not just him—even the wall and furniture and rug in that painting had infections and plagues.

Disgusting. Yet near as many got hypnotized by it as by the nudes.

But that was none of a guard's business, long as the visitors didn't touch the painting, or touch themselves. Maleekwa hated seeing some perv with his hand way deep in his pocket, hated having to go up to the perv and tell him, "Sir, you'll have to leave now."

Didn't think she'd have that problem with the little dude, gentleman in a fine black pinstripe suit, who'd been staring at Dorian Gray for twenty minutes. The look he was giving Dorian Gray wasn't freaky horny. Just kinda sad, like far, far away sad.

Shit. Wasn't too hard to guess why.

Hey Dor, how's it hanging, and oozing, and bleeding?

I know, I know, been a while, mea culpa, but things have gotten hectic, and complicated and scary beyond belief. You know if possible I would've been here sooner. You know you're the only one I can talk to. And you know how much it means to me to verify no matter how putrid my skin gets, yours is worse. And always will be. Ivan Albright really was a genius.

Good thing Ivan's dead. No chance I'll have to murder him.

That's right, five years in, business is booming, profits are incredible. So Tommy Tesca has lost his mind. He wants to bring in an outside investor, someone who can plunk down millions.

Wait. Gets better. Tommy's not tapping any old venture capitalist. He's got his heart set on going partners with Gianni Mastrizzi.

What do you mean, "What is a Gianni Mastrizzi?" Dorian, all due respect, you live in Chicago. You should keep current on the civic fundamentals.

Mastrizzi is the heavy of heavies in the Chicago Outfit. Old school, butchered his way to the top. No offense, Dor, this guy's rep is worse than yours.

Well shit yeah I tried to talk Tommy out of this, I'm not a complete idiot. Which is why I caved when he said he'd snap my fuckin' head off if I didn't shut up.

No point arguing. There's something insanely important to Tommy about getting in with the Lord High Mobster, no matter how stupid and risky that has to be.

So tomorrow we meet with Gianni Mastrizzi—and his son Lou, who I hear has an MBA, a sophisticate who hasn't whacked nearly as many people as the Old Man.

For some reason it doesn't matter to Tommy that if the Mastrizzis buy in, we'll be working with guys who'll bury us if any little thing goes wrong. Or maybe even if it all goes right.

Oh c'mon, Dorian—what "upside" do you think I'm missing?

Oh. Right. If this deal goes down I'll be done with murdering merely important artists. I'll be murdering great ones.

Thanks Dor. Always count on you to keep things in perspective.

The gentleman with the fine suit and the foul skin gave the disgusting freak in the painting this fond, unhappy little smile.

Oh. Oh, Lord.

Maybe that poor man ain't spending time 'cause he likes to look at that painting. Maybe it was because that painting was looking at him, and not a soul else could stand to.

EIGHTEEN / 2012

It was 8:40 PM when they got back to the office. Husak was still there, and on the phone. He waved Mark and Doonie into his office.

"Uh-huh. Right. Yessir. Uh-huh." Husak hung up a little too hard. Complained, "You'd think Ditka and Jordan got whacked. HQ's been lit up by the national media, plus Europe, especially Holland." Husak eyed Doonie. "And our perp's already got a cute name—The Art Critic."

"That was fast," Mark commented, blandly.

Husak kept staring at Doonie. "It was on Karl Winnie's blog."

"Reporters," Doonie scoffed. "Winnie pulls the name out of his ass but says he got it from a cop, fools his editor into thinking he's got sources."

Husak wearily demanded, "Just tell me Winnie's source didn't use that term in front of the bereaved."

"Loo!" Doonie snorted, offended.

"Small blessings. So watcha got?"

Mark and Doonie briefed Husak.

Husak said, "The Ken doll and the Yellow Submarine are kinda arty; this JaneDoe is worth a look."

Doonie took Gilson and Voorsts. Pulled their communications, looking to see if they'd been in touch with one another or a common third party.

Mark took JaneDoe.

But first Mark put in a call to the POD unit. Police Observation Device. Spy cams. The policeman's friend. Twelve hundred of them, attached to light poles and buildings across the great city of Chicago.

Mark requested a survey of footage from every camera within a mile of the two crime scenes, for two hours before and after each murder. If they spotted the same car or pedestrian near both locations, might be a magic bullet.

Mark went through JaneDoe's communications and financials. Hit the databases, looking for anything hinky in her past. Nada.

Mark searched for murders with a dildo sodomy signature. Squat.

A search for any unsolved artist homicide spat out Laurie Desh.

Mark expanded the search to include any artist death nationwide that merited a police investigation, starting the year Desh went down, 2005.

In 2006 in Wisconsin, Richard Struger fell off his bike, knocked himself out or broke his neck, then got run over by a train. Sort of strange accident. Which made it sort of typical; every year dozens of people manage to snuff themselves in improbable ways.

In Los Angeles in 2009, Harold Pruitt took a fall off a roof. There was no evidence Pruitt was suicidal. No intoxication or physical evidence that pointed to an accident. But also no evidence he was pushed.

In 2010 in Taos, Ella Stark passed away in her sleep. Stark was 83 and had emphysema; coroner ruled she'd simply stopped breathing.

The police report noted a small mystery: Alfred, Stark's black Lab, was gone. Neighbors said the dog had never before run off.

To one neighbor, the dog's disappearance suggested Ella Stark's spirit had entered Alfred and he/she was now running free. To Mark, who hadn't done mescaline since college, it suggested the possibility of a break-in which Alfred had made a fatal effort to thwart. Same possibility occurred to the Taos cops. But a search of the premises found nothing had been stolen or disturbed. And no puddle of retriever blood.

Which put Mark back where he started, with Laurie Desh being the only verified unsolved artist homicide.

Like Gilson and Voorsts, it happened in Chicago. Unlike them, Desh was female, and there'd been no oral decoration. But Desh might be an early work by a serial whose kinks escalated over time.

Tomorrow morning Mark and Doonie should make that visit to Desh's art dealer, Dale—

Husak lumbered out of his office and asked, "Got any hits?" He was wearing his raincoat.

Doonie said, "Nope. Gilson and Voorsts weren't phone pals. And no mutual third party. Also, GR result came back on JaneDoe—negative." Doonie glanced at Mark.

Mark understood; Doon wanted him to establish he wasn't defending JaneDoe. "Negative but not conclusive," Mark cautioned. "She works with dyes and glue, got a box of latex gloves. Far as her phones, in the past year JaneDoe made one call to the Taylor-Voorsts household landline, but she traded calls with Hal Taylor's cell—her relationship was with him, not Voorsts."

"Then go home," Husak ordered. "Just been notified we got a 7 AM meet tomorrow, to organize a task force. Its us and Area Four— and an FBI liaison."

"Feebs, over just two vics?" Doonie asked.

"Apparently the Dutch don't have that many great painters left— their Prime Minister called the White House, who jingled the Mayor, who was already unhappy about Chicago's new rep as the artist murder capital of the world. Go home. Sleep fast."

Husak headed out the door, intent on obeying his own order.

Doonie looked at Mark. "Drink?"

As if it were actually a question.

JaneDoe would be Topic A at tomorrow's meeting, with the FBI.

"I'm buying," Mark told Doonie.

"No shit."

NINETEEN / 2010

The brand-new STS rolled west through the darkness, into the promised land.

The gleaming eight-cylinder beast came to rest in a well-lit driveway, alongside a security intercom. The driver's window whooshed down. A meaty hand emerged and a thick finger jabbed a button.

Ten long seconds later a disinterested metallic voice said, "Yeah?"

"It's Tesca. Tommy Tesca," he specified.

No reply. The gate slid open, granting entrance to a small private parking lot behind ZeeZeeZ Bowl-A-Rama in Downer's Grove.

Heavy steel door in the back of the building. Security cameras.

Inside the steel door, a pat-down.

Tommy and Dale are led down to the basement beneath the lanes, then to a sub-basement and into an office where, soon as the door shuts, the racket from the bowling overhead just fucking disappears. And where not just the Son, but the Father, are waiting to hear what Tommy Tesca has to say.

Heh.

Spent most of his life eating Mastrizzi shit, but now he's here. ZeeZeeZ. Private sit-down. Not just with Lou The MBA Boy, but also the Old Man himself, Gianni Mastrizzi, that vicious cocksucker with eyes like a dead snake. Gianni had this hairless reptile skull that was too small for his body, which somehow made him more threatening.

Tommy was cousin to the Mastrizzis. Twice removed, but family. But he was not a made man. Just some shark kicking taxes up the chain. All 'cause back when Tommy was seventeen he had this little fuckup, burglary gone wrong.

Like he went into the house of someone he shouldn't've, honest mistake, no idea this rich Polack fuck was connected.

Worse, the cops caught Tommy.

Tommy's mom went crying to Gianni Mastrizzi. The Old Man came through, got Tommy's case dumped.

Ever since, the Old Man saw Tommy as nothing but ass-pain. Even the son, Lou, who as kids Tommy and him got along, Lou since then acts like he can't see or hear Tommy.

Till now.

Now it's Tommy sitting with his cousins, sipping scotch and explaining what a fantastic thing great art is.

You buy paintings by some genius, he turns into some dead genius, then you flip the paintings for two, three times what you paid.

Next Tommy explains the rules that keep the scam safe.

String out the buys over months, wait three-six months before you whack the artist, then string out the sales.

Whack older artists—their shit is worth more, and it's easier to make it look like a natural event.

Don't hit Chicago artists, too close to home and makes a pattern. Same reason, don't hit more than one artist in any city, heh.

Tommy saw no need to mention it was Dale came up with those rules. Little leprosy-face dweeb was only at this meet because Lou needed to hear every sorry-ass detail about the paperwork.

But, credit where it's due, when Dale starts describing the fucking house of financial mirrors he built to move the money, cover the tracks and duck the taxes, The MBA Boy's into it.

Dale and Tommy created an offshore corporation. An art consulting firm, with offshore bank accounts.

Next they set up six offshore shell companies. Each one hires the art consultant firm to buy one painting—by wire, no face-to-face, nobody's name used. Then these six shells peddle the paintings back and forth between each other till anyone trying to follow the money gets fucking dizzy. Then each company sells its painting, months apart, to legit collectors.

After Dale finished, Tommy, as the man in charge, got the last word.

"Bottom line, beauty of the art market is, the more expensive the painting, the huger the jump when the artist dies. Each time around

I bought pricier shit, and each time, my margins went up. So… Heh?"

Father and Son stared at him. It lasted maybe five seconds. Felt long and deep as the Grand Canyon.

Lou said, "We'll think it over."

Tommy looked at Gianni. Mr. Dead Snake Eyes had not spoken this whole meeting and his face never showed a thing. Good. Time to worry with Gianni is when he smiles at you.

The MBA Boy stands, meeting over. Lou shakes Tommy's hand, says, "This is an interesting operation."

Tommy knows Lou ain't being polite, 'cause Lou's never worried about being polite to Tommy.

Jesus fuck. The hook is set. Tommy is in. He is in.

Then Lou shakes Dale's hand. "Thank you. Impressive presentation."

The fuck? Tommy gets *interesting*, Dale gets *Thank you* and *impressive*? A cold anger leapt inside Tommy, along with this sick feeling—

He clamped down. Don't go fucking paranoid. This is the Mastrizzis being the kinda assholes they are. Letting Tommy know, until he delivers heavy dollars, to them he's the same fuckup he was at seventeen.

Fine. What's gonna happen is, Tommy's gonna get rich, the Mastrizzis are gonna get richer, and Tommy's gonna be inside.

Trusted.

Made.

Or else. Or fucking else.

TWENTY / 2012

Mark lived on Sheridan, in a high-rise just past the north end of Lakeshore Drive. It was after two when, weary and unsober, he got back to his one-bedroom apartment and crawled into his one bed. But, disobeying Husak's order, Mark didn't sleep fast. Too busy interrogating the ceiling, demanding an explanation why, soon as he ID'd JaneDoe, he hadn't told Husak: *Loo, in 2008 I had a relationship with the ass tattoo Barbie. Someone else will have to interview her.*

And then he parlays that initial stupidity by going dog-wild? Knowing, even while he was burying his face in her crotch, that if he waited till this case was cleared, JaneDoe and her crotch would still be there.

Why?

The ceiling suggested: Gale.

Really? His ex-girlfriend gets fiancéed, so he's gotta go screw anyone, right away?

Shit, if it was just about getting laid he would've called Carrie Eli... except he couldn't. Carrie wasn't available.

Mark and Carrie met in college. Lust at first sight. Never led to love. Just lifelong friendship, with sleepovers. But only when neither was in a real relationship.

Assistant State's Attorney Carrie Eli's idea of a real relationship was to fall in love with a married man—she was a workaholic commitophobe to a degree that made Mark look like a stone romantic. And Carrie was quite pleased with her current somebody else's husband.

Shit.

Maybe Mark could request a therapeutic exemption—right, call Carrie at—Christ, 3:37 AM—and hope her married boyfriend isn't there. Hi, mind if I drop by for a mercy fuck to take my mind off my sex life?

But, shit, wasn't the sex that was bothering him. It was his lack of professionalism—

His landline rang. He answered, "Bergman."

"I'm sorry," Carrie Eli said. "Hope I—"

"I'm awake. You all right?"

"I'm in my car across the street."

Carrie gave Mark a perfunctory peck, strode past him and headed for the bedroom, steaming mad, peeling off her clothes.

"Let me guess," Mark said, trailing her, "your boyfriend's hooked up with a girl younger and more solvent than you, and for her he's actually going to divorce his wife."

"No, I'm used to that." Carrie yanked off her bra and angrily flung it across the room. "This is serious. This putz, with the wedding ring and the eighteen pictures of his daughters in his phone, is—" she spat the epithet: "—*not married*! Those were stunt kids! Nieces!"

Mark cracked up.

Carrie thrust a hand in Mark's robe and grabbed his dick. "Stop laughing and what happens next won't hurt."

"But it's funny," he insisted. "You found a guy who's marriage avoidance program is even more robust than yours. You've met your soul-mate."

"Not true! I'm honest! And not the point! The point is he runs this lounge lizard scam and *I fell for it*! I'm too, too—*everything*—for that! *Fuck*!" She shook her head. "Don't hate him near as much as I hate feeling like a total idiot. Y'know?"

"Yeah," Mark sighed, "I know that feeling." He enfolded her in his arms.

Then the bed grabbed them, tore off Mark's robe and Carrie's panties, and Carrie, on a mission, was furiously, urgently all over Mark. Climbed aboard, slammed down hard, and again, and again-again-againagainagainagain...

Slowed. Stopped. Eyed him.

"What?" Mark asked.

"You're distracted. You're almost never distracted."

"Distracted," Mark scoffed.

He treated Carrie to twenty minutes of the deranged, bed-damaging opposite of distracted.

Sank back into the pillows, soaked, panting, and, oh fucking finally, empty-headed, floating off to sleep.

Carrie snuggled alongside. Gave him a tender kiss on the cheek. Laid her head on his shoulder.

Whispered, *"Who is she?"*

TWENTY-ONE / 2010

Smothering the old woman was a piece of cake, but then they noticed her dog had stopped breathing, too.

Son of a bitch had been snoring like a lawnmower when Tommy and Dale snuck in, but now the Lab was as inert as if it was his face that had been underneath a pillow with a three-hundred pound mobster on top.

"Ah shit," Dale muttered, as he kept checking Alfred for a pulse that kept not being there. Unfuckingbelievable. First time they'd ever had a screw-up and it happens with three-point-seven million bucks of Mastrizzi money on the line.

Ella Stark lived alone, on a secluded hillside outside of Taos, New Mexico.

Two things you can count on when sneaking into a house in the middle of the night in the rural southwest:

1) The owner, even if—especially if—she's an eighty-three-year-old stoner with emphysema, will have a gun handy.

2) There will be a dog who will bark his ass off.

Earlier that evening Dale had plodded by dressed as a hiker, and flipped a spiked meatball onto the property. He'd immersed himself in veterinary pharmacology until he'd determined the perfect sleeping dose for a dog Alfred's size.

Perfect for a younger, healthier dog Alfred's size.

Dale looked up at Tommy. "We have to bury him."

"Doggie funeral, heh?" Tommy said, amused. In the months since the Mastrizzis bought in, Tommy had morphed into Forrest Gumpino, suffused with an optimism so bulletproof the only excuse for it was mental impairment. Especially at a moment like this.

If a woman with Ella Stark's pulmonary difficulties is found cold with her loyal mutt gazing mournfully at her, she died in her sleep of natural causes. If there's a poisoned dog next the bed, she died of murder.

Fortunately Dale had become obsessive about planning for contingencies. He brought a tarp and a shovel.

They wrapped Alfred in the tarp and deposited him in the trunk of Tommy's still newish STS. A dead dog in the trunk would've peeved the shit out of Tommy. But not Gumpino.

"Least we don't haveta chop him up. Ever tell ya how much hassle it is to take a grown man apart without power tools?"

They drove till pavement gave way to dirt and they arrived at the desolate contingency dog disposal site Dale had scouted months earlier, when he'd been shadowing Ella Stark and designing the hit.

Tommy got stuck doing most of the shoveling because they had to get Alfred underground before dawn. When the interment was complete, Tommy was sweat-soaked, filthy, wheezing, and in a good mood.

"*Requiescat in pace*, Al," Gumpino intoned, making a whimsical sign of the cross.

Dale was beginning to suspect Tommy was bipolar.

The pitch meeting with the Mastrizzis had been followed by three weeks of tense silence, during which Tommy had been as surly as something that lived under a bridge and ate children.

Then they got The Big Call. The Mastrizzis bought in. Not just bought in, dove in. Lou Mastrizzi took an enthusiastic interest, working directly with Tommy and Dale.

The Big Call was a mood elevator that turned the seething troll back into normal Tommy. Months of repeatedly being in Lou's presence was a hallucinatory that turned normal Tommy into Forrest Gumpino.

As they drove away from Alfred's grave, Dale said, "Sorry."

"For what? The thing went good."

"Unless Alfred being missing raises a red flag."

"Cause why, he's the first dog ever run off?"

"Cops don't believe in coincidence."

"Which still leaves 'em with fuck-all for who done it or why. Oh man, lookit the colors those mountains turn in this sunrise. Someone should paint that."

"I believe there have been one or two New Mexico sunrise paintings. Tommy, if the cops open a murder investigation, you think the Mastrizzis will see it the way you do?"

"Sure. Look, Dalie-boy, nothin' to be scared, Gianni's not gonna shoot you over a doggie OD. Tell you what's gonna happen. Coupla hours from now the maid finds Ella Stark dead. The price of Stark's shit goes through the fucking roof. You and me make a boatload of money, and the Mastrizzis make fifty boatloads... And then..."

Gumpino fell silent, gazing into the lurid pastel sky, visions of Mafia-plums dancing in his head.

The coroner ruled natural causes.

Ella Stark was a towering figure, a living link to her mentor, Georgia O'Keefe. During the art trophy boom of the go-go 1980s the tab for major Stark canvases crossed into seven-figure territory and never looked back. During the next two decades, with her output slowed by age and illness, Stark's paintings had grown more fungible by the minute.

When she died the price of her shit went through the fucking roof.

Boatload after boatload after boatload of money was dumped into accounts in the Caymans, Switzerland and Liechtenstein.

In River Forest, Lou Mastrizzi was pleased.

Gianni Mastrizzi was pleased. But not satisfied. The Old Man liked the profit margin. But he thought the pace was too slow and the operation too risky. Said if they ran the scam over and over there would inevitably be a fuck-up.

Lou Mastrizzi told Tommy and Dale what the Old Man decided.

There would be one final score. Massive. An eight-figure investment. And then they'd shut down, forever.

Lou would be managing this one, in detail. Said the prep had to be perfect. Even if it took years.

Dale started the research.

Lou held regular planning sessions with Dale and Tommy.

Then only with Dale.

Not only was Tommy excluded from the meets; he could tell Dale was withholding information. Which had to be at The MBA Boy's orders.

Forrest Gumpino imploded. Plummeted past normal Tommy, straight into seething troll.

Dale dreaded being alone with the seething troll.

Dale dreaded saying anything to Lou about the troll, because he couldn't be sure what the result would be.

Dale's left eye began to bulge.

TWENTY-TWO / 2012

Mark ran the shower too hot and stayed in too long, to cleanse the scratches an enraged Carrie had clawed into his back, and to boil away the absurd notion an amused Carrie had deposited in his skull.

If Carrie sensed a little distractedness in Mark, it wasn't love. It was preoccupation with his total idiot romp with JaneDoe and its resulting complications. The latest of which was scheduled to commence in twenty minutes.

The task force launch party was a dressier affair than Mark anticipated.

The role of toastmaster, normally a gig for a Captain, was played by Daryl Langan, Deputy Chief of Field Group B. The Deputy Chief's presence put the cops on notice these artist murders were not merely crimes against humanity, they were crimes against the Mayor's image. Plus which, someone in custom-tailored blues with brass stars on the epaulets would provide bureaucratic counterweight to the FBI agents.

There were two of them, and their hair was perfect. Grey-white, wavy and receding into a widow's peak on the fiftyish senior agent, Sten Ostergaard. Straight, thick and surfer-blond on boyishly handsome Nick Rarey.

Special Agent Ostergaard liaised by announcing the FBI's most brainiac profiler had taken a red-eye from D.C. and was at this moment on his way in from O'Hare.

Deputy Chief Langan announced the task force would work out of this office, Area Three, with Lieutenant Husak in command.

Langan introduced Detective Bergman, who'd brief on Gilson, followed by Detective Hsu, who'd brief Voorsts.

Bergman recited the highlights, ending with JaneDoe's connection to both Gilson and Voorsts, and her lack of an alibi for either crime. Information which was in his written report, had any cops or Feds bothered to do their homework.

Mark was about to hand off to Wendy Hsu when young Agent Rarey raised a question.

"Thank you, Detective Bergman, just one, um—how did you determine the doll was a representation of JaneDoe?"

The baby-faced Fed *had* read Mark's report. And spotted a detail that wasn't in it.

"One of the other—live—Barbies recognized the doll's hair and red leather—" Mark didn't get to complete the fib.

He was saved by a man who blew into the room, waved at the Feds and boomed, "Don't let me interrupt!"

"No problem," Mark assured him. "Welcome to Chicago, Doctor...?"

He was in his forties, medium height, pugnacious jaw, shaggy hair poking out of a Kangol beret, aviator shades, three-piece herringbone suit, black cowboy shirt, turquoise bracelet, alligator boots. He pulled off the shades and gave Mark a wink. Said, "Bard Hillkirk." Took a quick look around to see how many cops recognized his name.

Hillkirk manfully hid his disappointment and strode to the Feebs and Langan. He murmured to Langan, who nodded, then took the floor.

"Thank you," Langan told Mark. "Hsu—" Langan held up a hand, gesturing for her to wait. "Dr. Hillkirk has worked up a profile, which we need to get to right away." He turned to Hillkirk. "Don't worry, we'll have you back at O'Hare on time. A chopper if necessary."

Mark and Doonie exchanged a look. Doonie crossed his arms and waited to be impressed. Mark slipped out his phone.

Hillkirk stepped front and center. "Sorry about cutting in line, I'm due in Osaka. Haven't written the profile yet—I'll do that on the plane and email it. But I prefer to connect face to face. Don't have to tell you how important that is," he told them.

Mark's browser told him Hillkirk was a consultant at The House That J. Edgar Built. Doctorate in Abnormal Psych from the University of Wyoming.

"Someone has dubbed our perp The Art Critic. I'd call her—or him—The Tsarina. Those phallic inserts are conquest, not criticism.

"The Tsarina is a woman or gay. Her goal: To be a great artist. The Tsarina lusts for that so hard she can't waste time achieving it through decades of incremental progress. The Tsarina is leaping directly to greatness by turning great artists into pieces of her own work.

"She's a loner. Resentful of authority. Possibly—probably—promiscuous.

"Obviously, she fancies herself an artist. Perhaps is one, but not on the exalted plane of Gilson or Voorsts: True genius, a status upon which The Tsarina is fixated.

"Look for someone on the outer edge of the victims' social circle. Groupies, volunteers. Gallery staff. Students who took classes from the victims. Even," Hillkirk flashed a cynical grin, "art critics, who are all artist wannabes.

"There is an outside chance The Tsarina wasn't an acquaintance. But since there's no forced entry... No. The Tsarina knew both victims." Hillkirk nodded in agreement with himself. "Any questions?"

Not from Mark. Mark was clear on what Hillkirk had just done.

Hsu asked, "Dr. Hillkirk, you're certain the perp is a woman or gay. How did you arrive at that?"

"I'll put it in the written version. If I start expounding on analytical process, I'll miss my flight to Osaka, and by tomorrow you and I will be on the Attorney General's shit list," Hillkirk bragged.

Mark decided to ask a question, on the off chance it might make Hillkirk miss his plane. "We did find one unsolved previous local artist murd—"

"Yes, in your report, six-seven years ago, female, garroted... " Hillkirk squinted in concentration. "Laurie Kash!"

"Desh."

"Really? Hmm. But to answer your next question—no, that murder's not connected. I don't see congruent precursor pathology that would mature to fit The Tsarina. Digging into the—Desh—homicide would be a waste of time."

An alarm beeped in Hillkirk's pocket. He silenced his phone.

Agent Rarey whisked him out the door.

Hsu briefed Voorsts: No fingerprints. Canvas of the neighbors drew a blank. The Yellow Submarine vibrator was an old, unlicensed collectible from a magical mystery manufacturer. Teams would check sex shops and second-hand stores to see if it had been purchased locally.

Langan told the room, "All right. This JaneDoe is the only link between the vics, and she fits the profile to a T." The Deputy Chief of Field Group B gave Lieutenant Husak a hard significant look. "You'll have whatever resources you need, and focus *all* of them on her."

Then Langan hustled out like a man in a hurry to get to the breakfast he'd skipped to get to this meeting on time. A man in too much of a hurry to notice something that was obvious to Mark.

JaneDoe didn't fit the profile to a T. The profile fit her to a T.

Fucking Hillkirk. He hadn't worked up a profile, he'd placed a bet. He'd read Mark's report, decided JaneDoe was the odds-on favorite. Tailored a profile so specific that if the cops did bust her it'd make Hillkirk look like a goddamn psychic.

And fucking Langan. That look he gave Husak was an easy read. *JaneDoe's your perp. Make it happen, fast.*

Husak issued assignments. "Bergman and Dunegan are the primaries. Hsu and Montero will—"

As Husak worked his way down the list, Mark looked at Doonie, silently putting the question to him. Mark said he'd fess up if JaneDoe became a suspect. Which she just did. Without a shred of serious evidence.

Doonie gave his head a small, firm shake: *No. Too late.*

Same way Mark saw it.

The issue wasn't Mark's career. Fuck Mark's career. Minor collateral damage compared to what JaneDoe was looking at.

Her having sex with Mark wasn't just any old sex; she seduced the detective interviewing her about Gilson's murder. Classic sociopath chutzpah. The news JaneDoe had humped Detective Bergman would add a whole mess of momentum to the suddenly real danger of her getting railroaded.

Only way to prevent that was to find the actual Art Critic, fast. While working twenty-six hours a day investigating JaneDoe.

TWENTY-THREE / 2011

Oh, Lord, thought Maleekwa Pritchard-Varney, observing the well-dressed man communing with Dorian Gray. Hard to believe a complexion that nasty had managed to get worse. And one of his eyes had gone bulgy.

The museum guard and the poor man had struck up a nodding acquaintance. She'd nod when he walked in, and he'd return it.

She decided this time she'd say goodbye. A word and a smile. A friendly face who wasn't put off by his. Well in fact she was, but, she was a Christian woman, and the poor man's afflictions weren't his faul—

His hand. His left hand. He'd been the whole time with that hand stuck in his pocket. Was she so distracted by his skin—Maleekwa tried to picture his other visits, think if he always stood that way, hand in pocket. Was he all along touching himself?

Isn't there any way I can join you up there, Dorian? C'mon, I've gotten repulsive enough—I could play a servant, maybe offering you a rotting puppy on a platter?

No, Dor, I'm not implying you belong in a velvet painting with poker-playing dogs. I'm implying I'm desperate to be someplace Tommy can't get at me.

He keeps giving me this mega-troll stare, like he's wishing he had a kitchen sink so large he could fit my head in the disposal.

No, Dor, that's not masochistic whimsy. It's logical terror.

All his life Tommy dreams of getting in with the Mastrizzis. Then Tommy has his inspiration, his kill-the-artist business plan. Boom, dream comes true.

And it's a handful of turds.

He was sure the Mastrizzis would finally think he was smart. Instead the Mastrizzis think I'm smart and Tommy was lucky to bump into me.

Worse, they steal his shiny toy. He's gone from being boss to being muscle. Meanwhile, I work with Lou Mastrizzi. Who trusts me to invest twenty million dollars.

No, Dorian, I'm not relishing how the man who ground off my finger is being humiliated. I am concerned. I'm concerned shitless.

Tommy and I will each bet a half-million on this final throw; the Mastrizzis are putting up fourteen. And here's the insane part: They insisted on adding another five mil from an investor—like what this needed was more risk, another partner we have to trust.

Guy named Jay Branko. Friend of Lou's. Branko owns a huge construction firm, gets city contracts, hires union workers controlled by the Mastrizzis.

Now, with the troll already seething, the sensible thing would be to not tell him we're taking on this other investor. But the Old Man does tell Tommy, just for the pleasure of informing him there's no need for him to know the investor's name.

So of course Tommy shows up at my place and demands to know who the fuck this secret investor is.

I tell him, "I can't. The Mastrizzis would kill me."

Tommy's glaring. Nostrils quivering. Ready tear my throat out with his teeth.

But instead of killing and eating me he pats me on the cheek. Goes and washes the hand that touched my eczema. Then goes into my room and pisses on my bed. Leaves, without washing his hands.

And now the troll's mood is about to get shittier.

Our final target is Damian Jung. A colossus of modern British painting. And, at seventy-six, an age-appropriate candidate for sudden death. Best of all—don't know how much auction gossip you pick up around here—Jung's stuff is cosmically expensive. Last year one of his classics went for thirty-nine mil; we're talking bidding wars between major museums and minor Saudi royalty. Too rich for even the Mastrizzis.

So we're buying minor works, in the two to six million range. After Jung's tragic demise we'll maximize profits by selling one painting a year.

Which brings us to the details of that tragic demise.

Jung loathes the U.S. Almost never visits. But Jung does take a ski vacation in Zermatt every January. Seventy-six, he should know better. It's dangerous out there.

Thing is, Zermatt's tiny; a Swiss zillionaire playpen. Tommy Tesca would not be inconspicuous in Zermatt.

Lou says no problem. Lou has a line on a high-end Euro-hitter.

I say problem. On top of not being told Branko's name, Tommy's also had his troll-panties in a twist over Lou telling him he doesn't need to know the name of the target until it's time to prep the hit. Now Tommy's about to hear he can't do the hit or even be told who the target is. Tommy's been reduced from boss to muscle to silent micro-partner, who isn't entitled to know where his money's invested.

So I've asked Lou to break the insulting news gently. Throw Tommy a bone. What he craves: To feel like your cousin again. Take him to a Bulls game, or better yet, to some family thing.

What? Dorian! I'm shocked you'd accuse me of setting Tommy up. Never crossed my mind the Mastrizzis—especially the Old Man— might decide killing Tommy would be easier than trying to raise Tommy's self-esteem.

Far as Maleekwa could tell the hand in the man's pocket never moved. But his chest gave a heave. And then he does this cold little grin. Had he just finished…?

All that time she spent feeling bad for him. Offered up prayers. And now this.

She had to at least let him know she knew. Bust his damn afterglow.

The man started to leave. Turned to his left. Did the instinctive thing to maintain balance when turning left, which was to pull his left hand out of his pocket. Just for an instant.

Long enough. Maleekwa saw. The middle finger was gone except for a gruesome stub. The fingers alongside the stub were scarred, and bent at nauseating angles. He'd been *hiding* his hand, and she'd been *this* close to accusing—

The poor man was coming her way. Looking at her. He'd seen her reaction, the horror on her face. *Mercy.*

Maleekwa said, from the core of her generous, deeply embarrassed being, "Have a blessed day, sir."

"From your lips to the Old Man's ears," he replied.

TWENTY-FOUR / 2012

M ark, Doonie, Hsu and Montero convened in Lieutenant Husak's office. Husak was ordering a countywide dildo hunt for the source of the Yellow Submarine—

Mark's cell burbled. He excused himself and stepped out of the office.

It was Carrie—calling from the desk phone of Assistant State's Attorney Carrie Eli.

"Hello, Counselor."

"Detective," Carrie responded. "I regret to inform you that for the first time in my life, I'm the one who has to apologize for not being able to get it up."

"Get what up? "

"A subpoena to tap JaneDoe's phones and computers. The judge was all, *insufficient cause*. Wants us to bring him stuff that smells more like evidence."

"You caught this case."

"Obviously. And obviously I should've placed this call to Husak, but this way you're the one who has to give him the bad news."

To Mark, the cops not getting to tap JaneDoe's communications was good news; never know when she might mention bonking Detective Bergman.

Mark informed Husak, "Judge turned down the wiretap subpoena."

"Surprise," Husak muttered, unsurprised. "Put 24/7 surveillance on JaneDoe."

"Shame me and Bergman can't help on that," Doonie dead-panned, reminding Husak that JaneDoe knew their faces. It sounded like Doon was gloating about avoiding shit-work. Mark knew Doon was gloating about avoiding the possibility of JaneDoe spotting them and publicly planting a kiss on one or the other.

Another bullet dodged.

Until Husak said, "You two get the fun job. Bring her in and re-interview her. In depth."

Fuck. Mark pictured grilling JaneDoe while Husak observed from the other side of the mirror. She makes one slip-up, a joke, a look...

"Lieutenant," Mark said, "if Doonie and I go at her a third time, she walks in knowing we like her. But if Hsu calls JaneDoe, says *Hey, I'm the primary on Voorsts, I need to ask you some follow-up, but I'm slammed, would you mind coming down...*"

"Uh-huh," Husak nodded. "JaneDoe thinks she's just a witness, plus maybe we get the woman to woman comfort zone."

Doonie gave Mark a complimentary look.

He'd put them on the safe side of the mirror. Sort of.

Wendy Hsu ushered JaneDoe into a 12th District interrogation bin. Husak, Doonie and Mark were in the observation room. Mark observed JaneDoe had already made a mistake. She'd accepted a cup of coffee.

JaneDoe sat. Took a sip of official police-issue heartburn. Placed the cup off to one side, to minimize the risk of absentmindedly picking it up.

Hsu began with the dinner at Gerd Voorsts' place. Asked about the relationship between Gilson and Voorsts. Hsu then asked about all the dinner guests.

But JaneDoe was the subject; Hsu was sizing her up. And getting her yakking. Sometimes a mouth builds momentum and moves faster than its mind.

When there were no diners left to dissect, Hsu moved on to, "How was the relationship between Gerd and his boyfriend?"

JaneDoe darkened. "No. Forget it. Hal and Gerd were happy."

Control yourself, Mark thought, in JaneDoe's direction.

"And I talked to Hal this morning," JaneDoe continued. "Said he was out of town when it happened."

"Which we confirmed," Hsu replied. "But spouses have been known to hire someone to pull the trigger."

"So your theory is Hal paid this hired gun to kill Bobby Gilson first, for practice?" JaneDoe's expression was one degree shy of a sneer.

Behind the glass, Husak said, "Fits the profile—resentful of authority."

"What artist isn't," Mark said.

"What cop isn't," Doonie added.

Husak didn't respond. He focused on the interrogation room, where Hsu was responding to JaneDoe's insult with shrewd amusement.

"My theory is, consider everything. Fr'instance, I checked out your website. I like your stuff." Hsu grinned. "Honest. Off the record. Those costumes are way cool—I wanna see somebody wear one."

JaneDoe's near-sneer twitched into a near-grin, and she mumbled an embarrassed, "Thanks."

My, how unexpected praise can blow open a young artist's dopamine floodgates, Mark thought. *Be careful kid, Wendy Hsu is good.*

Hsu, enthused, queried JaneDoe about her work. Soon JaneDoe had her phone out and they were giggling at photos of her latest creatures.

Husak looked at Mark. "Another fit with the profile: Those Halloween costumes ain't ever gonna make JaneDoe a major artist like Gilson and Voorsts."

"A century ago that's what they said about imagists and abstractionists like Gilson and Voorsts," Mark parried. "Lieutenant, remember how Hillkirk ducked Hsu's question about why he thought the perp was a woman, said he'd explain it in the report? His written explanation is a one-sentence pile of psychobabble."

"Now you're an expert on medical jargon?"

"Nope. I forwarded the profile to Dr. Duxler. She said Hillkirk's one-line justification was horseshit—her exact medical jargon."

Husak scowled. "If you think the profile's horseshit, don't give me dick-measuring shrinks, gimme proof."

"That mean we can look at that murder from 2005, Laurie Desh?"

Husak, sounding like a cop who resents authority, said, "Langan's orders are we work JaneDoe and nothing but." Husak returned his attention to the interview.

Hsu was saying, "Sounds like a breakthrough year."

JaneDoe confided, "My dealer informed me I don't make costumes. I make 'interactive bio-kinetic sculptures.' Which I need to go get bio-kinetic on."

"Well, there is one more thing."

"Oh." JaneDoe shot a baleful glance at her cup of sour puppyshit-brown liquid. Now also tepid and stale.

"I know," Hsu sympathized. "There's an Intelligentsia down the—"

"That's okay. What's your one more question?"

"I'd like to hear a little bit about you and Robert Gilson."

JaneDoe sat up straighter. Her jaw tightened. Green eyes narrowed.

A moment Mark had seen a lot of. The one where the realization grabs and squeezes: *I'm not a witness, I'm a suspect, they're out to get me.* A moment that normally was one of Mark's favorites.

JaneDoe stared a hole in Hsu. Said, "I have to go now."

"Ten more minutes."

JaneDoe frostily declared, "There's nothing I can tell you I didn't already tell Ma—"

Behind the mirror, Mark and Doonie stiffened—*Don't use my/ his first name!*

—JaneDoe caught herself, slurred the *Ma* sound into— "Mauhhmmmm, y'know, Detectives, uhmmm—," as if groping for the names.

"Bergman," Hsu prompted, "and—"

"—Dunegan, right."

Lieutenant Husak didn't notice Detectives Bergman and Dunegan exhale in unison.

"They went over the me-and-Bobby thing in excruciating detail," JaneDoe informed Hsu, with flat finality.

"I know. But sometimes, fresh ears."

"You can read their report, with fresh eyes." JaneDoe pushed back her chair and stood. "If you're concerned your colleagues left anything out—" she stared into the mirror "—go ask them."

JaneDoe picked up the cup of coffee sewage. With defiant eyes fixed on the mirror, she drained it. Plunked the empty cup down, told Hsu, "Thanks." And left.

Mark wondered if JaneDoe understood, or cared, she'd just made herself even better liked.

Mark watched Husak, to scope his reaction.

Husak's reaction was to whip out his cell and make a call. Said, "Husak. She's leaving now… Okay… Good." He hung up.

"You worried the guys are gonna miss a six foot tall babe drivin' a red truck?" Doonie asked, assuming Husak had alerted the team tailing JaneDoe.

"I called the FBI," Husak explained. "Let them know she's leaving. While JaneDoe was here they've been bugging her apartment, to go with the taps they put on her phones and computer."

"They got a Federal warrant?" Mark asked. "Off what?"

"Voorsts donated to radical lefty groups and Palestinian charities. The Feds told a FISA judge they're investigating to see if his murder's got national security issues."

"Fuuuck," Doonie crooned in admiration. He gave Mark a wry look.

Yeah. Now the real fun starts. Here's where they find out if JaneDoe happens to be America's only twenty-five-year-old who could multi-orgasm with a cop who's investigating her for two murders, and not share. With anyone. In person, on the phone, or online.

TWENTY-SIX / 2011

Lou Mastrizzi's kid sister Bobbi gave birth, which provided the perfect occasion for Lou to massage Tommy Tesca's ego. Which had been Dale Phipps' fervent suggestion.

Normally Lou would say fuck it, Tesca would have to deal. Tesca knew if he made waves...

Though what waves could Tesca make? If Tesca was so humiliated he'd blow off his profits in order to deny the Mastrizzis theirs, he might sabotage the operation. But how? Tesca couldn't blow the whistle—he'd go down for multiple murder raps. So...?

Oh. Right. Tesca could kill Dale Phipps. Little guy was the lynchpin to the whole deal.

So that's what Dale was worried about.

Okay. We could clip Tesca. But then the cops would investigate Tesca, and who knows where that would lead.

With twenty million—maybe double that in profits—at stake, better safe than sorry. Feed Tesca a treat.

Lou had that, thanks to his sister popping out her third: Invite Tesca to the christening. All it would cost was one more face to feed—Tesca was a widower, with no kids—and Tesca would live his wet dream. He'd be on the inside with the Mastrizzis, even if it was only for the christening of a girl.

Just needed to clear the invite with Dad. The Old Man, who regarded most of humanity as a taller, heavier species of head lice, had special contempt for Tommy Tesca. Dad never said why, and Lou learned young never to ask Dad to explain himself.

But Gianni was also the ultimate pragmatist. When Lou asked if they should whack Tesca or invite him to the christening, the Old Man pondered it for a moment.

Said, "Maybe he'll stay after and help do the dishes."

Lou wasn't surprised Tommy Tesca showed up at church wearing a new suit. Lou was surprised, pleasantly, the suit wasn't goombah glam. More like top of the line Brooks Brothers. Ace consultant Dale Phipps strikes again, Lou surmised, grinning.

Tesca thought the grin was for him.

Tesca floated through the ceremony exuding an angelic glow, as if being in church were a religious experience. And that, Lou prophesied, would be but the entry-level ecstasy; transcendence would be attained when Tesca was received in the holy of holies, Lou's walled estate in River Forest.

And yea, so it came to pass. Behold Tesca the mighty artist-slayer, breaking bread with the Mastrizzi generations. Tesca kissing the cheeks of Mastrizzi women and cooing over the Mastrizzi infant. Tesca shmoozing with Mastrizzi lieutenants, made men, who were too solid to come out and ask what the fuck Tommy Tesca was doing there.

They joked with the nobody loan shark as if he were one of the guys. Threw in casual questions about what he'd been up to lately. Tesca replied with a sly grin, "Same old, same old." Clearly the best fucking party of his life.

Which got even better when Lou invited Tesca for a chat in what Lou called his humidor—a weatherized gazebo nestled among large old trees at the far side of the back yard. The two of them ambled out there in full view of the Outfit's upper management. Bliss.

"I'm not allowed to light up in the house since we had kids," Lou explained, as they settled into throne-sized leather chairs. He sloshed eighty-year-old cognac into snifters. "Here's to healthy living."

Tommy chuckled.

They fired up exotic thigh-rolled Cubans that made Cohibas look generic.

"Fidel's own stash," Lou joked.

Tesca puffed, sighed with operatic pleasure. Thanked Lou for the cigar, and, for the eighth time, the honor of being invited to the sprinkling of Bobbi's latest.

Lou murmured, *"Non c'e' di che."* It's nothing.

Obeisance completed, Tesca asked, with a shrewd twinkle, "So, you picked the genius whose value I go increase?"

"Uh-huh." Lou took a puff. Exhaled a long, elegant cloud. "Thing is, Tommy, this genius lives in Europe."

Tesca thought for a moment. "Fine," he assured Lou, with deep determination. And even deeper anticipation.

Fuck. The asshole is fitting himself out with a tux, a Walther and an Aston Martin. Three-hundred-pound Guido Bond of the Cicero Secret Service.

"Tommy... That's a whole other world. Has to be someone local. Fits in, speaks three-four languages. Has resources in place."

"Lou—I can handle this."

"Tommy, no." Said almost the way you'd say it to a dog. With about as much effect.

"I have done how many of these bastards now," Tesca protested, "without any blowback, *at all*, heh?!"

"Not in Europe."

Tesca flushed, getting angry. Which was not acceptable

"Think," Lou commanded. "This is the only way that makes sense. And the work will be up to your standard—we've got a line on a high-end pro."

The joy drained out of Tesca's soul. Along with the blood from his face. Turned pale as a Norwegian heart attack.

No such luck.

Tesca, not trusting himself to look at Lou, stared at the floor. "This outside pro. He'll have us by the balls."

"Shooter never meets us, never knows who we are."

"Someone will," Tesca insisted, still studying the floor. "The cut-out."

"He's a gentleman of proven discretion. Makes good money and wants to live to spend it. You think the Old Man and I are idiots?"

Tesca flinched. Took a breath. Surrendered to reality. Raised his head. Whispered, "Never." Tesca tried to puff on his super-stogie but it was out. "Just, heh, like you said, I was thinking things through."

"Always important."

"Always… So, who's the artist?"

Ah fuck. "Tommy, c'mon. Long as you're not the shooter, there's no need."

"*What!?!*"

"Tommy—"

"My own fuckin' operation I can't be trusted!?"

Lou studied Tesca from a great, detached, utterly unthreatened height. Long enough for Tesca to start to worry.

Lou said, slowly, "Look around. Look where you are."

Tesca took the advice and the threat to heart. Put away his glower. Finished his cognac.

Said, "Heh."

Thinking all the guests were gone, Lou and Gianni were alone in the den, discussing plans for Mom's upcoming surprise 65th birthday bash, when in walks Tommy Tesca. Shit, maybe he *was* gonna stay and do dishes.

Lou stood; the Old Man remained seated.

Tesca thanked Lou again.

Lou thanked Tesca for coming. Hoped he had a good time.

Tesca nodded. Then just stood there. Looking at Gianni.

Oh shit, Tesca's not going to… Yes he is. Poor dumb fuck.

"Gianni, could I have a word?" Tesca murmured; subservient, but insistent. "I—"

"No one gives a fuck what you have to say," the Old Man rasped. "You don't wanna put your money in this deal, you can stick it up your ass. Either way, only time I wanna see your lips move is when you pray nothing happens to Dale Phipps."

Tesca's lips pumped silently, like a suffocating fish's. He managed to mumble, "I'd never—swear to God."

Impassive reptile eyes impaled Tesca. "Smart. 'Cause your mama ain't around no more to save you." Then the eyes went human and things got worse. "A fine, *fine* woman," Gianni reminisced, as a narrow lopsided grin creased his face. An ugly, boastful schoolyard sneer.

The implication went through Tesca like a harpoon.

Lou tensed, preparing to slam a forearm into Tesca's throat.

But Tesca was paralyzed.

"Bye, Tommy," Gianni said. "Been a *pleasure.*"

Somehow Tesca found the strength to lumber away.

Shit. Dad fucked Tommy's mother. Which for the Old Man rendered Tommy lower than pigeon crap.

That was so Dad.

Lou looked at the Old Man and raised an eyebrow, silently asking the obvious about Tesca's future.

"Nah, he'll eat it," Gianni declared, with a grin. Genuine grin. Most sincere satisfaction he'd shown all day.

TWENTY-SEVEN / 2012

Mark began his workday. Turned his computer on. Stared across the room at JaneDoe's photo on the murder board, linked by arrows to photos of two corpses. And here we go. Mark pulled up links to the overnight field reports. One was the surveillance log from the cops shadowing JaneDoe. The other was a transcript of the FBI bugs and taps on JaneDoe. Always save the best for last; Mark started with the surveillance log.

4:17 PM Subject left Area Four in her vehicle. 4:43 PM Subject arrived at her residence. 10:49 PM Subject drove to Logan Square and entered the apartment of Kate Scott and husband Greg Neal. 11:50 PM, all three took a taxi to a dance club. 4:08 AM, Subject and her companions returned to the Scott-Neal apartment. All three emerged at 12:49 PM and went to Ina's restaurant for breakfast. At 2:11 PM the Subject drove back to her residence.

Which added up to JaneDoe being so spooked by the realization she was a murder suspect that she couldn't spend the night alone. A normal reaction for an innocent person. Or a guilty one.

Mark clicked on the link to the Feebs' eavesdropping.

A gripping read. Mark gave it five stars. Page-turning suspense and a happy ending: JaneDoe hadn't said anything serial killerish. Or anything about being on a first-name, pants-down basis with a Detective Bergman.

Unless JaneDoe *had* said something about sleeping with Mark, and the FBI had redacted it, so Mark wouldn't know they were on to him. That's what he'd do if he were them.

Should he have his apartment and phones swept? If so, how often? It's a bitch to determine what's sensible in a situation where logic and paranoia are nearly identical twins.

Fuck it. What he could do is do his job.

Which was to go interview JaneDoe's friends and associates.

Doonie and Hsu had worked up a list and split it. Doonie handed Mark their half. Mark read the names.

Anyone else watching would've sworn Mark's face didn't move. Doonie quietly asked, "Who?"

Mark gave his head a microscopic shake: *Not here.*

Mark called the POD techs who'd been scanning the street camera files. Maybe in the last five minutes they'd spotted a pedestrian or vehicle that'd been near both crime scenes. If that person wasn't JaneDoe, Mark could blow off these interviews and start chasing someone who might actually be the perp.

Turned out the techs had suspended the wide survey. They'd been ordered to go back through all the footage looking only for JaneDoe and her red 2011 Subaru Forester.

Mark and Doonie got into their black 2009 Crown Vic.

Mark said, "Remember that vintage bowling shirt I gave Patty for her thirteenth birthday?"

"You mean the one she wore every damn day after you got shot, 'cause her wearing it was the only thing keeping you alive?"

"Got it at this vintage store I'd gone to with JaneDoe—back then, Janvier. She introduced me to the owner, they're good buddies. Couple weeks later I went back, to find a present for Patty. The owner recognized me, remembered my name. We had a nice chat."

Doonie scanned the list. "Lila Kasey, proprietor of Pandora's Rerun."

"Uh-huh."

"And Kasey knew that you and Janvier…?"

"Yup."

Doonie shrugged. "When we get to her place you'll stay in the car."

First stop was the Marla Kretz Gallery.

JaneDoe's art dealer was tiny, high energy and no nonsense; in her 60s and hadn't bothered with a plastic surgeon. When Doonie asked what she knew about JaneDoe's relationship with Robert Gilson, Kretz cut to the chase.

"You suspect Janey? Jesus. Waste of time."

"Could you tell us some specifics about why?" Doonie requested.

"Specifically, artists are being slaughtered and you guys—how can I put this—are running around with your heads tucked firmly up your backsides."

"Regular part of the job," Doonie confirmed. "Look, it's natural you want to protect your client—"

Kretz laughed—two short sharp barks. "Oh darling, if this were about protecting my income, I'd be trying to frame her. If you arrested JaneDoe for murder her price would triple."

When they got back in the car, Mark said, "That thing about JaneDoe's price tripling."

Doonie eyed Mark. "You think Kretz would kill two guys on the off chance we'd bust JaneDoe for it?"

"What these two killings goosed is the value of the paintings by the two vics."

"A collector who's trying to cash in kills the artists and sticks Ken and the Beatles in their mouths, so we'll think psycho," Doonie mused. "There a way to find out if someone owns a bunch of Gilsons and Voorsts, and just started selling 'em?"

"Dunno. I'll check with Claudel." Mark said, referring to Detective Janet Claudel, Robbery's art crime specialist.

Mark and Doonie interviewed the next three names on their JaneDoe friends and associates list. None said anything that moved the needle on whether JaneDoe was or wasn't The Art Critic.

Just one more stop to make.

TWENTY-EIGHT / 2012

Lila Kasey's store was on Milwaukee, between North and Armitage. Heart of Bucktown, a neighborhood that had upscaled from blue collar to arty to gentrified in the blink of a decade.

So Pandora's Rerun was now on one of the busiest retail stretches on the North Side. So the cops had no luck finding legal parking. Fortunately there was a hydrant in front of the store. Mark squeezed the big Ford into the space.

Doonie got out and ambled into the store.

Mark communed with his cell. Its spam blocker was snoozing on the job; first email was a sympathetic stranger offering to upscale Mark's tiny penis—

Tap tap tap. Passenger side window.

Friendly face. Mid-fifties. Large alt-stylish woman, large retro sunglasses, large chunky jewelry, large coffee in one hand, a half-smoked Dunhill in the other.

She mouthed, "Mark?"

Busted.

He lowered the passenger window. "Hi."

"Thought it was you," she said, pleased. "Good thing I can't smoke in my own store, might've missed you."

Behind her, Doonie emerged from Pandora's Rerun and asked, "Can I help you, Miss?"

The woman straightened up, turned to face Doonie. Mark got out and said, "My partner, Detective Dunegan. Doon, Lila Kasey."

"Ah," Doonie commented. Told Mark, "I'll guard the car."

Mark stepped onto the sidewalk. "Actually, Ms. Kasey—"

"Lila."

"—we're here to see you."

"Me?"

"We're working the Art Critic murders."

"What could I possibly..." Lila trailed off, thought a moment. "Mind if we walk around the block?" she asked, waggling her not quite finished ciggie.

"Sure," Mark agreed.

Ray of hope, her not wanting to talk in the store, where her staff could overhear.

As they strolled, Mark told Lila, "We're doing background on people who knew both victims. JaneDoe's one of them."

Lila stopped. Said, "Uh-huh." As in, a suspicion confirmed. She dropped the glowing butt, crushed it beneath her faux-tigerskin ankle boot, lit another and resumed walking. Said, "No way JaneDoe's a murderer. What else you wanna know?"

"How did she get along with Gilson? And Voorsts?"

"Fine, I think. She didn't talk much about either one."

"Never mentioned having a thing with Bobby Gilson?"

"Nope. If it had been a serious affair, I would've heard about it," Lila said, pointedly eyeing Mark.

Mark asked, "When was the last time you communicated with her?"

"Maybe a month."

So Lila didn't know Mark had recently slept with JaneDoe. One item he wouldn't have to worry about Lila giving away.

Before Mark could get to his next question, Lila asked, "Have you, uh, questioned her yourself?"

"Yeah."

"Huh," Lila grunted, gazing at him thoughtfully.

They went up a side street. Came to a pocket park. Lila sat on a bench. The detective joined her, waited for her to resume interrogating him.

"Way back when, she told me you were a good guy." A pensive drag on the Dunhill. "Took it a little hard when you two split. Wasn't blaming you—not more than you deserved. JaneDoe knew it was about her drugs. So she enjoyed the shit out of setting up a weed bust to help you make that witness talk."

Mark said, "You're the first person I've met whom JaneDoe confides to about her private life."

"I'm the big sister she never had. So yeah, she does open up to me—not about every casual quickie, just the rare guy who means something." Lila let Mark chew on that. "She was a bit hurt when she did you that favor, then you came back from L.A. with some gorgeous rich girl... How's that going?"

"It's gone."

"Yeah, well, falling in love ain't that hard, but finding a tolerable roommate's damn near impossible," Lila commiserated, with rueful authority.

"For some of us even the falling in love part isn't a piece of cake."

Lila pulled out a fresh cigarette, studied Mark as she lit it off the one she was smoking. Said, cautiously, "It's weird, you working these murders."

"Luck of the draw."

"I didn't mean weird you caught the case. I meant weird you haven't told your superiors about you and JaneDoe."

Mark made no comment on Lila's comment.

"I'm wondering why you're keeping that secret," she went on. "You've questioned JaneDoe, so she knows you're working these murders, but she obviously hasn't given away anything about you and her, which would have gotten your ass kicked off the case... She must think you're on her side."

Mark, in a serious official tone, replied, "This is an ongoing investigation. It's important you not tell anyone about this interview. Especially her."

Lila nodded. "Got it."

"That needs to be a no exceptions no-shit fully adult 'Got it'. "

"Honey, my dad was a Streets & San supervisor. And a precinct captain."

"Thank you for your cooperation," Mark said, meaning it.

"You're welcome," Lila replied, meaning it. "Last thing I want," she explained, "is for it to come out the detective and the murder suspect are hiding the fact they once spent months fucking each other cross-eyed. You'd look pussy-whipped and she'd look like the bad girl who'd done it."

Lila put a hand on Mark's thigh. Gave it an appreciative squeeze. Sighed, "Lucky her."

Lila removed her hand and let Mark and his thigh get back to work.

TWENTY-NINE / 2011

Walk *he fucked your mother, he fucked your mother,* don't look around, heh, just keep moving out the door *he fucked your mother, he fucked your mother.*

In the car, turn the key *he fucked your mother.* Drive *he fucked your mother. Motherfucker fucked your mother and you didn't kill him, sitting there letting you know hefuckedyourmotherhefuckedyourmotherhefuckedyourmother.*

Driving, driving nowhere except away from Lou Mastrizzi's house and Lou Mastrizzi's father *he fucked your mother, he...*

Shit. *That* had been Gianni's price for saving Tommy from that B&E beef back when.

Tommy could see it. Mom would do anything for her son. And Gianni knew Mom musta been—hungry. Tommy's bastard dad had run off while she was pregnant. Then alone all those years. With men looking, wanting. Face like a horse, but that body. Ugly girl with great tits, we all been down that street, 'course Gianni would want—

God! *I* wanted...

Out of nowhere, that memory. It'd been gone, hadn't come around once this last twenty years.

He's twelve. Playing basketball, goes down hard, head smacks the blacktop, wakes up in the Emergency. That night at home, Mom's sitting on his bed, all weepy-happy her boy's still alive, she's holding him to her, got his face pressed against those... And his hand, his hand is just nuts to know what it feels like, and the hand reaches up and touches—*Oh fuck Mom shoves him away hard, gives this insane look, hauls off and smacks—*

A barrage of fast loud thump-thump-thumps shuddered the Caddie, which was no longer on pavement and Tommy stomped the brakes, the car screeched and yawed and came to rest with the

front right wheel in this drainage ditch along this goddamn suburban forest preserve road and Tommy was thinking, *Gianni fucked my
mother and made me remember this shit, and he stole my business and
I didn't kill him.*

Tommy drank. Beat himself up for not breaking the Old Man's
neck then and there.

But that would've been suicide.

Tommy drank some more. Beat the crap out of some guy in a bar.

Beat the crap out of a couple of deadbeat clients. Guys who were
a couple of bucks light.

Made Tommy feel better. For a couple of hours. Then he'd go back
to trying to figure a way to whack Gianni Mastrizzi.

Best go old school. Show nothing. Let Gianni think you're a pussy,
he got nothin' to be afraid of.

Fuck.

The Old Man did have nothing to be afraid of.

Only way Tommy could see to get to Gianni was strap on a bomb
and go Al Qaeda. And hope it worked. Tommy would die not knowing whether he'd killed the motherfucker.

He could hire it done.

Have to be serious shooters. Badass Colombians. Who would
charge Tommy every penny he had, to take on Gianni fucking
Mastrizzi... Then turn around and sell out Tommy's ass to Mastrizzi.
Which would be the only safe thing for the shooters to do.

Fucking Colombians.

THIRTY / 2011

Tommy is in a studio apartment. Spiffy renovated warehouse in River North. He's there to school a deadbeat. Young yuppie fuck. Soon's Tommy walks in he knows the kid's got no excuse. Tommy's pretty sure the painting over the couch is worth the four grand the kid owes.

Trying to stall, the kid asks does he want a brew and goes to the fridge. Tommy follows. Looks at the sink. Flashes on that time he used the disposal on Dale. Back before Dale had Mastrizzi protection.

The young yuppie fuck goes to hand Tommy a Duvel. Tommy grabs the kid's wrist, yanks him to the sink and jams his hand into the disposal. The kid screams and pisses himself...

...Tommy doesn't hear, doesn't smell, is barely aware of the young yuppie fuck. Tommy is elsewhere, gone inside a moment like nothing he's ever—The thing just appears in his head, complete, he SEES, sees all of it, everything he hadda do, and how it would play out—it's like the inside of his brain is all bright, lit up like a stadium for a night game, and his gut, his gut knows the glow in his head is right. This is better than Gianni dead, this is Gianni alive and eating shit—and Tommy grabbing back his business, and turning a profit... And then Tommy's gonna have to disappear, forever. Which he is okay with. He would retire a satisfied man.

Tommy grins. The young yuppie fuck faints. Tommy takes the painting from over the couch and marches off to war.

Tommy informed Dale he wouldn't be putting money into this last project. Gianni Mastrizzi would take that to mean Tommy was such a weakling he'd let his hurt feelings get in the way of a big score.

Tommy studied the files of possible targets Dale had assembled over the years. Only one was any use—the first Dale ever made, way back when. Because that was the only list that had Chicago artists. Tommy's plan would only work if he could move fast; so all the hits hadda be in one city.

This would violate Dale's—and now the Mastrizzis'—rule: No hits in town. Heh. Tommy was gonna show those cocksuckers what their candyass rules were worth.

Tommy only liked one name on Dale's 2005 list. Tommy made Robert Gilson Target Number One, then started researching today's Chicago artists.

Found a great Number Two. Gerd Voorsts.

There was no clear winner for Number Three; only some half-assed possibilities, none especially profitable. But Tommy needed three, to make sure it looked like a serial killer. That would piss on another rule: Only ever whack one artist at a time. Tommy would kill three—and prove it was a fuckin' advantage, 'cause the cops would think serial and look for some freak.

And also, heh, there'd be the big fuck-you. On the third corpse Tommy was gonna put a note, cool psycho shit like, *"I'm bored here. Going to Europe to kill a real artist. And this time you won't know it was me, or even a murder."*

Heh. Probably the Chicago cops keep the note secret, and warn the European cops to dig heavy into every artist who dies. So Gianni will end up busted for his big-ass multi-million score.

Or the cops *do* publish the note, which means Gianni's big finale is fucked, he has to call it off.

Either way, the Old Man will know it was Tommy who fucked him. Who else would kill three artists in Chicago, and know to give away the Mastrizzis' big Europe operation? Gianni would know this was Tommy's revenge for stealing his business.

As far as revenge for Gianni fucking his mother... Well, that had been the other huge part of Tommy's amazing brain flash: There's nothing Tommy could do, or, more important, had to do, about Mom spreading for Mastrizzi. That had been her own decision.

Just like her slapping Tommy that time for what his hand did.

Tommy sold everything, house, car. Left town without telling anyone. Which he knew the Mastrizzis, heh, would take to mean he was so humiliated he couldn't even live in the same city with them.

Tommy moved to Indianapolis, where nobody knew him. Nobody who knows anybody lives in Indianapolis.

Legally changed his name. Got a passport.

Set up offshore accounts and started buying art, anonymously.

Flew to Brazil. Rented a nice little apartment in Sao Paulo.

Flew back to Indianapolis. Snuck into Chicago time to time, to tail his artists, plan his hits.

Settled on his third and final target. Since he couldn't find another big-money score, Tommy picked the artist who'd be easiest to clip. Hot young bitch called herself JaneDoe.

THIRTY-ONE / 2012

On her way home from the interrogation JaneDoe drove more carefully than she had since, oh, ever. Not so much as a pump-fake at a stop sign. Couldn't risk a traffic ticket. Like somehow that would make her look nervous and guilty. Of murder. Shit. Being an actual suspect wasn't amusing. She wondered how criminals put up with paranoia of this density. Ten minutes of this was worse than a year of being an unknown artist. Well, six months.

JaneDoe quit kidding herself she was gonna get anything done. Called Kate and Greg, her best friends from art school, told them she required a night of dancing. Said she didn't wanna talk about why.

JaneDoe spent the night at Kate and Greg's. Had a nostalgic three-way. Followed by a blissfully irresponsible breakfast at Ina's. Whole wheat oatmeal pancakes with blueberries, and a side of andouille sausage. Happy density.

By the time she got home JaneDoe knew what her next piece was gonna be. Got busy.

Marla Kretz called; cops had been around, asking about JaneDoe's connections to the Art Critic victims.

Ice crusted JaneDoe's innards, until she asked the names of the cops, and Marla said, "Dunegan and Bergman. Why?"

The ice thawed. "Same guys talked to me. They're checking on anyone who knew Bobby and Gerd, 'cause they don't have anything else to go on."

"What it sounded like," Marla agreed. "Ignore those clowns and get back to work. Bring me more pieces, *schnell!*"

"*Jahwol, mein Fuhrer.*"

JaneDoe hung up. Okay. Mark and Doonie being the ones investigating her was a relief. No way those two are gonna let me get framed. In fact one of those cops is totally into me, even if he can't admit it yet.

JaneDoe grinned and plunged back into assembling her new creature: Foam Mark, her interactive bio-kinetic tribute to poor over-qualified underemotional Detective Bergman.

Foam Mark was coming together fast, easy. Like the best ones do.

Phone rang. It was Drago Djanovic, the MCA curator who'd put JaneDoe's sculptures in the New Chicagart show, back when they were mere costumes.

Drags told her detectives had been to see him. They were interviewing everyone who, like Drags, had been at that dinner with Bobby and Gerd. But they mostly asked about JaneDoe.

JaneDoe asked the cops' names. Drags said Dunegan and Bergman.

JaneDoe told Drags no problem, the cops are just fishing.

JaneDoe turned off the ringers on her phones and went back to work.

Foam Mark turned cranky, stopped coming together fast and easy. JaneDoe took a break. Checked her messages.

There was a text from Kate: Keep gttg yr vmail. Cops here tdy xing me&G bout u. Re: Art Critic. WTF? CALL ME.

JaneDoe called. Told Kate, "Those two cops, Bergman and Dunegan, are just fishing."

"These were named Hsu and Montero."

JaneDoe took a breath, steadied her voice. "Yeah, well, shift must've changed. Nothing to worry, really."

Except there are cops besides Mark and Doonie investigating me.

JaneDoe smoked a joint and decided to run some errands. Maybe stop somewhere for a cocktail. Good to get out of the house.

Hated being out of the house.

Treated herself to expensive takeout. *Cavatelli Di Ricotta Al Sugo Di Caprioli e Funghi*. Pasta with venison and mushroom ragu.

Took it home, washed it down with a 1990 Barolo, a recent gift from the delighted Robo-Zeeb in Milan. A real special-occasion wine. Like the day you find out you're the target of a serial killer investigation.

She felt a little sodden after dinner. Almost did some coke, but—eccch! Too jangly. She didn't even want caffeine.

Got in bed. Read for a minute and a half; couldn't concentrate. Turned out the lights.

Couldn't sleep.

Luckily still had a third of a bottle of Barolo, and weed. That'll cure insomnia.

Not.

Ambien time. That'll cure insomnia.

THIRTY-TWO / 2012

How come I know what you want, but you don't, JaneDoe asked Mark. Wait, you do know, you just—Chime!—won't admit it, she growled, frustrated, and punched him, and her fist sank into his chest because his chest turned to foam rubber, which frustrated her even more, they were naked and it felt right except Mark wouldn't admit what he wanted and when she hit him he kept turning gooey, flashing between Real Mark and Foam Mark—Chime! Chime!—Now she and Real Mark were naked on a giant mirror in an interrogation room with terrible coffee, except the mirror turned warm, liquid, clear Caribbean blue, so the Chime! *chimey thing must be a steel drum—Her sonofa-*bitch doorbell Chimed!

"Gunnncchh!" JaneDoe heard herself snort, clottedly, as she jerked half-awake, fragments of her annoyingly obvious dream slosh-ing around in her skull.

If she opened her eyes she could see what time it was. She tried, but her heart wasn't in it. Whoever was abusing her doorbell would give up and go away. All she had to do was not move. None of her friends would ring at this hour. Whatever this hour was.

Chime! Chime! Chime! Chime!

What kind of fucking goon—? JaneDoe, using her fingers, hauled open her eyelids. Blinked away a gummy blur, stared at the clock.

8:42 AM; the goon was definitely not one of her friends.

Shit. She could've bought one of the lofts on the upper three floors. Those shared a common entrance, which had an intercom. JaneDoe had the lone ground floor unit, which offered the convenience of no stairs to climb, plus a private front door. But the inconvenience of no intercom. So JaneDoe couldn't pick up the phone, tell the goon, "I'm not home, fuck you and die," hang up and parachute back into Ambienland.

Instead she had to haul her butt off her best friend, the first brand-new mattress she ever owned, first mattress that ever truly understood her, and plod all the way to her front door to peep through the peephole.

The goon was the big burly variety, wearing a suit. She only saw his back—now that she was out of bed and at the door the prick was giving up and leaving—

JaneDoe was so pissed he'd yanked her out of Ambienland she yelled, through the locked door—"HEY! Who the fuck are you!?!"

The goon turned—looked Italian and had some club-like thing in his fist—and someone rushed up behind him, with—

A *TV camera*?!?!

"Miss Doe? Miss Doe?" the goon asked, excited, talking into the club. "Al DeNardi, Fox News. Can we—"

"No!" Ah shit, shit, shit. Only one reason a fucking Fox scumbag would be at her door.

Through the peephole she saw DeNardi paste on a hammy scowl, eyes narrowed, teeth clenched. He threw a quick look back at the camera, so his audience would see what a dead ringer his scowl was for Clint Eastwood's, then bellowed at the door, "Miss Doe! MISS DOE!"

When DeNardi didn't get an instant reply he rapped indignantly on the door, which was way more Clint than indignantly fingering a doorbell.

"Miss Doe!" DeNardi demanded of the door, "Are you—*The Art Critic*?!"

After a moment the voice behind the door said, "No, I'm the interactive bio-kinetic sculptorette."

She told herself this would seem really fucking funny someday.

She told herself she was about to find out if it was true no publicity is bad publicity.

She told herself there was no reason to be scared.

THIRTY-THREE / 2012

The lead detectives on the Art Critic case showed up for work less than a minute apart. Sat at their facing desks and got down to business.

Mark said, "G'morning."

"No it ain't," Doonie warned. "Phyl's bitching it's almost two months you were over for dinner."

"Tell Phyl soon as we clear this I'm showing up for dinner, even if she doesn't invite me."

"You tell her that. She loves it when it sounds like you're flirting with her."

Business done, they went to work.

Mark put in a call to Janet Claudel, the art theft specialist. Asked if she could trace sales of works by Gilson and Voorsts.

"I will try," Claudel promised. "This is great—thank you—never thought I'd catch a homicide—you think JaneDoe's been investing in the vics?"

"No idea, but it seems worth finding out if anybody was," Mark said.

"I'll get right on it—but, fair warning, tracking art sales is dicey—there *are* databases, but not every auction house and gallery participates—and those that do never give the names of anonymous buyers and sellers—plus which there's no way to know about paintings that change hands between private collectors. But anyway—this is so cool—I'll get back to you soon as I've got anything."

Mark returned to his morning routine. He started with the FBI taps. A number of JaneDoe's friends had phoned to say they'd been questioned by the cops. Lila Kasey wasn't one of them. Solid citizen.

Mark opened the task force overnights. The first report was on The Hunt For Yellow Submarine.

The TV stars had gotten nothing off the Yellow Sub. The paint was chipped, indicating repeated vigorous use. But there were no prints or trace. The Yellow Sub had not only been wiped down, it had been immersed in rubbing alcohol. The perp wasn't taking any chances with where that thing had been.

Cook County's finest were busting ass to find the last place that thing had been. Cops across the city and the suburbs were checking porn shops, kitsch shops, collectible shops, pawn shops and online. So far no hits.

On to the POD report: results were in from the search for a money-shot of JaneDoe or her Forester at either crime scene. Total blank. Now the unit could resume doing what Mark asked for in the first place, a search for *any* vehicle—

His phone rang. The surveillance team sitting on JaneDoe's place. A Fox News truck had parked, spat out a reporter and cameraman, who rang the doorbell, then interviewed the closed door, then banged on it—Oops, two more news vans just pulled up.

Mark alerted the district watch commander to scramble the crowd control.

He turned the TV on: BREAKING NEWS—POSSIBLE ART CRITIC SUSPECT!

Right. With cops questioning dozens of people about JaneDoe's relations with the murder victims, some were going to tweet about it.

He checked. Twitter, Facebook and blogs were exploding with JaneDoe. A gossip site had launched a poll where people could vote on whether JaneDoe was The Art Critic.

By noon JaneDoe's block was the site of a Woodstockian siege-fest. Her corner was thronged with media vans, video bloggers, murder groupies, random gawkers, a guy peddling T-shirts that said *Kill All The Art Critics*, and, Mark hoped, someone was giving away hits of the brown acid.

JaneDoe was alone inside. Mark knew that because Special Agent Nick Rarey, cheerful, having a great time, began phoning Mark hourly summaries of the FBI taps: Several of JaneDoe's friends offered to come be with her, but she thanked them and instructed them to stay away. She told them the moment any visitor walked out her door the media would be on them like flies on shit. Told them there was nothing to worry about, she was going to get mad publicity out of this.

Latest update from Rarey: JaneDoe hired a lawyer, over the phone. No way she was going to let herself get lens-raped by running the media gauntlet to get to the lawyer's office, so the lawyer was on his way over.

Rarey assured Mark the FBI mikes would be turned off whenever JaneDoe communicated with her attorney. Listening in would violate lawyer-client privilege, which would blow any prosecution of JaneDoe all to hell, if the defense found out about it.

"*Sure* they won't be listening," Doonie mocked.

"Meanwhile," Mark muttered, "what next?"

"Shit out of ideas," Doonie conceded.

Time to visit Lieutenant Husak. If he was shit out of ideas too, maybe he'd let them spend a coupla minutes looking at Laurie Desh.

The Lieutenant was watching TV. The Grace Natchez Show. Natchez was the star crime shrieker for a cable news network, solving felonies at a glance. Unraveling motive from a single factoid. Venting darkly when police dragged their feet about arresting her designated perp.

At the moment Natchez was playing forensic art critic, snarling at pictures of JaneDoe's creations, explaining how these sicko costumes were a roadmap of a serial killer's mind.

Husak told Mark and Doonie, "Hang on a minute, I wanna see this," as Natchez segued to a special guest, Professor Bard Hillkirk, who was attending a conference in Dubai, where he'd graciously agreed to stay up until 3 AM so he could snag himself some national airtime back home.

"Professor, I have reliable information you provided Chicago police with a profile of The Art Critic!"

Hillkirk gave a modest shrug. "It's out of policy to comment."

"C'mon, really?! Okay, okay—just hypothetically, does JaneDoe fit a profile you *might* do of this killer?!"

A coy grin. "Sorry."

"Then why the heck did you come on my show?!"

A flicker of panic crossed Hillkirk's face, until his charm app rebooted. With a boyish duck of the head, he confided, "Well, I can tell you, insiders aren't calling this perp The Art Critic. Insiders refer to her as The Tsarina."

Husak groused, "*Insiders*? You're in fucking Dubai." He hit the mute button. "What you insiders got for me?"

Mark said, "Not one thing that makes JaneDoe The Art Critic, or The Tsarina."

"But she's got the world crawling up her ass now anyway," Doonie noted.

"Yeah," Husak said, "and Langan likes that. The more pressure, the sooner she cracks."

Mark said, "Right, but, Loo, steada me and Doonie sitting around waiting to hear cracking noises—" Mark's cell rang. He answered. Listened. Said, "We're on our way."

"Cracking noises?" Husak asked.

"Sonar ping off the Yellow Submarine."

THIRTY-FOUR / 2011-2012

For Tommy's plan to work he hadda sell the serial killer angle. Popping three artists probably does the trick. And Tommy did what that little leprosy-face fuck did when planning a hit. Research.

He rented serial killer movies. Second one in, bam—there's this scientist cop saying, "Serials almost always have a signature. Just like an artist signs his canvas." Just like an artist! Heh!

Tommy decided he needed a signature that was fast, easy and did not involve carving. You could chop off a pinkie easy. But that means a butcher knife, then taking the bloody finger and finding a place to ditch it. And the DNA-smeared knife.

Or maybe he could just leave the finger—stick it in the guy's mouth. Weird, heh. That works.

But instead of a wet messy body part he'd have to lop off, why not something dry he could just bring with him? Like…

A cigar? Nah. Nothing weird about a cigar in the mouth.

Heh. Hadda give this some thought.

Tommy is tailing Gerd Voorsts, learning the geezer's routine. He's walking up Michigan, on the block south of the bridge where there's those tourist shops selling team souvenirs.

A window display stops Tommy cold. A Cubs cap surrounded by those miniature little Cubs bats. And next to them, a Sox cap and bats.

That's it. Tommy could get three miniature little Sox bats—no, wrong, he's a Sox fan, don't wanna leave that clue. Plus which Cubs fans are gay—the cops would think they know why the killer stuck it in the guy's mouth.

Wait. His third target's a woman. So okay. One Cubs bat. Then a different dildo-type thing for each artist.

Shit, one of them could just *be* a dildo.

After six porn shops Tommy was fed up. All the dildos were plain and boring, or ugly and stupid. A vibrator with a spinning feather-duster-thingy on top does not say serial killer.

Tommy gave up. Started browsing second-hand stores and pawn shops, looking for any goddamn object the right size and shape.

Wouldn't ya know, soon's he quits looking for his dream dildo he finds it. Crappy second-hand joint in Forest Park, ten miles west of the Loop. A drab blue-collar 'burb from where you could see the skyscrapers downtown but know they had nothing to do with you.

The store is a dusty jumble. So's the owner, tired old fart sitting behind the counter watching horse-race reruns on a tiny TV.

Guy raises a bushy eyebrow at Tommy. "Help you?"

"Just browsin'."

The old fart goes back to watching yesterday's races.

Tommy browses. On a shelf cluttered with chipped figurines, tarnished cocktail shakers, ratty wind-up hula dancers, a dented aluminum tray embossed with a map of *The Ozarks, Mountain Paradise...* There it is, leaning against a rusty *Grease II* lunchbox: a Yellow Submarine vibrator. The paint job's all scratched, but you can make out John, Paul, George and Ringo peering out the portholes. Yeah, yeah, yeah, ye-ahhhh.

Tommy walks past it. Does a quick scan of another shelf, and leaves.

Later that day, a gaunt homeless guy with greasy pants, meth sores, brown teeth and booze breath limped into the store. Looked around, spotted the Yellow Submarine. Brought it to the counter, asked the price. Fifteen. To the owner's surprise, the bum pulled out a twenty.

Two down, one to go. Tommy decided he'd use the Cubs bat on Gilson, the Yellow Submarine on Voorsts, then, for JaneDoe...

Tommy burned time looking for some third signature that would fit with the Cubs and the Beatles.

Almost bought a pennywhistle but it was too small, and didn't have any brand name, let alone a famous faggy brand-name. Almost bought a bicycle pump but it was too big and had a faggy brand-name no one heard of.

Tommy finished all his other preparations. It was time to start popping artists. He decided, worst comes to worst, he'd buy a miniature Blackhawks hockey stick to put in JaneDoe's mouth.

Heh! Worked out Tommy didn't have to settle. Within seconds of slitting Robert Gilson's throat, problem solved. The first dead genius on the list was such a freaky bastard he'd made with his own hands the perfect signature to use on him. Tommy saw the naked Barbie and it was love at first sight. No!—the Ken!

Ken was perfuckingfection! Way fuckin' sicker.

"Thanks, heh," Tommy told Gilson, waving the Ken doll in front of the dead man's blank trout eyes.

How lucky is it, the day Tommy whacks this sick fuck, what the guy is painting is these dolls, Barbie with her blonde bush and Ken with his purple-vein hard-on? Fuckin'-ay: Ken, the Beatles, the Cubs. Went together somehow, like there was some message. Tommy grinned, imagining the cops trying to figure out what the hell that message was.

Tommy pulled Gilson's mouth open and inserted Ken, feet-first. Went in a little too far; looked, for some reason, just kinda *off*. Heh.

Tommy slid Ken out a bit, so his stiff shlong rested on Gilson's upper lip. Tommy stepped back, assessed his work. Awright. Now Ken and Gilson were staring at each other. Great stuff. Truly fuckin' weird.

And, cherry on the cake, unlike the fifteen-dollar Yellow Sub and five-dollar miniature Cubs bat, Ken was free.

Tommy left Gilson's studio in a terrific mood. Looking forward to whacking the next two, imagining exactly how far in he'd place the Yellow Sub and the Cubs bat.

THIRTY-FIVE / 2012

The Forest Park cops had no trouble pinpointing when the Yellow Sub had been purchased: twenty-four days ago. Ron Coomber, the proprietor of Bargains & Treasures, saw no point in splurging on a computer, but kept a scrupulous handwritten ledger, "Because I don't need no tax problems with the IRA."

Identifying the purchaser was another story.

"Some bum looked like all the other bums." The specifics Coomber could recall: white, skinny, medium height, lousy skin, worse teeth, baseball cap, and greasy pants. As for age: "A bum. Coulda been thirty, coulda been fifty."

When Mark and Doonie arrived the cops were an hour into canvassing the town's skinny white homeless guys. So far no results.

Could be The Art Critic put on a costume and makeup. Or he'd hired a homeless guy and then killed him. Mark's money was on #2.

Mark and Doonie visited Bargains & Treasures to see if they could jog the owner's memory.

Ron Coomber looked to be seventy years old and sounded as if he'd spent the last sixty in a sour mood. Had small bloodshot eyes and enormous weirdly mobile gray eyebrows, a pair of scraggly beasts living on his forehead.

When the detectives asked about the Yellow Sub, Coomber scowled and his brows crouched, two small wolves threatening to pounce.

"Look, I already told those other cops everything I remember. Ev-ree-thing. There ain't any more than that."

"You'd be surprised," Mark coaxed, "how much stuff can pop up if you—"

"I'm old, nothin' pops up. It was a month ago. And I get a lotta people comin' through."

A doubtful proposition, but Doonie nodded sympathetically. "Yeah, but only one buys the Fab Four vibrator. You notice if he had a tattoo—"

"If I seen I woulda said. Look, did my civil duty, ain't fair all I get for it is cop after cop standing here scaring customers away."

"Nah, that wouldn't be fair," Doonie commiserated. "Sooner we get through a coupla questions, sooner we get outta here."

The threat backfired. Ron Coomber folded his arms, flexed defiant eyebrow-wolves at Doonie, then turned his attention to his TV. The detectives were dead to him.

Mark glanced around. "Hey—a *Grease II* lunchbox." He fetched it and plunked it down in front of the old man. "I had one of these," he lied.

"Who knows, maybe that exact one," Doonie suggested.

"How much?" Mark asked.

Coomber, without looking up from the TV, muttered, "Ten."

"Reasonable."

Coomber deigned to look at him.

Mark pulled out a ten. Extended the bill partway toward the old man. "When the bum handed you his cash, you notice a tattoo on his hand or arm?"

Coomber stared at the ten. Shook his head.

Mark gave him the bill.

As Coomber took the ten he froze. Pointed at Mark's wrist. "A cast—he had this dirty old cast on his wrist, stickin' out his sleeve, came up around the bottom of his thumb."

"What color was the sleeve?"

Coomber shrugged. "You wanna bag for that?"

Mark nodded. He pulled out a picture of JaneDoe. "She ever been in the store?"

Coomber eyed the photo. "Nah. But who knows, she mighta. These days, girls, I'm careful not to stare, don't wanna get sued for sexual enhancement." He handed Mark a plastic bag.

"Thanks," Mark said. "Was there anybody else who looked at the Yellow Submarine? Earlier that day, or the day before?"

Coomber scowled, offended at being extorted for more than ten dollars' worth of effort—

His eyebrow beasts leapt. "A guy—I remember now, yeah, 'cause the day the bum bought that thing, it was the second time—In the morning, the submarine catches this guy's eye, and when it hits him he's starin' at a Beatles penal device, he does this—" his eyebrows mimed surprise. "Gets embarrassed and moved on, right out the door."

"What he look like?"

"White, and… big. Don't ask what he's wearing. Sunglasses."

"What kinda big?" Doonie asked.

"Sorta like you, only… even a little bigger, and…"

"Fatter?" Doonie suggested.

Furry eyebrows shrugged a what-you-gonna-do apology.

THIRTY-SIX / 2012

Mark left a voicemail telling Kaz to search for a white male with a cast on the right wrist who'd turned up in an area morgue, starting twenty-four days ago.

A Forest Park sergeant took Mark and Doonie on a re-canvass of the local homeless, to find out if anyone remembered a guy with a cast.

In a camp hidden behind foliage on the flanks of the expressway they met Tony and Roz, who knew exactly the guy.

Tony said the prick with the cast was hitting on Roz.

Roz told the cops that never happened, Tony got psycho when anyone talked to her.

Tony warned Roz not to call him crazy.

Roz told him he was psycho jealous and he knew it.

Mark and Doonie got between them before the hitting started.

Tony and Roz agreed the guy was named Buddy. Tony was sure Buddy was from Arkansas. Roz swore it was Vermont.

Mark and Doonie got back to the office just as Kaz won the lottery. Last week a white male, cast on the right wrist, greasy pants, was found in a shallow grave in the MacQueen Forest Preserve, way the hell up past DeKalb.

The corpse had been in the ground two-three weeks. Tox, organ damage, abscesses and dental disaster indicated chronic booze and speed abuse, but the COD was a broken neck.

His prints were in the system; busted for turning tricks back when he was better-looking. Dennis Lovesey. Age forty-two. From Utah.

The DeKalb County Sheriff had no leads on who killed him or why.

The Forest Park cops showed photos of Dennis to Tony and Roz, who confirmed he was Buddy.

The Forest Park cops showed the photos to Ron Coomber and asked if this was the man who purchased the Yellow Submarine.

"Coulda been. Sure. Maybe."

"Drove seventy miles to dump the body—he's fat but he ain't lazy," Doonie concluded, when he and Mark briefed Lieutenant Husak.

"All we know about the fat guy is he glanced at the Yellow Sub," Husak corrected. "No proof he's the one who hired the homeless guy to buy it. JaneDoe coulda hired him."

"Owner said she'd never been in."

"This owner who wouldn't be sure who it was if you showed him a picture of himself?" Husak countered. "And as for killing the homeless guy—JaneDoe's a big healthy girl, she could break a man's neck."

"Yeah," Mark agreed, "she could."

But now he was a millimeter closer to being able to prove she hadn't.

All he had to do was sort through every large overweight white male in Chicago.

THIRTY-SEVEN / 2012

It was the Laurie Desh death whammy all over again: Dale is having perfectly good sex, and Tommy Tesca leaps out of a tabletop electronic device.

This time Dale was no longer living with Soosie. Soon after going into the artist-slaughtering business Dale had done the right thing and broken up with her. Which was also the practical thing; no way to explain to Soosie why he kept disappearing for weeks, and why he suddenly had money.

This time Dale was in his office. Lou had set Dale up with a respectable front, as an Esthetic Impact consultant, whom the Mastrizzis' many acquaintances in the business world hired to class up their office walls. Turning murderer was the tragedy of Dale's life, but turning corporate interior decorator felt like its low point.

Dale was at his desk, receiving oral affection from a professional under the desk; a healthy fee was the only reason a woman would touch someone whose complexion was as unhealthy as Dale's.

Dale had left his computer on, and, even as his lava was fixing to go all Vesuvius, he couldn't resist a glance. Saw a news flash from ArtAlarm.Com: ROBERT GILSON MURDERED.

Vesuvius went dormant.

Dale phoned Lou Mastrizzi and told him they needed to speak.

They were tooling up Lakeshore Drive in Lou's two-day-old Maserati Quattroporte, which had that new-car smell and that newly-swept-for-bugs sense of security.

"So what's up?" Lou asked, with his eternal sense of security. No matter what, Lou exuded the unruffled, amused demeanor of a man utterly comfortable in his spa-polished skin. Lou enjoyed his life, and yours too.

"Tommy Tesca is in town murdering artists."

"Robert Gilson? Heard it on the radio while I was driving over."

Dale nodded. "Now we know why Tommy disappeared last year."

"Why you so sure this was Tommy?"

"Seven years ago Gilson was on the first list of targets I made—the only list with Chicagoans on it."

Lou mulled that. "If it is Tesca—why?"

"Money. And to show us up; he's breaking the rule about not killing where we live. If I'm right, he also won't wait a year before killing another one. And even if he doesn't..."

A sad grin from Lou. "The asshole's gonna get caught."

At which point the only bargaining chips the asshole could offer the cops would be Dale and the Mastrizzis.

"Okay," Lou continued. "Still could turn out someone else popped Gilson, but I'll track Tesca down. If it was Tommy, we'll get to him before the cops do." Making that sound simple as Googling the nearest Banana Republic.

"Good," Dale replied, trying to match Lou's casual confidence. Failing, dismally.

Lou gave Dale an amused, sympathetic glance. Exited at Belmont, took a right turn into Lincoln Park and pulled to the curb. Unbuckled his seat belt. Asked, "Ever drive a Mazz?"

The Mastrizzi muscle hunting Tommy Tesca came up with exactly nothing. It had been thirteen months since Tesca's family or friends heard from him. Nobody knew why Tommy left or where to. Fell off the Earth.

Lou unleashed his best hacker.

There was no credit-card trail. Tommy must've paid cash for everything. But the cyber-hound sniffed out a year-old court filing in Indiana. Thomas Tesca, born in Cicero, Illinois, currently a resident of Indianapolis, petitioned for a change of name.

Petition granted. He was now Jonathan Davis.

Davis's address turned out to be a postal box. Lou's muscle checked the box rental joint. Tesca had terminated the box soon as he became Davis.

The muscle scoured Indianapolis. Nothing.

Then it became obvious why they were having no luck finding Tommy Tesca aka Jonathan Davis in Indiana.

Gerd Voorsts got shot in the head. Tommy was still in Chicago.

Dale began carrying a gun. Totally illegal. Didn't care.

Dale also completed the purchase of a six-mil Damian Jung canvas. He met with Lou and their investor, Jay Branko, at Branko's office, to brief them on the acquisition; the only way they talked business was face-to face.

In the elevator after the meeting, Lou gave Dale a wry look, leaned close and whispered, "Holster bulge."

Lou treated Dale to dinner. Alinea, a trip to high-tech foodie heaven.

The first hour was all small talk, as they ate their way through the tasting menu's cascade of gastro-engineered delicacies and perfectly paired wines. Nine courses in, Lou judged Dale to be un-tense enough to digest the main course.

Lou advised Dale that carrying an unlicensed weapon was an unacceptable risk. Advised Dale not to doubt they'd find Jonathan Davis, soon. Advised Dale to concentrate on their project. Informed Dale the only thing to worry about was what color he wanted his Maserati to be. Because, when this ultimate deal went down, a Mazz was going to be Dale's bonus.

Dale, as advised, laid awake all night concentrating on how this ultimate deal would go down. How, when Tommy was safely dead, and Damian Jung was safely dead, and all Jung's paintings had been safely cashed in at a fabulous profit... Dale would be the only man alive who could implicate the Mastrizzis.

Dale bought a smaller carry piece and a subtler holster.

He put his original gun in the nightstand by his bed. Another gun in his desk at work. Another under the driver's seat of his Prius.

And two more in an emergency escape kit, which he'd begun assembling the day he'd gone partners with the Mastrizzis.

And maybe it was just superstitious, but given the manner in which he'd found out about Laurie Desh, and now Robert Gilson, Dale decided to stop having sex until Tommy Tesca was dead.

THIRTY-EIGHT / 2012

ime to quit fiddling with the goddamn dildo and leave. But Tommy couldn't make up his mind between having only John and Paul's faces show, or to include Ringo's. More of a laugh with Ringo showing, heh?

But when Tommy pulled the Yellow Submarine up so Ringo was sticking out above Gerd Voorsts' skinny dead lips, the dildo got wobbly; Tommy didn't want to risk it falling out of Voorsts' mouth before the cops found it and got some good shots of it.

Tommy wondered if he could use a shoelace or something to tie Voorsts' jaw shut.

Rejected that. Would look preposterous.

Fuck. Better safe than sorry. Tommy pushed the Yellow Sub down until it was securely wedged. Still looked pretty decent. Yeah. Fine.

Tommy was halfway up the basement stairs when he stopped, pissed at himself for being such a goddamn wimp. Why the fuck bother going to all this trouble—paying that junkie creep to buy the perfect signature dildo, then whacking the creep and driving to almost fucking Wisconsin to bury him—and then settle for doing a half-assed job? Heh?

Fuck that. If he left it like this it'd make him crazy.

He stomped back down the stairs. Pondered the body in the tub. Visualized. Hehhhhhh...

Tommy slid the Yellow Submarine out so that Ringo's face showed. Fucker started to fall outta Voorsts' mouth again.

So Tommy slowly, slowly, eased it down, one fucking little fraction of an inch at a time...

Holy Mother, there it was. The Yellow Sub was in there solid, no wobble, with just enough of Ringo's puss sticking out so you could tell it was him. In fact it was cooler with just half his face showing—like

Ringo was playing peek-a-boo from inside this dead genius' mouth.

Tommy treated himself to a long gaze at how great this came out. Soaking it in. Imagining the looks on the cops' faces. What would go through their minds.

Fuuu-uck. What a buzz.

Tommy left feeling, what—*lighter* than he had since, shit, *years.* Heh!

Tommy's best mood in years lasted until late the next afternoon.

The problem wasn't being cooped up in a mobile home out past Elgin, an hour and a half outside the city, in by-God corn-growing goat-fucking meth-cooking farm country. This was a good hide-out. Place the cops and the Mastrizzis wouldn't look, a shit-hole trailer park where the residents were mostly farm workers who were mostly illegal and totally into nobody getting nosy about anybody's particulars.

What killed Tommy's buzz was watching hours of news without a single goddamn word about Voorsts. For the first time in his life Tommy found himself frustrated by the fact no one had found the body of someone he'd popped.

Getting the Yellow Sub just right had been a rush. But after a while, knowing he'd done such good work and no one was seeing it, that was just fucking annoying.

He opened a fresh bottle of Scotch. Balvenie Doublewood, heh, first-class single malt Dale Phipps turned him onto. Dalie-boy did have his moments. But mainly Dale had his pile a fuckin' tightass rules, and here's to breaking one more: Tommy poured the Balvenie over ice.

The 21-year-old hooch spread through Tommy like a cloud of warm silk, and when it got to his brain it whispered, *When you whack JaneDoe, how far in you gonna push the Cubs bat?*

Well, thing is, Tommy explained to the Balvenie, no way to tell until he had the bitch dead and saw how the miniature Cubs bat worked with her mouth, and—he learned this from Gilson and Voorsts—the way the bat goes with JaneDoe's whole face, heh? Just have to go with what feels—

Fucking finally! Gerd Voorsts was dead. For real, on TV. Bulletin on a local newscast. Which meant the cops, maybe this very minute, were photographing the Yellow Submarine, from every angle.

Tommy's benign buzz flowed back in.

Then got even better.

The Channel 2 anchor said the magic words: "Chuck, any confirmation from police we're looking at a *serial killer*?"

Chuck said, "Investigators are considering the possibility this was indeed perhaps the work of a serial killer."

They cut to live chopper shots of a crowd outside Voorsts' house. Tommy channel-surfed; four local channels were also going live, with choppers.

Within minutes the combination of magic words and aerial photography hooked CNN: "In Chicago, a serial killer is targeting major artists."

Because CNN was in, the other cable news networks had to jump on it. Started showing clips of art snobs back in Voorsts' hometown, Holland, freaking out.

Tommy poured another heretical Balvenie on the rocks. Raised the glass. "You watchin', Dalie-Boy? Lou? Gianni? Heh?" Knocked back the Scotch. Yeah! This could not be happening better.

Except...

Over the next few hours the cops as usual refused to cough up any details. Tommy expected that; they'd kept the Ken doll secret, so no way they'd blab about the Yellow Submarine.

But sitting here watching the news, realizing millions of people were tuned in, but it might be years before any of them got to see his work... bothered him.

Until he learned he had an official serial killer secret identity.

Fuckin'-ay! He was *The Art Critic*. These were *The Art Critic Murders*, now and forever. Famous shit.

At ten PM nearly every local and national newscast opened with some variation of: "Another killer review from Chicago's Art Critic!"

Every dumb-shit station using the same fucking line. But ya

couldn't blame 'em. *Killer review.* Funny.

Funny? Shit! This was off the charts. He had the cops completely suckered. Was pissing on the Mastrizzis. Was gonna retire rich, and invisible.

Invisible, and yet a fucking star.

Though that did bump up the risk factor. With all this publicity, whacking JaneDoe might turn out a little trickier than he figured, 'cause now every artist in town would be shitting bricks. Taking precautions.

Fuck it—price of fame, heh? The Art Critic was stoked. Whole world was hot to see to his next *killer review.* No way was he gonna disappoint.

THIRTY-NINE / 2012

They were in Carrie's bed, the Assistant State's Attorney stretched luxuriously against Mark as he confided the problems he was having finding a large fat white male.

Mark told Carrie about the databases refusing to spit out one intriguing large fat white male murderer, sexual predator, painter, art critic or art professor. Mark even pulled the driver's license of the possible suspect from the Desh file. Dale Phipps was five-six, a hundred-forty pounds. And that, Mark told Carrie, that's when he decided to call it a night.

Mark did not tell Carrie how, at 1:48 AM, frustrated in every way, he'd put his computer to sleep, pulled out his cell phone and... almost called JaneDoe. Christ.

"Great," Carrie said, "you're spending the night with me because you couldn't find a serial killer to spend it with."

"Also because you're big fun, and big smart."

"So you only have sex with me so you can get to talk to me?"

"Guilty. Tell me how to find the fat man of my dreams."

"Wellll..." Carrie drawled, and, as she pondered the problem, began absentmindedly rolling Mark's balls as if they were large warm worry beads. "Maybe it's a large fat white male who's fixated on Gilson and Voorsts but can't afford their paintings—then why didn't he take any? Because he can't bring home evidence he's the killer. But then he still doesn't have their paintings, so fuck me," Carrie declared, punctuating it with an annoyed tug on her worry beads.

"Ow."

"Sorry." She resumed her gentle meditational rolling. "What if The Art Critic is an art critic? Must be a lotta fat white guys in that subculture."

"But none with priors. And I can't go interview them, find out where they were the time of the murders. Husak gets pissed when I even mention looking for alternative suspects."

"So…" Carrie's fingers began to juggle a little faster, "the way you'll be allowed to investigate someone else is to prove JaneDoe isn't the perp."

"There isn't any proof that she isn't."

"Then what makes you certain it's not her?"

Carrie's fingers went still; she'd felt him tense.

Mark said, "Look at her sculpture—the Ken doll and the Yellow Sub don't match the look, the whole sensibility of her work."

Carrie resumed gently—cagily—rolling Mark's balls. "What's JaneDoe like?"

A short silence took a while to crawl by.

Mark said, "Arty." He traced a finger up Carrie's inner thigh. "Impulsive." His fingertip began drawing lazy circles on Carrie's clitoris. "Innocent." He slid two fingers inside her and slowly flexed them. Carrie eased one of her own fingers in between his. Mark's cell rang.

It was the surveillance team. They'd busted a guy in the alley behind JaneDoe's building trying to break into a rear window of her apartment.

FORTY / 2012

The Art Critic strolled into the south end of the alley, looking like he belonged there. He was in meter-reader drag, a ComEd uniform complete with hard-hat, photo ID and a data recorder.

The Art Critic checked the rear of JaneDoe's building. JaneDoe's red SUV was in the fenced-in parking lot.

He patted his breast pocket. Miniature Cubs bat was there. Patted his back pocket. The psycho note about going to Europe to kill a real artist was there.

He put on clear, colorless latex gloves.

Ladies and germs, boys and girls, The Art Critic will now deliver his final killer review.

It was 8:10 AM. JaneDoe would still be asleep. Groggy as hell when she came to the front door. People answer when it's a guy from the electric company saying there's a problem with your meter, and maybe a safety issue.

She'd be grateful when he explained: *Sorry to bother you, lady, but your meter's showing crazy high usage, didn't wanna go enter those numbers and stick you with a humongous bill, not till I asked if you really been using this much,* and he'd raise the data recorder like to show her the reading, but she'd see the gun under it, and wham bam he backs her in, closes the door and tonight he's on a plane to Brazil.

The Art Critic left the alley and headed up the sidewalk toward JaneDoe's front door, which was in the front corner of the building. As he went, he glanced across the street, kitty-corner, to where he liked to park when he cased her place, 'cause it had a view of her front door, and past it to where her Subaru exited the alley—*The fuck?!*

There was a dark green Crown Vic parked in Tommy's favorite spot. Two guys in the front seat who were nothing but plainclothes cops. Both of 'em looking at Tommy.

His heart hammered and bile danced up the back of his tongue. He fought an urge to turn and go back into the alley. Don't draw attention, heh. Keep going. Just a dumbfuck meter-reader on his dumbfuck route.

He passed JaneDoe's door, turned the corner and headed north. His mind on fire: *Why the cops sitting on her? They know she was his next target? How would they?!?! Maybe they put protection on every artist in Chicago? No that's fuckin' ridiculous.*

Tommy kept walking. Took off the ComEd helmet and ID. Zigzagged back to where he was parked. Got in his car. Put the key in the ignition. Almost gagged up his breakfast.

our hours later, Tommy, wearing a suit, was parked a half-block behind the Crown Vic. Had to find out if it really was JaneDoe the cops were watching.

JaneDoe's red Forester pulled out of the alley.

The Crown Vic followed. Tommy followed the Crown Vic. Motherfuck. The cops were all over JaneDoe.

Tommy had been turning his head inside out trying to think how the cops coulda found out she was his target. Came up with squat.

If the cops weren't tailing her to protect her, then what?

The Forester headed north on Halsted. Followed by the cops. Followed by Tommy.

The Forester turned west on Adams. North on Racine. Then parked. By the 12th District police station.

The Crown Vic parked down the block.

Tommy kept driving. In his rear-view he saw JaneDoe walk into the police station.

Tommy cancelled his flight to Brazil. Spent a long serious night in his trailer. Red wine and coffee.

What was JaneDoe doing in the cop shop? The cops like her for something? Or was she there to discuss her security detail?

Question is what's the smart move for Tommy here. No way can he clip JaneDoe with cops babysitting her. Does he wait, see if they give up and go home? Or does he right now fuck off to Brazil? His safest move.

But if he doesn't kill her he's blowing off the profit he'd make on those two fucking costumes of hers, heh, costumes he'd laid out eighteen grand for. Small change compared to what he was gonna make off Gilson and Voorsts, but shit, whatever he earns on this play has to

last the rest of his life… And it works better if he whacks three artists instead of two. The media goes more nuts, the value of each dead
genius goes up.

So question is, how long's it take the cops to back off of JaneDoe?

Even bigger question, how much longer can Tommy risk staying
here? He hadda figure by now the Mastrizzis know it's him. Hadda
figure they got guns looking. Gianni fucking Mastrizzi and his smug
little cunt of a son—wait—shit!

If Tommy doesn't kill JaneDoe he doesn't get to leave the psycho
note saying he's going to kill some huge artist in Europe. If he doesn't
leave that note, he hasn't fucked up Gianni's last huge play.

He could mail the note.

Nah. Cops couldn't be certain who sent it. Only way they know
for sure is they find it on dead JaneDoe with a toy Cubs bat in her
mouth.

Tommy fell asleep thinking, heh, he was gonna hang in a while.

Tommy woke up thinking, get real. Time to get the hell outta
Dodge.

Yeah. Something this fuckin' important, this calls for a morning
decision. Rested, calm, your brain's back between your ears steada
drooped over your balls.

He called the airline. Fly outta Milwaukee that afternoon, catch a
red-eye from Miami to Sao Paulo.

He made coffee. Turned on the tube. Discovered the cops sitting
on JaneDoe's place had been joined by a herd of fucking TV news
crews. And gawkers. Must be a hundred cocksuckers surrounding
JaneDoe's place.

Every channel, reporters were saying JaneDoe was The Art Critic.

Giving her all the credit for Tommy's fucking work.

FORTY-TWO / 2012

etective Mark Bergman wasn't a happy man when he walked into the interrogation room at 4:47 AM. Didn't like that some twit tried to crawl in JaneDoe's rear window. Didn't like that his fingers still smelled faintly of Assistant State's Attorney. Didn't like that the white male on the other side of the table was a five-nine, hundred-sixty-pound, twenty-year-old twit and not a large fat serial killer.

The kid, however, was delighted to be under arrest. "I'm a journalist!" he proclaimed as Mark sat down, not waiting for a question.

"You're Kenneth Nazarian of Glendale, California, journalism undergrad at Northwestern. Which professor taught you to use a bolt-cutter on the security grate over someone's window?"

"Thomas Jefferson! A total access free press is democracy's proctoscope."

"Yeah, I remember reading that one on his monument. Thing is, reactionary legislators went and made breaking and entering a felony."

"If the mainstream press had done its job I wouldn't have had to take it to the next level. Media gave up on her, dude, else I never would've been able to sneak into that alley."

That last part was true. The camera crews and gawkers besieging JaneDoe's building began to drift away after twenty-four hours of her refusing to show herself. After forty-eight hours, the last two crews left to cover a Vince Vaughn premiere. The remaining the gawkers went home, there being no chance of getting their faces on the news.

Only the police surveillance remained.

"How'd you get past the cops?"

"Easy," Nazarian preened. "From where your guys are parked they can see the entrances to the alley, but they can't see into it. So I scammed my way into the apartment building across the alley from

130

JaneDoe's building. Went up to the roof. Laid low. Around 2:45 I saw her lights go out. Waited half an hour, climbed down the fire escape and walked across the alley to JaneDoe's rear window."

"Expect to get an interview if you got inside? 'This isn't a home invasion, Ms. Alleged Serial Killer, it's Tom Jefferson's proctoscope'?"

"Dude, you're thinking old school," Nazarian scolded. "She was *asleep*. I was gonna shoot infra-red, inside a serial killer's pitch-dark lair, maybe get footage of her sleeping. *Blair Witch* goes paparazzi— I'da been famous. Still will be, thanks to getting busted. Bet you a hundred I am viral—could we take a quick look at your phone?"

Mark stared at him.

Nazarian sighed, annoyed. Then, hunting for details to use when he was allowed to start blogging: "How'd I get caught? Was she not asleep?"

Not for long. JaneDoe had been jolted awake by the racket democracy's proctoscope was making with his bolt cutters. She called 911. Before the operator could dispatch a patrol car, the Feds tapping JaneDoe's phone had alerted the surveillance team.

Mark said, "Your attorney will have access to the incident report after you're booked."

"Excellent. We do that now? Can you video the booking?"

Mark stared at him.

"Oh, dude, welcome to the 21st century. My trial's gonna be huge"—Nazarian mimed a gigantic headline—*"First Amendment versus tight sphincter letter-of-the-law!* Hey, you'll be in my video— when the trial's over you can say how you feel about being forced to bust me."

Mark said, "First Amendment? Doesn't cover the intent-to-distribute amounts of grass, coke and X we found in your car. Mandatory fifteen. On each count."

"Wha—my ass! *There was nothing in my car*," Nazarian shrieked, in a whiny falsetto. "Two cans of Red Bull in the back seat! There were no fucking drugs in my car!"

Mark stood. "Welcome to Chicago. Dude."

Which was bullshit. But Mark couldn't slug the little shit. Making him spend twenty-four hours in a cage freaking out over nonexistent drug charges would have to do.

"I want a lawyer!"

"Gonna hire a good one, or one who looks good on camera?"

The question stumped Nazarian.

Mark started to leave. As Mark reached the door Nazarian wailed, "Why you picking on me?! *She's* the one who murders artists, *she's* the one being an asshole not engaging with the press! *She brought this on herself!*"

Mark turned. His expression made Nazarian flinch.

Then the realization hit Mark. He gave the kid an evil grin.

Nazarian thought that meant the beating was about to begin, so he started screaming, "Help! Help me!! Somebody please he's killing me!!!"

Mark left the interrogation room in an improved mood. *She brought this on herself.* Idiot, why you been shielding her when you should've been using her?

FORTY-THREE / 2012

When Lieutenant Husak got to his office that morning, Bergman and Doonie were standing by his desk. Couple of big dogs with their leashes in their mouths, begging to go for a walk.

Husak, who'd seen the preliminary report on the alley incident on his computer at home, said, "G'morning. We confirm Nazarian's alibis for the times of the murders?"

Mark nodded. "He's not a serial killer, he's just the future of journalism."

"So what's the big news you can't wait to hit me with," Husak asked.

"I fucked up," Mark said.

Husak raised an eyebrow.

Mark said, "When I wanted to look into the Desh case, that artist murder from seven years ago? I spaced on the most important fact."

"More important than the fact you wanted to violate Langan's order we only look at JaneDoe?"

"Much. Loo, in my initial interview with her, back before she was a suspect... It was JaneDoe who told me about the Laurie Desh case."

Pointing the cops at the 2005 corpse of her debut victim would fit the FBI's profile of an arrogant serial killer lusting for recognition.

Husak went stone-faced and asked, too quietly, "Three weeks. How the fuck's that slip your mind three weeks?"

Mark's theory consisted of, "I..."

"Had one mother of a big-ass brain cramp," Doonie explained. "Seven years, it's about fuckin' time. Now I know he's human. The other big change is, starting right now, the only beef Langan is gonna have about us looking at the Desh case is if we don't get right the fuck on it."

FORTY-FOUR / 2012

The seething troll was hunkered down in his trailer, watching TV. Watching how JaneDoe was cashing in on the retarded cocksucker world thinkin' *she* was The Art Critic.

JaneDoe's art dealer was telling how she just sold all three weirdass JaneDoe costumes in her gallery. Sticker price had been eleven grand each, no takers, now suddenly they fly out the door for twenty-eight grand.

Upside, though, those two JaneDoe costumes Tommy bought, nine grand apiece, were now good for twenty-eight apiece.

This with JaneDoe still alive. So imagine if Tommy could make a visit.

Heh.

Fuck the cops. Fuck the Mastrizzis. Tommy would give it a few days, see if he could figure a way to kill the shit out of JaneDoe.

Turned out the reporters staking out JaneDoe's place had the attention span of a gnat. Couple days and they're gone.

Tommy did a drive-by. The cops were still sitting on JaneDoe.

Got worse.

That night some college kid YouTube fuckwad gets busted trying to break into JaneDoe's.

So now there's a shitload more cops sitting on JaneDoe. And some reporters are back.

That was the reality. Wasn't gonna change anytime soon.

Unless Tommy got creative.

FORTY-FIVE / 2012

ale was back in the Maserati with Lou. But this time it was Lou who'd called, his voice dark with concern. A first.

They'd been driving several minutes and Lou hadn't said a word.

"What's up," Dale finally ventured, hoping he hadn't committed a life-threatening breach of etiquette.

"Jay." Lou spat the syllable. "Jay's turned six kinds of pussy."

"Uh-huh," Dale said. Hoping he was wrong about what was coming next.

Jay Branko Jr., president of JB Structural, was a brawny big-armed banger who'd single-handedly fought his way up his mother's birth canal to inherit a major construction company. Like many of the tough guys in the tough business of building things the size of bridges and skyscrapers, Branko's default demeanor was human bulldozer. Which would swell into enraged sadistic bulldozer if Branko was confronted about his pussiness.

"You're going to go calm him down." Lou's voice dropped an octave. "'Cause I'm done trying."

"Any advice on the best way to do that?"

Lou looked at Dale. "Make sure Jay understands: I'm. Done. Trying."

Christ. Dale had just been assigned to issue a Mob ultimatum to a nasty heavy-hitter tycoon. So Dale hadn't committed a life-threatening breach of etiquette. He'd been given a life-threatening promotion.

When Dale walked into Branko's office Branko remained seated behind his desk. Grunted "Hi" and pointed for Dale to take the chair across the desk. In earlier meetings they'd sat by the coffee table.

Dale got right to business. "Lou said you had some concerns."

"What I have is a more sensible approach. Even if Damian Jung doesn't have a ski accident, our paintings are getting more valuable every day, right?"

"Right."

"So we leave Jung be, stay patient, cash in a painting every three-four years. The profits are a little less, but we won't be taking a stupid risk."

"The profits would be exponentially less. And the gentlemen you've invested with don't take stupid risks."

"Did they catch Tesca?"

"They will."

"Yeah? You know this because?"

"The cops aren't looking for Tesca. They think JaneDoe is The Art Critic."

"Maybe. You wanna play maybe? Maybe the cops do get to him first."

"Tesca can't give them your name."

Branko shot Dale a threatening smirk. "He can give them your name."

"At which point our friends—or you—would make me disappear," Dale replied, unfazed, outlining a business contingency. "If I were worried the cops might grab Tesca, I'd be making myself disappear, instead of sitting here talking to you."

Not what Branko expected. His smirk wavered. "Even if the cops never find Tesca we got problems," Branko countered, in a pouty snarl. "He's a moron. He'll leave a money trail, the cops will find out he was buying and selling work by the artists he killed. *The cops will be onto the scam.*"

"So? We're not morons, we haven't left a trail."

"*So,* you fucking moron idiot smug turd, from then on when Jung—or any bigass artist—dies, the police will be all over it."

"Swiss cops won't link a knifing and a shooting in Chicago with a seventy-eight-year-old having a ski accident in Zermatt."

"More fucking maybes! Jung's seventy-fucking-eight, we do the sensible fucking thing, we just stay patient!" Branko yelled.

"Not practical. Because, A) Jung could live to a hundred, and,

B)…" Dale enunciated slowly, making clear this was a warning, "…
That is not our deal."

Branko's eyes narrowed and his cheeks flushed. But instead of
leaping across the desk, picking Dale up and throwing him through
the 60th-floor window, he snarled, "When it's my five million, the
deal is what I say it is. And tell Lou this is the last time I discuss this
with an errand boy—*no!*—you stay the fuck out of this. I'll tell him."

"Jay," Dale said, a kindly uncle attempting to demystify one-plus-
one for a slow nephew, "Lou's trying to protect you. Which is why I'm
here, repeating everything Lou is really fucking done explaining to
you. Might not be the best idea to keep bothering him, let alone issue
an ultimatum, because…" Dale gave Branko a cold look. "Ever met
the Old Man?"

Branko glared.

Dale held Branko's glare. Waited for the big bad stud to think it
through.

*Would Gianni kill me for arguing to change the plan? Is this
little Halloween-face prick yanking my chain?... This little Halloween-
face prick has planned and pulled off a bunch of murders... I never
have.*

Branko blinked.

amn, that was fun.

More than fun. Much, much more.

Dale walked the fifteen blocks to his office. Too stoked to sit in a cab.

Oh man. Jay Branko throws down. Dale smokes him.

More important, Dale wins his personal bottom line: The Damian Jung project stays alive. Long as that stays alive, Dale stays alive. Gives him years to refine his disappearing act. Which will work.

Because Dale Phipps was for motherfucking real. He was a winner. Didn't matter at what. Being good at anything, succeeding at *anything*, made you a man. Whether that thing was noble, or it was eczema-stoking barbarism, didn't count for shit.

Dorian Gray was gonna be unbearable when he heard poor naïve Dale finally arrived at that simple truth.

Yeah, well, fuck Dor and the Victorian parable he rode in on. Dale took out his iPod, inserted the buds, goosed the volume to Primordial Brain Massage and dialed up some Muddy Waters pile-driver whomp.

Bah-wadda, thonk-thonk-thonk! Bah-wadda, thonk-thonk-thonk!

Right down State Street, *thonk-thonk*! To Tree Studios, *thonk-thonk*! That cool old building, *thonk-thonk*! Old dark wood doors, *thonk-thonk*! With frosted glass, *thonk-thonk*! Right through his door, *thonk-thonk*! Into his lobby, *thonk-thonk* where his receptionist, Kylie, said something Dale couldn't hear, as she gestured at the two men waiting for him.

A tall handsome one in his thirties and a beefy fiftyish slob. Dale figured them for middle management drones from some waste disposal firm that had been ordered to hire him.

The younger drone started to speak, as Dale pulled out his

ear-buds—

"—tective Bergman and this is Detective Dunegan. We're looking into possible connections between the Art Critic murders and Laurie Desh."

The floor tilted. The air turned gray. Dale struggled against a barrage of urges to moan, puke, flee, faint. Managed to squelch them.

But a fart snuck out. A long thin staccato blattering that rose in pitch to somehow sound like a frightened question-mark.

Troy left Thalken's Corner early, around one-forty AM.

Most nights Troy hung out till the bar closed. Tonight he got chased out by a fantastically edible young thing he'd been looking forward to feasting on.

She'd been fine during the part where they were nameless strangers on adjoining stools.

She'd been fine during the part where nameless strangers became Larissa and Troy.

Then came the part where Larissa found out the name that came after Troy was Horowitz, yes that Troy Horowitz, the sculptor, and Larissa told Troy how much she loved his work and wanted to know if he was freaked out by this whole Art Critic thing, did he think JaneDoe was The Art Critic, did he know JaneDoe, what do other artists think, are all the artists leaving town or barricading their homes and carrying guns?

Larissa was panting to talk about the stuff Troy and his friends had been talking about, constantly, repetitively, obsessively, pathetically, masochistically, banally and frighteningly, for weeks, so now the mere mention of the topic filled Troy with an unnerving schizo blend of boredom and dread.

He glanced at his watch, put down an extra ten for the bartender and stood up.

Larissa rotated her stool so she was facing Troy. Gazed up into his eyes. Purred, "Leaving?" Not a question. An offer.

An offer of the meal Troy had spent the last hour coaxing onto his plate. And, gazing down at Larissa's plummy lips and buttery cleavage, one he deeply craved.

But he knew what she'd keep talking about between courses. All night. And maybe at breakfast.

"Nice meetin' ya," he sighed, and left.

As Troy went out Thalken's front door and down the steps he suffered a twinge of non-buyer's remorse.

First, because he'd violated the lesson his forty-three years on Earth had taught him about sex: you don't regret the things you did do nearly as much as the things you didn't do.

Second, because Bobby and Gerd had been killed while they were home alone. Troy was going home alone, when Larissa would have made an annoying but succulent human shield.

But, Troy reminded himself for the billionth time, unlike Bobby and Gerd, his place had steel doors, motion detectors, floodlights, and alarms that would blast sirens while silently summoning security goons. He'd gone whole hog eight years ago after the place had been burgled, a load of expensive tools stolen. Back then the converted body shop had just been his studio, but since his divorce it was also home. A much safer one than the house he'd shared with The Bitch and The Brats, and just a two-and-a-half block walk from a neighborhood bar where Troy was the star regul—

"*Freeze*," a harsh hiss from a huge guy who surged out of a narrow dark walkway, stuck a gun in Troy's face and clamped a crushing hand on his throat.

Troy gave a tiny nod.

The man was wearing a nylon ski mask. Thank God. Robbery.

The huge mugger yanked Troy into the walkway and shoved him against the wall.

"Stay quiet, you don't get hurt."

Troy nodded again. Just cooperate—*Gloves! Why's a mugger wearing latex gl*—

A startlingly beautiful light flashed in the gun barrel and Troy's brain stopped.

Many months ago Troy Horowitz and JaneDoe had been the finalists in the contest to become Tesca Target Number Three.

Financially, Horowitz was the better prospect. But he lived in a fucking fortress. The only place Tommy saw to nail Horowitz was walking home from the corner tavern where Horowitz hung, late, four-five nights a week.

Tommy didn't like clipping people outdoors. Never knew who was watching, who might come by.

So JaneDoe got the nod.

But things had changed.

So here Tommy was, out-fucking-doors, whacking some genius whose art he never even had a chance to stock up on.

Tommy pulled the dead sculptor's jaw down and stuck a souvenir miniature of the Hancock Building in his mouth. The base was too wide to fit, so the building had to go in upside down.

Looked like crap. Pissed Tommy off. Had an urge to take his Hancock Building and go.

Couldn't. Even if this one wasn't up to his usual standard, it got the main job done.

Soon as those cocksucker retard cops find this they'll know The Art Critic ain't JaneDoe.

And they will get the hell off her doorstep.

FORTY-EIGHT / 2012

Mark just barely recognized Dale Phipps from his driver's license photo; his face looked like it had been pranked by a horror movie make-up crew.

But it was Phipps who was shocked by Mark and Doonie. He blanched and blew a fart.

That happens. Even to people who aren't guilty of something worth arresting them for.

Phipps gave an apologetic nod, and ushered the cops into his office. He invited Mark and Doonie to sit as he hurried behind his desk like a man seeking safety behind a moat. Obviously nervous. But not interestingly.

Cops are connoisseurs of nervous. This was garden-variety. Except maybe for Phipps keeping his left hand in his pocket the entire time, even after he sat.

Soon as his butt landed in the chair Phipps blurted, "Is there some connection between Laurie's death and the Art Critic murders?"

"The profession of all three victims," Mark replied, giving no sign Phipps had just goosed the Nervous-ometer by trying to find out what the cops knew. "Did Laurie Desh and JaneDoe know each other?"

"Not that I was aware of. But young artists go to a lot of the same parties, bars—and openings, if only for the free wine and snacks."

"Was there anyone who had a reason to want Laurie Desh gone?"

"Nobody." Phipps massaged the brow above a bulging bloodshot eye. "As I told the detectives back then."

"Everybody pisses somebody off," Doonie insisted. "Any jilted exes?"

Phipps shook his head. "Not far as I knew. But we didn't see much of each other the last year-and-half of her life."

"After she blew you off and went with the Jacob Ruby Gallery in Manhattan?" Mark asked, hard, to see what brand of nervous it provoked.

"Yes, after that," Phipps answered. "And yes of course there were some hurt feelings at fir—"

"And some lost profits," Mark cut in.

"See," Doonie amiably pointed out, "Laurie did piss somebody off."

"I—" Phipps stopped, reset. "You've obviously read the file, so you know what I told the detectives. Of course I was upset, but not for long. What Laurie did was business as usual." Phipps looked at Doonie, then at Mark. "I did not kill Laurie Desh. You know that, because you know I was with my girlfriend when it happened."

"And girlfriends never lie," Mark said.

"She's an ex-girlfriend now. Ask her again."

"Good idea," Mark said. "Did you know Robert Gilson or Gerd Voorsts?"

"Everybody knew Bobby. I never met Voorsts."

Doonie asked, "Did Laurie Desh know them?"

"Bobby, for sure. I have no idea if she knew Voorsts."

"Do you know of anyone," Mark asked, "who knew all three? Someone Desh, Gilson and Voorsts had in common?"

Phipps blatted out another weak fart. He blushed, his rashes glowing darkly. "Sorry."

"We're professionals," Mark assured him. "So you *do* know someone?"

"What? Um, no, I, I can't think of anyone."

"You had this expression like you did." Not exactly; it was the fart.

Phipps shook his head. "No, no one, at all—I cannot help you there, honest," he apologized, holding out both hands in an instinctive gesture of sincerity.

It was the first time Phipps' left hand emerged from his pocket.

Mark and Doonie's eyes snapped to that hand.

There was no weapon in it. And no middle finger, except for a squat stump, and the fingers next to it were failed pretzels.

Phipps reddened and he yanked both hands down behind his desk.

Christ. The skin, the eye, the fingers—Phipps was probably nervous around anybody, let alone cops... And yet he was prospering in a business that was all about personal contact. "Well, thank you for your time, Mr. Phipps," Mark said, pretending he was done.

"Anything I can do."

"And," Mark gestured at the well-appointed office, "congratulations on the way you've rebounded from bankruptcy."

Phipps gave a modest duck of the head. "Thanks."

"How did you get into the esthetic impact consulting business?"

Bingo—another gassy blat.

Phipps covered his mouth with his undamaged right hand, through which he murmured, "Sorry, I'm—too much coffee this morning—sorry."

"Hell," Doonie confided, "had a partner with your same coffee troubles, only worse. Eight hours a day stuck in a car with him playing trombone. Closest I been to shooting a fellow officer."

Phipps searched for an appropriate response. Settled on, "Oh."

"So," Doonie urged, "you were saying how you got to be a, watchamacallit?"

"Esthetic..." He sighed. "Interior decorator. Well..." As Phipps struggled to answer that simple question his eyes darted back and forth, which gave the bulging one a fishlike quality. "...After my gallery went bust—"

Mark's cell rang. "Excuse me." He took the call. "Bergman... Right. We're on our way." He hung up. "Thank you for your cooperation," Mark stood. Promised Phipps, "We'll talk more soon."

Doonie waited till they were walking down the hallway, out of earshot of Phipps' office, before asking, "Something good?"

"For JaneDoe, yeah. For the sculptor who just turned up dead, no."

"There an Art Critic signature?"

"Looks like."

"So JaneDoe's off the hook... And you two..." Doonie grinned in happy anticipation.

FORTY-NINE / 2012

21-year-old Dottie Lang and Maxx, her terrier mutt, were having a totally usual walk when Maxx went gonzo yappy and tried to charge up a walkway. Dottie figured he'd spotted a rat. She had no intention of chasing rats anywhere, forget in that narrow dark passage between two grungy old buildings.

But Maxx's terrier-berserker switch had been thrown. He kept lunging back toward the walkway, manically scrabbling at the sidewalk, growling and whipping his head back and forth. Dottie was afraid Maxx was going to break his neck or at least rip out a toenail. She surrendered, and Maxx dragged her to something almost as gross as a live rat.

Dottie jerked to a halt. Began to back away. Stopped. Stared. With that thing in his mouth, it took a moment. But she recognized him; Troy, that sculptor dude who always sat on the end stool at Thalken's, hitting on anything with big boobs, so he'd never talked much to Dottie—holy shit! *Troy was an artist.* So this must—

Dottie yanked out her cell and took a picture.

Came out dark. She pressed Low Light and got a couple of better shots.

Then she hauled Maxx out to the sidewalk and called 911.

The dispatcher offered to stay on the line with her until the cops arrived. Dottie said that's okay, hung up, and started posting.

After uploading twice, Dottie froze: She could've *sold* these pictures.

Too late. Her life had been *You feel it, you message it.* Her thumbs ruled.

So what. This works. These pictures were totally viral. Maybe historic. Tonight she'd be on TV, rocking the news.

And OMG, Maxx was gonna be a hero.

Dottie's thumbs galloped back into action.

FIFTY / 2012

They had just pulled away from the Tree Studios building when Mark realized what the finest part of the day was going to be.

Doonie noticed Mark trying not to grin. "What?"

"JaneDoe won't be off the Art Critic hook unless she has a solid alibi for this murder."

It took Doon maybe two seconds. He loosed a pleased, wicked moan when he got there: JaneDoe's alibi would be provided by her 24/7 CPD and FBI surveillance teams.

Okay, back to work. "Assuming the Art Critic didn't fuck up this time and leave his home address," Mark said, "we need to go at Phipps again, soon."

"Yeah, he sure as shit was holding back."

"Not just about Desh," Mark noted. "First fart came when he heard we were Homicide, second came when I asked if he knew someone connected to all three vics."

"Uh-huh," Doonie nodded, "and the third fart was when we asked how he got from being broke to sitting pretty. So we look at his money—"

Doonie's cell rang.

"Dunegan... Thanks, Loo." He snapped the phone shut. "Husak sent us something."

Doonie used the dashboard-mounted laptop to open Husak's email.

Two photos of the vic. He had an entry wound in his forehead and a miniature Hancock Building in his mouth. The Hancock was inserted upside down, a slight departure from the signature. But that wasn't why Husak had treated them to this preview.

The photos weren't police issue. They were on a Facebook page belonging to a 21-year-old waitress and her little dog, who'd just updated their status to: TODAY'S GRACE NATCHEZ GUEST STARS!

Dottie and Maxx had discovered the dead artist a few blocks north of Lake Street, a mile west of the Loop. The Market District, a semi-gritty neighborhood where produce distributors and light industry once thrived by servicing wealthy lakefront wards. In the 1970s its core businesses started going obsolete and belly-up. It made a comeback in the '90s. Media firms spilled in from the Loop, bringing a sprinkling of trendy restaurants, edgy galleries and hipoisie bars. But there was no shaking off the ingrained drabness of side streets dominated by weary factories, warehouses and tenements that had been collecting soot since the first half of the previous century.

At the moment, one side street was glamorized by a corpse, a herd of camera trucks, news choppers dancing overhead, and a gleaming limo waiting to spirit Dottie and Maxx away to a cable news bureau for their exclusive interview with Grace Natchez, who was on the phone in her dressing room in New York, raging at her field producer in Chicago to "get that little slut in the limo or my exclusive's gonna be about as exclusive as a fucking toilet seat at the back end of a 737!"

Dottie and Maxx were bathing in questions shouted by a phalanx of frantic reporters when Natchez's field producer sidled up and whispered in Dottie's ear: *"If we don't leave right now there won't be time for our make-up genius to do you before you go on camera!"*

Dottie squealed a quick "G'bye!" to the press and plopped into the limo, just as Detectives Bergman and Dunegan walked past. They entered the police-tape perimeter around the entry to the fatal walkway, which the TV Stars had tented with blue plastic sheeting to shield the vic from cameras. Now that the whole world had already seen what was in his mouth.

Under the tenting they found Wendy Hsu and Jim Montero hanging out with the guest of honor; this being Area Four, Hsu and Montero had been first in.

"Troy Horowitz, 44, sculptor," Montero informed Mark and Doonie. "Last seen leaving a nearby tavern at 1:40 AM, presumably walking to his residence, a block north of here."

Mark and Doonie studied the Hancock Building insertion.

Doonie said, "Exactly like his Facebook photo."

"Now there's a first," Mark said. "But also, first time the toy was inserted upside down."

"Because the base is too wide to fit in the guy's mouth," Doonie shrugged.

"First time the perp made that kind of mistake" Mark pointed out. "Also, the effect isn't as—whimsical as the others."

"Everyone has a off day," Doonie ruled.

"Yeah," Hsu chimed in, "I think it's him again."

"Probably," Mark said. "But it's also the first outdoor kill—though that might make sense—the Critic's a victim of his own success, every artist in town is too paranoid to let a stranger in."

"Especially Horowitz," Montero said. "Tavern owner says Horowitz's studio has security like a fucking bank. Street was the only place to get at him."

"Yeah," Mark admitted.

The variations between this and the other two kills were minor and explicable. This was The Art Critic. Not because that's who Mark wanted it to be. But because that's who logic said it was.

Time to go find out if Deputy Chief Langan was into logic this week.

FIFTY-ONE / 2012

When Mark and Doonie walked into Husak's office he was watching TV with Special Agent Nick Rarey, the competent young Feeb who'd noticed the key detail missing in Mark's account of how he ID'd the JaneDoe Barbie.

At the task force meeting Rarey maintained the regulation FBI cyborg demeanor. Here by himself with no supervisor to perform for, the blond baby-faced agent came across like a precocious college kid who'd lucked into a cool summer job as an FBI agent.

"Detectives," Rarey grinned, giving a casual fist pump.

Husak flung up a different gesture: a warning to not interrupt the TV.

A cable newscast. The anchor, sharing the screen with a close-up of a dead sculptor sucking on the Hancock Building, was incredulously asking, "Police *still* won't say if this is another Art Critic murder?"

Cut to a reporter at the crime scene: "All the statement says is—" she read text off her phone—" 'The evidence is being processed.' "

"Has there been word," the anchor wondered, "about whether any of the other victims had also been, um, violated with a miniature skyscraper?"

"Police won't comment on details."

"This one will," Doonie said. "It's the fuckin' Art Critic."

Husak muted the TV. "Probably."

"Got my vote," young Agent Rarey cheerfully declared.

"Deputy Chief Langan," Husak prophesied, "is gonna say this resembles the Art Critic's signature but the penmanship's shaky."

Doonie said, "Yeah, but," and ran the reasons why the outdoor thing and upside down thing made sense.

Husak replied, "Langan will want to hold off until ballistics come back. A match with the weapon that killed Voorsts would nail it."

"Even if it's not a match," Mark said, "the Art Critic's good for this. He's thorough enough to not use the same piece twice."

"I agree," Rarey chimed in. "And, bottom line, between our taps and your surveillance we know JaneDoe was home when Horowitz took that bullet."

Mark and Doonie did not grin or trade a look.

"We need to get after the real Art Critic," Rarey concluded.

"It is possible JaneDoe is the real Art Critic," Husak said, dutifully, without enthusiasm, "and this was a copycat. I see three ways that could happen: One, Horowitz was killed by a cop who knew the signature. Two, a cop leaked the signature. Three, JaneDoe has a disciple whose mission was to whack Horowitz if JaneDoe ever got busted."

"All of which I—and, almost as important, my boss—rate crazy improbable," Rarey said.

"Me too," Husak glumly admitted.

Mark sympathized. Husak was the one who'd have to advise the thin-skinned Langan it was time to cancel his order to look at nobody but JaneDoe, preventing a hunt for the real perp, a mistake which maybe got Troy Horowitz killed.

"Gentleman," Husak said, inviting the three of them to leave his office so he could make that touchy call.

Mark, the last one out, took care to shut the door gently.

Rarey asked, "Mind if I hang with you guys while we wait for the verdict?"

"Grab a chair," Mark said.

Rarey rolled a chair up alongside their desks.

Mark said, "Agent Rarey—"

"Nick," Rarey insisted.

"Nick, I get the feeling today's murder doesn't make you unhappy," Mark observed, not giving away his own huge lack of unhappiness about it.

"I never liked JaneDoe for this," Rarey confided.

"So you came over to help stick it to Langan?" Doonie asked.

"Dr. Hillkirk liked JaneDoe just as much as Langan did. So our hotshot profiler screwed the pooch too."

"A dog show you're enjoying," Mark suggested.

A wry grin. "The good doctor is held in—astonishingly—high regard by certain very senior officials."

"So," Mark said, "field guys know Hillkirk's a quack, but he's a political hire with serious protection."

"You might think that. I couldn't possibly comment."

Mark grinned. *"House Of Cards."*

Rarey nodded. Doonie frowned.

"Most awesome TV show ever," Rarey told him.

Doonie looked at Mark.

"A British thing, on PBS," Mark explained.

"Okay," Doonie sighed, pushing back from his desk. "I gotta piss. You girls talk among yourselves."

Watching Doon walk away, Rarey guessed, "Sox fan?"

Mark nodded. "How long you been in the Chicago bureau?"

"Eleven months. Best American city I've been in."

"Where you from?"

"Silver Spring. I'm government issue. Dad's an Assistant Secretary of the Treasury, Mom's a lawyer at State."

Shit. Not only was the kid sharp, he was an insider. Born on the Federal fast track.

Mark asked, "How did your folks take it when you were fourteen and informed them you were going to be a professional skateboarder?"

"Aw c'mon Mark, too easy. White suburban teenager, you knew it hadda be skateboarder or rapper. My actual shameful secret: I do not have the first fucking clue where to look for the Art Critic. You got anything?"

Mark had Dale Phipps. But no way Mark was going to blab to the FBI about the guilt-farter before he briefed Husak.

Mark shook his head. "Back to the grind, see if anything connects Horowitz to the other vics."

Husak poked his head out of his office and announced, "We're good. Langan wanted to stall, but Downtown's not gonna take that

PR hit. The C of D's gonna issue a statement saying the Art Critic did Horowitz and JaneDoe did not. Give her lawyer a heads-up," Husak instructed Mark, and, turtle-like, retracted his head into his office.

Mark began searching for the lawyer's phone number.

"Damn," Rarey sighed.

Something about the way that sounded made Mark look at him.

"Having to go through her lawyer," Rarey explained. "JaneDoe is a total scorcher. Shame you don't get to give her the good news, in person," Rarey said, giving Mark a meaningful look. Slightly threatening and thoroughly pleased.

The way a cop is when he's just put the hammer down.

JaneDoe did say something. The FBI did have it on tape. The FBI did redact the transcript.

Well, shit, no wonder Rarey was in such a sunny mood. Had Hillkirk with egg on his face, Mark with his nuts in a vise.

That's a fun day.

FIFTY-TWO / 2012

The seething troll is in his mobile cave gazing into his digital fire.

The vision conjured by the fire is Grace Natchez, sneering at a guest who's been ungracious enough to remind Natchez she'd claimed to see a roadmap of a deranged killer's mind in JaneDoe's sculptures.

"I never said that!" Natchez snaps. "I just said she made twisted sicko art—and I was only reporting a diagnosis supplied by a reputable—*supposedly* reputable—criminologist!"

Bullshit, thinks the troll, you make up shit like that every day.

Natchez touches her earpiece. "Finally! The young woman who discovered the victim and took the picture that busted this story wide open is in our Chicago studio!"

The screen fills with a photo of dead Troy Horowitz accessorized with a miniature Hancock Building.

The troll is conflicted. His work is on worldwide display. But it's his worst, heh. His one sloppy job, and that's the only one the world sees.

But it does mean his plan is working.

"And now, Dottie Lang and her brave canine companion Maxx in an *exclusive* interview!"

The troll has already seen the skinny skank and her furry rat on every channel. He lowers the volume. Takes a swig of Balvenie. Assesses the battleground:

The cops don't worry him. But Gianni Snake-Eyes and Lou The MBA Boy, by now they must've... Fuck those cocksuckers. He's been ten steps ahead of their sorry asses this whole—

"HEH!" the troll shouts, and slaps his forehead, as the thunderbolt strikes.

His work is done! He can head for Brazil... Fuck! He was so lasered in on getting to that JaneDoe bitch he forgot how to count to fucking *three.* He hadda whack three artists to convince the cops he was a serial killer, heh? So now it's time to pack his fuckin' b—

The back end of the thunderbolt hits. Physically. A punch in the gut that makes the troll grunt and wrap his arms across his belly, fists clenched: *He didn't plant the note on Horowitz!*

The psycho note that says he's going to Europe to kill a big-time artist, which would fuck the Mastrizzis' huge last score! Which was the whole fucking point of this whole fucking thing, but the troll's had such a hard-on about pinning that note on JaneDoe it never occurred to his dumb ass, leave the note on Horowitz and it's game fuckin' over.

Shit... No choice now but to hang in here and finish JaneDoe.

And that thought has a strangely calming effect. Fuck it, spilt milk. Because, haveta admit, he's goddamn fine with the fact his date with JaneDoe is still on... Heh... Maybe his mind didn't actually forget the note, his mind kept itself from remembering the note because this was the way it hadda be...

The troll's musings are interrupted by the muffled sound of Grace Natchez braying about Breaking News!

The troll turns up the volume: The police say the Horowitz murder is an Art Critic killing. And JanefuckingDoe is no longer a person of interest.

The troll grins. JaneDoe's surveillance team is history.

The show cuts to a live feed outside JaneDoe's building.

Fuck! The goddamn camera crews are back. A reporter informs Natchez that JaneDoe's lawyer just entered her apartment, and before going in he made a statement that he'd be making a statement after conferring with his client.

"Is *JaneDoe* going to face the media?!" Natchez demands.

"Her attorney said *he'd* be issuing the statement."

"I thought so!" Natchez crows. "Well if JaneDoe wants to prove she isn't more than a little *off*, she *has* to appear, she *will* appear, herself, in person! Soon!"

The troll hopes to fucking Christ the horse-face old whack-job's prediction comes true. Sooner JaneDoe throws meat to the jackals, sooner they leave her be.

And then he goes at her, fast. Has to get to her before the Mastrizzis get to him... Heh. An inspiration hits, shouldering aside concerns about the Mastrizzis.

The troll decides, if there's time, he'll get two more miniature Cubs bats. He'll put one in her mouth, one in her cunt and one up her ass.

His grand finale, pizza resistance or whatever the fuck they call it.

FIFTY-THREE / 2012

Mark slid Nick Rarey's business card into his pocket.

Rarey, on his way out, issued an upbeat "See ya" to Doonie, who was returning from the john.

"Friendly kid," Doonie said to Mark. "Thought he'd never leave."

"We all have to get busy. Downtown is about to issue an official 'Oops'."

Mark phoned JaneDoe's attorney and alerted him to the upcoming Oops, then he and Doonie went to brief Husak on Dale Phipps.

"Good," Husak growled, relieved to be back doing something that had the possibility of being useful. "Even if you don't find anything to squeeze Phipps with, go at him again soon."

"And can we check out that list of fat white art aficionados?" Mark asked.

"Work your case the way you see it."

"Awesome."

Mark removed JaneDoe's photo from the murder board. He assigned the overweight aficionados list to Kimbrough. He ordered the POD unit to scan for a large fat white male near all three crime scenes at the times of the murders.

Doonie took Dale's financials.

Mark took Dale's phones. Mark was multi-tasking; his eyes scrolled through Dale's calls while his mind scrolled through the implications of Rarey's business card. On it was a handwritten phone number Rarey "asked" Mark to call when he got off work tonight. No matter how late.

What did the FBI want? He couldn't give them much on this case they weren't already getting in task force updates. They must be looking for a heftier payoff—deploying him as a snitch on one of their eternal probes of Chicago pols, Chicago cops, Chicago businesses, Chicago unions, Chicago trees and squirrels—

Mark got a hit off Dale's phone records: in 2005, when Dale's gallery was going under, he traded calls with one Thomas Tesca, who was in the system. A booking photo from 1995 showed a thick-featured, scowling young thug busted for misdemeanor assault allegedly connected to loan sharking; case got kicked when the vic refused to testify.

So, Dale made the classic drowning businessman mistake of asking a shark for a lifeline. Good place to start when Mark and Doonie question Dale—

"Hey," Doonie, said, directing Mark's attention to a TV on the wall.

Live news: JaneDoe's attorney reading a statement in front of her building.

JaneDoe. Mark had to talk to her, soon. But the FBI bugs would, you bet, remain hot until the Feds could get into her place and remove them. Mark didn't want to be overheard talking to JaneDoe until he found out the quality of the cards the FBI were holding. They might be bluffing; no point handing them confirmation of something they suspected but couldn't prove.

Mark had to contact JaneDoe when she was outside her loft, and without using a phone or email. He had an idea how.

Mark's phone rang. "Bergman."

"Hsu. Canvas turned up a fat man sighting."

"How good a look?"

"Not very. The walkway where Horowitz died goes through to the next block. A local had just parked his car and turned off the engine, when he sees a huge dude—white, wearing a black coat and watch cap—come out of the walkway. The witness wasn't up for meeting this ape who lurks between buildings at two AM, so he sat real still in his dark car and didn't get out till the ape went around the corner."

"No description of the face?"

"Nothing. The big guy moved fast, walked away with his back to our witness."

"Our witness got a glimpse of the face when the fat man came out of the walkway," Mark insisted. "Bring him in, put him with mug shots, a sketch artist, a hypnotist and a bartender, turn him upside down and shake him till some details fall out."

FIFTY-FOUR / 2012

What a fucking miserable morning," Dale lamented.

"You abuse my hospitality, Dale. Lately you visit only when you're overwrought. An affliction for which I've repeatedly prescribed opium, which advice you've repeatedly ignored," Dorian sniffed.

"Being blitzed and immobile is not my best option for surviving this."

"Perhaps you over-value survival."

"Perhaps, but I'm in no rush to find out. Please, Dor."

"Very well. Whine on."

"This fucking miserable morning started out fucking great, with me crushing Jay Branko. But that was a karmic trick, to set up my crash when detectives showed up—asking about Laurie Desh, and how I started my new business!"

"I assume you dazzled them with your wit."

"More like alerted them with my flatulence. But they left in a hurry. Why? Because dumb-shit Tommy whacked Troy Horowitz!"

"Is that inconvenient?"

"Yes! Now the cops realize JaneDoe isn't The Art Critic. And they promised they'd be seeing me again... But none of that is close to being the most fucking miserable thing. That would be this decision I need to make, fast: Do I tell Lou about my visit from the cops?!?!"

"So decide."

"Easy for you to say. Look, if Lou ever finds out I kept it secret... But if I do tell Lou the cops questioned me, that makes me an instant liability."

"Obviously. Which dictates the obvious decision: Keeping it secret is your best chance they'll refrain from slaughtering you until the project is comple—"

Dale's burner phone rang. Lou. Dale told Lou, "I need a minute," apologized to the nice lady security guard for having forgotten to turn off his phone, and hustled out to a stairwell where he could talk.

Dale got into Lou's Maserati.

"We have a lead," Lou said, and started driving.

"Can you say what it is?"

"My hacker didn't find a vehicle registered to 'Jonathan Davis' at the Indiana DMV, so he looked at bordering states. Jonathan bought a year-old SUV in Iowa but never registered it in Indiana. Been driving it on the Iowa temp slip."

"So if we tracked him to Indiana, we'd come up dry looking for his vehicle," Dale said. "Shrewd."

"Not enough. My PI talked to the used car dealer. Jonathan made sure the SUV had a trailer hitch."

"He's in a trailer park. We got him."

"We've got a couple of hundred trailer parks in the tri-county area. We're working outward from downtown. No hits yet. But we've got a black 2011 Suburban, tinted windows, trailer hitch, no plates and a driver the size of a baby whale."

"Thanks for driving into town to let me know."

"I'm here about Branko. How'd it go this morning?"

Dale's turn to deliver good news: "Jay huffed and puffed, but came to Jesus."

"He hasn't called you since the news broke about Horowitz?"

"Not a peep."

Lou gave Dale a sage nod. "Well done."

Dale gave a modest duck of the head.

"But with Tesca staging this new hit," Lou continued, "I know Jay's bouncing off the walls. So you let him know we've got a lead and we're closing in."

"I give him any details?"

"Just the basics: *Lou knows the car Tommy's driving and has an idea where he's holing up.*"

"Got it." Yeah. Long as Lou kept freezing Jay out, communicating only through Dale, Jay would know he was still on thin ice. He'd stay scared and careful.

Lou dropped Dale off on Lower Michigan Avenue, a short walk from Branko's office.

Dale watched the Mazz drive out of sight. He hadn't told Lou the bad news: The cops had been to see him.

I followed your expert advice, Dorian.

Dale thought he heard something that might have been a distant snicker.

Dale pulled out his burner, called Branko and informed him he was on his way over with good news.

Branko snarled *Yeah* and hung up.

Dale snorted, amused. Compared to Tesca, the cops and the Mastrizzis, Jay Branko was about as threatening as a Renoir pastel.

FIFTY-FIVE / 2012

Dale didn't sit. Walked into Jay Branko's office, delivered Lou's message and left.

Lou's message forced Jay to quit dicking around and make the decision he'd been stewing about since Dale's first visit. If the Mastrizzis were closing in on Tesca, Branko's window of opportunity for killing Dale was about to slam shut.

Even with Tesca just having whacked his third artist, the Mastrizzis still had their Sicilian hearts set on killing Damian Jung. Like after this Art Critic mediagasm, the cops wouldn't be all over the sudden death of a fucking huge art superstar, "accident" or no.

Eliminating Dale was the only way to stop Lou from launching this payload of atomic stupid. Lou couldn't take Dale's place—Lou couldn't be certain which paintings to buy, and was too smart to personally do the buying. He'd have to find a new art expert, who was cool with murder and could be trusted with tens of millions of dollars. Good luck with that.

Problem: Branko couldn't have Lou suspecting it was him who killed Phipps.

Solution: Frame Tesca. Which would be difficult if Tesca died before Phipps. So it was now or never.

Jay needed a shooter who had no connection to the Outfit—Irish? Russian? Albanian?—and who worked fast.

Jay had some phone numbers; you don't run a heavy construction business without every form of heavy muscle. But he'd have to find the right guy right away. Tonight.

And even then, say he finds a shooter who does the job. The shooter could dime Jay to the Mastrizzis. Which means after the shooter takes out Phipps, Jay has to have someone take out the shooter.

Lotta moving parts. Kinda sucks. But so does going to jail

if—when—the Jung hit goes sideways.

Which is the worse risk?

He went dead still for a few seconds. Or maybe minutes.

He ordered his secretary to hold his calls and cancel his appointments. He went looking for a shooter.

And this wasn't, Jay assured Jay, about how that smarmy pus-face dwarf twice today waltzed out of here thinking he'd made me his bitch.

FIFTY-SIX / 2012

JaneDoe adored William J. Potinkin. No surprise; the lawyer had been recommended by Lila Kasey. Potinkin was half-Irish, half-Jewish. Small, old and skinny—the way a five-foot-five strand of rusty barbed wire is.

Potinkin carved a path through the media scrum, slipped through JaneDoe's door, accepted a kiss on the cheek, looked her over, recognized she was wearing her idea of conservative clothing, and said, "Forget it."

"But—"

"You're not going out there today." Potinkin headed for the kitchen. He preferred hard chairs.

JaneDoe followed, protesting, "William J, I'm not staying under media house arrest any more. It's obvious I'm not the Art Critic."

"Not entirely, not until the police catch the real one." Potinkin said, taking a seat at the kitchen table. "You gonna offer me a seltzer or let me die of thirst?"

"Die of thirst." JaneDoe went to the refrigerator and grabbed a bottle of Gerolsteiner.

"You only have to stay locked up one more day."

"*Why*? That mob of gossip zombies isn't gonna leave me alone until they get to chew on my brain, so I'm gonna go feed them," JaneDoe said, plunking down a glass of sparkling water.

"You're not ready and the optics are wrong."

"Ready for what? They ask questions, I answer. Far as optics—" she gestured at her clothes"—I'm in my respectable plain-Jane outfit."

"That's what you think. Not that it would matter what you've got on if you went out there. It'd look like a perp walk, pure screaming chaos, you getting machine-gunned by questions, you'd get rattled—"

"No I wouldn't."

"—and you'd start sounding evasive, the darting eyes, the trapped animal looking to run and hide—because you're not prepared, you don't know what you must say and what you must not—and you haven't rehearsed the most sincere way of saying it. But because I'm a great attorney and magnificent humanist and your check didn't bounce, I'm going to save you. Tomorrow evening you'll do a dignified interview with one of our esteemed local TV news anchors—winner to be determined by the quality of the ass-kissing they'll be doing to land you."

"Your ass or mine?"

"Guess. Tomorrow morning I'll prep you the way I would for a cross-examination. And my PR maven and her stylist will dress you."

"What's wrong with what I'm wearing?"

"The interview will go beautifully, the audience will see what a warm, wonderful young woman you are, and the rest of the media will lose interest because you'll have answered all the juicy questions."

JaneDoe took a swig of Gerolsteiner from the bottle. Took another swig. Surrendered. "I'm all yours."

"I know. There is one more thing."

"Yes, William J?"

"It remains imperative you keep your recent love life secret. If it became public now it would muddy the narrative. Cast doubt on your innocence."

"How?"

"It suggests a scenario in which you are the Art Critic, and your lover, who knows your M.O., tries to save you by murdering Troy Horowitz. So you two stay away from each other—completely, no calls or emails—until the cops catch the real Art Critic."

JaneDoe thought that over. Asked, "What if they never catch him?"

Potinkin went to JaneDoe. Kissed her on the cheek. Said, "Nine AM. I'll bring bagels and lox."

JaneDoe turned on her TV to watch William J deliver his statement to the camera mob outside her door. After the first sentence she muted the sound.

She went to her work table and removed the drop cloth under which Foam Mark was hiding. She studied him, unable to decide if he was completed.

JaneDoe picked up her cell. Put it down. Stared at it.

She could disguise it as a business call. *Detective Bergman, I'm calling about... Considering what I've been through, I'd appreciate it if you kept me updated on your investigation.*

Shit. Was it worth the risk, just to hear his voice? Yeah, it was.

She reached for the phone again. Stopped. Wondered if Mark was feeling the same way—it was worth the risk. Would he call her, just to hear her voice?

FIFTY-SEVEN / 2012

Mark's phone rang. "Bergman."

Silence… Then the harsh "*GHGHGRRRGMMM!*" of a throat being cleared, followed by intermittent gagging: "S-s—*gahaakkch!*—sorry—protein bar—crumbs."

"That's what it sounded like," Mark said.

Guy Stutz, the head POD tech, rasped, "Good news—I'm sending—*gwuukk!*—vid—*grechhem*!!!!!"

"Just send it. Then drink some water."

"What was that?" Doonie asked.

"Stutz is dying, but he sent a parting gift."

They watched the traffic-cam video.

Doonie said, "I'll put out an APB."

"Wanna nail down one detail first."

Mark phoned Hsu.

Soon as Mark identified himself, Hsu leapt in with the answer to what she presumed would be Mark's question: "The witness can't give us a face. Just a broad nose, maybe. That's all: A possible broad nose."

"I'll take it. That's not what I'm calling about. Witness know what time it was when he saw the perp?"

"Exactly 1:42 AM."

"Exactly?"

"He checked the dashboard clock right before he looked up and saw the big guy. What you got?"

"At 1:42 your witness saw the big guy emerge from the walkway, go to the corner and turn west, walking toward Racine. Two minutes later, at 1:44, a POD shows a black 2011 Chevy Suburban emerging from Racine, turning east onto Lake."

"Driven by a big guy with a possible broad nose?"

"Can't tell. Windows are tinted. And no plates."

"*Still*," Hsu purred, pleased.

"Yeah," Mark agreed.

Doonie issued an APB on the Suburban, noting the driver might be a very large man, armed, and wearing all black.

Meanwhile, POD techs would be scanning footage from Lake Street to see if they could track the Suburban. Other techs would be checking the previous Art Critic crime scenes; this morning's search hadn't turned up any shots of a large fat male pedestrian, but now they'd be looking for the Suburban.

Mark and Doonie were updating Husak when Mark's cell rang. Stutz again, having survived the protein bar.

Stutz tracked the Suburban heading west on the Eisenhower. Out of the city and down onto suburban streets, out where the cameras weren't.

Husak said, "We still don't know for sure that's the Art Critic's truck. Find anything to squeeze Phipps?"

"Nothin' yet," Doonie said. "But we still got a pile of Phipps's shit to shovel through."

"Well then."

Mark and Doonie resumed shoveling.

Finished a little before 9 PM, having found nothing in Phipps' lifetime paper trail they could bash him with.

Doonie shrugged. "One hard question and he'll be farting his head off."

Mark nodded. "Go at him first thing tomorrow."

Doonie yawned. "Yeah I'm done. Long fuckin' day. Feels like a week since we talked to Phipps this morn—"

Mark received a third call from Stutz.

Mark listened, hung up. Told Doonie, "PODs just found a shot of the Suburban six blocks from Voorsts' house—twenty minutes before Voorsts got popped."

Confirmation the Suburban was The Art Critic's ride. They were chasing the right vehicle.

"It's burgers and bourbon time," Doonie ruled.

True, normally. Not tonight. Mark's long fuckin' day wasn't over. Still had to go meet Nick Rarey and find out exactly what the Feds had on him.

Mark said, "I'm gonna hang in here—still have to write today's task force update."

Doonie complained, "You're getting old," and left.

Mark bashed out the update, got in his car and went to a pay phone. Called Lila Kasey and asked if she could meet for a quick private chat.

FIFTY-EIGHT / 2012

They talked in Mark's car.

As usual, Lila Kasey was dressed like Joan Crawford on acid and chain-smoking like it was 1952.

Mark asked if she'd be willing to deliver a message to JaneDoe.

Lila peered at him thoughtfully, took a drag on her Dunhill. Exhaled. Said, "JaneDoe's phones are tapped. If they weren't, you'd be using a pay phone instead of using me."

"Gets better. Not only would you have to talk to her in person—you can't talk in her house."

Took Lila maybe a second to decipher that one. "You bastards."

"Not us bastards. The FBI bastards."

"Well that makes all the difference."

"So you'll do it."

Lila gave him a stern look. "Why did you wait until now to warn her?"

"How? Tomorrow will be the first time she sets foot outside her house."

Lila processed that. Stubbed out a spent cigarette and lit a fresh one. Asked, "Anything else you want me to tell her?"

"She can't contact me. She has to wait until I can get in touch… Which might not be until this case gets wrapped up."

"Christ. The FBI's going to keep spying on her *until this case gets wrapped up*?"

"Probably not. But I'm not sure."

"But she's no longer a suspect!"

"But they're still the FBI. And this case is still open."

Lila sighed. "So all you're asking is for me to tell JaneDoe she won't be seeing you anytime soon, and the reason is her phones are tapped and her home is bugged, and will be, for we don't know how long."

"Wanna borrow a helmet and body armor?"

"They come in leopard skin?"

"Someday," Mark promised. He handed Lila a burner phone and explained how he wanted her to handle things tomorrow.

When Mark finished, Lila asked, quietly, "There anything *personal* you want me to tell her?"

Five thick, rich seconds later, Mark whispered, "Yes."

Lila gave him a pleased little grin, kissed his cheek and got out of the car.

FIFTY-NINE / 2012

Rarey picked up on the first ring and issued a friendly, "Hey, Mark."

"Where you at?"

"The Ambassador East, room Six-Twen—"

"Wrong." There'd be cameras in Rarey's room. "We'll talk in my car."

"It's cool how you say that as if the decision were up to you."

"Be on the northwest corner of Astor and Goethe." Pronouncing the last word *Go-thee*, as required by local custom.

After a moment, Rarey said, "You do know the world outside Chicago refers to the great man as *Gert-uh*."

"We don't hold it against them. Ten minutes."

Rarey got into Mark's car, closed the door and wrinkled his nose. "Didn't take you for a smoker. Or was it someone else?"

"Palms flat against the roof."

Rarey grinned and complied. Mark patted him down. Didn't find a wire. But he did fish a disposable lighter out of Rarey's jacket pocket.

"It's a genuine Bic," Rarey said.

Mark tossed the lighter out the window and put the car in gear. "Don't hide a recorder in a genuine Bic unless you're also carrying something to smoke."

"Whatever you say, Dad."

"Did you a favor. Your boss isn't only looking to get tape on me. He needs to hear how you handle being a handler. Now you can lie about how well you did."

"I never lie."

"Good. What do you think you have?"

"You and JaneDoe."

"What about me and JaneDoe?"

Rarey pumped his right index finger into his curled left fist.

"So you're a mime."

Rarey pulled an envelope out of a breast pocket. "Transcript of the relevant conversation."

"So you're a mime who can type. I wanna hear the original vocals."

Rarey took out his wallet, extracted a thumb drive, and placed it in the center armrest compartment.

"I told Ostergaard this was going to happen," Rarey confided, pleased.

SIXTY / 2012

Mark got home and went straight to the fridge. He hadn't eaten since inhaling a sandwich at his desk that afternoon. Plus which, if the first thing he did was rush to the computer to hear what the FBI had on him, he wouldn't respect himself in the morning.

He found rotisserie chicken leftovers that were, what, four, five days old? No, eight or ten. He feasted on a can of tuna and a beer.

Mark moseyed over to the computer, checked his email, checked the Cubs' box score... plugged in the thumb drive, put on headphones and listened to what made the Feebs think they owned him.

The audio quality was awesome. FBI bugs were way more evolved than anything in the CPD toolkit.

But the FBI's editing was Neanderthal subtle. Mark could tell JaneDoe had been having a conversation, and the other person had been deleted.

Whoever cut the tape tried to make it sound as if JaneDoe were delivering a halting monolog. But her inflections said she'd been responding to questions.

"The lead detective is a guy named Mark Bergman, and, four years ago we had a brief affair... Hadn't seen him since. But then, right after Bobby Gilson was killed, Mark realized one of the Barbie totems might be me, and he came over here to question me and, uh—spent the night... Since then, except for police business when there were other cops around, we haven't seen each other. Or communicated."

Well all right. The Feebs only had one of his nuts in a vise.

This wasn't JaneDoe blabbing to a friend. That would've been stoned, glib, intimate—JaneDoe being herself. This was JaneDoe being soberly informative. JaneDoe briefing the one person who needed to know about Mark, and whom it was safe to tell.

Her lawyer.

The FBI had let their bugs gobble up privileged conversations.

Advantage Bergman; the FBI couldn't threaten Mark with criminal charges. The illegally obtained evidence wouldn't be admissible, against him. But it would be admissible as hell as evidence the FBI violated the law—and be an engraved invitation to William J. Potinkin to bite them in the wallet.

So the worst the Feebs could do to Mark was end his career. They could accomplish that by leaking this recording to the CPD.

Which meant, bottom line, the FBI had zero leverage… if Mark could handle not being a cop any more.

Fuck yeah. Especially if the only alternative was to be the FBI's tub toy.

The operative word being *only*.

Mark got some sleep.

SIXTY-ONE / 2012

A t 1:36 AM Dale Phipps made up his mind.

He inserted a thumb drive. Downloaded the files.

Inserted another thumb drive. Downloaded the files.

Inserted another thumb drive. Downloaded the files.

Jay Branko told the shooter his unusual requirements, which Jay prayed wouldn't be deal-breakers: "You have to put something in his mouth. And he has to die in the next forty-eight hours."

Zerbjka stared at Branko for a few seconds. Asked, "He has security?"

"No. And he lives alone." That last part was a guess, but Jay figured no one could stomach waking up to Dale Phipps' face.

"Very risking, to do such things in such hurry," the bullet-headed Serb observed.

"Fifty thousand. Half up front."

Zerbjka shook his head. "Fifty up front."

Fuck. "Fine."

"How soon you put this cash in hand?"

"Inside of an hour."

"Sonbitch will be dead inside forty-eight. Maybe sooner. At which time you bring another fifty."

"And if he's not dead?"

"It means job was not possible."

"How do I know you won't sit on your ass for two days and pocket the easiest fifty grand of all time?"

"Because one hundred thousand is prettier number. Therefore is ninety-nine per cent chance this poor bastard will die. And is one thousand per cent chance you rich bastard will die, if again you insult Zerbjka, hokay?"

Hokay. You got the right attitude, Zerbjka. You also better walk the walk, because if you botch it the Mastrizzis will barbeque the both of us.

Lou told Gianni, "We've checked every trailer park within an hour-and-a-half of downtown."

"Look farther out."

"Okay. But, Dad, I gotta wonder if Tesca would drag his fat ass two hours in and two hours back every time he comes to the city."

"Don't misunderestimate the fat fuck. Lookin' to fuck us in the ass with no grease and he's gettin' away with it, so far," Gianni noted.

Lou suppressed a grin; first time the Old Man ever utters a good word about Tesca, and what earns Dad's approval is Tesca going on a suicidal revenge mission.

"True," Lou acknowledged. "But not much longer."

Gianni knocked wood. And his lips tightened into a cold, hungry grin.

Poor Cousin Tommy.

There was no TV news at this hour, so Tommy was scowling at porn with the sound off and listening to news radio.

Neither was providing satisfaction. Might as well turn them the fuck off and nod out. Tommy let go of his floppy dick and reached for the radio. The radio struck first, stopping him with the magic words: "A new development in The Art Critic case."

Tommy's hand returned to his crotch.

"Avant-garde sculptor JaneDoe hasn't left her apartment since she became the prime suspect in the Art Critic murders. Yesterday, despite police declaring she's no longer a suspect, JaneDoe remained in seclusion. But tonight, on our sister station, WPLZ–TV, JaneDoe will break her silence. The intriguing young artist will appear on the 6 PM newscast, giving an in-depth, exclusive interview to anchor Grant Mosher."

"Atta girl," Tommy rumbled, giving his dick a triumphant squeeze.

In depth. Smart. Second she finishes that interview she's old news. All those hyenas around her place move on.

And Tommy moves in.

Yes. Finally. It's gonna happen. Yes. Gonna. Gonna.

His meat woke up. Tommy sagged back against the pillows, contemplatively massaging himself, laying plans.

SIXTY-TWO / 2012

Mark's phone rang at 7:01 AM.

"G'morning, Mark! Which corner do I go stand on this time?"

This time Rarey was carrying a pack of cigarettes but no lighter.

"Couldn't resist," he grinned.

Mark chucked the cigarettes out the window.

"No need to litter," Rarey scolded. "We weren't going to risk you throwing away another expensive piece of equipment."

Mark put the car in gear and headed for Lakeshore Drive.

Rarey continued, "But this does confirm you have even more trouble than I do resisting a good time. After hearing the recording, you have to admit that."

Mark remained silent, eyes on the road. Like a man who was pained, conflicted, trying to delay the moment when he'd cave.

"Mark, us FBI pricks *will* use that tape. Or bury it. Up to you."

Mark quietly asked, "What do you want?"

"Not that much. We want credit for breaking this case. We'd like to get there first, make the bust, if possible. You can help with that."

Mark gave a small resigned sigh, like a man who'd just heard something which confirmed his suspicions. Which it did: this trivial gig was to saddle-break him, make him easier to ride where the FBI really wanted to go.

Mark, like a man acknowledging his freedom has just expired, informed his handler, "First thing I'm doing today is going at Dale Phipps."

"Intriguing guy. But we haven't found anything hinky on him, yet."

"You've been looking at Phipps?"

"Dawg, a few weeks back you came up with an interesting theory.

Has your art cop found any purchases of works by Gilson and Voorsts before they died, or sales since?"

"No." Mark shot a hard look at Rarey. Sons of bitches had leads they'd been holding back.

"Hey c'mon, eyes on the road."

"This is a fucking murder investigation," Mark warned.

Rarey's grin expanded. "And the Bureau has a little more reach than your one-woman art squad. Wanna take a guess what we found?"

Mark cut hard across two lanes of traffic, exited the Drive, stopped at the first empty stretch of curb and glared.

Unruffled, the youngster informed Mark, "In the past year dealers in this country and Europe purchased four Gilsons and three Voorsts. All on behalf of anonymous clients. When we asked for names, the European dealers politely advised us to piss off. However, a couple of patriotic American dealers didn't want us FBI pricks or our IRS friends mad at them. The patriots slipped us the names of the buyers."

Instead of telling Mark what those names were, Rarey glanced around the busy intersection. "Awfully public spot. Let's get back on the Drive," he ordered, asserting his authority, which, like most things, amused him.

Mark snapped a vicious chop to the bottom edge of Rarey's kneecap.

"AH!" Rarey grabbed his knee and gasped percussively—"Ah-ah-ah! Shit! Ah! Goddamn it, Mark... Okay, okay," Rarey conceded, massaging his knee. "The buyers were two shell companies. Not unusual. Except, one is named Lougian and the other is Gianlou." He paused to see if Mark got the implications.

Mark nodded for Rarey to go on.

"They share a home address, in the Caymans. And all the payments were wired from two banks, one in the Caymans, one in Liechtenstien. And all the art was shipped to the same storage facility in Switzerland."

"What about Horowitz?"

Rarey shook his head. "All recent Horowitz sales have been to respectable buyers who used their real names."

"If the Art Critic didn't invest in Horowitz, why bother killing him?"

"For art's sake?" Rarey hypothesized.

"You able to trace ownership of the shell companies and bank accounts?"

A defeated shrug. "This is why the better class of criminal is so fond of the Caymans and Liechtenstien."

"Dale Phipps have any links to these companies?"

"Not that we can find. When you question Phipps you should smack him with the names Lougian and Gianlou, see if he flinches."

"I can't do that unless—"

"We provide this info officially, otherwise you couldn't explain how you know it." Rarey grinned. "That memo will show up soon as I report how well our conversation went."

Mark asked, "If I'd said no, would the FBI have kept these leads secret from us?"

"But you didn't," Rarey said. He flexed his knee. Grimaced. But kept flexing. "It's fine, I won't need crutches." He straightened up and looked at Mark. "Just, one last detail." His face went serious. "Don't hit me again."

"Don't insist on it again."

Rarey gave a wry nod. He eased himself out of the car. Limped down the block, pulling out his cell. Calling Ostergaard to let him know Detective Bergman was all theirs.

SIXTY-THREE / 2012

When Mark walked in, Doonie was already at his desk.
Doonie greeted him with, "You check your email the last ten minutes?"

Mark shook his head.

"Exciting shit." Doonie swiveled his monitor to face Mark.

It was the promised FBI memo on the past year's purchases of Gilson and Voorsts paintings.

"You called it two weeks back," Doonie mused. "Our guy ain't some psychopath fuck."

"No, he's a Chicago psychopath fuck: a serial killer with a business plan. Any sightings of his Suburban?"

Doonie shook his head. "And this is the best Hsu's witness could do, even after a session with Merlin the Hypnotist."

Doonie tapped keys. The FBI report was replaced by a sketch of a generic fat guy with a slightly broad nose and a watch cap pulled down to his eyebrows.

Getting back to the exciting shit, Mark said, "So, Gianlou and Lougian?"

"Yeah," Doonie agreed.

Gianni and Lou were the first names of the Mastrizzis, the Outfit's boss and boss apparent.

"If the Mastrizzis were buying paintings then killing the artists, they wouldn't put their names on the purchasing entities," Mark said.

"The Art Critic did it in case we ever got this far. Point us at the Outfit, send us on a goose chase."

"Yup." Mark nodded at the uninformative sketch of the generic fat guy. "Who's this lunatic who's purposely getting Gianni Mastrizzi mad at him?"

"Let's ask Dale Phipps and see if he farts."

Before they left, Doonie put in a request to Gang Crimes for any info they had linking the Mastrizzis to Dale Phipps and/or the exciting world of fine art.

And Mark emailed Janet Claudel, the art squad, asking her to find out if any Chicago gallery had sold to Lougian or Gianlou.

Hoping to catch Dale before he left for work, Mark and Doonie got to Dale's home at 8:15. It was in Logan Square, a semi-blue collar, semi-gentrified northside neighborhood where the continued presence of semi-active Hispanic gangs was keeping real estate prices semi-reasonable.

Dale lived in a 1950s walk-up brick building that had been surgically enhanced during the renovation boom of the 90s, its smallish A-cup apartments enlarged into C-cup condos.

Dale wasn't in his. Or wasn't responding to the intercom.

Mark and Doonie hung out in the vestibule of the building's locked front door in hopes that a resident would exit the building.

One did. A young father with twin infants in a double-wide stroller. He propped the door open with one arm and was about to start wrestling the stroller through—

Mark grabbed the door and held it open.

Doonie smiled at the babies. "They're beautiful," he told the young dad. "And then they learn to talk," he warned.

The young dad and his future tormentors went on their way.

Mark and Doonie went up to the fourth floor, where they knocked on Dale Phipps' door. No answer.

SIXTY-FOUR / 2012

Dale's office door was as unresponsive as his apartment door had been.

Doonie checked his watch. Twenty after nine. "Maybe art guys don't open at nine."

"They do if their clients are corporations that keep business hours."

"We're open! We're open!" a woman shouted. It was Phipps' receptionist, hurrying down the hallway, rummaging in her purse. "Sorry, sorry, we usually open at nine." She flashed a genuine grin. Mainly at Mark. "Nice to see you again, Detectives, uhh…"

"Bergman and Dunegan. Nice to see you too, Miss Doyle."

Mark's remembering her name had the desired effect.

She sighed, embarrassed, but twinkling with pleasure. Miss Doyle twinkled well; she was twenty-something, slim, with pixie-short red hair, stylish dark green eyeglasses, porcelain skin dusted with pale freckles, and a grin bracketed by deep dimples. As she resumed trawling the depths of her vast purse, Mark checked for the hopeful little leer Doon would be giving him. Yeah, there it was.

"*Finally,*" Miss Doyle murmured as she excavated the office keys. She ushered the cops in, asking, "Can I make you some coffee? We have an espresso machine. Please, because, not only was I late, but— Mr. Phipps won't be in."

"Is Mr. Phipps ill?" Mark asked.

"No, just a little intense. Not intense *mean*—he's very nice— intense *moody*. Sometimes he just needs to be out of the office. Like, this morning, I got an email to cancel his appointments, he wouldn't be in till this afternoon, or maybe tomorrow." She gave Mark an adorable apologetic look.

"Do you know where he goes?"

"He never says."

"Would you mind calling and letting him know we need to speak to him?"

"Of course—but it'll go to voicemail. He doesn't pick up during his—private times."

"Does he get back to you?"

"Never. He'll wait till he gets back to the office—oh—wait—one time, he did call back… There was all this clattering, and he apologized, said he was in the cafeteria at the Art Institute—sorry I forgot that."

"But then you remembered," Mark pointed out.

That earned another twinkle. "But I don't know if the Art Institute's where he usually goes. For sure he's not there now—"

"Because it doesn't open until ten," Mark said. A shared moment. Mark handed her his card. "When you get his voicemail, please tell him to him call me, right away."

Miss Doyle phoned. Left the message. Hung up. Said, "Sure you don't want coffee—I make a reasonably awesome latte."

"Very kind, but no thanks."

"Well—here," she said, offering his card back.

Mark said, "Keep it."

Miss Doyle gave him a knee-buckling grin; no twinkle, just pure smoldering pixie.

"To make sure Mr. Phipps has my number, in case he deletes your voicemail," Mark clarified, all business.

Miss Doyle's grin faded.

Out on the street Mark explained, before Doonie could voice his disappointment, "I was only flirting with Miss Doyle to get her talking about Phipps."

"But you didn't have to break her heart there at the end," Doonie complained.

"Better than breaking it over the phone if she called."

Doonie raised an eyebrow. "So this thing with you and JaneDoe is fuckin' serious."

Mark didn't reply. He got in the car, called in a request for a trace on Dale Phipps' cell phone location.

No joy. The GPS was switched off, and Phipps hadn't used the phone, so there were no cell tower hits.

"Any point going to the Art Institute when it opens?" Doonie wondered.

"No guarantee that's his hang. And even if Phipps does go there today, you know how huge that place is… Don't you? You have been there?"

"Sure. They made us go in sixth grade."

"The bastards. Let's visit Dale's ex-girlfriend."

Soosie Smith. Hyper-expensive Gold Coast address.

SIXTY-FIVE / 2012

Will this take long? I have Kabbalah class in twenty minutes."

"We'll keep it brief. We're trying to locate Dale Phipps, and—"

"Dale?! Why?"

"We're investigating the Art Critic murders, and—"

"Dale's the Art Critic?!?!!!"

"No—no he's not. We want to consult with him about the art business, but we can't find him."

"Oh. Well, I totally do not know where Dale might be, I mean, he broke, he *destroyed* my heart, we were together two years and four and-a-half months, then he just walked out, and the only time I've seen him since was a year ago, in the lobby at Victory Gardens during intermission. It was like a movie: our eyes meet across this crowded lobby, and we're both like seriously freaked, and I'm thinking, *Should I?* but Dale *runs* out the door. Which was kind of a relief, 'cause, omigod, his *face*. Like too gross to look at, even if he'd been a stranger, much less this just elegant man I was deeply in love with and I'm still so mad at. Y'know?"

"Uh-huh. So Dale didn't have any—facial issues, when you met him?"

"Dale was handsome—well except for his mangled hand, but his face was so intelligent and sensitive."

"What happened to his hand?"

"Some loan shark did it. Dale's gallery got in trouble and he made some bad choices—I paid off the debt, I, I *saved* Dale, and then he…"

"Was this loan shark named…" Mark visualized booking sheet of the shark Phipps had traded calls with, "…Tesca?"

"Dale never said."

"Is there anyone Dale's close to, family or friends?"

"Nobody, his family's gone, his best friend was Walt Egan, and

Dale disappeared on Walt when he disappeared on me. By that point Dale had awful rashes, maybe that's why, he was worried I'd be like, repulsed. But I loved him, and… Though, I'm not sure I could live with a face who looks the way Dale's does now. Does that make me a bad person? I mean, he is soooo gross—almost as if that Dorian Black thing Dale said came true."

"Dorian—you mean Gray? Dorian Gray?"

"Yes, thanks, right."

"Who the fuck's—pardon my French—who's Dorian Gray?" Doonie asked.

"Later. You were saying, Miss Smith?"

"It was our last night together, which of course I had *no idea* at the time—I was telling Dale, look, I will take you to the best doctors in the world. But Dale was like, 'Wouldn't help, this might not be a medical problem,' and I was like, 'What else could it be?' Dale says, 'Might be a Dorian Gray problem,' and I knew what he meant because he'd streamed this old black and white movie. So I said, 'But you haven't done terrible things like he did…' Dale just gave me this weird little smile… And next morning, poof! Gone… Oh, God, reliving all this Dale drama—you guys are the first time I've talked about it with anyone besides my friends, my therapist or my Mom… I totally need to be at Kabbalah. Sorry I couldn't help."

"But you did. Big-time."

"Big-time?" Donnie scoffed as they headed down the hall to the elevator. "How?"

"She reminded me about Dale's loan shark—I'll call Gang Crimes, see if Tesca worked for the Mastrizzis. And, much more important—Soosie just forced you to make a second visit to the Art Institute."

SIXTY-SIX / 2012

So I left a copy with my lawyer and one in my safe deposit. And now I'm gonna hide myself as well. This is goodbye, Dorian. Last time we speak face to hideous face.

No, Dor, this isn't one of my 'hilarious attempts at humor'.

No, it's not a 'failure of nerve, and worse, a failure of style.' It's a triumph of logic. There's a fatal flaw in me playing the waiting game, hoping Lou never finds out the cops questioned me. The flaw being, if Lou does find out, he's not going to tell me. I will not know Lou knows, and has decided to kill me, until the moment some thug—

"Dale, my frient!" a large shaven-headed thug exclaimed as he threw an arm around Dale the way an old frient would, except for the way his fingers dug into Dale's shoulder. "So sorry being late, but is only few minutes and is all Bob's fault hennyway," Shaved Head joshed, indicating a tall thin greasy-haired guy in sunglasses and a long black leather coat standing on the other side of Dale.

Shaved Head whispered, "Grin and say hokay."

"Hey, Bob," Dale managed, with a vaguely grin-like lip-twitch.

"We should go," Shaved Head insisted. "Is best not to keep wives waiting, no?"

The museum guard, the robust African-American woman who'd been shocked by the sight of Dale's hand and been super-nice to him since, was watching.

As the three men walked towards her—Shaved Head with his arm around Dale, and Bob directly behind Dale—the guard gave Dale a questioning look.

"So, Dale," Shaved Head inquired as they walked, "your kids doing hokay in schoo—"

The guard stepped in front of them, blocking their exit. "Are you all right, sir?" she asked Dale.

"Sure," Shaved Head answered, "we going for terrific lunch."

The guard glanced at the hand gripping Dale's shoulder. "Sir, would you please let go of this gentleman?"

"Excuse?"

"Please remove your hand from—"

"Oh! Sure, sure," Shaved Head nodded, releasing Dale. "Dale, please explain to this nice lady you and me are frients."

"Yeah, exactly," Dale said, his eyes locked on hers.

"So thank you miss, have nice day."

"Just a moment," the guard said, gesturing with her left hand for them to stay, while with her right she plucked her radio off her belt.

Shaved Head grabbed the radio out of her hand and gave her a threatening glare.

She dropped-kicked him in the nuts.

He doubled over, letting go of the radio and Dale.

Dale ran.

Bob started to chase but the guard stuck her foot out and tripped him and Bob did a face-plant on the hardwood parquet.

Shaved Head slugged the guard in the temple and she went down.

As Dale dashed out of the gallery he took a sharp left, heading for the stairs, but that didn't work because he slammed into an old guy in a wheelchair. Dale, the chair and the old guy went sprawling.

Shaved Head, clutching his groin, ran-limped after Dale.

SIXTY-SEVEN / 2012

They'd parked across the street from Pheeps' building at 6:00 AM. Vuk, the wheelman, stayed in the car. Zerbjka and Slobo went to the front door. The apartment numbers weren't listed, just the fokking intercom dial codes—if they got in the building they wouldn't know which place was his.

They went back to the car.

The target finally dragged his ass out the door a little before eight. By then there were too many people on the street to snatch Pheeps.

Zerbjka couldn't pop Pheeps from a distance; he had to shuff a toy building in Pheeps' mouth.

Zerbjka and Slobo tailed Pheeps, with Vuk trailing in car. Pheeps entered Logan Square el station. They followed.

The platform was too crowded. The train was too crowded.

Slobo stayed on the phone with Vuk, who was driving, following the Blue Line route.

Pheeps got off at Lake, in the Loop, where the sidewalks were as crowded as the damn el, and cops all over. Pheeps walked to one of the shiny office towers on Wacker. High fokking security. Visitors had to sign at desk.

When Pheeps cleared security and headed for the elevators Zerbjka and Slobo were still in line. Pheeps got on elevator, along with ten more fokks. No way to know which floor Pheeps got off.

Hokay, Zerbjka could find out where Pheeps went by reading the register.

As Zerbjka got to the desk the security guy flipped the register to a new, blank page.

Hour later Pheeps comes out, walks to LaSalle. Goes into fine old building, stone walls with big brass bars over the windows. A bank.

Zerbjka strolls in. Spots Pheeps being buzzed through fancy

brass gate to marble staircase that goes to basement—to safe deposit. Zerbjka can't follow.

Pheeps leaves bank, walks east on Adams. Crosses Michigan Avenue. Trailing at a discreet distance, Zerbjka and Slobo step into the street as the light turns red, have to run like madmen through eight fokking lanes of traffic. They get to other side alive and follow Pheeps into giant old mooseem. Art Institute. Huge fokking building.

SIXTY-EIGHT : 2012

Zerbjka and Slobo went up wide stone steps and into lobby, in time to spot Pheeps flashing membership at uniformed guard. The guard waved Pheeps through checkpoint into mooseem.

Zerbjka and Slobo went to checkpoint and the guard asked for their tickets. Zerbjka pulled out a fifty. The guard pointed to long room on their left where there were ticket counters. Fokking American boy scout.

Zerbjka saw Pheeps walk past this huge three-story zig-zag staircase, under huge skylight. Pheeps walked past huge zig-zag stairs and into small lobby on far side.

Zerbjka and Slobo went into ticket room—was this long fokking line. Sheet. Branko said Pheeps had small office, only a receptionist. If the lazy fokk would go there, they could kill both, bim-bam, all done. Why didn't Pheeps go to his office? Had he made them?

Slobo's phone vibrated. It was Vuk, saying Art Institute was gigantic, two whole blocks, and only street parking was on rear side, on Columbus Drive. Vuk waits there.

Zerbjka took the phone and told Vuk—in Serbian—keep engine running, they were going to grab Pheeps.

Slobo muttered, in Serbian, **"Here? With all these people? We have the rest of today and all tomorrow."**

But Zerbjka didn't have tomorrow. Tomorrow was his wife's niece's wedding. If Zerbjka doesn't show at wedding, this confirms wife's suspicion he's banging her sister's daughter.

"If you're too pussy to handle this shrimp," Zerbjka sneered, **"you should leave, go buy yourself a pretty dress."**

They grabbed maps of mooseem—place was size of fokking palace—and hustled past huge zig-zag staircase to the small lobby

Pheeps entered. There were three goddamn galleries off it: left, right and straight ahead. Straight ahead was biggest gallery, very long, like tunnel. Zerbjka checked map—tunnel led to whole other section of palace, and on the end is—fokk!—exit to Columbus Drive.

They hurried through the tunnel-gallery. There were two aisles, one on either side of a row of glass display cases that ran up the middle of the room. Zerbjka and Slobo each took an aisle. No art crap in this gallery—was loaded with old-time armor and weapons. Big-ass swords, daggers, axes. Zerbjka scanned the gallery, hoping to spot Pheeps. All he spotted was Slobo looking at the fancy bootcher tools with hungry grin, dreaming what he could do with one of those.

They exited into a wide corridor that was perpendicular to the tunnel-gallery. Either end of this corridor connected to other corridors.

Zerbjka checked map; left corridor went to exit. They rushed down it and out onto Columbus. Pheeps was nowhere. Sheet! Only hope was Pheeps stayed inside.

They returned to wide corridor, the one perpendicular to the tunnel. At the south were two small staircases leading up, and between them a staircase leading down. All the stairs went to bunch of galleries. This place was nightmare.

Where would Pheeps go? Branko said Pheeps was modern art consultant. Zerbjka consulted map. Small staircases went up to American Modern Art 1900-1950.

Zerbjka and Slobo climbed the half-flight of stairs to a mezzanine: a rectangle of four corridors, overlooking a small interior courtyard below, which was full of statues. The sides of the mezzanine were lined with wide entryways to gallery after gallery. They headed for the nearest.

Sheet, talk of nightmare—first thing they see in gallery is painting of this horrible gray zombie monster—

And Pheeps. Staring at zombie.

Pheeps was so in love with this zombie puke he didn't notice Zerbjka was there until Zerbjka put a grip on "Dale, my frient."

They start to leave, old frients having nice chat—

Mooseem guard is in their face, fat black beetch giving Zerbjka this Dirty Harry face.

Zerbjka made nice but she pulled out walkie-talkie, and he grabbed it from her, but she kicked his balls halfway up his neck, Pheeps ran, Slobo started to chase but fat beetch tripped Slobo, and Zerbjka, bent over, his balls screaming for revenge, whipped a roundhouse right to her temple—

A big crashing noise from corridor, and yelling—

Slobo tried to stand—got far as his knees—gasped and grabbed his nose. Broken, gushing blood.

Zerbjka staggered forward, each step a stab of pain.

SIXTY-NINE / 2012

G randpa! Grand*pa*!!!" shrieked the young woman who'd been pushing the wheelchair, as Dale frantically disentangled himself from
Grandpa, who'd landed on top of him. Dale shoved the frail old man
off, too hard for the young woman's taste—she yelled "Son of a bitch!"
and kicked Dale in the chest, knocking him on his ass, as—

Shaved Head lurched out of the gallery—

Dale, seated on the floor, managed to pull his gun—

Shaved Head paused—

The girl saw Dale's gun and flung herself protectively on Grandpa,
who moaned, "OWW! Godammit!" as—

Shaved Head reached into his jacket—

Dale fired—

Shaved Head grabbed his left arm and dropped to his knees—

Dale scrambled to his feet and rushed to the stairs, where something smashed into his leg from behind, sending him sliding and
tumbling down the short flight, accompanied by the wheelchair,
which Shaved Head had flung at him.

Dale was aware of screams and panic erupting around him, but
his concentration was on getting upright, while watching the top of
the stairs, where—

Shaved Head, huge gun in hand, peeked out from where he was
pressed against the wall at the top of the staircase, and—

Dale fired—Shaved Head drew back but stuck his hand around
the corner, aiming down in Dale's direction and squeezed off two
quick rounds—

Dale scrambled into an alcove right next to him, where there was
an elevator and a flight of stairs leading up to the second floor.

Dale was halfway up the stairs when he heard thudding feet
entering the alcove, so he fired two shots down toward the alcove,

then resumed climbing. At the top of the stairs was a right turn onto another, broader staircase—

BLAM! BLAM! Two shots from Shaved Head below, reaching around the alcove wall and firing blind in Dale's direction—

Then someone down there was bellowing—"Police! Drop the gun! Drop the fucking—"

More gunfire—Dale's heart leapt: *Cops!*

But as Dale ran up the broad staircase and into *Europe Before 1900,* he heard a heavy grunting creature pounding up the stairs.

SEVENTY / 2012

The route to Dorian Gray went through Gunsaulus Hall, which 13-year-old Mark had thought of as Gunslaughter Hall, because of the ornate wheel-lock pistols and blunderbusses in its display cases. And those Three Musketeers firearms were the least of it. The bulk of the gallery was devoted to more venerable goodies, the Age of Chivalry's most romantic achievements: armor with spiked elbows, broadswords, daggers, maces, axes, hammers, pikes.

Doonie did a subtle double-take as they entered Gunslaughter Hall. He slowed, came to a halt at a display of pikes. Dark wooden shafts about twelve feet long. Some tipped with two-foot long blades that sprouted vicious barbs. Some tipped with an axe head topped by a foot-long serrated spike.

"Now that's art," Doonie ruled.

"Yeah, one of those, you could gut a man easy as gutting a trout."

There was a distant clatter, followed by a woman's shocked yelp.

Then a gunshot—the hell?—frightened shrieks, and people were running into the far end of the Hall.

Mark and Doonie pulled their guns and began running toward them—

Another clatter, more gunshots and screams—

A panicky mass of people poured into that end of the Hall, desperate to flee the gunfight, but the ones in front saw the two armed men running at them, screamed and jerked to an abrupt stop. The crowd behind crashed into them and the surge of bodies tumbled like a wave hitting a shore.

"Police! Stay down, stay down!" Mark yelled, waving his badge, as he and Doonie picked their way through—

As they reached the east end of Gunslaughter Hall there were two more echoey bangs, off to the right. The cops flattened against the wall next to the exit, Doonie calling in a *Shots Fired* as Mark peeked into the corridor—

Caught a glimpse of a man—bear-thick, shaved head, black leather sport coat, gripping a gun in one hand and his balls in his other, bloody hand—lumbering into an alcove.

Mark went to the alcove—

Shots sounded inside the alcove—

"POLICE! DROP THE GUN DROP THE FUCKING—" Doonie bellowed from behind Mark as—

Bullets crashed into the wall next to Mark's head—he dropped into a crouch as—

Behind him, Doonie's gun roared—

Mark looked left, saw a tall thin long-haired man with a bloody nose retreating up a short staircase—Mark and Doonie threw shots but the tall guy was gone—

Mark and Doonie traded a quick look—hadda go after both these fucks.

Doonie started edging toward the short stairway up which the second shooter had disappeared.

Mark eased into the alcove. As Mark started up the stairs there was an eruption of crowd-panic shrieks from above. Mark swung into a broader staircase, his gun aimed up at—

A clutch of terrified museum-goers rushing out of a wide entrance to the third-floor galleries—the museum-goers saw Mark and froze—

"Police!" Mark yelled, lowering his gun and pointing at his badge, which he'd hung on his breast pocket, "I'm a cop! Easy!"

There were only eight or ten people, so this time the ones in back managed to stop before they bashed into the ones in front, fortunate, because the ones in front would've been knocked down a flight of steps.

Mark raced up the stairs and flattened against the wall alongside the entrance. Look backed to check on the museum-goers—they were frozen on the stairs, staring up at him.

"Go to the alcove—and stay there!"

They obeyed, except for a teenage boy who scampered back up

the steps and flattened himself against the wall on the other side of the entrance, across from Mark. Scared, but in a fun way, buzzed about being in this video game.

Mark's new partner held up two fingers and stage-whispered, "Two guys, both male."

"Thanks get your ass outta here."

"Big one chasing a small one. Both have g—"

Shots blasted somewhere up ahead—the teenager flinched, clutched his abdomen and slid to the floor.

"You hit?" Mark asked.

The teenager shook his head. Not wounded. But wanting to die. His bowels had let go.

"Welcome to the club," Mark told him, and swiveled through the entrance to *Europe before 1900*, snapping into a combat stance and scanning the gallery. Nobody.

But he could hear shit happening up ahead.

SEVENTY-ONE / 2012

There is a craft to displaying art. *Europe Before 1900* was a long series of connecting galleries. Some were single large rooms, others were divided down the middle to create small side-by-side galleries. And the entryways feeding visitors from one gallery to the next were asymmetrical—some wide, some narrow, some set in the middle of a wall, some set in the right or left corner of a wall. This gave each gallery a distinctive configuration, and imposed a meandering pattern on foot-traffic that's more interesting than walking a straight line from one identical room to the next.

The layout wasn't kind to Dale Phipps, whose only concern was speed. Dale ran into the first gallery, skidded to a halt, made a 90-degree left turn and ran into the gallery alongside this one, then made a 90-degree right. Those two galleries were empty, because the sound of gunfire had inspired everyone to flee. The problem was most had run in the same direction Dale was running, but not as fast. He caught up the with tail end of the crowd in the third gallery, a cluster of slow-moving oldsters shuffling through the entry to the fourth gallery.

Dale shoved past the oldsters—some canes but no goddamn wheelchairs—and into the fourth gallery, which was—

Worse. On the other side of the room a tangled scrum was competing to shove their way into the fifth gallery. *Shit!*—the galleries at the far end of this section held the Greatest Impressionist Hits—Van Gogh, Monet, Seurat, Lautrec—always fucking mobbed—must be a traffic jam backed up all the way from there to here—but it was Dale's only way out, unless he wanted to turn and shoot it out with Shaved Head.

Dale shot it out with the ceiling, firing a round to get people's attention, then yelled for them to get the fuck out of his way. Dale charged into the fifth gallery, which was—

Much worse. His gunshot had thrown the art lovers into full-on bestial panic. There were few in Dale's way when he ran in because almost everyone was jammed in the left-hand corner of the far side of the room, clawing to get into the sixth gallery—the narrow entry was blocked by a writhing pile of the fallen. People were fighting to scramble over the pile, but the seething mass of bodies grabbed and kicked at them, so more people fell and made the pile higher—

Dale heard shrieks, thuds and feral basso grunts behind him—Shaved Head knocking people out of his way—

Dale ran at the writhing pile—he'd run hurdles in high school, only JV but he had passable technique—shortened his final stride, kicked his lead leg high, planted his rear foot and launched—

Got the height but not the distance. The writhing pile was considerably wider than a track hurdle. Dale's front foot landed on a guy's chest and the guy grabbed Dale's leg and yanked—Dale landed on his back on top of the writhing pile, and saw—

Shaved Head coming through the entry on the kitty-corner far side of the fifth gallery—

Flat on his back on top of the pile, Dale fired wildly—

Shaved Head pulled back into the fourth gallery—

Dale screamed "Stop moving! Stop!" and the people beneath him obeyed, which allowed Dale to roll onto his stomach, aim at the kitty-corner entryway behind which Shaved Head had retreated, and squeeze off—

Three sickeningly hollow clicks. Gun empty.

Shaved Head emerged, grinning, his gun leveled at Dale—

"FREEZE! DON'T FUCKING MOVE!!!" an unseen heaven-sent cop yelled from behind Shaved Head.

Shaved Head froze.

Dale scrambled off the pile and into the sixth gallery, popped the empty clip and, faster than he'd ever managed with his maimed left hand, jammed home a fresh clip—

Shots went off behind him. Dale hop-scotched across people who'd sensibly flung themselves to the floor, and shoved his way into the crowded Greatest Impressionist Hits galleries, brandishing his reloaded pistol.

SEVENTY-TWO/ 2012

Two shots from up ahead. As Mark hustled across the third gallery toward the fourth, a small stampede of terrified people rushed out of that gallery—

They saw Mark and his gun—screamed—Mark pointed to his badge and hissed "Police! Police! SHHH!" He hurried to the next entryway, flattened against the wall and looked into the fourth gallery—

People were proned out on the floor, covering their heads and whimpering—except for one guy who was on his feet, squirming against a wall, as if trying to hump his way through it—

And on the far side, at the entry to the fifth gallery, the Bald Bear was pointing his gun at someone in the fifth—

"FREEZE! DON'T FUCKING MOVE!!!"

Bald Bear froze.

The man humping the wall decided it was now safe to get the hell out, so he launched himself off his beloved and ran toward Mark—

Bald Bear whirled—

Mark couldn't shoot, the wall-humper was in his line of fire, rushing straight at him—

Mark grabbed the wall-humper's arm and yanked him down, pulling the wall-humper backward with him into the third gallery as Bald Bear pumped a few rounds—

Mark scrambled back to the entryway and looked—Bald Bear was gone—

Behind Mark a woman began groaning and someone yelled "She's hit! She's hit!"

A thirtyish woman was curled on the floor, clutching a bloody bicep. Mark rushed to her, yelling, "Is anyone a doctor?!"

Nope, just sprinters—everyone was fleeing. Mark intercepted the wall-humper—"Stay!"—and pulled him to the floor alongside the wounded woman.

Mark handed the woman his handkerchief. "Keep pressure on the wound," he instructed, whipped off his tie, made a tourniquet and yanked it tight.

Mark handed the end of the tie to the wall-humper. "Keep this tight. *And don't you fucking leave her.*" Mark told the woman, "Don't move, okay? Help's gonna be here soon."

That should be true—even if cops outside weren't able to fight their way through the manic flesh torrent that'd be pouring out of the main exits, there were loading docks and side—

Gunshots—far off, downstairs. Just two guns: Doonie one-on-one with the tall thin shooter. Shit, no reinforcements yet.

Mark resumed chasing Bald Bear, and the "small one" the Bear was chasing. Dale Phipps was small.

Dale's gun, aided by his face, cleared a path through the Greatest Impressionist Hits, from which he emerged into an enormous gallery, the hub of this wing. It overlooked the Grand Staircase, which led down to the main exits.

But it was a no-go zone.

The Grand Staircase was a huge open atrium space. Four small stairways zig-zagged down to two small landings, which in turn fed into a central landing, from which two wide stairways led to the ground floor. The hordes swarming down those upper four narrow stairways had met in head-on collisions at the two small landings. The effects rippled back up to the top. The result was Grand Ant Hill, thrashing mounds of fallen, frantic, fractured people strewn across the stairs.

Dale looked around—there! He shoved his way into a corridor leading to European Decorative Arts, on the far side of which was another staircase to the ground floor.

The European Decorative Arts galleries were jammed with people equally desperate to get to that stairway. But Dale was the only one waving a 9mm VIP pass.

This stairway was 1970s modern, a steeply curved corkscrew swoop of steps suspended in the center of a two-story space, with only thin metal railings between you and the open air. Slightly scary. People were descending at a sane pace.

Sane was unacceptably slow. Dale fired another shot and screamed "FREEZE! NOBODY MOVE! STOP MOVING!" at the people on curved stairway. They obeyed.

Dale hurried down, picking his way between people frozen in place, white-knuckling the handrails. Wasn't easy to squeeze between some of them—*God, the number of fat people in this country*—

An eruption of screams from above, accompanied by a man bellowing "Moof! Moof! Moof!"—

Dale began leaping down two, three stairs at a time. Had one last fatty to clear—Dale lost his footing, bounced off a planetary rump, went airborne and splatted full-length on the hardwood floor at the foot of the stairs—

Ah shit the gun slammed out of Dale's hand and skittered away—he reached for it—

BLAM! A bullet exploded the parquet in front of Dale, peppering his outstretched hand with splinters—

"DON'T MOOF!"

Dale didn't, except for slowly looking up.

Shaved Head was descending the curving stairs, keeping his weapon aimed as he weaved around the hippos pressed against the handrails, many with their eyes squeezed shut in hopes that might convince Shaved Head, or themselves, they weren't really there.

Shaved Head stepped off the staircase and loomed over Dale.

"On your niece!"

"On my?—Oh." Dale pushed himself up onto his knees.

"Hands behind head!"

Dale complied. *This mean he's not going to shoot me?*

"Open you mouth!"

Dale opened.

Shaved Head shoved a miniature Hancock Building in Dale's mouth.

Oh. They're trying to pin it on Tesca.

Shaved Head grinned and placed the muzzle of his gun an inch from Dale's forehead.

SEVENTY-FOUR / 2012

ark tracked Bald Bear by the gunshots and screams.

Mark came to a suspended corkscrew staircase jammed with cringing people, and down at the foot of the stairs Bald Bear was about to shoot Dale Phipps, on his knees with a Hancock Building in his mouth—

No time to aim and the angle sucked but Mark's bullet slammed into the top of the Bear's collarbone. The thick beast went down. Squirming, groaning, but not visible.

Mark's view was blocked by people on the curved staircase. He hustled down a few steps to where he could see—

Bald Bear, curled on the floor, gushing blood, in major pain, but still holding his gun—

"Drop it! *Put it the fuck down!*"

Bald Bear grinned at Mark.

"Right now," Mark advised, "or you're dead."

Bald Bear slowly placed the gun on the floor beside him. Didn't take his hand off of it.

Out of the corner of his eye Mark saw Dale pull the Hancock out of his mouth and get to his feet. "Dale, STAY!"

Dale stopped—

Bald Bear raised his weapon surprisingly fast for a half-dead guy—

Mark put two in Bald Bear's chest—

Dale dashed toward a tall marble-trimmed entry to a gallery—

"DALE!!!" Mark flicked his gun in Dale's direction—Dale paused—made eye contact with Mark—resumed running—

Mark didn't shoot. Resumed aiming at Bald Bear, and navigated down through the corkscrew stairway's human obstacle course.

Bald Bear was flat on his back in a pond of blood, arms flung out

Jesus-wide, but his gun was still in his hand and he still wasn't a hundred per cent dead. He was muttering darkly in a foreign language. Hurling curses, the only weapon he could still fire.

Just to make sure, Mark stepped on the rugged bastard's wrist and pulled the gun out of his hand.

The rugged bastard stopped muttering and agonizingly raised his head, glaring, grinding his jaw, searching for his last dying glob of saliva. He found it and tried to spit at Mark. The bloody sputum just dribbled over his lower lip and the effort killed him.

Mark pocketed the gun and started to go after Phipps—

Gunshots from somewhere behind him, not too far off. Sustained fire, Doonie trading with the second shooter. Mark did a one-eighty and ran hard.

SEVENTY-FIVE / 2012

As Doonie came out of the long hall he saw a skinny bloody-nosed goon shooting at Mark, so Doonie returned fire fast as he could.

Missed, and the goon disappeared up a short staircase.

Doonie and Mark traded a nod and each went after his guy.

Doonie sidestepped a fallen wheelchair at the foot of the stairs, eased up the steps, peered over the top—didn't see the shooter.

What he saw was a rectangular mezzanine, its outer walls lined with galleries. The center of the mezzanine was an atrium under a skylight held up by old-fashioned marble columns.

On the floor right in front of Doonie was a good-looking young broad laying on top of some lucky geezer.

Doonie started to ask, "Which—"

"That way," the young broad snapped, like she was pissed about the level of service she was getting, "down those stairs!"

She pointed to the rear of the mezzanine, where a staircase went down to an interior courtyard. Doonie hustled toward it but skidded to a halt when he heard a screech from below—he looked down—the interior courtyard was full of sculptures and two tourists babbling "Pleasedon'tshoot pleasedon'tshoot—" at the skinny goon, who was hissing "Shut up! Shut up!" and pointing his gun at them—

"FREEZE!" Doonie roared, aiming down at—

The skinny goon whirled and fired up at Doonie—

Doonie held fire because he couldn't risk hitting the tourists. He pulled back, then peeked down. Saw the goon retreating into one of the galleries that lined the sides of the inner courtyard, as the tourists ran the hell away, up the courtyard's front stairs.

Doonie scoped the situation: the stairs the goon had taken at the rear of the mezzanine led down to the rear of the inner courtyard. But if Doonie went down those rear stairs, the goon would run out the front stairs.

So Doonie rushed down the front mezzanine stairs, which came out next to the stairs leading down to the front of the inner courtyard. Doonie edged down into the courtyard—

The goon leaned out of a gallery and fired—missed Doonie but killed a small statue, as—

Doonie snapped off shots—

The goon grabbed his leg and fell back into the gallery.

Doonie hurried into an adjacent gallery. On its far wall there was an entry to the goon's gallery. Doonie went there and—

Nobody.

But a trail of blood led to the next gallery. Doonie nearly took a bullet when he poked his head into it. Doonie pulled back sharply—bullets tore through the flimsy gallery wall next to him—he hit the deck.

He heard movement.

Doonie hoisted himself to his feet, saw the goon heading up the rear stairs, back to the mezzanine.

Doonie chased him—goon had a shot-up leg, even Doonie should be able to run this asshole down.

But when Doon hustled up the rear stairs and looked across the mezzanine—no chance for a shot, the goon was already speed-gimping down the *front* mezzanine stairs. Skinny prick, gunshot leg and all, was faster than him.

At least the young broad and the geezer were gone—she must've dragged him away.

Doonie ran to the front of the mezzanine. Looked down—*shit*—a glimpse of the skinny prick as he ran into the long hall.

Doonie heaved his beerbelly down the stairs and hustled to the hall's entrance. Took a breath and moved in—

Nobody. The walls of the long hall were lined with display cases, and the center of the hall was divided into two aisles by a row of free-standing glass display cases, alternating with a bunch of fucking knights and horses in tin suits.

But the goon hadda be in there; not enough time for even a quick gimp to make it to the exit way down at the other end. And he was bleeding.

Doonie followed the blood up the right aisle—

The skinny prick's gun snapped out from behind a suit of armor—

The bullets missed Doonie and blew out the front of the display case behind him—Doonie returned fire—

The goon dove into the left aisle—popped up a second later, shooting through one of the display cases in the middle of the hall—

Doonie stood his ground and shot back—

The glass sides of the display case between them collapsed, and—

One of Doonie's bullets smashed the gun out of the goon's hand!

They both froze, shared a *Did that cowboy shit just happen?* moment—Doonie grinned at the goon—

Who looked down at an eighteen-inch ceremonial dagger in the shattered case in front of him—

Doonie yelled "Don't!" but the goon was already wrenching the dagger loose from its fastenings, and Doonie fired—

Click. Empty.

Doonie popped the clip and pulled out another—

The gimpy goon managed to step up into the shattered display case and used his good leg to launch himself—

He landed on Doonie, who dropped his empty gun and grabbed the goon's knife-arm with both hands as they crashed backward into the shattered display case behind Doonie, the corpulent cop landing inside the case, on his back with the goon on top of him, pressing hard on the dagger, the point an inch from Doonie's eye—

Using his weight advantage, Doonie rolled over, so he was on top—and using that same tonnage, leaning down, Doonie began to move the goon's dagger—

The goon began punching Doonie's head with his left hand—

Doonie knocked the goon's fist aside and Doonie's hand came down on a thick round wooden handle—

But the handle was fastened to the display by metal loops—

Doonie yanked—

The dagger point waggled upward toward his fucking eye—

The handle Doonie was yanking at tore free and Doonie swung some heavy thing at the goon's head—

Mark charged into the west entrance of Gunslaughter—

Forty feet away, Doonie was inside a display case straddling the skinny goon, who was trying to shove a dagger into Doonie's—

Mark stopped short and raised his gun—

Doonie bashed the goon with a mace. A fucking mace. A sploosh of blood, goo, hair and bone erupted from the goon's skull, and he went limp.

As Mark hurried to them, Doonie looked at the heavy thing in his hand, seeing for the first time what it was.

Mark asked, "You hurt?"

Doonie gazed at the wet part of the mace for a few seconds. Looked at Mark. "I shot the gun out of his hand, then killed him with a, a, whatchamacallit."

"Mace."

"Uh-huh… This is a great museum." Doonie slid out of the case and stood, gripping his mace.

"Your back is bleeding."

Doon flexed his shoulders and winced. "Might be a coupla little pieces of glass in there."

Mark checked the goon's pulse. "He's not dead."

"Fuck," Doonie complained.

Mark picked up Doonie's gun and full clip, inserted the clip and handed it to him. "I gotta go after Phipps."

"PUT DOWN THE GUN HANDS IN THE AIR PUT DOWN THE FUCKING GUN SHOW YOUR HANDS," a bunch of unis and SWATs screamed as they flooded into the Hall, weapons leveled.

Mark pointed at the badge on his breast pocket. "We're cops," he said, and gestured at Doonie. Four of the unis were veterans, which meant at least two should recognize Doon. They did.

Mark told the senior SWAT, "In addition to that"—the gory mess in the display case—"we got one shooter dead, and their target, who's probably left the building: Dale Phipps, white male, five-six, light hair, horrible skin, bulging left eye. I need backup."

The head SWAT radioed Dale Phipps' description to the scene commander outside.

Mark and three SWATs ran back the way Mark had come.

When they arrived at the curved staircase the dead Bald Bear was going viral. Most of the art lovers had fled. Five were clustered around the corpse, posing for photos, and one was holding the miniature Hancock—

"Put that the fuck down!" Mark roared—

The art lovers did a mass flinch-and-yelp as they saw Mark and his three beefy pals with assault rifles—

The art lover holding the Hancock quickly laid it on the floor. "Sorry sorry sorry." He pointed to Dale's gun on the floor nearby. "I didn't touch the gun."

Mark told one SWAT, "Secure the scene," and signaled the others to follow him into the gallery where Phipps had gone.

Native American Art, but no Phipps. It led to another gallery: African Art, no Phipps, but an emergency exit.

Mark and the SWATs emerged onto Jackson Street. The street was blocked at both ends by patrol cars. Mark nodded for one SWAT to go east to Columbus, while he and the other SWAT ran west toward the cops blocking Michigan, Mark barking out a description of Phipps to them as he approached.

A Sergeant said, "Yeah, came through three-four minutes ago."

"See which way he went?"

"Into that." The Sergeant made a despairing gesture at what was behind him.

Mark and the SWAT ran up the museum's front steps to get a better view. Police had barricaded the sidewalk and cordoned off a narrow corridor across Michigan Avenue directly in front of the museum, so emergency vehicles could get through by coming down Adams.

Nothing was gonna get through the churning human bog filling the rest of Michigan Avenue; outside the corridor formed by the police barriers, all eight of the avenue's lanes were jammed with people, and the immobile cars and buses trapped by them, as thousands exiting the museum were joined by thousands rushing toward it, anxious not to miss the show.

Mark scanned the seething mass. Useless. Couldn't pick out an individual—

"That's him! That's the cop who killed the bad guy!"

A cluster of weight-challenged art lovers who'd been on the curved staircase were being interviewed by a cluster of news crews—several of the art lovers were pointing at Mark—reporters and cameramen knocked over a barricade and stampeded toward Mark, shouting, filming and snapping stills as they ran—

"Shoot them or something," Mark instructed the SWAT, then turned and trotted up the steps into the museum, pulling out his phone and calling Husak to tell him to get teams to Phipps' residence and office, fast.

SEVENTY-SEVEN / 2012

Lou and Gianni spent some quality father-son time watching TV news together, then Lou took out his burner and called Dale's burner. No answer. Tried Dale's regular cell. No answer.

What a fucking roller coaster of a morning.

Started on a high: Lou's men located Tommy Tesca's trailer park. Tesca wasn't there, but a neighbor ID'd his photo and confirmed his ride was a black Suburban.

Lou's men tossed the trailer; didn't find anything that told where Tesca had gone, but found a back-up hard drive and a couple of thumb drives they were now examining. Meanwhile Lou put eyes on the trailer, and the entrance to the park, and the road leading to it.

And then, while Lou was at Dad's telling him the good news, the Art Institute happened.

Two morons tried to snatch a guy in the crowded museum, but got into it with him—and with a couple of cops. The morons end up one dead and one close to it, and their target gets away.

And it turns out the dead moron was carrying a miniature Hancock just like the one Tesca used for his last Art Critic gig.

And, nail in the coffin, witnesses described the target who was supposed to eat the Hancock as a guy who happens to have Dale Phipps' height, build and remarkable complexion.

So now in addition to finding and killing Tesca before the cops found him, they had to find and kill Dale before the cops found *him*.

Then it was gonna be Jay Branko's turn.

Had to be Jay who pulled this shit. Only other person who might want to whack Dale was Tommy, for the exact same reason as Jay: to sabotage the big European score.

But Tommy sure as shit did not match the descriptions of either museum moron. And Tommy sure as shit wouldn't have paid good money to have those monkeys pull this lame-brain stunt.

Jay would. Jay would hire morons to pop Dale and leave that thing in his mouth, trying to pin the hit on Tommy. Jay had his head far enough up his ass to believe Lou and Gianni would fall for it.

"You want to hold off going at Branko?" Lou asked, because with the Old Man it was best to state your opinion in the form of a request for his decision.

Gianni stared at Lou.

The silence was punishment, Gianni whipping his son for not having been man enough to intimidate Branko out of ever trying this.

When the Old Man was done, he asked—challenged—"Can you sell Branko on we're not after him?"

"I can get his hopes up." Lou's burner rang. "Speak of the devil."

Gianni nodded for Lou to take the call. Sat there assessing Lou's performance.

Lou put the phone to his ear and said, with his trademark nonchalance, "Hey dude, was just about to call. You believe this shit? I'm hoping the museum's liability coverage isn't with our company."

SEVENTY-EIGHT / 20120

Jay Branko had to knock back a couple of vodkas to get his brain to do something besides scream he should *right now* grab a plane to the ass end of nowhere and never come back.

Fuck! FUCK! What was wrong with Zerbjka? What kind of stupid—fuck it, no time for that. Had to figure how to play this.

Would the Mastrizzis assume it was Jay who hired this clown-act hit? He'd for sure cross their minds. But they couldn't be certain, long as he plays it cool… He should phone Lou, read the vibe. Besides, after this disaster, if Jay didn't touch base, that'd be suspicious.

Jay dialed.

It rang.

Rang again.

Rang again. *If Lou doesn't pick up, does that mean—*

Rang aga—

"Hey dude, was just about to call. You believe this shit? I'm hoping the museum's liability coverage isn't with our company."

Same old Lou—banter, you dumb fuck. "You own an insurance company? Which one?"

"Never mind. You recognize the description of the man who got away?"

"How could I not. Gotta be the little guy."

"Gotta be. The clincher is the souvenir the shooter was putting in the little guy's mouth. That's the fat guy's signature, a final Fuck You, make sure we knew this was him."

They think it's Tesca!—maybe. "That's what I figured. But… Why wouldn't the fat guy just do it himself?" *Good one, like you got nothing to be afraid of.*

Lou chuckled. "Dude, the little guy would spot the fat guy a mile off. Hadda hire an unfamiliar face."

"Right."

"And speaking of the fat guy—good news—we're close."

"Close?"

"Very. Just a matter of time."

"Boo-yah." *I could get away with this—if Lou kills Tesca without talking to him first.* "And, the little guy?"

"Isn't answering his phone. But we'll find him."

"And then?"

"Send him far, far away."

"Right," Jay sighed. "Shit, bro, when people say the art world is exciting…"

"You thought that meant humping skinny girls in the bathroom at gallery openings. Me too. I'll call when there's news," Lou promised.

There'd been nothing in Lou's voice except Lou's usual voice, so… this could be as good as it sounded. The Mastrizzis believe Tesca hired the hit on Phipps. Soon they'll kill Tesca, then Phipps. This shit's gonna work out.

Or… Lou telling me what I want to hear means they're setting me up, and I do have to grab the first plane to the ass end of nowhere.

Jay re-ran and re-ran the conversation, searching for a tell.

SEVENTY-NINE / 2012

Sorry," William J. Potinkin said, as he checked the caller ID, "I have to take this."

"Thank God," JaneDoe replied. They were two hours into Potinkin putting her through TV interview boot camp. And soon Potinkin's stylist would show up with a load of Nice Girl clothes—

"Turn on the TV," Potinkin ordered.

"Why?"

"The Art Critic might be dead."

JaneDoe grabbed the remote.

Holy crap. There'd been running gun battles in the Art Institute.

Witnesses fleeing the museum said a gunman tried to murder someone and stick a miniature Hancock Building in his mouth—just like the Art Critic did with Troy Horowitz. But before the would-be killer could finish, he'd been shot to death by a cop.

An accomplice of the possible Art Critic was badly wounded, and the injury toll to museum-goers trampled in a rush to escape was estimated to be in the hundreds.

It got weirder. The intended victim had a gun and had been trading shots with the possible Art Critic. After the cop saved his life, the man fled. Witnesses said he was white, short, slender, had some sort of indescribable skin disease and a bulging eye.

Police weren't saying if they knew the identity of the intended victim, or the possible Art Critic and his accomplice.

Police did confirm *this* officer—footage of a plainclothes cop on the museum steps—was the one who'd killed the possible Art Critic. Officials had yet to release the officer's name.

JaneDoe released it. "That's Mark."

"Hmm," Potinkin grunted sagely. "Not the ugliest cop ever."

"Yeah," JaneDoe agreed, but what she was thinking was: *Gunfight?*

Four years ago Mark almost died when he got shot busting another murderous fuckwad. This time there was blood on Mark's shirt but he didn't look wounded. Just intense, even for him. Well shit, he'd been shot at—*again*... and... and...

JaneDoe stared at Potinkin.

"No," Potinkin ordered. "Not till this is over."

JaneDoe stared at Potinkin.

"No," he repeated. "You can bump into each other at Whole Foods and fall in love when this is finished. Not before. Not one word."

Right. True. But...

Her cell rang. Lila Kasey, wanting to know how JaneDoe was doing, and was there anything she could do, maybe come over and keep JaneDoe company, and drive her to the TV station so she didn't have to deal with that?

Oh Christ yeah. Potinkin had hired a car but fuck that. Lila was a rock. Having Lila here would make it easier for JaneDoe to deal with everything: Potinkin. Potinkin's stylist. The TV interview. And Mark.

Lila was JaneDoe's only friend who knew about her thing with Mark four years ago. JaneDoe hadn't told Lila about current events. That might have to change. *Gunfight.* The word had taken up residence in the pit of JaneDoe's stomach. She was reaching the point where if she couldn't talk to Mark she'd have to talk about him.

EIGHTY / 2012

A detectives relieved Mark of his weapon, then had to be walked through every move of the firefight.

Then came the obligatory micro-detailed debrief, in which they parsed the specific dispositions of the bystanders (especially the wounded one) and dissected Mark's decision-making before firing every shot. Each bullet was a potential truck-bomb's worth of liability damage.

But for some reason—perhaps because the shooting and stampeding began before Mark and Doonie drew their guns, and the museum's security footage confirmed Mark's account—the IA guys only questioned Mark a little over two hours.

Soon as it ended Mark called the ER. The doctors were finished harvesting glass from Doonie's back. Doonie had been declared unfit to return to work, but fit to return to the Art Institute and walk IA through his own debriefing marathon.

The goon Doonie brained was in a coma.

First thing Mark noticed when he got back to the office were the changes on the murder board. At the top was a photo of Mark, labeled WYATT, and one of Doonie, labeled THOR.

Wyatt asked what progress had been in made in finding Dale Phipps.

None. Hadn't turned up at his office or apartment—where his Prius had been found, lonely and unused, in the garage.

Kaz and Kimbrough were re-examining Phipps' particulars for clues about who might want him dead, and where he might run. Techs were unpacking hard drives from Phipps' office and apartment.

Husak had released Dale Phipps' name to the media, along with a close-up lifted from a museum security cam.

As far as the shooters: The dead guy's wallet said he was Antonije Zerbjka, a Serb with a green card. His fingerprints said he was Dejan Zupljanicz, a Serb with an intercontinental rap sheet.

The coma guy was Slobovan Zaentz. He wasn't talking, but a snitch reported there was a third member of Zerbjka's crew—a wheel-man. Detectives were interviewing associates, friends and family.

No buzz about who'd hired the hit.

As far as the main attraction: There'd been no new sightings of the Art Critic's Suburban.

Agent Rarey showed up. Said the FBI had been stonewalled by the Liechtenstien and Caribbean banks; there was no money trail.

The Feds had found no link between the Mastrizzis and the Lougian and Gianlou shell companies.

IA—in what Husak declared a land speed record—pronounced the shoot righteous and returned Mark's weapon. But Wyatt Bergman was obliged to report for a psych eval, within 48 hours.

Sure thing.

Mark and Rarey were in Husak's office theorizing about what the hell the attempt on Phipps might have to do with the Art Critic. There was a quick knock and Doonie walked in. All three men rose.

"No hugs," Doonie warned. "Till the stitches come out I'm only takin' compliments and drinks."

"Good job today, great to see you alive," Husak said. "Go home."

"I'll sit quiet and listen," Doonie promised, easing down onto a couch. "What're we talkin' about?"

"For starters," Husak said, "the media and god knows how many voters are obsessing over whether or not Zerbjka is—was—the Art Critic. HQ wants definitive yes or no evidence they can announce, or at least a strong opinion they can leak."

"Zerbjka's not him," Mark declared. "The Critic kills artists. Plus which the Critic never uses the same totem twice—our Serbian friend didn't know that."

Husak nodded. "This does read like Zerbjka tried to pin this hit on the Critic."

"Speaking of the Hancock, and the fact the Critic kills artists to cash in," Mark said, "we have to revisit Horowitz. There's no record of the Critic buying Horowitz sculptures. If the Critic was the doer, what was his motive?"

"Maybe the Critic wanted us to know he's not her," Doonie said, pointing at the TV on Husak's wall.

JaneDoe was doing her interview on the 5 o'clock news.

"Can we unmute the sound?" Rarey asked.

Husak gave the young agent a weary squint. "We're working."

"So are my people," Rarey said. "When JaneDoe left her house to go to the TV station, we went in. The bugs and taps are gone."

Rarey kept his eyes on Husak while he said that. Not even a glance at Mark. No way Rarey was going to endanger his asset by indicating JaneDoe's debugged apartment was of special interest to him.

Not that Rarey's asset was going to trust Rarey's claim the bugs were gone.

Mark took a brief look at the screen. The interview seemed to be going well. JaneDoe looked relaxed, sincere. Innocent and enjoying it.

Mark would have to wait to find out if his plan was working and JaneDoe had accepted Lila Casey's offer of a lift to the studio.

He'd instructed Lila not to give JaneDoe his message until after the interview; no telling how far and wide she'd erupt when she found out all her recent conversations, emails and bowel movements had been recorded by a Federal agency.

Mark had told Lila not to call until late tonight to let him know how it went.

Mark was pretty sure JaneDoe would want to see him.

But he wasn't certain.

He had to work at not looking at the TV.

ou's cyber guy downloaded Tesca's hard drive and tickled its clit until its encryption melted away. Files gushed forth.

The miserable shit had named his shell companies Lougian and Gianlou.

There was detailed purchase and shipping data, along with descriptions and photos of the art. Tesca's two most recent acquisitions made Lou's day.

"Liz Paul" was a female Gibson guitar.

"Reflectoraptor" was a predatory dinosaur whose skin was made of curved, deeply colored Mylar mirrors; get near him and you got hit with a barrage of dark, distorted funhouse views of yourself.

Both pieces were functional costumes, which the text called Bio-Kinetic Interactive Sculptures.

The artist was the luscious young woman the cops had mistaken for Tommy Tesca.

When in fact JaneDoe clearly was Tommy's next target.

EIGHTY-TWO / 2012

William J. Potinkin informed JaneDoe she'd knocked it out of the park. Lila agreed. So did the blogosphere; by halfway through the interview, JaneDoe's consensus identity had morphed from Arty Bizarre Murder Suspect to Wrongly Accused Edgy Buzz Babe.

And she'd answered all the juicy personal questions about her *feelings*; the rest of the media would quit camping on her doorstep now that all they could hope for were sloppy seconds.

Potinkin invited JaneDoe and Lila to One Sixty Blue for a celebratory dinner.

As they were being seated, JaneDoe got a call from her dealer, Marla Kretz. Marla congratulated her for not coming off like a crazy artist, and warned her not to party too hard, tomorrow she had to get back to work; interview highlights had been posted on YouTube, and Marla was hearing from collectors, worldwide, offering insane money to be first in line.

A cork popped. The sommelier poured a '98 Deutz *blanc de blancs*. Potinkin offered a toast to innocent, talented, young, beautiful, tall clients and deductible business meals.

The food was brilliant, the wines off the hook, the mood pagan-pure exultation. Even after eating her dessert and half of Lila's, JaneDoe weighed a thousand pounds less than she had since the moment her life had gone Kafka.

But.

Tonight would not end with Mark in her bed. Or even on her phone.

Thank god Lila was here.

JaneDoe slid into the passenger seat of Lila's Volvo station wagon. The valet wished the ladies an especially sincere "Safe ride home" as he closed the door.

"Don't worry," Lila told JaneDoe, "I'm not as drunk as you look."

JaneDoe squeezed Lila's hand. "Thank you."

Lila gave a dismissive shrug.

JaneDoe said, "Nightcap at my place, so we can *talk*."

Lila gave her a sympathetic little grin.

Sympathetic but—equivocal, JaneDoe thought. Like, wary. Like Lila's concerned I'm crashing off my pagan-pure exultation and about to crumble into loony little pieces. Not gonna happen, Lila, I'm fine, just need to fire up a joint and talk about Mark for a few hours. In fact it's gonna amuse the shit out of you when you hear what's been going on with me and Detective Bergman.

They pulled out of the parking lot. Lila turned right and headed north.

JaneDoe grinned. "You sure you're not as drunk as I look? My place is the other way."

"We're going to my place."

"But I've got Humboldt Train Wreck."

"Yeah but we can't talk at your pl—I mean, don't worry, I've got plenty—"

"We can't talk at my place? *Why*?"

Lila hesitated. "I'll explain when we get—"

"*Now*. Right. Now."

Lila pulled to the curb. Took the kind of slow deep breath people do right before diving off the high board.

"I would've called you today and offered to help in any case. But, also... I saw Mark last night. He wants to see you."

"Then why doesn't he just call me? If he's worried about his phone records, he can use a pay..." The realization gave her guts a playful squeeze. "Shit my phones are tapped those goddamn fucking pigs."

"Not cop pigs, FBI pigs."

"Well then."

"Aaaand, so is your computer. And they've been reading your mail."

"Wha—*Fuck!*"

"Also... your apartment's bugged."

JaneDoe turned white, turned red and loosed a volley of screams and sobs and punched the dashboard, again, and again again again, until she stopped to use her sleeve to wipe away tears and snot.

Lila handed her a wad of tissues. "Mark says—"

"I've been fucking raped. They've been in my home, spying on every single..." She pounded the dashboard some more.

"He said the FBI is going to remove all the b—"

"I can't stay there tonight."

"You don't have to."

"Can't stay there till I've had the place disinfected with a fucking blowtorch."

Lila squeezed JaneDoe's arm. "Mi casa is su casa long as you want, sweetie."

They hugged. Lila's hug was maternal. JaneDoe's was distracted. Too many emotions slam-dancing inside her.

They drove in silence. The buildings lining the streets seemed to JaneDoe like the walls of a World War One trench, and the Volvo was this tiny wretched creature scuttling along the cold muddy bottom.

"He should've warned me," she whispered to the trench, and Lila, and herself, and him.

EIGHTY-FOUR / 2006

Two fucking hours parked down the block from One Sixty Blue, MJ's fancy fuckin' restaurant, like MJ ain't phat enough, heh, the eight-figure salary he useta get, and the eight-figure endorsements, that schmeiss Nike sends MJ every time some kid gets mugged for his Air Jordans and cries till Mommy buys him a new pair.

The goddamn Volvo finally pulled out of the restaurant lot.

Hope MJ cooked you a great supper, hon, 'cause it's your last.

He put the Suburban in gear and followed—

Crap!—the Volvo suddenly pulled over.

There was no place to park behind them, he had to drive past.

He parked on the next block. Cut his lights. Watched in his rear-view.

They didn't get out of the Volvo. Just sat there, lights on, engine running.

Had they made him?

The Volvo started driving again.

Bucktown. The Volvo went up a driveway alongside an old-fashioned three-flat.

Tommy got lucky. There was a spot to park right across from it.

JaneDoe and the big beatnik broad came walking up the driveway and went in the front door. Minute later the lights went on in the top floor apartment.

Tommy went and looked at the front door. It had an old-fashioned intercom—there was no mirror, kind that hides a TV camera. The name on the third floor was Lila Kasey.

Tommy got back in his truck. Waited another couple hours. The lights in the apartment were still on.

The news on the radio, as it had been all day, was still in fucking heat about the shit went down at the Art Institute. Somebody tried to whack Dale. And planned to pin it on Tommy. And the cop who waxed the shooter was working the Art Critic murders.

Heh? Couldn't figure what the fuck that might be about. But it couldn't be good.

Tommy had to get this fuckin' shit over with, go be a fat happy ghost in Brazil.

Screwed a silencer onto a .40-cal Sig Sauer.

Tough luck, Lila Kasey. And anybody the fuck else was dumb enough to be up there with JaneDoe.

EIGHTY-FIVE / 2012

ow is it we release *that* face to the media," Nick Rarey wondered, gazing at the umpteenth broadcast of Dale Phipps' unique epidermal plaguescape, "and nobody spots him?"

"He's indoors or wearing a burka," Mark said.

"Or a mummy costume," the wunderkind theorized. He was seated directly across from Mark, at Doonie's desk.

Mark had blackmailed Doonie into leaving when he noticed blood on the back of Doonie's shirt; Doonie's stitched-up cuts were oozing. Mark ordered a uni to drive Doon home.

Doonie protested that a little leakage was normal.

"Don't make me call Phyl," Mark warned.

"Fuckin' snitch," Doon groused. But he went, rather than let his wife come down and drag him off in front of the whole delighted squad.

In the hours since—it was after 11 PM—no leads had developed on Dale, or the Serbian wheelman, or—

Kimbrough whooped. Everyone stared at Kimmie staring at her computer. She'd been working the phones, calling every number in Dale's records. She said, "I may be looking at the Art Critic."

Mark led the stampede to Kimbrough's desk.

"Plowed my way back to 2005, saw this loan shark Phipps kept calling—"

"Tesca," Mark said. Crap! After the shoot-out he'd totally blanked on—

"Thomas 'Tommy' Tesca," Kimbrough nodded. "But back when you saw his sheet, we didn't have *this*."

Kimmie's screen showed the sketch of the hefty guy with the broad nose who probably shot Horowitz, next to Tesca's mug shot.

The guy in the booking photo was twenty years younger and

slimmer than the guy in the sketch. But—

Mark ran Tesca: No current address or phone. DMV said Tesca sold his Cadillac last year, currently had no vehicle registered in Illinois.

Mark put out an APB, and told Gang Crimes he needed a full-court press on all things Tommy Tesca.

Rarey searched FBI's confidential Mob database. Not a nibble; Tesca wasn't enough of a player to make it onto the radar.

A long half-hour later Mark got a call from Ed Nardelli, the senior Outfit genealogist at Gang Crimes. Nardelli was home but he'd been in touch with his CIs.

"Nobody's seen Tesca for over a year," Nardelli reported. "Rumor was maybe he pissed off Gianni Mastrizzi. Tesca's a cousin, but wasn't a made guy; word is the Old Man never had much use for him. And here's the good part—"

Mark didn't interrupt to say that the name Mastrizzi was already a good part—

"—last few weeks Mastrizzi soldiers have been lookin' for Tommy."

"Shi-i-t."

"You're welcome. What's Tesca got to do with the Art Critic?"

"Maybe everything. Keep that to yourself and keep digging. Anything Tesca's been up to since 2005, and any fucking thing about him and the Mastrizzis. "

"Gianni Mastrizzi and dead artists," Nardelli chuckled. "I am all over it."

As Mark hung up, Rarey, seated at Doonie's computer, announced, "Indianapolis! Ten months ago a court granted Thomas Tesca a name change. He is now Jonathan Davis."

"Current address?"

"A commercial mailbox. What'd you just hear that made you so happy?"

Mark gestured for Rarey to wait while he issued an amended APB for Tommy Tesca aka Jonathan Davis.

Mark motioned Rarey to follow him into Husak's office, where

Mark updated them. When Mark got to Mastrizzi, Rarey let out a small pleased groan. Serial killers are nice, but for the FBI, bringing down a Capone-sized mob boss is a re-enactment of the First Crusade.

"Has to be something there," Husak agreed, "the Critic's shell companies named Gianlou and Lougian, and Tesca being their cousin—"

"A black sheep cousin, who's trying to frame them," Rarey cut in. "And if they're after him it means they know what he's up to, they know about the art scam. Please let it be because they're in on it."

"Tesca can tell us—and so can Phipps, if we get to them before the Mastrizzis do," Mark said. "Though I don't think it was a mob hit on Dale today—no way Mastrizzi hires those kamikaze Serbs."

"Then who did?" Rarey wondered.

Husak shrugged.

Mark's cell rang.

Janet Claudel, art crimes. "I've got something amazing," she crowed.

"Good, what?"

"Just heard back from one of the last galleries on my list—three months ago they sold two pieces to Lougian LLC. Which were shipped to a Swiss—"

"Which gallery what artist!?!?"

"Marla Kretz, and—not gonna believe this—the artist was JaneDoe. I mean what are the odds—"

But Mark had already hung up, barked "JaneDoe is his next target!" at Husak, who grabbed a phone and ordered units to her place, as Mark called JaneDoe's cell. It went to voicemail.

"This is Detective Bergman. If you're home do not let anyone in until police officers arrive. They're on their way, this is serious, no fucking around. If you hear this message, *call me right now.*"

Mark tried JaneDoe's landline; nothing.

He told Rarey, "Call Potinkin, ask if he knows where she went when she left the TV station."

Mark called Lila Kasey's phone. Got voicemail. Left a message that he needed to contact JaneDoe right now, she was in danger.

Mark called the burner he'd given Lila. That went to voicemail too.

Mark emailed and texted JaneDoe and Lila.

Husak yelled, "JaneDoe's not home!"

Mark's phone rang. "Bergman!"

An excited POD tech. "Got a hit on the Suburban—1400 block of West Randolph, turning north onto Ogden."

"When?"

"Couple of hours ago, 9:28 PM. We're running Ogden footage, see if we can track—"

"Mark!" Rarey interrupted.

"What?"

"Potinkin had dinner with JaneDoe at One Sixty Blue—"

"Shit!" *One Sixty Blue was at Randolph and Ogden—*

"—and she left with her friend Lila, about 9:30. Lila's car."

Mark checked Lila's address, ordered the nearest units to converge, told Husak, "The Critic's Suburban was following JaneDoe and Lila Kasey when they left dinner—Kasey lives in Bucktown—scramble a goddamn chopper," and ran out the door, with young Rarey matching Mark step for step while also phoning his superiors.

EIGHTY-SIX / 2012

T he women were ensconced in opposite corners of Lila's museum-quality Deco couch, where JaneDoe settled when she was able to stop pacing and ranting.

"Janey, it's after eleven, can I at least check my mes—"

"Nope," JaneDoe insisted, "the phones stay off, the computer stays off, and Detective Bergman can just... wonder."

"So will all the other people whose messages I'm not returning," Lila pointed out, and refilled JaneDoe's glass.

JaneDoe shrugged, unmoved by the collateral damage. After hours of drinking, smoking and venting she remained awake, enraged, and adamant about maintaining the digital blackout she'd decreed the moment they walked into Lila's apartment.

"Sweetie," Lila pleaded, "if I could just—"

"No!... Sorry," JaneDoe sighed. "I'm being a bitch, but tonight I need to be."

"Nah, you're just worried that if—when—Mark calls, you'll grab the phone out of my hand and start screaming at him."

"No, I'm looking forward to screaming at him. But not till I decide exactly what about. There's so much to choose from."

"So don't choose. Scream all of it." Lila offered the burner phone to JaneDoe.

JaneDoe stared at the burner as if she expected it to sprout fangs at one end and rattles at the other. She said, quietly, "Four years ago, when Mark and I ended it, it was on the phone—well, Mark wanted to do it in person, but I blew him off. No big deal. Just another man done gone..." She re-lit a roach, took a deep toke. "Then... He goes to California, gets shot and doesn't wake up for a week... Shit, Lila, I was useless, sick to my stomach that whole week."

"Love."

"Up the ass," JaneDoe agreed. "And, *and,* while Mark's out there recuperating, I help close this hit-and-run he and Doonie were working. But when Mark gets home he's got this California girl in his suitcase, and all I get from him is this one quick thank-you call." JaneDoe glared at the burner. "Fucking phone. Four years later it rings again, but the reason he's calling is I'm a witness in a murder investigation, and then fuck me I'm the *suspect,* and the fucking FBI is bugging my home, phones, email, my whole fucking *life,* and Mark doesn't even try to fucking warn me."

"How? You weren't setting foot outside your bugged house."

"He could've written it down and had you bring it to me."

"At which point you would've remained calm and silent?"

"Fucking yeah! And then, *then* I would've known not to go and... Lila, I told Potinkin, out loud, about me and Mark. So the FBI, and maybe Mark's bosses, know..."

"Mark won't blame you for that."

"He better fucking not, *it's his fault!* He-should-have-fuck-ing-warned-me!"

"Tell him that," Lila said, tossing the burner to JaneDoe.

Reflex reaction: JaneDoe caught it.

"Number One on the speed dial," Lila murmured.

JaneDoe eyed the burner, still not convinced it wasn't a dormant form of rattlesnake.

She decided to risk it. Turned the phone on. It woke, sang its Hello tune. No fangs.

JaneDoe aimed her index finger at the 1—

Lila's landline rang—a phone connected only to the downstairs intercom.

JaneDoe froze.

Lila relaxed into a stoned beneficent Cheshire grin. "Wonder who that is."

"Son of a bitch," JaneDoe whispered, and plunked the burner down.

Lila reached over to the side table to pick up the intercom phone—

"Don't answer it," JaneDoe demanded.

"He needs to know we're okay."

"Don't buzz him in."

Lila put the receiver to her ear and said, "Hello?... Hello?" Her Cheshire grin faded. "Hello? Who's there?" She shrugged at JaneDoe. Gave it one last, "Hello?" Hung up. "Some punk," Lila theorized.

"Named Bergman."

"He drove over here to ring my doorbell and run?"

There was a screech of tires from the street.

"There he goes," JaneDoe crooned.

"Couldn'ta been Mark," Lila insisted. She went to the bay window overlooking the street. Peered down, trying to see up the block. "Gone, whoever it was."

"*Mark*. Rang your doorbell, then got a police alert about a cat up a tree. Zoom, bye-bye... And that," JaneDoe declared, her voice thick with prophesy, "is what it'd always be. Life with an addict. The badge, the gun, the rush."

"He's a lot more than that. And thirty-five, and lonely."

"Yeah, typical junkie."

The women stared at each other across the room, and... Helicopter rotors. Far off but coming fast. Then a police siren. Then more sirens, a baying pack headed this way, until their howls were drowned by the thudda-thud roar of a chopper settling into a window-rattling hover directly overhead, and a harsh white light blasted the street in front of Lila's house—

She looked out the window. The spotlight was nailed to a black SUV parked directly across from her front door—

Patrol cars hurtled in from both ends of the one-way street and screeched to a halt. Three cops threw their car doors open and crouched behind them, guns leveled at the SUV. A fourth cop ran to Lila's front door and rang-rang-rang-rang-rang her intercom.

JaneDoe, who was closest to the intercom phone, made no move to pick it up.

The cop below began pounding the door and bellowing, "POLICE! POLICE OPEN UP!"

Lila looked at JaneDoe and issued a seriously impressed, "Holy crap."

"Yeah… How'm I gonna compete with that?" JaneDoe dared her wise old friend to explain.

EIGHTY-SEVEN / 2012

Mark didn't splatter the boozy jaywalker on Belmont or ram the bus on California. Missed both with millimeters to spare.

Nick Rarey said nothing. Thoroughly enjoying the high-speed siren-and-sparklers ride. But when Mark laced between stopped cars and fishtailed into a left turn against a red light onto Milwaukee, where vehicles were still moving, Rarey was moved to comment.

"Ah, love," he sighed, sounding equal parts amused by Mark's ardor and concerned about surviving Mark's driving.

Mark gave no sign of having heard Rarey, or, moments later, a radio squawk reporting the good news that the subjects were unharmed. He floored it all the way.

Skidded to a halt at the scene. A SWAT team was setting up a perimeter around the Suburban, and unis were evacuating the block's residents.

Mark and Rarey hurried to the military-serious SWAT commander, who was trying to determine if there was anyone in the Suburban by issuing bullhorn commands to "step out of the vehicle!"

Wasn't getting a response.

Mark introduced himself and asked, "Anybody see him get in the truck?"

"No."

"The building been swept?" Mark asked, indicating Lila's three-flat.

"Been cleared basement to roof," the SWAT commander told him.

"The subjects been evacuated?"

The SWAT commander gave his head one crisp shake. "Got unis guarding them—didn't want to bring 'em out till we know where our psycho perp is. Or isn't," he said, returning his gaze to the Art Critic's truck.

Mark studied the Suburban. The tint on its windows was so heavy the bleaching glare of the helicopter's spotlight didn't penetrate.

The SWATs' night-vision wasn't showing a thermal signature inside the vehicle, but the goggles weren't reliably sensitive enough to rule out a man crouched low behind the truck's doors.

The SWAT commander told Mark, "Frodo's on the way." Frodo being one of the Department's miniature robo-tanks, employed to inspect dicey locations. "Be here in ten minutes."

Which meant ten minutes or maybe thirty. And then Frodo's wizards would get him moving anytime from instantly to a wide range of not instantly.

"Need to know if Tesca's in there," Mark said, "or if he ran when he saw the chopper and realized we made his truck. If he's gone we need to get after him."

The SWAT commander said, "Not risking my men for that. Just you and me. And you go first."

"Me too," Rarey volunteered, to make sure the FBI would share credit for the bust.

Which would be broadcast live—news choppers were swarming, and camera vans were piling up at either end of the block.

Mark and Rarey strapped on Kevlar. They and the SWAT commander rushed the Suburban.

Mark grabbed the driver's door handle and yanked.

The door opened—Mark lunged in, sweeping his flashlight and muzzle through the SUV.

"Clear!"

Mark withdrew from the SUV, whipped out his phone and ordered balls-out ground and aerial searches of the vicinity. He asked the SWAT commander, "The subjects see or hear him?"

"Subject said her doorbell rang—haven't heard the details, been busy since I got here," the SWAT commander replied. Then added, with what might have been a shadow of a hint of a grin, "Been running my ass off all day, thanks to you."

Right. The Art Institute gala this morning, a million years ago.

"You can buy me a drink when you cash the overtime," Mark

said. "Which apartment are the subjects in?" As if he didn't know.

"Third floor."

Mark looked up at it.

Yup, that's where JaneDoe was.

Standing in the front room's bay window.

Alive.

Looking down at Mark.

Looking up at her.

He heard the SWAT commander yell, "Tell those assholes get her the hell out of that window!"

A moment later Mark saw JaneDoe react to something said by someone behind her, then a uni put himself between JaneDoe and the window.

Mark murmured "Thanks" to the SWAT commander, for issuing the order Mark should have.

"*De nada*," the SWAT commander said, regarding Mark with what was definitely a shadow of a hint of empathy. "You're having the mother of all fucking crazy fucking endless days."

"True."

And the next part of that endless day would be Mark interviewing the subjects, Lila Kasey and JaneDoe.

With Agent Rarey at Mark's side, relishing the moment.

EIGHTY-EIGHT / 2012

L ate at night, climbing the stairs to Lila's apartment to see JaneDoe. Just as planned. Except for how this secret reunion was gonna take place in front of Mark's happy FBI handler.

And except for how JaneDoe's reaction to the news about the FBI bugs had been worse than Mark's worst-case imaginings. So much so, she and Lila hadn't been answering or looking at their phones and computers.

Mark had no idea how JaneDoe was about to react to being forced to look at him, let alone him accompanied by one of her FBI buggers. Coming right after she'd been a minute or two away from getting murdered. Goosed by the epic amount of booze and weed she'd surely been doing.

The aroma in Lila's apartment was awesome. Got awesomer as they entered the living room, where JaneDoe and Lila were seated on the couch. They, their empty bottles of Hospices De Nuits, and their ashtrays full of Dunhill stubs and fat roaches were guarded by a sergeant and two unis armed with street-sweepers. Good weapon for decimating serial killers, not much defense against second-hand smoke.

As Mark and Rarey walked in, Lila stood and said, "Hello." Her expression neutral. Not giving Mark any kind of meaningful look.

JaneDoe remained seated, wineglass in hand, giving Mark a look so meaningful a dead man could pick up on it. Fortunately the look's most obvious meaning was *I hate you,* which the unis would take to be business as usual.

"Ms. Kasey, JaneDoe," Mark said. "Sorry your big evening turned out this way. Glad no one got hurt."

"Detective Bergman, the knight in dull black armor," JaneDoe drawled, referring to his Kevlar and so much more. "Catch the Art Critic yet?"

"No," Mark said. "I understand he tried to get in here."

"Maybe," Lila said. "Someone rang the intercom but when I picked it up they didn't answer."

JaneDoe frowned at Rarey, as it dawned on her Mark's partner was totally not Doonie. "Is Detective Dunegan all right? Was he the officer who got hurt at the Art Institute?"

"Cuts and bruises. He's okay." Mark returned to Lila before Rarey had a chance to introduce himself. "Did you hear anything—breathing, any noises?"

Lila shook her head. "Nothing. But a minute later we heard squealing tires, someone peeling off down the street, big hurry."

Fuck. "Did you see—"

"No. Whoever it was was gone."

"What makes you so sure," JaneDoe demanded, "the Art Critic was after me? I mean considering you used to think I was him."

"His SUV followed you from the restaurant, and now it's parked across the street," Mark told her.

"Why the fuck didn't you bust him before he got here?"

"We just recently spotted him on the tapes, then found out from your attorney where you'd eaten dinner."

"We tried to warn you by phoning and messaging—but you weren't responding," Rarey said, going right at the curious part of the women's behavior.

JaneDoe educated the naïf: "Not responding is a response."

"To what?" Rarey wondered.

Lila, bless her, jumped in. "JaneDoe's been harassed by the media for weeks, tonight needed to be pure celebration. No intrusions."

Mark said, "Speaking of the media—"

"That's not a Chicago badge," JaneDoe noted, squinting at Rarey's shield.

He grinned. "Special Agent Nicolas Rarey, FBI."

JaneDoe went dead still. Deciding exactly what she was going t—

"Speaking of the media," Mark repeated, "they're out in force. But they don't know who you are, yet. For your privacy and safety, let me sneak both of you out of here and put you in a guarded hotel room for a couple of days."

"And if we haven't nailed the perp by then," Rarey promised, "my people can extend your stay."

JaneDoe locked eyes with Rarey.

"My privacy means that much to the FBI?"

"Yes," Mark cut in, "which is why Agent Rarey and I have to go chase down this creep. So if you ladies will excuse us."

"Don't count on it," JaneDoe warned.

EIGHTY-NINE / 2012

As Mark and his ebullient young handler walked back to the car Mark called the POD unit: "Drop whatever you're doing and see if any vehicles tailed the Suburban from One Sixty Blue to Kasey's house. Thanks."

Rarey grinned. "The Mastrizzis are looking for Tesca, and now Tesca disappears from Kasey's doorstep in a blaze of squealing tires. I love this case."

"You amused by the possibility they got to him before we did?" Mark asked as they got in the car.

"No, but I am enjoying the ride," Rarey said, buckling his harness. "Besides, maybe those weren't Mastrizzi tires. Maybe Tesca had an accomplice, who picked him up."

Mark started driving.

"Or," Rarey continued, "maybe Tesca fled on foot, the squealing tires had nothing to do with him."

"Wanna put money on either of those?"

"Shit no. But if the Mastrizzis did grab him—not ideal, but not a disaster."

"Except for the part where Tesca could've told us why Gianni and Lou were after him, maybe connect them to his Whack An Artist game."

"We can nail them for Tesca's murder."

"Call me when you find Tesca's corpse. It'll be next to Hoffa's. You'll get to sew two Mafia merit badges on your sash and make Eagle Agent."

Rarey studied him. "You in such a jolly mood because Tesca might be gone... or because JaneDoe kept kneeing you in the balls just now?"

"Tesca."

"Okay. But still, dude—why's she so angry at you? Why wouldn't she be happy to finally see her man?"

"Maybe she was faking it to make all you other cops think I'm just another pig she hates."

"Maybe. But why did JaneDoe especially hate me?"

"You're the supposedly smarter FBI, but you've been helping make her life hell instead of busting the guy who nearly killed her tonight."

"But that crack about the FBI being concerned about her privacy… Sounded almost as if she knew about the bugs."

"Nick, if I were stupid enough to violate FISA secrecy statutes by warning JaneDoe, I would've been smart enough to do it *before* she had a chance to blab about her and me."

Rarey gave a wry, equivocal shrug.

"Tell you, what, though," Mark said. "If it turns out you lied about removing the bugs, I'm gonna be pissed off enough to inform her lawyer."

Rarey considered that. Grinned. "See? You're having fun too."

orture. Until tonight it had been just a word. Tonight he was learning pain was a living thing, sentient lava studded with broken
glass, blistering its way through his veins, howling mockery at his
helplessness, turning every single second into a slow nightmare. And
Jay Branko had been like this for three hours. Alone in his office.
With nothing to ease his torment.

Booze or pills weren't options. Jay couldn't afford to be buzzed
if Lou called with news about Tesca; Jay's life depended on how he
handled that call.

If it came. The Mastrizzis might not catch Tesca tonight. Or ever.
Or maybe they already had caught Tesca, and learned Tesca hadn't
put that hit on Dale Phipps. So there wouldn't be a phone call. Just a
bullet or an explosion when Jay went down to the garage and got in
his car.

Could Lou arrange a hit so fast? Unlikely. Maybe Jay was safe
tonight no matter what.

Shit no. That's the kind of lazy assumption—

His burner rang.

Showtime.

Jay gathered himself. Answered with a relaxed, "Hey."

"Hey."

"How things?" Jay asked.

"Can't complain," Lou said. "Main deal is done, and we're getting
after that little side deal."

"My man! Now that is the shit. "

"I am, and it is. I'll be in touch when there's more news."

"I know it'll be good."

"Awright. Now you sound like the old you."

"C'mon, bro, that was just due diligence, me on the sensible business tip. My thang. But you gotta know I'm down with you, my bruthah, knew you'd make the smart call, and tonight's the proof."

"Damn straight. So you hang loose."

"Always."

Jay hung up, sighed, and vomited in the wastebasket.

Lou hung up and looked at his father.

Gianni raised a questioning eyebrow.

"Jay was kissing ass and putting his heart in it."

Gianni grinned. Somewhere an angel died, and three more turned in their harps and took early retirement.

NINETY-ONE / 2006

ello?... Hellohhhhhhhhhhhhhhhhhhhhhh..."
G'bye.

Lila's words and Tommy Tesca flowed away from each other, Lila's voice turning blurry gray and getting sucked like smoke back up into the intercom, simultaneously with Tommy being sucked down a gooey black drain that opened seconds after the needle jabbed his neck, he tried to fight but someone stole his bones and he was pouring down the soft soft black drain and then he was the blackness.

He woke shrieking. His bones had returned. Someone was hammering on his finger. Then the other nine, one by one. Then some of his crushed fingers were ripped off.

Fuckin' huge hairy *cazzo* in no shirt and a rubber apron doing the job.

Next to the *cazzo*, also in an apron, staring down at Tommy, was bald, bony old Vin The Blacksmith Santoro. Got the nickname back in the day for the number he did on a horse trainer. He was one of the Outfit senior citizens who'd been at the christening at Lou Mastrizzi's house, wondering why the fuck Tommy was there. The Blacksmith was Gianni Mastrizzi's oldest, closest, most loyal tool.

"Hiya Tommy." He let out a bemused snort. "Who'd'a thunk a useless fat turd like you, get so fuckin' famous." The Blacksmith gave Tommy an approving pat on the cheek, then removed his eyes.

And on and on. And on.

The Blacksmith and the *cazzo* gave Tommy a sendoff a saint would envy. When they'd worked themselves to exhaustion and Tommy was three hundred pounds of breathing raw hamburger that was about to give up on the breathing, The Blacksmith sent the *cazzo* away.

The raw hamburger heard what sounded like a heavy metal door slam shut. The crap you notice at a time like this, heh.

The Blacksmith pulled up a chair and put his lips close to the raw hamburger's ear. Hissed, "Gianni says to tell ya 'bout the first time he fucked your big-tit whore mom. Long time ago, before you was born. Fucked her up the ass then fucked her in the cunt without wiping her shit off his dick. And that's how you happened, Tommy. That's what you're fuckin' made of... Gianni says if you'da turned out even a little bit like him you'da been a made man, you'd'a almost been family. But ya turned out the brown stuff on his dick."

The raw hamburger's weak, wheezy breathing quickened.

Then slowed.

But didn't stop.

Torn, bloody lips trembled their way into a sneer.

Tommy exhaled something too labored and faint for The Blacksmith to tell if it was words.

"Speak the fuck up." He placed his ear by Tommy's mouth.

"Ash... ash..."

"Ash?"

"Ash-kuh..." Tommy enunciating as best he could with most of his teeth gone or shattered.

"Ask?"

"Yesh... Yoo, yoo ash-kuh... myee *Da-duh*... " The word made Tommy chuckle and gag up blood. "Yoo ash-kuh myee Da-duh... how come, heh, he din' cu' yoo in onnuh... shcaw."

"Score? What score?"

"Bigges' fucshin' evuh... An', an' wuz all my 'dea-uh..."

"What idea? The fuck wuzzit?"

"Wush, wush... myee... myee, mash..."

"Your wha'?"

What remained of Tommy's lips formed a jagged grin.

"Mash...duh...peesh."

"The fuck?!?!" The Blacksmith demanded.

Tommy wouldn't say.

The Blacksmith thumped and pumped Tommy's chest.

Tommy just laid there being dead, mutilated and satisfied.

NINETY-TWO / 2012

The POD unit found footage of a beige van following Tesca's Suburban. Got a shot of the plate.

The plates came up stolen. And the beige van disappeared into the southwest 'burbs.

A snitch ID'd Vuk Stetenich—the Serbian wheelman. The FBI grabbed Stetenich at O'Hare as he was boarding a redeye for Frankfurt, connecting to Belgrade.

All the Feds got out of him was that Zerbjka's crew was hired by someone throwing around elephant dollars; best money Stetenich had ever almost made.

Dale Phipps' amazing face had gone viral. Resulting in two Phipps sightings.

Both turned out to be teenagers with killer acne who'd been dimed by witty classmates.

There was no clue as to where the real Dale Phipps was tonight. Mark and Rarey began assembling timelines matching where Dale, the other faces on the murder board and their money had been during the past seven years.

At 3 AM Mark and Rarey went to tell Husak what they'd come up with. Husak was asleep in his chair. But as Mark and Rarey began to back out of his office, Husak woke and, yawning, insisted they brief him.

Mark told the tale. Detectives had been interviewing anyone with a connection to Dale. One of Dale's ex-girlfriends said in 2005 Dale was so frantic for cash he'd taken back a Laurie Desh canvas he'd given her, so he could sell it to pay off his debts. This happened a few days before Desh was murdered, after which the value of Desh's paintings jumped.

Judging from Dale's phone records, the person he likely owed money to was loan shark Tommy Tesca. Judging from what happened next, the two of them likely became partners.

In 2005, a Wisconsin artist named Richard Struger died in a bicycle accident. Before his death, three Struger paintings had been bought by Dale on behalf of anonymous clients. Over the next year, the paintings sold at a whopping profit.

Shortly after that, the Caymans shell companies were incorporated. During each of the next four years, one American artist, whose works cost five-figure, then six-figure sums, died from what looked like natural causes or an accident. Always with same pattern of purchases before their deaths and sales afterward—and always through the offshore shells.

Then in 2011 an artist in New Mexico died in her sleep—but this artist's works cost over a million a pop. More money than Dale's and Tesca's shell companies could afford. But suddenly they're partnered with several new shell companies that do have seven-figure resources.

"The Mastrizzis have that kind of money," Husak, now almost fully awake, suggested.

"Uh-huh," Mark yawned, "and that's the year Dale's consulting firm starts signing clients that are Mastrizzi fronts and friends."

"So it's all peaches and cream," Husak mused, "but despite that, Tesca disappears, comes back as the Art Critic, and starts whacking artists."

"But not the quiet way he'd been doing it," Mark said. "He's killing in Chicago, every couple of weeks, not making it look like accidents, in fact leaving serial killer signatures that'll draw attention—and naming his offshores after Gianni and Lou Mastrizzi."

"Not only walks away from this profitable scam, he wrecks it," Husak mused.

"They musta hurt his feelings really bad," Rarey suggested.

"Yeah." Husak frowned. "But it wasn't Tesca who hired the Serbs to kill Dale—Tesca wouldn't have ordered them to use the Hancock.

And it ain't the Mastrizzis—never woulda hired those bozos. So, who?"

"Don't have a name," Mark said, "but I have a theory: Scared money. Every year Dale and Tesca kill a more expensive painter. If this year the price goes to eight figures per painting—"

"Might be too rich for even the Mastrizzis," Husak said.

Rarey nodded. "So they bring in an outside investor—who panics when the Art Critic starts blowing the cover off their scam—and since Mr. Scared Money knows Dale can identify him… Ka-pow," Rarey said, firing his index finger.

Mark glanced at his watch. "I'll leave a message for Nardelli, ask if there's a wealthy friend of the Mastrizzis they'd trust enough to cut in. Right now Nick and I are—" Mark yawned, "—gonna unpack that list of Mastrizzi-connected firms that hired Dale, see if we find a candidate."

"No," Husak ruled, "you're going home."

"Lieut—"

"The two of you look, sound and smell like a couple of half-dead frogs."

More like three-quarters. Mark gestured surrender. "Just one more thing, Loo. After what happened at the Art Institute today, the Mastrizzis—"

"—will be looking to whack Dale, before we can catch him," Husak said.

Husak and Mark shared a dour silence, neither of them wanting to say it out loud.

So Rarey did. "Hey, just 'cause the Mastrizzis got to Tesca before we did doesn't mean they're gonna beat us to Dale. We're gonna win this race," he predicted, yawning.

NINETY-THREE / 2012

Dale entered the walk-in storage unit. Closed the door and opened the wheeled luggage that held costumes, guns and money. And a laptop and two burner phones.

Dale dressed in a full-bag burka with a veiled eye slit. And gloves. He'd stuffed the middle finger of the left glove, so none of his tells were visible. And he'd honed a passable accent by putting in hours reciting along with YouTube videos of Middle Eastern women speaking English.

After paying cash for a ticket, the devout Muslim woman spent a tense hour in a Greyhound waiting room. The devout Muslim's tension worsened as she boarded the bus, dreading that someone would start speaking Arabic to her.

A middle aged black woman sat next to the devout Muslim. Then did her best to be sociable in English, a danger Dale presumed the burka would preclude.

Dale pretended to have almost no English. His affable companion made a valiant effort to carry the conversation, pulling out magazines and pointing to pictures of clothing, jewelry, celebrities, cars, then proudly showing cell-phone photos of her grandkids at Disney World, knocking herself out to connect with the bashful foreigner.

The bashful foreigner whispered, "Very thanks you. But must make sleep. Sorry. Sorry. Much, much tired."

The affable woman's eyes narrowed. She muttered a sarcastic, "Uh-huh," feelings bruised by what she knew was going down. Same old same old.

Dale felt like shit. Murder, money laundering, interior decorating and now casual racism. Dale made a silent vow to Allah that he'd send a big fat check to that museum guard who saved his life.

When the devout woman got off the bus she wasn't the only modestly dressed Muslim rolling a suitcase through the terminal. Which is why Dale had gone to Detroit; significant Middle Eastern population.

Dale took a cab with a Latino driver. Handed the driver a print-out bearing the name and address of a motel. The motel wasn't in an Arab-American neighborhood, where someone might try to chat him up. The motel did accept cash, a full week in advance plus a deposit to cover extras.

Dale ordered in a *halal* meal and washed it down with beers from the mini-bar—wearing gloves to he wouldn't leave prints. For the sake of dexterity he'd switched to a pair of latex gloves. But after a few hours sweat was pooling in the fingertips. Was there such a thing as trench finger? Dale went back to the cotton gloves from his burka ensemble.

The latex crisis dealt with, Dale resumed grappling with a some-what more disastrous complication: His face was all over TV and the web. He'd only prepared for hiding from the Mastrizzis. Not from them, the police, and much of the Earth's population.

He had fifteen thousand in cash. Plenty more in accounts and safe deposit boxes in the Caymans and Liechtenstien. Two passports, one in his name and one an alias. Unusable; both sported photos of his now famous face.

Shit. Dale had discovered a breathtakingly expensive Swiss clinic that specialized in deeply private facial renovations. But that plan assumed he'd be able to get his face to Switzerland. Now, best Dale could do was sneak into Canada and hire a bent plastic surgeon who did quality work, and wouldn't sell him to the Mastrizzis. Did they have bent surgeons in Canada? They must. Even Canada. But how do you find one?

Dale needed sleep. Turned out the lights. Closed his eyes.

No fucking way.

Dale turned the TV on. Breaking news: The Art Critic's vehicle had been found. But it was empty. Police refused to say if they had an idea where the Art Critic might be.

Dale had an idea where Tommy might be. Dale tried not to think of what the Mastrizzis were doing to Tommy at this moment. Tried to calmly assess his options to avoid that same treatment.

A) Negotiate with the Mastrizzis. Hope his carefully dispersed copies of their art transactions would provide enough leverage to save his life.

B) Negotiate with the cops. Hope they weren't too corrupt and/or incompetent to save his life.

C) Suicide. His only pain-free death option… Nah. Didn't have the stones. Plus he knew he'd die hearing the far-off sound of Dorian's derisive snickering…

Dorian. The museum.

The memories Dale had been repressing all day—easy enough while he was a hundred-forty-pounds of adrenaline obsessed with *escape*—came flooding in. The goon's hand clamping on his shoulder. Him fleeing, lungs heart head pounding. Shooting and being shot at, flailing through that madhouse crush of berserk tourists. Shaved Head leveling his gun at Dale's forehead. A bullet hitting Shaved Head instead of him. Then him running gasping terrified again.

When dawn came Dale was still awake, but the trembling had subsided.

NINETY-FOUR / 2012

The park bench the well-tailored English gentleman chose wasn't favored by tourists. Trees and a statue obstructed its view of an arrogantly pretty Swiss lake. They also obstructed tourists' view of the bench, which made it a favorite of young lovers and pot-heads.

Stephan Densford-Kent wasn't young, though he did sometimes smoke pot, and still owned a full head of sandy-colored hair only partially streaked with gray, and the ruddy-cheeked face of a charming, wrinkled, contentedly corrupt seventy-year-old schoolboy.

Soon after Densford-Kent sat he was joined by a casually but expensively dressed thirty-two-year-old. Not his lover or dealer. His favorite shooter.

Densford-Kent said, "A nearly perfect afternoon, don't you think?"

"Nearly. What's gone wrong?"

"The art project has been temporarily suspended."

"How temporarily?"

"To be determined. The client has a more pressing need."

"How pressing?"

"Extremely. Rush job. But far simpler than the project. The subject isn't famous. And there's no need to make it appear to be something other than it is."

"So it pays less."

"Merely your standard luxurious rate."

"Damn. But, seeing as how I hate to disappoint you, and I'm suddenly unemployed—I'm there. Soon as you tell me where 'there' is."

Densford-Kent gave the shooter a dubious, narrow-eyed look. "You will fly in, do the job, and leave."

"Where?"

A small, reluctant silence.

"Chicago."

With a bone-dry hint of amusement the shooter replied, "Not a problem."

"Have I your word you'll behave? I must believe that."

"Yes you must," the shooter agreed, "because you don't have anyone else available. If you did you wouldn't have contacted me."

"Cheeky cunt," Densford-Kent complained, fondly. He shook the shooter's hand, transferring a thumb drive containing a dossier on Jay Branko.

Took a couple of days, but Mark and Rarey figured out Mr. Scared Money's given name.

Dale Phipps' most lucrative client was JB Structural. A construction firm that regularly employed a subcontractor whose major shareholder was a trust controlled by the Mastrizzis. JB also favored a trucking firm owned by a Mastrizzi cousin, and construction unions whose execs were Mastrizzi blood brothers.

JB Structural was owned by Jay Branko. According to Ed Nardelli, Branko's deceased father and Gianni Mastrizzi had always played well together. A meaningful relationship their sons were emulating.

Rarey turned up an FBI surveillance photo of Lou Mastrizzi playing golf in a foursome that included Branko. At a country club to which they both belonged.

Branko owned a luxury box at the United Center. Three doors down from Lou's.

Branko could afford a multi-million investment in buying art and murdering the artist. Which also meant, for Jay, handing a hit man a briefcase full of hundreds wasn't elephant dollars, it was loose change.

But wait, that's not all Mark got when he rush-ordered his very own copy of JB's financials. Mark also received, at no extra charge, this priceless bonus data: JB's most lucrative contracts were with the city and county. Deals you don't land unless you're seriously wired into Chicago's political heavyweights.

JB Structural was a nexus of shadowy, complex, big-dollar interactions between the Outfit and the Machine.

When Mark and Rarey laid it out for Husak, Rarey exulted, with a touching blend of joy, ambition and bulletproof youth, "This could be huuuge."

"Yes it could," Husak said, to Mark, quietly. A warning.

NINETY-SIX / 2012

I f any other subcontractor pulled this shit, Jay Branko would've fired the son of a bitch, sued his balls off and gone at his shin with a tire iron. All Jay could do to Todd Sullivan, of Sullivan Brothers Concrete, was chew him out. Todd was married to a niece of Cousin Eddie, the second most dangerous man in City Hall. Piss Eddie off, and bye-bye government contracts—like this one, to retrofit crumbling overpasses on the Dan Ryan. A job on which Cousin Eddie's nephew-in-law had been pouring substandard concrete.

"Goddamnit, Todd! Women, children and Aldermen drive across those goddamn things. If one of those fuckers collapses—"

"Ain't gonna happen," Sullivan scoffed.

"—you and me end up broke and living in a cage with big black cocks in our mouths. *That's* what ain't gonna happen, 'cause you're gonna rip out that mud you poured and re-do every fucking inch."

Sullivan shrugged. "If that's what you want."

"And you're gonna eat every fucking dime."

"Dream on."

Jay dreamed of a tire iron hitting bone. "Every fucking dime."

"Nah. Tell you what, show of good faith, twenty-five percent discount." Sullivan gave him a sour, defiant grin. "Final offer."

"You eat the cost, and I don't inform Cousin Eddie you've been pulling shit that's gonna kill voters. Final offer."

The defiance drained out of Sullivan's face.

That's right, you dumb fuck, that Cousin Eddie shit cuts both ways.

After the dumb fuck left Jay's office, Jay leaned back in his chair, feeling human again. It had been two days since his conversation with Lou. The call had gone well. But did that mean things were okay, or that Lou was playing him? Jay had been obsessing about how much danger he was or wasn't in—

His secretary buzzed. There was a Homicide detective and an FBI agent asking to see him.

Christ. So busy pissing his pants about the Mastrizzis he hadn't given much thought to the police. No point; Zerbjka, the only shooter who'd met Jay, was dead.

Then what the hell were they here about? A cop *and* a Fed?

"I'm Detective Bergman, and this is Special Agent Rarey."

"Gentlemen," Jay said, coming out from behind his desk to shake hands. "Can I get you something? Water, coffee, tea, soda, sports drinks, got the whole fuckin' 7-11 going on. When my dad built this place he'd put down shot glasses and pour without asking."

"Thanks, no," Bergman said. The cop was eyeing photos on the wall of Jay with the Mayor and other heavies.

"Please," Jay said, gesturing for them to sit at the coffee table; a secure, important man. Not a man with his brain blazing: *SHIT, it's that cop who took out Zerbjka, this is about Dale. But this fucking baby-faced Fed wouldn't be here about a local hit—more likely international stuff like the art scam—or my deals with the city?* "How can I help you?"

Bergman said, "We're trying to locate Dale Phipps. I understand you're one of Phipps' clients."

"My firm is. In fact Phipps stopped by a couple of times the past few weeks." Cops would find that in the security logs anyway. "Was pitching me some big lumpy steel sculpture."

"Remember the name of the sculptor?"

"No. Just that Phipps was advising me to shell out eighty grand for something looked like it came from a plane crash."

"Do you know of anyone who'd want Phipps dead?"

"If there was he never said."

"Phipps ever mention places he vacationed, a favorite getaway?"

Jay shook his head. "Wasn't like we were buddies. Only ever talked business."

"Got it. Thank you for your time, Mr. Branko."

"Anything I can do, Detective."

"If Phipps gets in touch, please let me know," Bergman said, handing Branko his card.

"Immediately," Jay promised.

Bergman and Rarey started to leave. Bergman stopped. "Oh—one more thing. How did you choose Phipps?"

Jay's stomach sank. He furrowed his brow, trying to look perplexed. "Uh… Someone recommended…"

"You don't remember who?"

"It was… couple, three years ago, trade show at McCormick…" Jay flashed a sheepish grin. "I'm at this bar, late, six or seven of us… Somebody wrote 'Dale Phipps' on a napkin… Sorry."

"Which trade show?"

"The construction technologies expo—I think. Been through hundreds of those damn things."

"But I assume your secretary has a record of every damn one."

Jay's gut churned. He had no clue if Bergman had believed him. Cop had a poker face like a Chinese banker.

And what the fuck was that teenage FBI prick about? Never said a word. Sat there with that snarky smirk, eyeballing Jay like he was a fucking specimen on a slide. The fuck the FBI want with me?

Christ. Gonna have to tell Lou. Bad enough a cop was asking about Dale. But the motherfucking FBI? The Outfit's favorite guys.

Shit, shit, *shit*. No way around it. If Jay doesn't tell Lou the cops *and the FBI* were here, he's dead. Which he might be anyway when he tells Lou they were asking who introduced him to Phipps. Because that person was Lou.

Jay took out a shot glass. Opened a bottle of vodka and took a swig from the bottle.

He pulled out his burner. Went to thumb Lou's number—*No!*

Had to make one other call first. Also risky. But also Jay's only possible leverage. The one guy who might have reason and enough juice to protect him.

Jay phoned Cousin Eddie.

id it work?" Husak asked.

"Yeah," Mark told his boss, "when I asked Branko who introduced him to Phipps, he began quietly, discreetly shitting bricks."

Mark had to drop some pressure on Branko, because there was no hard evidence linking him to the attempted hit on Phipps.

The surviving Serb couldn't ID Branko. And Branko's fiscals showed no money trail; whatever upfront cash he'd paid Zerbjka hadn't come out of a bank account.

Cops armed with search warrants had tossed Zerbjka's house, car and place of business—Zerbjka was landlord of a former tavern that housed a Serb social club, The Partizan Sporting Association. The cops found some naughty assault weapons, but not the prize: Branko's cash. If Branko's fingerprints were on the money, Mark could've hauled Branko's ass in.

So Mark's only move was to toss the Phipps grenade and see if Branko detonated. Mark was betting Branko would rush to inform Lou Mastrizzi that a cop—and a Fed—had dropped in and asked a magic question.

That was a conversation Branko and Mastrizzi wouldn't have on any phone. Which is why the cops had Branko under surveillance, and the FBI put eyes on Lou. With luck, they'd get photographic evidence of Branko meeting Lou. In any case, it'd be interesting to see what the stress did to that relationship.

Nick Rarey was so enthused about the broader implications of Branko's discreet brick-shitting (the Outfit + Chicago Politicians!) that he gave up monitoring Mark, and returned to his own office to monitor the surveillance on Lou, and to help map JB Structural's maze of deals, hoping to find a trail of contract crumbs that led from

City Hall on one side to Outfit-infected contractors and unions on the other.

Tommy Tesca and Dale Phipps remained invisible. In Tesca's case the condition was probably permanent; Ed Nardelli's informants reported that Mastrizzi's soldiers had stopped looking for Tesca and returned to their regularly scheduled felonies.

JaneDoe stubbornly remained on Mark's mind.

JaneDoe and Lila had refused to move to a hotel. JaneDoe spent the night at Lila's, waiting for the reporters swarming the block to move on. Which the reporters did, after the cops announced they had no idea why the Art Critic abandoned his vehicle there, because none of the block's residents was an artist.

Mark, who knew JaneDoe wouldn't go home if the FBI bugs were still in place, phoned Lila, burner to burner. Asked Lila to tell JaneDoe the bugs were gone. And that JaneDoe should remain vigilant, but there were indications the Art Critic had left town.

Lila said, "JaneDoe's in the shower—I'm gonna go hand her the phone."

"Don't—I can't talk now."

"Well… Is there anything else—like, you wanna arrange another, more private get-together with her than that last one?"

"Not yet."

Lila sighed, "Okay," in a tone that conveyed disappointment in Mark's poor judgment, and urged him to reconsider, implying JaneDoe was getting unhappier by the minute, and if Mark didn't put his arms around her soon, he might never, not that Lila was going to meddle by offering advice Mark would be wise to take to heart.

NINETY-EIGHT / 2012

ranko left his office at 7:43 PM. Went home. Not to his house in Kenilworth. To a pied-a-terre he kept in a Streeterville high-rise.

At 12:21 AM Branko's car emerged from the building's garage.

Branko drove to Bridgeport, parked, and at 12:38 AM entered Teddy Flynn's, a venerable Irish saloon that was sandwiched between the equally venerable Lyden & O'Leary Mortuary on one side and Scanlon Brothers Electrical & Plumbing Supplies on the other.

The first unit following Branko parked across the street. The second and third units parked at either end of the alley behind Teddy Flynn's, in case Branko tried slipping out the back.

A few minutes later Detective Wendy Hsu strolled into Flynn's and looked around, as if expecting to meet someone. She didn't spot Branko, so she took a seat at the bar and ordered a light beer. Took a sip, checked her watch, looked around the room again.

The bartender asked, "You not gettin' stood up, are you darlin'?"

Hsu admitted, "No, this is my bad. I'm late. Has a beefy hunk of a guy, forty, wavy dark blond hair, brown leather jacket, been in?"

The bartender shook his head.

But a wrinkled white-haired stud one stool down from Hsu said, "I seen him. Chugged a shot and headed for the gents. Been in there a while."

The bartender scowled at the wrinkled white-haired stud, who chose not to notice the warning. "Don't worry hon," the erotic geriatric comforted Hsu, "if he fell in, I'll stand ya a drink."

"Maybe when I get back from the lady's," she grinned.

Hsu went to the rear of the bar; bathrooms on the left, a staircase leading down to a basement on the right.

Hsu put on a goofy inebriated grin and mistakenly lurched into the men's room. It was empty. She went to the staircase. A sign above it said PRIVATE. She peered down the stairs—

"No bathrooms down there, darlin'."

The bartender. Standing right behind her.

"Thanks." Hsu went into the lady's room, informed the wire on her wrist that the bartender had made her, and Branko was in the basement.

Hsu finished her beer, slapped down an extra ten, told the bartender to pour the wrinkled white-haired stud a drink, and left.

Forty-eight minutes later Branko emerged from Flynn's and drove back to Streeterville. Hsu and Montero tailed him. The second unit sat on the front of Flynn's, the third unit sat on the alley. The bar closed at 3 AM. Lou Mastrizzi wasn't among the exiting customers.

Next morning Mark phoned Rarey, to check on Lou Mastrizzi's whereabouts last night. Rarey said Lou left his home at 11:39 PM, arrived at the Mastrizzi HQ beneath ZeeZeeZ bowling alley in Downer's Grove at 12:26 AM, emerged at 2:47 and drove home.

It was physically impossible for Lou Mastrizzi to have been at Teddy Flynn's while Branko was there.

"So who the fuck did Branko meet?" Husak wondered.

Mark thought it over. "I'll call Doonie."

"Bridgeport," Husak nodded, recognizing the logic.

Doonie laughed. "The guy who Branko met with never came outta Teddy Flynn's' cause the guy never set foot in the joint."

"Ah crap," Mark moaned, having an idea what was coming.

"During Prohibition, Flynn's was a big-time speak called Mabel's. Basement's fulla rabbit holes. These hidden doors, connect to the basements of Scanlon's Plumbing on one side and Lyden's meat locker on the other. The guy Branko met was in one of those."

"And we'll never know which of Lou's guys it was."

"None. Least nobody Italian. I'm thinkin' Irish. 'Cause the type a hardhead Hibernians who own that block are still pissed about Torrio whacking O'Banion in 1924. I'll see ya at work tomorrow."

"Doctor cleared you?"

"Not the one I saw today. Got a 9 AM tomorrow with Dr. Bobby Ryan."

Mark phoned Ed Nardelli. "Gianni and Lou got any close Irish friends?"

"Not that they'd trust with *this* shit."

If Doonie's theoretical Irishman wasn't a friend of the Mastrizzis, he must be a friend of Branko's. What Irishman is Branko tight with who has enough clout to handle *this* shit?

Gangster? Cop? Pol?

NINETY-NINE / 2012

"Might be a gangster or a cop if Branko was looking for protection from the Mastrizzis," Husak mused. "For protection from us, it'd be a pol or someone who owns a few. But I don't want you chasing Doonie's phantom Irishman. Any new ideas for going at Branko?"

"Just an old one," Mark said. "I'm gonna re-toss Zerbjka's home and club, see if the guys missed anything—" the burner vibrated in Mark's coat pocket—he silenced it— "when they searched for Branko's down payment."

Husak waited to see if Mark took the call, which Mark would if it were business.

Mark didn't.

Husak made a shooing gesture. "Go on, call her back."

Mark gave Husak a small rueful nod, acknowledging yeah, Loo, you're right, it's a woman.

Mark went to the parking lot and called Lila back. Lila picked up in the middle of the third ring—

"Hi, Detective," JaneDoe said. A warm and threatening purr.

A split-second of shock at the unexpected voice, then the sound of it filled Mark, his whole body.

"Hi."

"Called at a bad moment just before, didn't I," she drawled.

"This is a good moment," Mark said.

"Shame there have been so few. I'm home. How's tonight?"

Tonight...? "Yeah. After eleven. Should work."

"Should?"

"I will do everything I can to make sure it does."

"But shit happens."

"Right now, a lot of it."

"I've noticed that."

"And, like it or not," Mark quietly noted, "sometimes it's shit I have to deal with right away."

"Yes I am," JaneDoe informed him.

Mark read an interview Kaz and Kimmie did with the wheelman, Vuk Stetenich, prior to searching Zerbjka's home and business.

Stetenich claimed Zerbjka hadn't paid him any upfront—Zee was a mean crazy prick you didn't mess with about shit like that. The other thing Stetenich was adamant about was how Zee's wife Roza was the last person Zee'd've trusted to know where he hid his money. Fucking hated each other, those two.

Mark went to the Partizan Sporting Association.

ONE HUNDRED / 2012

The social club was in Eastside, a far southeast district whose steel mills had been a magnet for Balkan immigrants in the early 1900s.

By the early 2000s the mills had emigrated to China. Along the lakefront, the neighborhood was sprouting sleek condo towers and townhomes. Inland, the neighborhood was a throwback cityscape of aging bungalows and low-rise apartments.

The Partizan Sporting Association was housed in what had been a corner tavern, in a 1930s two-story brick four-flat.

The club was near-empty. Nobody was watching the video of Partizan soccer triumphs silently flowing across two huge flatscreens. There were a couple of tables of old guys playing cards and nursing beers. There were a couple of late-teen guys trying to look hard enough to be in a crew like Zerbjka's, soon as they tore themselves away from the arcade shooter game. The bartender was sixty, fat and texting. Mark handed him the search warrant.

"Again?" the bartender wearily marveled.

"Again," Mark sympathized.

The bartender gestured for Mark to go, do what you will, and resumed texting.

Mark, aided by a trio of unis, worked from the roof down. Nothing up there but a satellite dish decorated with pigeon graffiti.

The second floor was a small apartment that had been converted to an office. There was a safe hidden inside a lower cabinet in the kitchen; the first searchers had found a few grand in it, none bearing Branko's prints.

In the floor under Zerbjka's office chair there was a hiding space where Kaz and Kimmie had found two machine pistols. Mark's and the unis' re-inspection of the walls, floors, ceilings, furniture and fixtures proved Kaz and Kimmie hadn't missed a thing.

Mark let the unis search the tavern on the ground floor. He didn't see Zerbjka hiding his money in a public space.

Mark went to the basement. Metal beer kegs. Broken barstools. Cartons of glassware, toilet paper, cleaning supplies, bulbs, paint cans, Partizan T-shirts. A padlocked closet, which Mark opened with a key provided by the bartender. Nothing inside but cases of booze.

On the opposite wall, the one facing the alley, was the furnace. The concrete floor around it was stained black. On the wall behind the furnace there was a bricked-in square where a coal chute used to be; the building was as old as it looked—

Like from Prohibition. When this place must have been a speak.

Mark went to the wall that separated the tavern basement from the basement of the adjoining apartments. That wall was lined with historic dead appliances. A 1960s brute of a restaurant refrigerator. A 1970s earth-tone brown washing machine and matching dryer.

Mark inspected inside each relic. Nothing. He tried to move the refrigerator but it barely budged; wasn't an object under which you'd hide something you might want to get at in a hurry, by yourself.

The washing machine was lighter. Mark tipped it forward, looked underneath and saw a steel plate set into the concrete floor. He moved the washer aside.

There was a handle in the steel plate. Mark swung the plate up. Beneath it crumbling brick steps led down to what had been a tunnel to the next basement. Hurray for civic traditions.

The entrance to the tunnel was bricked up. There was a three-foot-square dirt floor in front of the bricked-up tunnel. Most of the dirt floor was covered by a filthy old sheet of masonite.

Mark lifted the ancient masonite.

Found a very modern floor safe.

ONE HUNDRED-ONE / 2012

The Department's #1 Ace Expert Champion Safe-Cracking TV Star put down his drill, grasped the safe's handle, shot Mark an aristocratically confident look and tugged. The handle turned, the bolts snicked back, the TV Star opened the safe, pressed a button on his watch and informed Mark, "One minute fifty-three seconds."

"Shame it took you ninety-seven minutes fourteen-point-six seconds to get here," Mark muttered, peering into the safe. He pulled out a Trader Joe's reusable shopping bag. It was filled with bundles of reusable hundred dollar bills.

Mark handed the money to a rookie TV Star. Told her, "Lights and siren all the way to the lab. Walk in the door and start processing."

"Yessir."

The rookie TV Star hustled up the basement stairs. Mark was right behind, pulling out his cell and contacting the surveillance unit.

Jim Montero answered. They were tailing Branko, who was heading west on the 88. They just passed Downer's Grove.

Shit; Branko was outside Chicago's jurisdiction. Mark told Montero to let him know soon as Branko got where he was going.

Mark got in his car, called Husak, told him about the cash and that he was going to catch up with the surveillance, so if the lab got a fingerprint hit Mark would be there to collect Branko. Or at least witness it—off Chicago turf, Mark would have to watch the FBI cuff Branko.

Mark hit the siren and called Rarey as he drove.

"Awesome!" Rarey shouted, and hung up.

Mark was charging up the Tri-State towards the 88 when Montero called to say Branko had exited the 88 and was heading south on State 56.

"Where the hell is that?" Mark asked.

"Little bit past Aurora."

"Jesus, where's he going?"

"Let you know soon as he stops."

Fuck. The dashboard clock said 7:56. And Mark was headed out past where God left his roller skates. Fuck.

Mark killed the siren and party lights, slowed to sixty-five, took out his burner and called JaneDoe.

She didn't pick up until the fifth ring. Said a quiet, wary, "Hi."

"Hi... Listen, I—"

"You're fucking kidding me."

"It's—"

She hung up.

Mark's regular phone rang.

Montero: "The eagle has landed. Wanna guess where?"

"No."

"He's going to Rambo-Land."

ONE HUNDRED-TWO / 2012

It was located in a hollow but was easy to find in the dark, its presence announced by the hard glow of stadium lights banging against the rural night sky.

But it wasn't a ballpark. It was a bulletpark. Had a couple of fixed-target shooting ranges, plus a 3-D feature attraction: The Prairie Storm Tactical Shooting Course, a walk-through firing range Built To Special Forces Specs. It was a Third Worldish village with automated Muslimish targets popping up from windows, doorways, rooftops, boulders, a wrecked Humvee and—Coppola homage—erupting from the middle of a pond.

There was no way two unmarked cars containing plainclothes cops could surreptitiously park in the lot and eyeball the place.

Wendy Hsu got into the back seat of the second car, which parked a quarter-mile up the road. Jim Montero drove into Prairie Storm alone, plunked down a VISA and bought himself the right to play in the fantasy SEAL league. He was next in line behind Branko.

Montero went to the waiting area and sat a few chairs away from Branko, who was staring at the floor.

Montero said, "Hi."

"Hi," Branko grunted.

"P226," Montero commented, referring to the weapon strapped to Branko's leg. "Nice piece."

"Thanks... Listen, nothing personal, I uh, need to focus."

Montero made a *no problem* gesture, and got interested in a copy of *Law Enforcement Weapons* magazine. Most of it was devoted to military-grade mass slaughter machines, of less interest to the average law enforcer than to the average survivalist who needed to prevent the black helicopters from fluoridating his freedom.

Branko's name was called. He headed out to the course.

Montero's phone rang. It was Hsu.

Montero said, "Hi Hon," as if greeting his wife and not the lesbian with whom he spent the majority of his waking hours and trusted with his life.

"Sorry sweetie, but Bergman and the FBI are here, and Bergman just got confirmation Branko's prints are all over the cash. We're coming to collect him, so you don't get to play with your gun tonight."

Damn.

Mark and Rarey introduced themselves to the owner, T. W. Mueller, who escorted them to the observation tower where a range master had a view of the tactical course.

Branko looked jittery out there, movements jerky and shots going wide as he reacted to each surprise.

"I can get on the PA, tell him to holster his weapon and come back to the office," Mueller offered.

Mark shook his head. "Let him finish."

"You don't want to let him know something's wrong, while he's out there with that Sig in his hand," Mueller surmised.

"Affirmative."

Branko would recognize Mark and Rarey, so two Feds and two cops waited for Branko inside the door where he'd re-enter the building. Mark and Rarey remained in the tower where they could keep an eye on Branko while he was on the course.

A mechanical Muslim swung out of an alley to Branko's left—he whirled and fired—nothing happened, he'd drained his clip. Branko popped the empty, slammed in a fresh load—too late, the bad guy had snapped back out of sight.

"Bummer, dude," Rarey sympathized, "drive all the way out here thinking this was going to make you feel safer..."

Branko came to a halt. The wrecked Humvee was directly ahead. Branko scanned both sides of the street, checking every door and window.

Branko edged forward, gun in a combat grip—

A terrorist popped out of the wrecked Humvee's turret—

This time Branko raised his weapon smoothly, took a moment to aim before—

Branko jerked backward and landed on his back, looking as if he'd just lost a gunfight with a plywood jihadi.

The wound in Branko's forehead and the blood leaking from it looked real. Mark was betting the shot was fired by a biological gunman somewhere in the darkness out past the far end of the tactical course.

ONE HUNDRED-THREE / 2012

The Kane County TV Star placed a tripod on the spot where Branko had been standing. There was a laser mounted on the tripod, raised to the exact height at which the bullet met Branko's forehead. The Kane County TV Star tilted the laser so it was at the exact angle of the entry wound. He turned the laser on. It pointed to the exact spot the bullet had been fired from.

Forty feet up the service ladder on a transmission tower a good 400 yards from the Prairie Storm Tactical Shooting Course.

Mark and Rarey worked through the night. Shuffled into Husak's office after 11 AM.

"According to Nardelli," Mark yawned, "nobody in Gianni's crew makes that shot. Hadda be a specialist."

"Yeah," Rarey enthused, "dude who makes that shot, you know he's gonna have a whole lotta game."

"So this specialist was also tailing Branko, but we didn't spot him," Husak groused.

"He wasn't tailing Branko," Mark declared. "No way the shooter finds that firing position in the dark. So—"

"He knew where Branko was going. How'd Branko make the reservation?" Husak asked.

"Online. Someone's been snooping on Branko's computer—TV Stars found spyware."

Husak's phone rang. He answered, listened and hung up. "Ballistics. The slug that killed Branko was a .300 Winchester magnum."

"No matches in the database," Rarey predicted.

"Nope."

"A whole lotta game," Rarey repeated, pleased to be adding a high-end assassin to the FBI's already yummy menu of targets.

There was a quick knock on the door and Doonie strolled in.

"Morning, gentlemen," Doonie said.

"Just barely," Husak said, with a pointed glance at his watch.

"Loo, I got here soon as the doc took his thumb out of his ass and pressed the back-to-work button. Hi," Doon said to Rarey, then looked at Mark and said, "You need a nap."

"Thanks Mom."

"Hey, you're not as young any more as he is," Doonie replied, indicating Rarey. "We find out who Branko met at Teddy Flynn's the other night?"

"Nope."

"So," Doonie mused, "Dale Phipps is all we got left, assuming the Mastrizzis ain't done him too."

"So Doon," Husak asked, "what's your idea for locating Dale?"

Doonie thought it over. "Let Mark sleep on it, see what he comes up with."

Mark went to Homicide's crash rack for a couple of hours.

When Mark returned he found Doonie staring accusingly at his computer.

"What?" Mark asked.

"Pure crap."

More forensics had come in. The shooter hadn't left prints or trace on the tower. Or footprints in the dirt around it; he'd pulled his car up to the tower's concrete base. The tread marks in the dirt were from middle-of-the-line Hankooks, found on millions of boring, nobody would give a second glance compact sedans.

"So what's your idea for finding Dale? "Doonie asked.

After a moment Mark said, "We knock off at six and grab a drink."

They knocked off at seven-forty, having made the same lack of progress they would have if they'd knocked off at six. Or five, or four.

Had their traditional working dinner, burgers and bourbon.

Mark inquired how Phyl and the kids were doing. Doonie caught him up. Mark asked how the cuts on Doonie's back were doing. Doonie said, "They only hurt when I talk about 'em. How's *our girl* doing?"

Mark gave an ambiguous shrug.

"You sayin' you ain't been in touch, or you have and things ain't so good?"

Mark said, "Only hurts when I talk about it."

So they discussed the case for a few minutes, then gave up on that too.

Mark tried to read a novel. His eyes dribbled down the page. Mark thought about calling JaneDoe.

No point. Even if she'd agree, it'd be insane to set up another visit; no way to be sure he'd be able to show. And that would be the end of things. Assuming things weren't dead already.

But they could talk on the phone, if JaneDoe didn't hang up when she heard his voice.

Or was she waiting for him to call? And getting angrier when he didn't.

Or should he just go over there right now—

Mark's landline rang. "Hello."

"Is that you, Detective Bergman?" A whispery voice.

"Who's calling?"

There was the sound of tense, trembly breathing. The voice finally brought itself to say, "Dale Phipps."

ONE HUNDRED-FOUR / 2012

Dale was watching as the morning news shows excitedly tore open the latest gift from the ratings gods: Chicago construction magnate Jay Branko had been assassinated by a sharpshooter—while Branko was blasting his way through a Special Forces combat arms course. The police were refusing to comment, freeing the networks' guest speculators to wallow in the obvious military and/or espionage implications.

Dale's emotions were mixed. On one hand Dale was pleased Lou had hired an exponentially more competent shooter to kill Jay than Jay had hired to kill Dale. On the other hand every last one of Lou's competent killers were now hunting Dale. On the third hand Dale was facing the hard fact his escape plan was a bust. Had no idea how to hire someone who could sneak him into Canada—even as a white male. Forget the results if he were a veiled Muslim woman.

Maybe he could find a place in the woods where he could sneak across on his own… As if he could navigate in the wilderness, let alone survive in it.

But he couldn't sit in this motel until his cash ran out or Lou's muscle showed up.

Dale wired money from a Liechtenstein account to his lawyer in the Caymans.

The Caymans lawyer contacted Chicago criminal attorney Ross Kurnit. Instructed Kurnit to buy a burner phone.

Dale called Kurnit. When the lawyer learned Dale would be ratting out the Mastrizzis, there was a moment of hesitation, then he upped his fee.

The Caymans lawyer wired a retainer to Kurnit. If the cops traced the payment, all they'd get was the routing number of a Caymans bank.

The veiled Muslim woman took a six-hour bus ride to Gary, Indiana. When the cops traced the cell tower her call came through, it wouldn't be in Detroit.

She took a cab to Indiana University Northwest. Campuses were less freaked out by diversity. And the cell tower wouldn't be at the bus station.

She found a funky vegan coffee house where people would be too hip to stare. Drank tea and chewed a chalky muffin, killing time and appetite until it was late enough to try contacting Detective Bergman at home.

Bergman's phone was unlisted, but it had taken only a couple of minutes online to find out he owned a condo. Plus the address, phone number and how much Bergman paid for his one-bedroom 820-square-foot unit.

The veiled Muslim woman went into one of the coffee house's unisex bathrooms. Locked the door. Phoned a cab company and asked for a pick-up in five minutes. Then she phoned Bergman.

"Who's calling?"

Her throat tightened. She forced herself to breathe. "Dale Phipps."

Two seconds of silence.

"It's good you called. Let's get you safe, tell me where you are and I'll bring you in."

"Not yet. I want full immunity."

"From what?"

"Everything I've ever done."

"What do I get?"

"Lou and Gianni. Murder, money laundering, tax evasion. And the name of their next target."

"That might work. How do I contact you?"

"You don't."

"You gonna call this phone?"

"Or your cell, or your office line. It'll vary."

Dale hung up. Took the cab to the bus station and returned to Detroit.

ONE HUNDRED-FIVE / 2012

First call Mark made was to tech services, to trace Dale's call. Second call was to the Gary, Indiana police.

Third was to Husak.

Husak picked up. "Yeah?" There was a TV playing.

"Sorry to call at home, Loo. I just got off the phone with Dale Phipps."

Husak said he'd kick the news up the chain, set up a meeting of the relevant parties for as early tomorrow as possible.

Fourth call Mark made was to Nick Rarey. It went to voicemail. Mark hung up and redialed. Voicemail. Mark hung up and redialed. Voicemail. Redial.

Rarey picked up, panting heavily. "This better be the best phone call ever, you prick."

"I've asked the Gary, Indiana cops to sweep the area around the cell tower Dale Phipps called me from fifteen minutes ago. Wouldn't hurt if you guys got down there too."

"Done! What'd he want?"

"A free ride and witness protection, in exchange for the Mastrizzis."

Rarey quietly luxuriated, "O-kayyyy."

"Nick, wipe the grin off your face," Mark advised. "Don't let her see how happy you are you stopped and answered the phone."

ONE HUNDRED-SIX / 2012

Mark briefed the well-dressed sober-faced visitors in Husak's office: senior FBI agent Sten Ostergaard, and Assistant U.S. Attorney Lee Kelley.

"My home and office lines are programmed to forward calls to my cell, so there's no way I can miss Phipps' call," Mark concluded, to assure the Feds the local yokels had all their digital ducks in a row.

The Feds then assured the yokels they'd have no problem getting their legal ducks in a row. All the statutes Phipps violated—except the murders—were federal. The Feds were fine with granting immunity on those if Phipps could deliver Mastrizzi father and son. After which Phipps disappears into witness protection, and, in the half-dozen states where Phipps was at the very least an accessory to murdering an artist, the local prosecutors would have to swallow it.

"Phipps' attorney should call me, fast," Kelley told Mark. "But tell Phipps if he can deliver Gianni and Lou, *don't wait for the paperwork*—I guarantee the deal, he should turn his ass in before it gets shot off."

"Got it," Mark said. He asked Ostergaard, "Any progress in Gary?"

"Nothing yet. You'll know soon as I do."

The meeting ended on that collegial note and the Feds made their exit.

"Get any sleep last night?" Husak asked.

"Enough." Mark turned to leave Husak's office. Saw Doonie seated at his desk, glowering across the room at three plainclothes cops who were walking into the bullpen: Two young ones, and a tall gaunt vet who had small eyes and a long face coated with three days' worth of gray-white stubble, which emphasized the desperation of the dark brown dye job on his comb-over.

The three detectives were heading for Husak's office.

"Langan sent us some fresh bodies," Husak explained.

"Sent us?" As in, *You didn't request?*

"Said he knew we've been burning it at both ends, wanted to make sure we had enough manpower."

"Generous," Mark observed. Wasn't a compliment.

"Don't look a gift horse," Husak advised.

As Mark returned to his desk, he saw Doonie exchange cold-eyed, nominal nods of recognition with the tall gaunt comb-over.

The three fresh bodies entered Husak's office.

"Who's the one you hate?" Mark asked Doonie.

"That's Phil Adams."

Adams… The lazy fuck who'd booted the Laurie Desh investigation. And was under the protection of no less than Cousin Eddie.

Doonie gave Mark a significant look, urging him to put it together.

Bridgeport. Two nights ago Jay Branko has that cloak and dagger meeting in Bridgeport with some theoretical clout-heavy Irishman.

Last night Branko gets shot.

This morning Cousin Eddie's pet rat gets assigned to this task force.

If Cousin Eddie asked to see the daily reports, DC Langan was the type who'd oblige. But that wasn't enough. Cousin Eddie needed real-time updates and boots on the ground. Why?

Mark said, "He needs to get to Dale."

Doonie agreed.

ONE HUNDRED-SEVEN / 2012

Husak ordered Mark to remain at his desk. If Phipps rang, Husak preferred Mark take the call here, not on his cell while driving a car or interviewing a witness. Husak also ordered Doonie to park his ass, because with those goddamn stitches in his back Doonie shoulda stayed home altogether.

Mark and Doonie spent the next five hours building a case for how they both shoulda stayed home altogether.

The Feds and the Gary, Indiana cops turned up squat on Phipps.

There was no progress on the Branko murder.

At 2:17 PM Nick Rarey called with the first good news of the day.

There was a coffee house in Gary two blocks from the cell tower. A woman, Dale's height, wearing a burka, had been there last night—at the time Dale called Mark. When Burka Woman left, there was a cab waiting.

The cab driver's log showed he dropped off Burka Woman two blocks from the bus station.

Security-cam in the waiting room showed Burka Woman sitting twenty minutes, then going out to board one of three red-eyes: Detroit, Chicago or Indianapolis. But the boarding area camera was on the fritz.

The Feds were trying to contact the drivers of the three buses to determine which one Burka Woman took; in the meantime agents in all three cities were checking the bus terminals for footage of Burka Woman disembarking.

Mark and Doonie went to Husak's office and gave him Rarey's news.

"I'm betting Detroit," Mark said. "Sizable Muslim community."

From behind Mark and Doonie, someone asked, "Phipps is in Detroit?"

It was Phil Adams, standing in the open doorway to Husak's office.

"We're not sure," Husak said. "You got something?"

"Nah, been dry-humping all day, just got back," Adams drawled.

Mark was keeping Adams away from the real investigation; he'd assigned Adams to re-interview Tesca's clueless family and associates. So the lack of results was no surprise. Neither was Adams knocking off at 2:35. Or Adams eavesdropping in Husak's doorway.

"Got anything else for me?" Adams asked Mark, half-heartedly pretending he wanted to get back to work—

Out in the bullpen Mark's desk phone rang, and micro-second later so did the cell in his pocket.

"Shut the door," Husak told Adams.

Adams decided that meant close the door behind him and join them in the office.

Doonie glared at Adams.

Mark put the call on speakerphone. "Bergman."

Dale said, "Hi. It's me. How'd my proposal go over?"

"Gangbusters."

"Good one."

"Thanks. If you can deliver, the Feds will give everything you asked for."

"Tell them to call Ross Kurnit."

"Done. The US Attorney says not to sweat the paperwork, he guarantees the deal. He wants you to do the sane thing, let the FBI bring you in right now."

"Soon as the paper is signed."

"Dale—"

"And *you* have to be the one who brings me in. I won't call again until I'm ready to go. See ya."

The line went dead.

Husak asked Mark, "Why you?"

Mark thought it over. "The museum. I saved his life, then when he ran I didn't shoot him."

Husak got a call from a phone tech: Phipps' call originated in

Lansing, Michigan.

Mark's cell rang again. Rarey, even happier than usual.

"Burka Woman's in Detroit, got footage of her getting off a bus this morn—"

"Dale just called from Lansing. Get people to the Lansing bus station—and the Detroit terminal, in case Burka Woman's already on her way back there—shit, you find out she's on any bus going anywhere, intercept the motherfucker."

ONE HUNDRED-EIGHT / 2012

That morning, an elderly man left Dale's motel on foot. Stopped a few blocks away and hailed a cab. The cab took him to the dispatch office of a car service. The elderly man paid cash to hire a town car, for a long drive. To the other side of the state.

About halfway, the elderly man told the driver to pull off in Lansing and stop at a Starbucks. Asked the driver to grab some coffees and sandwiches.

The old man remained in the town car, and phoned Mark Bergman.

The town car pulled up at a dock in Muskegon, on the eastern shore of Lake Michigan. The driver helped his passenger get out, then fetched the old gent's bag from the trunk.

The old gent had curly gray hair, and a beard covered most of his face and neck. The skin that showed was wrinkled and dotted with liver spots. There was a bandage on his temple, the kind you see on old folks who've had a melanoma removed. He was wearing big plastic goggle sunglasses, the kind old folks wear over their regular glasses. And he was short, Dale Phipps' height.

The old gent boarded a ferry headed across Lake Michigan to Milwaukee.

If any of the other passengers had taken a close look they might have noticed the hair was a wig, the beard was fake and the wrinkles latex. But who wants to take a close look at an old person.

ONE HUNDRED-NINE / 2012

Assistant US Attorney Lee Kelley called Ross Kurnit. Kurnit said he'd be right over, it was only a four-block walk.

Shortly after Kurnit exited his office building, a muscular man in a black suit and sunglasses approached him and said, "Mr. Kurnit."

Kurnit looked him over. "You FBI?"

"My superior would a appreciate a quick word," the man said, directing Kurnit's attention to a large sedan with tinted windows, parked at the curb.

Wasn't FBI; would've shown ID.

Might be a new client. Or an old one. Kurnit glanced around. A crowded Loop sidewalk, cops all around. Not a place for a snatch.

Kurnit nodded. The man escorted him to the car and opened the rear passenger door. Kurnit leaned down to see who was in there.

"Hey, Ross, how they hangin'?"

Kurnit carefully said, "Good. Yours?"

Cousin Eddie gave Kurnit a vulpine grin, and patted the seat alongside him.

Kurnit got in. The muscular man closed the door.

Cousin Eddie studied Kurnit, remained silent, forcing Kurnit to ask: "So to what do I owe the honor?"

"It's not an honor, it's serious," Cousin Eddie said. "Here's what you and your client are not gonna tell Kelley."

The trial lawyer's poker face failed just a little, a slight widening of the eyes. "Eddie—"

"Cut the crap. If your client's crazy enough to talk about certain living people, so be it. But your client does not finger the late Jay Branko. Your client erases every single file mentioning Branko. Your client never says Branko's name. And if Kelley asks about Branko, your client swears Branko never heard of this art shit. You clear on that?"

Kurnit blinked. "Yeah, I am. But I've never even met my client, I have no idea how he'll—"

"Your client will get this right. And a hundred grand will show up wherever he wants it. And you, Ross, are about to have a couple of career years." Cousin Eddie's voice went gunmetal. "But Ross, if you let your client fuck this up, I'm gonna be unhappy with you. And your client's gonna find out so-called witness protection is just another government program. You know what kind of ambitious cunts run those? I do. Intimately."

A stare. Cold stillness.

Kurnit's lips moved. "I'll convey that," he promised. "But Eddie, my client says he stashed—*not with me*—he stashed copies of his files—the complete files—to be made public if he suddenly dies."

"That's another downside of witness protection. You don't die; Joe Blow dies, in Moose Crap, Alaska. The Feds are only allowed to inform immediate family. Your client hasn't got any. Nobody he left those files with will know he's dead."

ONE HUNDRED-TEN / 2012

Mark took another nap. Beat spending the afternoon at his desk trying not to doze while awaiting the outcomes of the two frenzies ignited by Dale Phipps' latest call.

Frenzy #1 was investigative: the FBI scoured the roads between Lansing and Detroit in search of Burka Woman.

Frenzy #2 was bureaucratic. If the FBI failed to find Burka Woman, they'd have to wait for Dale Phipps to surrender. And Dale would only surrender to Detective Bergman, despite the fact Dale was entering Federal custody. Which raised an urgent issue: *Who'd be in command?*

Let the inter-agency games begin.

Mark slept through them. Woke refreshed, grabbed a coffee and ambled back to his desk. Where Doonie informed him the bureaucratic crisis had been resolved: If Dale surrendered within city limits, Husak would command, with Mark leading the pickup, backed by cops and FBI. If Dale surrendered outside Chicago, Ostergaard would command, with Mark leading the pickup, and everybody else being FBI.

"Except me," Doonie explained. "I told Husak to tell the Feds you said you weren't doin' this without me."

"Damn, I've been talking in my sleep again."

A little after 7 PM Nick Rarey phoned in the box score on Frenzy #1: Dale was pitching a shutout. Burka Woman hadn't shown up at any bus terminal. Or train terminal.

"She couldn't leave by plane," Rarey said. "No way Burka Woman—or Dale—gets through airport security. He's holed up or he's acquired a vehicle."

Mark said, "Dale's too smart to steal a car, those plates would be on every cop computer in the Midwest."

"But Dale can't rent, he'd have to show his license and credit card. We'll check the taxi and car services in Detroit."

"And he might not be Burka Woman any more—ask about anybody Dale's height with his face covered. Meantime, you know if Dale's lawyer and the U.S. Attorney have cut a deal?"

"I'll ask."

"Thanks." Mark put down the receiver and looked up at Phil Adams.

Adams had materialized halfway through the call, standing patiently by Mark's desk and pretending not to notice Doonie staring bullets at him.

"Sounds like the FBI ain't had much luck finding Phipps," Adams commented, to Mark.

"Yes it did," Doonie said. Low, hard.

"So, need me to hang in here?" Adams asked Mark.

"Nah," Doonie answered. "You have yourself a nice night."

Adams gave Doonie a sour grin. Told him, "You too, Bergman," and left.

Mark and Doonie looked at each other.

Mark said, "Halloran's."

alloran's was better than just noisy. It had retro high-backed booths, offering retro privacy. At this hour the booths were reserved for dinner customers. Worked for Mark, who had no plans. Worked for Doonie, whose dinner plans had called for him to meet Phyl and Patty over at Barbara's, the only of his seven sister-in-laws Doonie never warmed up to.

Mark and Doonie finished eating before talking about what they were there to talk about; Doonie's rule, if time ain't an issue you don't jump right in. He'd spent enough of his fucking life turning meals into work.

The niceties observed, Doonie parked his silverware on his plate and said, "Branko is why Phil Adams' Chinaman is so worried about Burka Woman."

Mark nodded. "That's what Branko's office wall says." He'd told Doonie about the photos. Branko with the Mayor; the chairman of the Cook County Democratic party; the Republican governor.

"But," Doonie mused, "only cards Dale's playing are Gianni and Lou."

"Because Branko's too dead to prosecute. But if Dale does have proof Branko partnered with the bent noses on murder-for-profit, the media's gonna go crazy on Branko's city contracts and that picture of him playing BFF with the Mayor."

"Haveta ask Dale about Branko next time we see him."

"If we get the chance. Gotta hand him to the Feds soon as we pick him up."

"Life," Doonie sagely complained.

"And," Mark said, "if we make the pickup in Chicago, Phil Adams can't be there."

"He won't."

"Ain't up to us." Mark finished his drink. "Think Husak will be down with it?"

"He better be. 'Cause if Husak don't cut Phil out of the loop, somebody's gonna have to put Phil in the hospital," Doonie said, with a hint of longing. "You done?" he asked, indicating Mark's leftover fries.

"Phyl—your Phyl—is gonna kill me," Mark predicted as he shoved his plate toward Doonie.

"Speakin' a deadly women," Doonie said as he sloshed extra ketchup onto the fries, "you been in touch with our girl?"

Mark took his time before answering. "She called to ask me over. I said yes. Then I hadda call back to cancel. She hung up on me."

"So when you gonna call again?"

"Not until this shit's over."

"Uh-huh." Doonie contemplatively munched a fry. "You afraid she's gonna hang up again, or that she won't?"

"Heavy," Mark deadpanned.

"Since Gale left you ain't been yourself."

"Who've I been?"

"Gale's gone, what, coupla years? How many women you seen since?"

Mark shrugged.

"In a good month you useta get busier than you been this last year."

"Sorry."

"And how many times you been over to our place since Gale?"

"Five, six—no—eight."

"My point."

Eight. As opposed to hanging with the Dunegans at least once or twice a month, for years.

Mark said, "Oh."

"*Oh,*" Doonie confirmed. "You got Phyl kinda concerned. And ya just turned me into fuckin' Oprah. Gonna go see can I still piss standing up." Doonie slid out of the booth and headed for the john.

Well, that... called for another round.

Mark scanned the room. Saw their waitress walk up to a table of ten and begin taking orders. Might take days.

Mark went to the bar. Busy place. Every stool filled, and a small mob of standees fondling cocktails while waiting for a table. Mark got as close to the bar as he could and waved to the bartender, who was filling a large order. The bartender gave Mark an efficient nod, yes I'm aware you exist.

"Have a seat, my work here is done."

A woman on the barstool Mark was standing behind. Attractive. About thirty. The adult version of thirty.

Mark said, "Thanks, I'm at a table."

"Ah. Slow waitress," the woman commiserated, or maybe teased. She put cash on the bar and stood.

"Overloaded waitress," Mark averred.

The woman rewarded Mark's defense of the damsel with an approving, subtly amused look. Large warm brown eyes. Frank, confident. But not an invitation. An assessment. Reading Mark. Way a cop would, almost. She didn't vibe cop. But something. And, there was this almost familiar—maybe the expression, or the eyes—

"What can I get you?" The bartender, suddenly there.

"Two Jack Daniels, rocks," Mark told the bartender, then returned his attention to—

She was walking away, threading through the crowd toward the door.

Mark watched. She didn't look back.

"New friend or blast from the past?" Doonie, showing up alongside Mark.

"Neither."

The bartender plunked down their drinks. "Fifteen."

"Goes on the tab for booth Seven." Mark picked up the drinks, handed one to Doonie and raised a toast: "Here's to you, Oprah."

"Suck my gray hairy balls," Doonie said, clinking.

ONE HUNDRED-TWELVE / 2012

Mark settled into the couch with a cold bottle of Goose Island, his cell, and his burner. He cued up *The Wild Bunch*. The uncut full length as God and Peckinpah intended version. Mark wouldn't be getting to sleep anytime soon, so here's to 139 minutes of his mind getting the hell out of his skull.

A gang rides into town, wearing cavalry uniforms. They dismount and deploy; half discreetly establish a perimeter around a bank, half march into the bank. Mark picked up the burner and… Turned it off. Put it in a desk drawer.

A posse of railroad detectives is hiding on a rooftop across from the bank. They ambush the gang, and a temperance parade gets caught in the crossfire. Mark can't call JaneDoe. If JaneDoe takes his call, a second later his cell will ring, it'll be Dale, and Mark will have to hang up on JaneD—

Mark's cell rang.

Not Dale. Nick Rarey. "Happen to be in the neighborhood, wondered if you'd be up for a nightcap."

"Good beer." Rarey took a contented swig.

"Yup."

"You wanted to hear about the US Attorney's first date with Dale's lawyer. Kurnit said Dale has files on all the transactions. And can testify about planning hits with Lou, including two sessions with Gianni. Plus he confirms Tesca originated the scam, got shoved out, went rogue, and the Mastrizzis were gunning for Tesca."

"And also for Dale."

"Yeah. But if I were the Mastrizzis I'd worry Dale hid copies of the files to be sent to the cops if he got whacked."

"That's what torture's for. Besides, the files show offshore companies that don't have Mastrizzi names on 'em. Might not stand up in court without Dale to connect the dots, *and* swear the Mastrizzis conspired on the murders. Speaking of trying to kill Dale—did Kurnit say if Branko was in on the art scam?"

Rarey shook his head. "Kurnit said the only names Dale dropped were Gianni and Lou. Kelley told him to ask Dale about Branko."

"Speaking of Dale, I assume you didn't get any hits off the Detroit taxis and town cars."

"Not so far." Rarey finished his beer, and returned to the topic dearest to FBI hearts—Branko being the Missing Link between the Outfit and City Hall. "You find it strange Dale isn't offering us Branko?"

"Dunno. Another beer?"

Rarey studied Mark. "Y'know, Mark, sometimes I get the feeling I've been feeding you more information than you've been feeding me."

"Pure paranoia. Got any leads on who shot Branko?"

Rarey grinned and so did Mark. He went to the kitchen and returned with beers.

Handed one to Rarey, who sighed. "We still got zip on the shooter. *Sláinte.*" Rarey took a long pull. "Got any leads on who Branko went to all that trouble to meet with in secret?"

"Zip," Mark lied.

No fucking way Mark was going to toss Cousin Eddie's name to the FBI and hope it doesn't get back to Eddie.

No fucking way Mark was going to trust anyone but Husak with the news he and Doonie suspected Cousin Eddie was the secret friend Branko met in Bridgeport. And how deeply interested Eddie was in Dale Phipps.

Mark got in bed, closed his eyes.

Dale. Branko. JaneDoe. The Mastrizzis. The FBI. JaneDoe. Tesca. Cousin Eddie. Adams. Husak. JaneDoe.

Mark gave up, went down to the exercise room and picked a fight with a gang of weight machines.

ONE HUNDRED-THIRTEEN / 2012

Jesus fuck. Dale glared at his phone, as if blaming it.

Kurnit had given him the good news about the meeting with the US Attorney. Then the news of how—in violation of Dale's instructions—he'd omitted any mention of Branko. And why.

Did Dale have to fire Kurnit and get a new lawyer? Shit. How long would that take? Time was not his friend.

Besides. If what Kurnit told him was true, it wouldn't matter who Dale's new attorney was. This Cousin Eddie character would get to him.

"He's fucking Godzilla," Kurnit swore.

Fucking Godzilla.

Fine. Screw it. Dale didn't need to mention Jay Branko. Dale would get full immunity without Jay.

Though that would mean he'd have to lie convincingly when the FBI interrogated him, then perjure himself in court if asked about Jay. It never fucking ends.

So what. Get to it. Erase Jay Branko from the files.

Shit. Even after Dale sanitized the thumb drives he had with him, the drives he'd left with his other lawyer and in his safe deposit box still contained the Branko data.

Little time bombs that could get him killed.

Or maybe little grenades he could save himself with.

Dale called Kurnit. Told him to tell Cousin Eddie he'd play along. But that if he died bad, even as Joe Blow in Moose Crap, he guarantees the full files, including the Branko data, would go public. If Cousin Eddie doubted that, he could go ask any cyber geek for at least three ways Dale could make it happen.

Dale didn't bother to communicate a similar threat to the Mastrizzis. They were gonna kill him no matter what, for all the things he could say about them, stuff that wasn't in the files.

ONE HUNDRED-FOURTEEN / 2012

Mark and Doonie went into Husak's office and closed the door. Turned out they weren't telling Husak anything that hadn't already crossed his mind. Husak knew what Phil Adams was. Said, "When we set the details for the Phipps pickup—"

Mark's cell rang. It was Rarey.

"Burka Woman is history and Grampa Phipps is in Wisconsin."

"Doonie and Lieutenant Husak are here," Mark said, switching to speakerphone.

"G'morning sir, Doonie," Rarey enthused. "Just heard from Detroit. Yesterday an old man, Dale's height, hired a town car, paid cash. The driver took him across the state—with a stop in Lansing at the exact time Dale phoned Mark—then to Muskegon, where a ferry was leaving for Milwaukee. Our people are checking footage at both ferry terminals."

"Driver give a description?"

"Curly gray hair and beard, big square bandage on the forehead, and rockin' a pair of those Generation AARP giant goggle sunglasses."

When the call ended, Doonie said, "Maybe the Feds will grab Dale in Milwaukee and we won't have nothin' to do with it."

"That would be the easy way around our problem," Husak said. Making *easy* sound even money with *unicorn*.

Mark said, "Right. So when we set the pickup, the where and when—"

"—will be strict need-to-know," Husak said. "You two are the only ones from this unit who'll be there. So no other detective on this task force, especially Phil Adams, needs to know."

"Thanks, Loo," Doonie said.

"*But*," Husak grumbled, "people above me in the chain of command will be told the where and when."

"That was my next question," Mark said. "Don't suppose there's a chance that—a certain senior officer—could be cut out of the loop?"

Husak shook his head.

Doonie shrugged. "Langan won't risk gettin' caught bein' the one who sets up Dale to get whacked. That's why Cousin Eddie hadda stick Phil in here."

Husak scowled. "You hope." Another unicorn.

Doonie didn't disagree.

Husak said, low, "I lied. One other detective does have to be at the pickup." He looked Doonie in the eye. "Been too long since I strapped on the Kevlar."

Doonie grinned. Can't beat having a boss who, when he can't cover your back with bureaucratic maneuvers, will do it with a pump shotgun.

ONE HUNDRED-FIFTEEN / 2012

Mark cleaned his gun.

Mark got an email from HR informing him he'd exceeded the time limit for doing his post-shooting psych eval. If he didn't report for the eval within 48 hours he'd be subject to suspension, frowns and disappointed sighs.

Husak, who as CO had been cc'd by HR, wrote back, stating Detective Bergman would report for an eval soon as he completed a high priority undercover assignment that could not be interrupted.

Which consisted of Mark sitting at his desk waiting for the phone to ring.

Mark's phone rang.

Rarey: Security-cam at the Milwaukee ferry terminal showed Grampa Phipps disembarking with a large wheeled suitcase. Another camera showed Grampa Phipps leaving the area on foot. After which the geriatric and his large luggage evaporated. But the FBI couldn't go public with a photo of Grampa Phipps; that'd tell the Mastrizzis where to look for him.

Mark looked around; Adams wasn't in the bullpen. Mark quietly asked Rarey to find out if Kurnit had gotten back to Kelley about what Dale had to say about Branko.

Mark wondered what JaneDoe was doing.

Mark and Doonie went to lunch at their Thai joint. A couple of minutes after they sat, Phil Adams wandered in, was surprised to see them, asked if it was okay he joined them.

Mark said sure.

During lunch Adams asked had they heard any scuttlebutt about what Phipps was offering the US Attorney.

Doonie said nah, all we heard was what you heard on the speakerphone in Husak's office.

When the check came Doonie grabbed it. Adams tried to give him a five. Doonie insisted, my pleasure.

Late in the afternoon Husak called Mark and Doonie in. Told them Kelley and Kurnit had finalized a deal. Kurnit had no idea when Phipps would contact Mark to arrange the pickup.

When Mark and Doonie returned to their desks, their lunch buddy Adams sauntered over. "Any news?"

"Some heavy shit," Mark confided. "HR just gave me 48 hours to diddle the shrink, or they pull my badge."

Adams twitched as Mark's *fuck you* sank in. Gave Mark a toxic smirk and stalked away.

Mark went down to the basement range and killed paper.
Re-cleaned his gun.

Mark ate dinner alone, at home.
Poured a bourbon. Put on music. Opened a book. His cell rang.
Rarey: "Dale's lawyer said Dale said Branko had nothing to do with the art scam—or the attempted hit on Dale. He was positive Branko had no reason to want him dead."

"Shit."

"*Shit* because you believe Dale, or *shit* you think he's lying?"

"*Shit* I'm not sure." Actually Mark was sure Dale was lying, and he didn't know of anyone but Cousin Eddie who might've gotten to Kurnit and Dale.

Mark thanked Rarey and got off the phone.
Finished his bourbon. Looked at the bottle, debating.
Decided to call JaneDoe and ask her to please talk to him.
His cell rang again.
"Hi, how soon can you get to Rockford?" Dale asked.

ONE HUNDRED-SIXTEEN / 2012

The old man stood on the sidewalk with his suitcase, nervously tapping his foot. His wheelman showed up twelve minutes late.

The wheelman was unaware this was a getaway from FBI and Outfit manhunts. He was a gregarious 27-year-old harmonica player named Flying Frog—*Call me Froggy!*—who was between gigs (nineteen months), owned a 1994 Sentra, and answered a craigslist ad for a driver to take an elderly traveler from Milwaukee to Janesville.

The old man sat in the back seat, explaining it made him feel he was traveling in style, and besides, it was safer in case of a crash—nothing personal, but he had no idea what kind of driver Froggy was.

What Dale really thought was safer was Froggy sitting with his back to him rather than next to him, with a close-up view of his wig, beard and make-up.

When they got to the highway Dale told Froggy he actually needed to go a little farther, over the state line, near Rockford—don't worry, he'd pay a bonus.

No problemo!

Dale had Froggy stop at a mall outside of Rockford and park at a sporting goods store. He gave Froggy cash and instructed him to buy a mountain bike. And of course collect another bonus.

Totally no problemo!

Froggy moved the suitcase from the trunk to the rear seat, and squeezed the bike into the trunk, securing the lid with bungee cords.

They headed away from Rockford, onto a county road, then onto a dirt jeep trail leading into woods adjacent to a state park. Dale told Froggy to stop. Handed Froggy cash that included the bonuses. Asked him to get the bike out of the trunk.

Froggy did. He pointed at the suitcase, which the old man had wrestled out of the back seat himself. "You can't carry that on the bike."

"Thank you for your pleasant company and safe driving. Time for you to go."

Froggy asked, "But you are in shape to ride, right?"

"Yes."

Froggy grinned, sly. "C'mon, what's up with the make-up and wig? You a spy?"

"Yes I am, and this is a matter of national security. So in exchange for your cooperation, by which I mean your silence—" Dale handed an envelope to Froggy "—your grateful government will award you an extra five hundred. Please verify the amount."

Froggy opened the envelope and began counting.

"And, " Dale said.

Froggy looked up. Dale was pointing a gun at his face.

"If you ever tell anyone about me, I will find out, and you will die. So will whoever you're with."

Tommy Tesca's line. What the fuck, Dale figured, worked on me. Worked on Froggy too.

Dale changed into bicycle gear. Stashed the suitcase behind some bushes. Strapped on a backpack containing his essentials.

He walked the bike out to the paved road. It began to drizzle. Dale began to ride. Five miles, to another dirt road, this one a long drive-way which led to the place where he'd lost his virginity. An isolated, cushy cabin owned by the parents of Justine Krause, with whom he'd shared a deep meaningful arousal, junior year at Francis Parker.

It had taken only a few minutes online to confirm the property was still owned by Justine's mom. Who never opened the cabin before Memorial Day, and not then unless it was a warm spring.

And if some younger, more weather-resistant Krauses happened to be in residence, well, Dale would spend some seriously crappy time hiding in the woods—the drizzle had matured into a pelting rain—until Bergman fetched him.

Because no fucking way was Dale going to turn himself in anywhere near any place big enough for the Mastrizzis to have an associate.

The cabin was unoccupied. Dale broke in. Removed the dregs of his rain-wrecked make-up. Showered. Dined on expired microwave ramen. Survived it.

When it was late and dark enough, he phoned Bergman.

"Hi, how soon can you get to Rockford?"

"First I have to assemble the backup, so, let's say I'll get there between eleven-thirty and midnight."

"Not too much backup! I don't want to draw attention."

"Just enough backup so nobody can fuck with us. Where exactly in Rockford are you?"

"I'm not. When you're a mile or two south of Rockford call me. I'll give you directions."

"Dale, be safer to tell me now—in case you have phone trouble, or I do, or who knows what. This way we're covered."

Dale said, "No." Gave Bergman his phone number and hung up.

ONE HUNDRED-SEVENTEEN / 2012

Lou hung up the phone and told Gianni, "He's near Rockford. Won't give the exact location until the cops get there. They'll be hitting the road in about thirty minutes." Then, somberly: "Three Chicago cops backed by eight to ten Feds."

Lou had been unusually blunt in opposing the Old Man on this one. Even if they got a clean shot and only hit Dale—far from guaranteed, winging it like this—doing it while Dale was surrounded by FBI would start a firefight.

Killing a witness is business. Killing FBI starts a war.

Gianni had been typically blunt. *This is our one crack at Phipps before he starts yapping. War? This FBI is pure pussy next to what it was under J. Edgar Faggot.*

But now that it was go time, Gianni was silent.

Father and son held each other's gaze. The son's face neutral. The father's granite.

Gianni said, "Make the call."

Lou could refuse. Or give the order, then go behind Gianni's back and rescind it.

Then he'd have to kill his father before his father killed him.

They stared into each other, sharing that thought, that most ancient father-son animal truth.

Lou made the call.

ONE HUNDRED-EIGHTEEN / 2012

As their Crown Vic splashed up the rain-slicked ramp to the 90, followed by an armored FBI SWAT van and an armored FBI Yukon, Doonie declared, "We're a fuckin' circus parade."

"Real Chicago-style parade—in a downpour," Rarey commented, from the back seat.

"Wasn't Chicago's idea to do this tonight, it was Dale's."

Rarey was riding with Mark and Doonie because Dale, despite refusing to surrender to anyone but Mark, was entering FBI custody. The agency insisted one of theirs be alongside Mark to take immediate possession.

Mark, who was driving, said, "Storm's supposed to be gone from Rockford by the time we get there."

Rarey asked, "You trust weather forecasts?"

"Always."

Those, the Cubs' chances, and true love.

They were ten minutes outside Rockford, heading northwest, when they drove out from under the eastbound storm. The night sky was still opaque with clouds, but they'd stopped pissing. Maybe the Cubs and true love could happen too.

Mark keyed his headset—the whole team was wired—to alert the command center, the FBI SWATs and Husak, who was in the van, that they should prepare to eavesdrop, because he was about to phone Dale.

Dale picked up a microsecond into the first ring, whispered a tense, "Hel—" and interrupted himself with two fast sharp farts "—lo."

"Hi," Mark said in his most therapeutically casual tone. "How's it going?"

After a moment Dale warily muttered, "Talk some more."

"C'mon, you know this is my voice." No reply. "So, wanna go grab a coffee?"

Silence. Doonie rolled his eyes, fed up with this paranoid dipshit.

"The hell with coffee," Mark coaxed, "we'll get you a drink. And a blow-job. And a pony. And lifetime job security and subsidized housing."

Dale made a reluctantly amused noise. "How the hell you end up a cop?"

"Long story, I'm not telling over the phone. Where the fuck are ya?"

Dale recited detailed directions. Warned Mark the driveway was a quarter-mile long. Told Mark to stop at the end of the driveway, facing the cabin, and wait. "*Do not call me,*" Dale ordered.

"Got it."

"You stop the car, you stay in it, and you *wait until I call you.*"

The line went dead.

"Fucker doesn't even say goodbye," Doonie groused.

Rarey, consulting a laptop, said, "He's approximately nineteen minutes from here."

"Secret FBI GPS?" Doonie wondered.

"Google Maps."

A large sedan blew past, had to be doing over ninety. A few seconds later a large van did the same.

Watching them disappear up the road, Doonie said, "Smokey's gonna be writing tickets or bagging bodies. Not that I seen one tonight."

Turned out Google's omniscience was less than; the highway exit Dale instructed Mark to take was blocked by a row of orange safety cones.

"Fucking perfect," Mark muttered. He sped north, leading the parade to the next exit, where they took an overpass to the other side of the highway, got on and drove back to the southbound side of the correct exit. Only lost about four minutes.

They zigged through a series of ever narrower and hillier county roads, splashing through poorly drained intersections.

The last of which led to Walon Road. It was undulating and unlit, which with tonight's low cloud deck meant darkness black and thick as used motor oil. Both sides of the road were heavily wooded, the shadowy trees and bushes flickering past in the spill from the headlights.

They found the dirt driveway. Which tonight meant rutted mudway, dotted with the occasional mini-swamp. One of which the Crown Vic got stuck in, rear wheels furiously whining in the muck.

"Could happen to anyone," Rarey consoled Mark.

The van behind them nudged the Crown Vic out of the miniswamp. Mark stayed in low gear, drove Mars-rover slow as he negotiated the remainder of the slopfest.

The driveway ended at a clearing. The clearing was a semi-circle, sprinkled with gravel to provide traction, but tonight the gravel mainly served as shoreline for a series of enormous puddles.

As instructed, Mark stopped at the clearing's edge, facing the cabin on the far side of the clearing.

The "cabin" was two stories tall and four bedrooms wide. Ten feet to the left of the cabin there was a garage three cars wide. Fifteen feet to the right of the cabin there was a tool shed three out-houses wide.

The Crown Vic's high beams did a decent job of illuminating the cabin, a feeble job of revealing the garage and tool shed, then the light crawled off to die in the woods beyond the buildings.

There were no lights on in the cabin.

The FBI van pulled up behind the cop car. Husak (alley-sweeper) and six FBI SWATs (assault rifles) got out and took flanking positions to either side of the Crown Vic.

The Yukon stopped ten feet back of the van. Three SWATs got out. A fourth SWAT had been dropped off near the entrance to the driveway so he could play rear guard, hiding in the trees and keeping an eye on the road.

The cops waited.

Dale didn't call.

Doonie grimaced at Mark.

"In the woods, nine o'clock! " a SWAT hissed over the radio.

The SWATs scanned the woods with their night-vision goggles. Nothing.

The SWAT commander asked, "Was that a visual?"

"Negative," the first voice replied, "I heard something rustle."

Mark turned his engine off. Moments later the van and Yukon fell silent.

Ears strained. In vain.

"Raccoon?" a third SWAT theorized—

A thunderclap. Everyone flinched—then relaxed, as their nervous systems made the audio analysis: the blast was an act of nature, not weaponry.

Nature began to drizzle. The drizzle fattened into full-on rain, as if nature opened a faucet. Basic Midwestern cloudburst.

Mark started his windshield wipers and his phone rang.

Mark said, "Hi, you had better be here."

"Why did you turn your engines off?"

"So we could hear if you farted. C'mon, time to go."

"Pull up in front of the tool shed, close as you can and still leave room to open your rear door, right in front of the shed door."

"On my way."

Mark drove across the clearing, skirting a large puddle whose depth he didn't want to find out. He eased to a halt in front of the tool shed, aligning the car's rear passenger-side door with the shed door.

Rarey, in the back seat, opened the car door and pulled back out of the way. The shed door flicked open. Dale, crouched low, hissed "Watch your feet!" and lunged headfirst into the narrow gap between the rear and front seats—Rarey pulling his legs up onto the seat a second ahead of Dale landing. Dale scrunched down on the floor of the car and barked, "Let's go!"

"First we gotta close the door," Rarey said, scooting across the rear seat to get at it.

Mark informed the SWATs, "We have the package. I'll pull up by the garage so your vehicles have room to get in here and turn around."

"No! Get moving, they can just back down the driveway," Dale demanded.

"Not happening, that road's a mess," Mark said. "If one of those trucks gets stuck, our exit is blocked." He put the car in gear.

"Dale," Doonie asked, "you gonna stay down there, whole way back to Chicago?"

"I don't know—stop! What're you doing?!"

"Patting you down," Rarey explained. He extracted a gun tucked into the small of Dale's back. "That's one."

"That's all, no other guns!" Dale snapped, remaining resolutely face-down.

Mark turned left in order to pull up alongside the gara—the car bucked as a rear wheel sank into a puddle—

"Turn over," Rarey ordered Dale.

"I don't have another gu—"

The car fishtailed out of the puddle—Mark released the gas pedal and turned into the skid, the car slowing but slewing sideways in slippery muck, as—

A definitively unnatural BAM-WHOOSHHH erupted from the forest and something flashed through the space the car had just been in, nicked a fender and caromed into the tool shed, which blew up.

"RPG!" a SWAT yelled on the headset—

A shitstorm of automatic weapons fire erupted.

ONE HUNDRED-NINETEEN / 2012

Mark floors it wheels spin impotent then bite and the car leaps bullets hiss out of the darkness from both sides and punch through sheet metal Rarey gasps in pain the windshield disintegrates Mark drives head down into the gap between the cabin and the burning shed stomps the brakes the car skids to a muddy stop with the front bumper nosed out past the rear of the cabin but the car's sheltered by the cabin on the left and burning shed on the right—

Mark and Doonie threw their doors open—"OUT!"—Mark bellowed at Dale, who was kissing the floor. Rarey writhed on the back seat clutching a leg, groaning loud enough to cut through the thrum of rain on the car and the warnings-orders-curses-howls filling Mark's headset, and the cluttered chatter of assault rifles hammering at each other, punctuated by the roar of a shotgun, *Husak's alive—*

Mark yanked the rear driver's-side door open, hauled out Dale, who flattened himself against the rear fender, crouched low.

Mark started to rush to the other side of the car, where Doonie was dragging Rarey out of the back seat and onto the muddy ground.

An RPG exploded into the far side of the cabin but the shockwave sent Mark sprawling flimsy as a sheet of paper, the cabin shuddered, the windows blew out, bits of glass showering the men but washing away in the downpour that was soaking them.

Dale was hugging mud. Mark grabbed Dale's arm—"Move!"—and dragged him around to the passenger side.

Rarey was shot in the thigh. Doonie was putting a tourniquet on—

Mark shoved Dale to Doonie and yelled, "Get him—" *Stop! Someone's listening in, only way the shooters could've known where—* Mark tore off his headset, then pulled Doonie's off and hissed, "Get Dale into the woods," pointing to the forest behind the cabin—only way open, shooters would be converging from both sides of the driveway. "I'll take Rarey!"

Doonie looked at Rarey, then Mark. But resisted the urge to shoot Dale so he could help carry the kid. Doonie hustled Dale into the dark sloppy woods.

Mark yanked Rarey's headset off and went to slide his arm under him—

"Go!" Rarey screamed, "You can't fucking carry me—GO!" Rarey shoved Mark away, rolled onto his stomach and dragged himself under the car. Snarled, "Don't lose my witness!"

"Shhh!" Mark hissed—the downpour was dousing the burning shed but the wounded flames threw enough light to reveal glimpses of three men wearing Kevlar, headsets and night vision goggles—which hopefully would be blinded by the flames if they looked Mark's way. Mark crouched, kneeling by the front fender. The shooters were to Mark's right, moving through the trees—in the direction Doonie and Dale had gone—Mark would be able to come up behind the shooters, but would have to get close enough to make sure he didn't waste bullets on their body armor. Mark took a breath and start—

"Whoa-fuck!" accompanied the *guish-guish-guish* of feet scrabbling to regain balance in mud, followed by the *thump* of a body whacking into the back wall of the cabin—to Mark's left, very close. The three shooters to his right were following the infrared signatures fleeing into the woods, correctly betting one was Dale—but this other shooter was coming from the left to check the car.

Mark went dead still. Seriously outgunned. Surprise and getting the first shot would have to do it—

The shooter stepped out from behind the cabin, scanning the shot-up car and the open space alongside the driver's side—he moved forward, in front of the car, toward the passenger side where Mark was crouched—

Frantic *blam-blam-blam-blam-blam-blams* exploded next to Mark and the shooter toppled screaming as hollowpoints from underneath the car shattered his ankles and, as he hit the ground, slammed into his arm and ripped through his throat and he shuddered and gurgled and stopped moving. Rarey's revenge.

Mark came out from behind the fender, checked the shooter's neck for a pulse. The artery throbbed twice then didn't.

"Good one," Mark complimented the underside of the car.

"Thank you," the underside of the car replied. "Go!"

Mark took the shooter's AR-15. Patted him down—shit—bastard was out of ammo clips. Mark yanked the night vision goggles off the bastard's head and rushed into the woods.

Rushed fast as he could without taking a header. The goggles reversed darkness into visibility, but it was dimly glowing negative outlines of trees and brush, blurred by wet lenses. And the forest floor was a treacherous pudding—

A burst from an automatic weapon somewhere up ahead, distant muzzle flashes flaring in Mark's goggles—

A four-shot reply from a handgun—*Doonie*—

All three assault rifles opened up—

Mark ran, slipping, lurching, but pounding forward—*there!*—Shooter One, his pale glowing back to Mark, firing into the darkness—

Mark tripped over a tree root, fell, crashing loudly into a bush, rolled off of it, bounced back up and—

A spray of bullets decimated the bush Mark had just been in—

Fired by Shooter Two, a glowing figure twenty yards to Mark's left—Mark loosed a burst at Shooter Two and the figure vanished behind a tree and Mark wheeled toward Shooter One—who was raising his weapon at Mark—

Mark's rifle spat first, Shooter One went down—

Mark dropped to his knees as Shooter Two slid out from behind his tree and opened up. Mark scooted to the side, popped up and his rifle dry-fired, empty—

Mark hit the dirt as another cloud of lead sizzled past. He dropped the useless rifle, pulled his handgun, heard Shooter Two pop an empty clip, snap in a new one, and, grunting with exertion, start bashing through a thick stand of brush that separated him from Mark.

Mark quick-crawled behind the nearest tree, pulled himself to his feet and ran. Shooter Two snapped off short bursts—Mark zig-zagged, bent low—

He caught a glimpse of a glowing figure forty yards ahead—Shooter Three, taking aim at him—

Mark dove—

Shooters Two and Three opened up—

Mark hugged mud, the crossfire chopped a sapling in half, slugs ricocheted off trees and rocks, the sapling crashed, a ricochet ripped into the mud inches from Mark's eye, the firing stopped and the shooters closed in from either side. Mark scrambled to his feet and hustled out from between the converging shooters. Took a quick look back—spotted Shooter Three—Mark snapped off two shots, Shooter Three ducked, Mark ran and Shooter Two opened up at Mark from the other side—

Mark hit the deck but there wasn't a deck—Mark tumbled down a steep slope—his gun hand slammed into a rock, the gun went flying, Mark kept tumbling, brambles gouged the side of his head and tore the goggles off.

He slid to a stop, beaten bloody by the foliage. His gun hand stiffening swelling hurting bad. Not that he had a gun. And he couldn't see shit in the rain and dark. He started crawling back up the slope, groping at the ground, maybe he'd get lucky, find the fucking thing—

He heard a harsh whisper, one of the shooters talking into his headset—

Mark froze...

A short burst tore past at steep angle, the shooter firing down from the top of the slope—

Mark rolled away, got up and ran a few steps, dove and hit the ground crawling fast as he could—

A large dark thing loomed in front of him. Fallen tree. Mark scrambled around the end of the trunk, a tangle of upended roots grasping at nothing. Dove behind it, putting the tree trunk between him and the shooter's night vision, and crawled fast—

The top of Mark's head bumped into something hard, metal, round—*gun muzzle*—he froze.

Nothing.

Slowly raised his head. The gun was in a hand at the end of an outstretched arm—Mark grabbed the hand—Doonie. Flat on his back, not moving—Mark surged forward, felt Doonie's neck—found a pulse.

Too fucking dark to see where Doon was hit—Mark ran a hand under Doonie's vest. No chest or gut wound. Mark touched Doonie's head. Sticky warm ooze coated Doon's forehead—

Cursing and thrashing—one of the shooters losing his footing on the slope Mark had tumbled down.

Mark extracted the gun from Doonie's hand. Doon had fired four rounds; six left. Mark fished two clips out of Doonie's pocket.

Checked Doonie's pulse again.

The term cold rage never made sense to Mark. Now it was him and he was it. Solidified. Pure.

Didn't make Mark able get a useful grip on the gun with his swollen right hand. But it steeled him enough to will that hand to grasp a flashlight—

One of the shooters murmured into his headset. Easier for Mark to hear now, the rain had thinned to a drizzle, lot less noisy. So was the firefight back at the cabin. The ferocity was leaking out of it, the shooting no longer non-stop. One side was winning.

Mark heard footsteps squishing towards the downed tree. He let the shooter get closer—

Mark sprang up, switching on the flashlight—

The shooter's peripheral vision caught Mark's movement but the flashlight glared in his goggles as he swung his gun in Mark's direction—

Mark put two slugs in the shooter's groin, because the torso was armored and Mark was in no shape to gamble on a left-handed head shot. The shooter dropped. Mark scrambled over the tree and got close enough so the head shot was no gamble. Put the writhing beast out of its misery but didn't have time to take its assault rifle because Shooter Three was slamming his way down the slope—

Mark ran. Bullets followed. They went wide. Shooter Three stopped firing and concentrated on catching up. Good, Mark wanted to get him the hell away from Doonie—

Another swarm of bullets—one gashed Mark's left arm and he fell. But there was a large tree a few feet ahead. Mark crawled around behind it. Stood. Felt for his flashlight—gone. Couldn't repeat that trick. He waited. Clutching Doonie's gun in his left hand, his swollen painful right hand steadying the left as best it could. Three rounds. Couldn't put in a new clip; Shooter Three was close enough to hear that, because Mark could hear him.

Cautious footsteps in sucking mud.

Pain sizzled in the wound on Mark's left arm. The arm began to tremble.

The steps paused, Shooter Three stopping to pan around with his night vision—

BrraaAAAAFFF!—a huge terrified fart from directly above, in the tree—

Mark sprang out from behind the tree just as Shooter Three, six feet away, began to walk a burst of bullets up through the branches—

Mark cranks two shots, one misses and one takes a chunk out of the base of the guy's neck, he spins and topples, trigger finger locked, rifle yammering till it runs dry—

Mark rushes forward to get close enough to make sure his last shot—

Shooter Three, on the ground, lashes out with his empty rifle, sweeping it at Mark's legs—

Mark fires the same moment the rifle whips into his ankle, Mark's bullet kills mud as he goes down hard and the empty gun bounces out of his hand—

Mark lands on his back and the guy, gushing blood but not dead yet, is on top of Mark, straddling him, pressing the rifle against Mark's windpipe, gripping the rifle with both hands and leaning into it, Mark is pushing back, trying to twist the barrel off his throat and he can't, he grabs at the guy's face, trying to find an eye, the guy jerks his head out of Mark's reach, Mark's gagging now, not enough oxygen left to do anything but yank the fighting knife out of the scabbard on the guy's leg and jam the knife under the Kevlar vest, shoving the serrated blade in and yanking it back and forth, the guy is roaring, insane with agony, but still crushing Mark's throat, until Mark rips the blade out of the guy's guts, swings it up hard and buries the knife in his ear. The guy pukes blood in Mark's face but he does die. Even slides off to the side as he collapses, so Mark, gagging, gasping for air, only has to struggle a little to shove the corpse off.

Mark laid there, wiping blood off his face with his shirtsleeve, waiting for the pain in his throat to subside enough so he could try standing up. It didn't, so he stood up anyway.

"You didn't kill me, asshole."

Shooter One, the first guy Mark had brought down, from a distance. Now Shooter One was only ten feet away, leaning against a tree, needing it, one arm hanging useless. But his other was aiming something at Mark.

Mark still had the knife in his hand. Slowly raised it. Instinct.

Shooter One's face was in darkness but there was an acid grin in his voice: "C'mon, do it. Come get me. Give you two steps before I sh—"

Shooter One lurched forward as a bullet hit the back of his skull. Stumbled almost like a live man before he splayed face-down.

Mark waited for the arrival of whoever—wait—he didn't hear the shot—silencer? Or not, his ears were ringing and his head was throbbing, maybe he missed the bang.

He stared into the darkness where the shot came from. Nobody showed. Mark leaned down and stripped the night vision goggles off the corpse—

"FREEZE!"

From behind him.

Husak's voice.

Mark tried to speak but only produced throat pain.

"Hands on your head! Hands on your head!"

Mark did that. Still holding the goggles.

"What's in your hand?! Show me what's—Bergman? Mark?"

Mark nodded, and turned around.

Made out dim outlines of Husak and two SWATs, wearing night

vision, hurrying towards him.

"You hurt?" Husak asked.

Mark pointed up into the tree and forced himself to croak, "Dale."

Husak and the SWATs looked up—

Mark grabbed Husak, rasped, "Doonie's down!" put on the dead man's goggles and started limping fast as he could in what he hoped was the right direction.

ONE HUNDRED-TWENTY / 2012

Doonie's skull wasn't fractured, just chipped. He'd been at a dead run when he took two slugs in the back. The Kevlar held but the impact launched him headfirst into a branch. Knocked him cold. Caused the concussion that saved his life. If Doonie had been conscious he would've resumed shooting and the three guys with assault rifles would've shredded him.

Soon as Mark knew Doonie would be okay, he'd emailed Phyl, saying he couldn't talk. (Didn't say why). A while later Husak phoned Phyl with details about Doon's imminent (relatively) minor surgery.

Mark got his shoulder sewn up, and his neck and throat scanned for structural damage—negative, despite the wide swathe of ugly bruises across his throat. One side of his face was badly scratched. Mark's right hand (bashed by a rock) had a cracked bone. His left ankle (bashed by a rifle barrel) was ugly but not broken. He could sort of walk. So after four hours of sleep he swallowed a breakfast pain pill and went back to the cabin to debrief the FBI on the firefight.

It was early evening by the time Mark returned to the Rockford trauma center where the team was being treated.

Phyl was standing by Doonie's bed when Mark limped in, croaked, "Hi," and gave the strapping, strong-featured woman a tender kiss on the cheek.

Phyl registered his limp, his voice, face, purple-black neck, contused right hand, the sling on his left arm. Gave Mark a pained and scolding look, then gave him an emotional but very careful hug.

"So," Doonie asked, "the fuck's goin' on with your throat?"

"What gave me away?" Mark deadpanned, his voice a rusty cement mixer.

"Lucky guess. The fuck happened?"

Mark glanced at Phyl. Shrugged. "Not much. Looks worse than it is."

Phyl arched her eyebrows: *Don't you give me that let's protect the little lady shit.*

Mark said, "Guy tried to crush my throat with his rifle."

Phyl gave a short sharp moan as the image hit her. Then she hit Mark, a jab to his healthy shoulder.

"I love you too," Mark replied.

"And that?" Doonie asked, pointing at the sling.

"Shoulder got nicked. How you feeling?"

"How do I look?" Doonie's skull was swathed in mummy wrap, with a bulge on his forehead from the padded bandage where the bone chip had been extracted. His complexion was light gray and his speech had a sedative furriness.

"No worse than usual."

"Right. So you believe the fuckin' doctor says I can't have a fuckin' drink for a fuckin' month?"

"You so much as look at a beer," Phyl vowed, "I will do things to your skull that fucking tree can only dream of."

"She thinks it's better I get hooked on the painkillers," Doonie complained.

"Smart," Mark complimented Phyl, putting his good arm around her. "We can shove him into rehab, not have him underfoot the next coupla months."

Doonie's eyes narrowed. "You two been messin' around?"

"Since the day we met," Phyl assured him.

"What I figured. How's Rarey?"

Mark said, "Busted thigh bone, lost some blood, but he's young. Killed a guy."

"Hunh," a pleasantly surprised grunt. "Husak?"

"Cracked rib where bullets hit his vest. And he got kissed on the cheek. Gonna have a sexy dueling scar."

"Husak sexy? Not enough scars in the world. And the dipshit?"

"Scrapes and bruises from climbing a wet tree in the dark. FBI flew him out of here before dawn."

"And the Feds who rode with us?"

Mark summarized. The SWATs were aces. Lost only one man despite getting jumped. Four FBI seriously wounded, but they'd make it. Everybody else was dinged but still standing.

The SWAT who bought it was the guard they'd posted at the entrance to the driveway. When the shit went down he circled in behind the shooters and nailed the fuck firing the RPG. Saved everybody's ass except his own.

There were seven dead shooters. But no prisoners, because the surviving shooters pulled out, and the FBI didn't chase; had casualties to tend to, their trucks were shot up, and oh yeah, their first priority was to come find out what was left of you me and Dale.

Doonie looked away, thinking. Looked back at Mark. "The shooters musta got there right before us. Had no time to search for Dale before we showed up."

Mark nodded.

Doonie muttered, "That car and van, passed us right after Dale called."

"And those cones blocking the exit ramp."

Doonie took a sip of water. Looked at Phyl. "Throat's all dry. Couldja run down the cafeteria and grab me a popsicle or something, hon?"

"No," Phyl said, glaring. "Doctor said no work, no stress. *None.*"

Silence.

Phyl and Doonie looked at each other like two people who'd spent twenty-seven years married to the right person.

Phyl turned to Mark. Said, "Five minutes." She gave Doonie's foot a grudgingly affectionate squeeze and left the room.

"We ID the dead shooters?" Doonie asked.

"Three American, ex-military, ex-Blackwater. Four Mexican, ex-military, wearing Zeta ink."

Doonie stewed. Said, "Langan dimed us."

"Yeah. But probably not to Cousin Eddie"

"Cousin Eddie's the one wants Dale not talkin' about Branko."

"Dale already isn't talking about Branko."

"Think Eddie wants ta gamble the little shit won't crack once the Feebs start bustin' his balls?"

Mark said, "I think going Full Metal Jacket on cops and FBI doesn't say Cousin Eddie. He likes invisible. So does Cousin Eddie's cousin."

Doonie sighed, disappointed in himself. "Fuckin' concussion... You're right, Langan's for rent, and the Mastrizzis gotta stop Dale. So Gianni goes for one last great big swing a the dick before he dies..."

After a moment Mark said, "I'll keep you posted. If you stay off the booze. Totally. For a month."

ONE HUNDRED-TWENTY-ONE / 2012

Mark was in the hospital cafeteria, about to have his third all-soup meal of the day. His throat wanted nothing to do with solids.

Before eating, Mark checked his cell: No missed messages.

During one of his few free minutes that afternoon Mark had tried to contact JaneDoe. His burner was at home, so fuck secrecy, he used his regular phone. Called JaneDoe's burner. Left a voicemail. Called her cell. Left a voicemail. Called her landline. *It had been disconnected.* Mark emailed and texted. No response.

Mark dipped the spoon into the soup—his phone vibrated, incoming text—Mark grabbed it.

Rarey.

Last Mark had checked on him, early this morning, the kid was out cold. Now he was asking Mark to come to his room.

Rarey was sitting up. His leg was immobilized. Had a laptop on his tray table. His eyes were a little glassy but had no trouble focusing on Mark's swollen multi-colored neck.

"Awesome impersonation of a turkey in heat."

Mark croaked, "Shit, you haven't had surgery yet—I was hoping for post-op zombie."

"Nope. Taking a chopper to Midway, then I hop a plane to Baltimore. There's this dude at Johns Hopkins who's the best orthopedic surgeon in the universe, and went to high school with my Dad."

"Uh-huh." Mark, indicating the laptop, complained, "You've been working."

"Haven't you, multiple wounds and all?"

"Yeah. What's wrong with us?"

Rarey grinned. "How'd those mercs know to follow us, and how did they listen in when Dale called?"

"You got something?"

"Daryl Langan was at home when Dale made his first call, telling you he was in Rockford. Right after that, a burner phone placed a call, *via the cell tower by Langan's house,* to a burner using a cell tower in Downer's Grove. Right next to ZeeZeeZ Bowlarama, home of the Mastrizzis' underground HQ."

Rarey paused to gauge Mark's reaction. Rarey gave up. "Langan and your other superiors gathered at your HQ to monitor the op. But Langan said he was having unpleasant stomach issues, so for everybody's sake he went to his office and listened on his computer. Thirty seconds after Dale's second call, giving us directions to the cabin, that same first burner made another call, this time *through your HQ tower,* to that same second burner at ZeeZeeZ."

Rarey held for applause.

Mark said, "That's not enough to indict Langan."

"It's enough to lean on him, see what happens."

"Nothing, unless he's had a sudden lobotomy and forgot to dispose of the burner."

"You really see Langan skating?"

"No." Mark rasped. Flat. Cold. "I see you doing brief interviews with everyone who had access to that feed, except Langan. I see you grilling Langan for six hours. After which I see you floating a rumor you're negotiating a deal for Langan to flip on the Mastrizzis."

As Mark's plan for the FBI to get Langan killed sunk in, Rarey's expression went uncharacteristically serious. Just for a moment. A grin returned. The small, sly grin of a man who'd heard what he'd been hoping to.

"Gotta love that hardcore Chicago pragmatism… And your Chicago status is about to get amazing. First you ace that shooter at the Art Institute, then you wipe out three mercs and save the witness who's gonna bring down one of the top Mob families in America."

"Only the boss and Junior. The Outfit will abide."

"Still. Medals, promotions, crazy publicity. Superhero cop, dude, you're gonna be hangin' with the upper echelon of your Department. And City Hall—what pol wouldn't want a Mark Bergman photo op—and Mark Bergman at the dinner table. The stories you could tell."

"Spit it out," Mark instructed.

"This afternoon," Rarey told him, "my people interviewed Dale. He swears Branko had nothing to do with the art murders. I think Dale's lying and his files have been sanitized. So do you."

"So?"

"Dale has to be doing this for someone who has a huge need to make the Branko connection disappear—and huge enough clout to get to Kurnit to get to Dale. The only guys who fit that profile are at the top of the Machine's food chain." Rarey again paused. Mark again said nothing. "Superhero cop is going to use his super-powers to get close to certain of those gentlemen."

Mark looked at his watch.

Rarey sighed. "Ah c'mon, Mark. You know my bosses are hard-core DC pragmatists. They'll Kryptonite your ass from superhero to disgraced, fired, and jailed."

"You got nothing puts me in jail. You tapped privileged conversations."

"Maybe. Still leaves disgraced and fired."

"Disgraced? More like cooler than shit. I'd improve from badass who wasted four heavies to badass who wasted four heavies and slept with a serial killer suspect and was right about her being innocent. All you can do," Mark croaked, "is get me fired."

"Which is why you'll say yes."

"No."

Rarey gave Mark an empathetic look: I feel ya bro, totally respect that you need to go down swinging.

Then he said, hard, "Mark, we both know you won't give up the job."

"Try me."

"You *can't* give up the job, because… What else have you got?"

Mark didn't know the answer. JaneDoe hadn't called back.

Rarey waited. Patiently. A new weapon in the wunderkind's arsenal.

Didn't work. There was a quick knock and a nurse entered, followed by a gurney propelled by a burly orderly.

"My ride's here," Rarey explained. "Want a lift? I can chopper you to Midway."

"Yeah. Thanks."

Sooner Mark got home the sooner he could head over to JaneDoe's apartment. The one with the disconnected phone.

ONE HUNDRED-TWENTY-TWO / 2012

Home at last. On the zero percent chance JaneDoe had phoned his burner, Mark fetched it from his desk, turned it on and, sure enough, didn't find the message she hadn't left.

Driving wasn't an option. Mark called a cab. Covered his neck with a light wool scarf before he left.

He buzzed, he knocked. He peered in a window. The lights were off.

He went round back to the alley, checked the parking lot. Seven vehicles, none of which was a red Subaru Forester.

Mark called Lila Kasey.

"Hello Mark."

"Hi. How you doing?"

"Christ, Mark, your voice—what happened?"

"Laryngitis."

"Uh-huh," Lila scoffed. "The news said that gunfight near Rockford had to do with your Art Critic case, and two Chicago cops were wounded, so I've been just a touch—you and your partner all right?"

"We're good. Thanks."

"Are you in a hospital?"

"No."

"Well that's something," Lila said. Stopped there. Waiting for him to broach the topic she knew he was calling about.

He broached. "Lila… Tell me where she is. Please."

A small soft silence.

Lila quietly said, "She left something for you."

Mark took a cab to Lila's.

Lila eyed a blotch of lurid skin that was bulging over the top edge of Mark's scarf. She reluctantly placed a set of keys in Mark's hand. Held his hand in both of hers. Advised, "You don't need to go there tonight."

Mark kissed Lila on the cheek and went back to JaneDoe's apartment.

Most of JaneDoe's things were still there.

And something human-shaped was sitting on the couch, hidden under a black sheet. There was an envelope propped on its lap. Addressed to Mark.

Dear Mark,

Lila's going to put my stuff into storage, and sell the furniture. If you want any of it, it's yours. Like I would've been. Was. Tried to be.

Could've sworn I was tough enough. Imagine my surprise.

Europe.

Turns out Paris wants to meet me. So does London. Frankfurt, Barcelona, Copenhagen, Milan and Lausanne. If my dealer can be believed. And I always do. So I'm off to make New Art for the Old World.

My last Chicago piece is under the sheet. It's yours. Whether you want it or not.

J.

Mark contemplated the lump under the black sheet.

He whipped the sheet off and flung it away, in what he hoped was a dramatic enough gesture to satisfy JaneDoe.

The foam costume—interactive bio-kinetic sculpture—wasn't one of JaneDoe's robot/animal/alien hybrids. It was fully human, almost.

It was him.

A Chicago cop. Wearing a real uniform.

But no hat. His hair was just like Mark's.

His face had no features. A blank oval. Wearing dark sunglasses.

There was no hand at the end of his right arm; there was a gun growing out of his wrist. Growing out of his left wrist was a daisy chain: three pairs of linked handcuffs, the first shiny silver, the second matte gray, the third jet black.

The front of his pants was packed with an enormously intriguing bulge.

There was a square hole in the left side of his chest. Suspended in the hole, where a heart would be, was a gold badge. There were two tiny LEDs imbedded in the center of the badge, pulsing red, then blue, then red, then blue.

Mark re-read JaneDoe's note.

Nothing in it said she didn't want him to chase her.

It said she needed to know how many thousand miles he'd chase her.

And, Mark was pretty sure, when he caught up with JaneDoe she'd need to hear what he'd say when she informed him she'd be living in Europe for at least a couple of years.

He needed to hear what he'd say, too.

Tomorrow he'd put in for indefinite leave and fly to Pari—

Mark's cell rang. Rarey. Mark took the call. "Hi. You all right?"

"I'm cruisin' at forty thousand feet."

"And exploiting your wounded-FBI-puppy status to get away with using your phone in front of the other passengers. Rude."

"You slander me, sir. I'm on a private jet."

"Which of your parents went to high school with the plane's owner?"

"Neither—Uncle Jeff's like thirty years older than my folks. Preliminary ballistics are in."

"Email it."

"Remember that wounded merc who was about to kill you, but took a round in the back of the head?"

"Vaguely."

"The slug in his brain didn't come from any of our weapons—"

"So it was friendly fire."

"And it isn't a match for any of the weapons we retrieved."

"It was friendly fire from one of the mercs who got away."

"Mark, we were all throwing mad lead. Every slug retrieved was one of *many* fired by every weapon in that firefight. Except that slug. It was the only round fired by this particular weapon."

"Which means the shooter ran out of ammo for his primary weapon, he pulls a back-up piece, fires one shot, kills his own guy, oh shit, and hauls ass."

"I don't think so. We got a match. This slug came from the same rifle that killed Jay Branko."

"Which means the pro who took out Branko was also one of the mercs who amb—"

No. Rarey was right. If that shooter had been one of the ambushers there'd be a pile of dead cops.

The pro who killed Branko for the Mastrizzis saved Mark from being killed by the Mastrizzis.

What the hell?

EPILOGUE

After the job was done she didn't leave Chicago. She did what Stephan Densford-Kent had worried she'd do.

She resumed The Hunt. Stalking Him. Learning Him. Getting right next to Him and toying with Him. Taking her time. Years. As many as necessary. Until she devised the perfect moment and method. Had to be perfect. Once in a lifetime, love of a lifetime perfect. Arthur perfect.

She tailed Him back to His apartment. He seemed to be in for the night. She had dinner and returned to her hotel. But an hour later she got an alert from the tracker she'd attached to His car.

He was headed in the general direction of her hotel. It was easy to pick Him up along the way.

She tailed Him to an office building in the west Loop. He drove into the building's underground garage. She parked down the block and waited.

While she was waiting, a black sedan parked across the street from the garage entrance. No one got out of the sedan.

An unmarked police car emerged from the garage, with Him at the wheel. His partner was riding shotgun and there was a third man in the back seat.

His unmarked car was followed by an armored van and an SUV with darkened windows.

The black sedan pulled out and tailed them. A moment later a large van—must have been waiting nearby—got in line behind the sedan; reinforcements.

Interesting.

She tailed the tailers.

Just south of Rockford the black sedan and large van suddenly hit the gas and sped past His convoy.

A couple of exits later He slowed, wanting to pull off—but the ramp was blocked. His convoy sped up. Got off at the next exit and drove across the overpass to get back on southbound.

She couldn't follow them through that maneuver without being noticed. She tore ass to the next exit, got back on southbound, took His exit and tracked Him by following the glow of the lights from His convoy. She cut her own lights when she began to catch up.

She pulled over as she neared an intersection where they'd just turned, and their glow paused. She walked to the intersection and peered down the road. Just in time to see the SUV entering a side road into the woods.

She got her gear out of the trunk. Put on boots and night vision. She entered the woods, moving quietly, aided by the pattering thrum of the steady rain. Which saved her life, because as she neared the place where His convoy was stopped, opposite a vacation home, she came up behind men hiding in the woods, aiming weapons at Him and His team.

His car began to move. It stopped at a shed near the house. Someone dove out of the shed and into the back seat.

He put the car in gear and a war erupted. He drove into the sheltered space between the shed and the house. The house exploded.

Three of the ambushers stopped shooting and ran in His direction.

She started to pursue but had to hit the dirt when SWATs blasted away at an ambusher she was passing behind—or maybe the SWATs were shooting at her, they had night vision.

She crawled until she was out of range of the driveway firefight. She got up and moved quickly toward a faint strobing of muzzle flashes deep in the woods.

When she got there He was still alive. But an idiot with an Uzi was about to change that. She removed the idiot.

Nobody but her gets to kill Mark Bergman.

Dina Velaros flew back to Switzerland, contemplating perfection.

NOTES

Dina Velaros is not that mysterious a character. Her life and motives are an open book. The book's title is *Shooters And Chasers*.

The Art Institute's collection of armor and weaponry was removed from Gunsaulus Hall in 2007. This novel is set in 2012. Fortunately it takes place in a slightly alternative universe, where the weaponry is still in Gunsaulus.

MATERIAL WITNESSES

First Draft First Responders: La Jaffe, Uncle Sheldon, Mighty Mike, the KamKels, Motorcycle Jim, T-Boze, Donna D, WorkDaveWork and RuleDawnRule.

Italian For Dummies Who Write Novels: Pacelli The Japanese Dancing Elvis, and Bonfante The Tuscan Tornado.

Police Procedures: Sergeant Karen Lemon of the Chicago PD was kind enough to provide details and data, so if there are any howling inaccuracies in this book's policework, it is all Sgt. Lemon's fault… No, wait—that's a howling inaccuracy. If any of the operational details are less than realistic, it's because I chose to blow off documentary authenticity in favor of cheap thrills, in order to satisfy you, the reader. So any errors are your fault.

ABOUT THE AUTHOR

Lenny Kleinfeld' first novel, *Shooters And Chasers,* was described by Kirkus Reviews as "A spellbinding debut."

Back before he was spellbinding he was a playwright in Chicago, where he was also a columnist for *Chicago* magazine. His fiction, articles, humor and reviews have appeared in *Playboy, Galaxy, Oui,* the *Chicago Reader,* the *Chicago Tribune,* the *New York Times* and the *Los Angeles Times.* In 1986 Mr. Kleinfeld sold a screenplay, and is currently three decades into a business trip to Los Angeles.

CPSIA information can be obtained
at www.ICGtesting.com
Printed in the USA
BVHW03s1835270218
509246BV00001B/138/P